# WAITING

## FRANK M. ROBINSON

## *Waiting*

"Frank M. Robinson, a wonderfully bold and inventive writer, has created a masterful work of fiction. *Waiting* is a novel of impeccably mounting suspense which leads to an utterly original revelation. Step by step, Robinson takes us on an absorbing and ever-deepening fairground ride and drops us through a startling trap door in evolutionary history."
—Peter Straub

"*Waiting* is a thriller with smarts, and it is a pleasure to recommend. Characters are richly detailed, and the plot twists are fascinating as well as credible in this very fine novel. Robinson creates terror in everyday settings—there is no safe harbor. *Waiting* is a novel of suspense that makes you think about the large questions of illusion and reality. What happens to your sense of self and its place in the world when you learn that someone you've known all your life is nothing like you knew. . . . Read *Waiting* with all the lights on and all the doors and windows locked, not that mere locks and lights will save you." —*Bay Area Reporter*

"A truly frightening and plausible story about another species of human beings, in hiding for 35,000 years and now ready to take control of the planet. . . . Robinson grips his readers by combining visceral fear with intellectual inquiry. This creepily credible tale will have his readers looking more closely at their so-called friends."
—*Publishers Weekly* (starred review)

"A thriller about the distant past and terrifying future, set in a vividly drawn San Francisco all too plausible."
—*Kirkus Reviews*

"Frank M. Robinson writes an ice-cold story of our future, yours and mine. Two million years of humanoid history point to one inevitable conclusion and now Robinson explores that coming event. Many of us will be involved, like it or not." —Wilson Tucker

"Rich with character, suspense, and constant surprise. This is one of the best chillers of the entire decade. It is guaranteed to give you nightmares. Reading this book was a pure pleasure." —Ed Gorman, *Mystery Scene*

Also by Frank M. Robinson

*The Power*
*The Dark Beyond the Stars*
*Death of a Marionette* (with Paul Hull)

# WAITING

## FRANK M. ROBINSON

**TOR®**

A TOM DOHERTY ASSOCIATES BOOK
NEW YORK

WAITING

Edited by David G. Hartwell

Quotation from "The Fire Apes," by Loren C. Eiseley, published in *Harper's* magazine for September 1949.

A Tor Book
Published by Tom Doherty Associates, LLC
175 Fifth Avenue
New York, NY 10010

www.tor.com

Tor® is a registered trademark of Tom Doherty Associates, LLC.

ISBN: 0-812-54164-2
Library of Congress Catalog Card Number: 98-47183

First edition: April 1999
First mass market edition: April 2000

Printed in the United States of America

0  9  8  7  6  5  4  3  2  1

This book is dedicated in loving memory to
my brother Mark,
who liked this story the best of all.

# NOTES AND ACKNOWLEDGMENTS

The author is indebted to the following for their suggestions and help in the research for *Waiting*:

Dr. Mark Hall of the anthropology department of the University of California at Berkeley for information relating to primitive man.

Pam and Terry Floyd for insights concerning the operation of hospital emergency rooms as well as medical practices in general.

Randy Alfred, who knows a great deal about a lot of things and especially about the operation of television newsrooms.

Richard Lupoff, fellow writer and pasta cook extraordinaire, for helpful suggestions regarding plotting, characterization, comma placement, and other esoterica of the storyteller's craft.

And last but far from least, my editor, David Hartwell, who helped make what I considered a good book even better.

For those readers who may wonder what makes a writer tick: I'm fond of didactic novels, books that inform as well as (hopefully) entertain. And yes, many of my characters reflect different aspects of myself. You pick which ones. And finally: Do I personally believe in the major premise of *Waiting*?

You bet.

—Frank M. Robinson
San Francisco
August 1998

*Sometimes at night I think one can feel even the pressure of mice waiting in the walls of old houses. All that concentrated life around us and above us, held in check, surging impatiently, ready for a new experiment, tired of us, waiting our passing. . . . It is perhaps significant that even we ourselves feel a growing inadequacy. Perhaps that is really the secret. Perhaps we are going away.*

—From "The Fire Apes," by Loren C. Eiseley

# THE BEGINNING

**Running . . .**

A stitch in his side had started to throb, and the chill night air burned when Shea sucked it into his lungs. He'd been half walking, half running, ever since he'd left Macy's. He'd suspected he was being followed when he got off at the Embarcadero station, the first stop that BART made in San Francisco. He'd even sensed it the moment he stepped onto the train in Berkeley, but that was ridiculous, and the few times he'd suddenly turned around, he hadn't seen anybody else at his end of the platform.

*It hadn't been much at first, just a growing sense of uneasiness, a feeling that somebody was watching him. He'd taken the escalator up to the street level by the Hyatt Regency, then decided to have a drink in its atrium. He was forty minutes early for the meeting; nobody would be at Soriano's yet and he hated sitting in a claustrophobic restaurant bar nursing a drink.*

*Halfway through his second scotch and soda he'd caught himself staring at the balconies above his head, searching for somebody hiding behind the vines that looped down from them. But all he'd seen was a maid pushing a cleaning cart on the sixth level, a few guests checking into their rooms, and a few more carrying coats and umbrellas, leaving for dinner or the theater.*

*He'd smiled to himself, thinking he was getting jumpy in his old age, but he couldn't shake the feeling that somebody had followed him from Berkeley and was somewhere in the atrium watching him. He'd tried to shrug it off, then became uneasy again at the thought that perhaps muggers had started to imitate carjackers, stalking their victims until they were alone and vulnerable.*

He turned up Larkin Street, ducking into a doorway to catch his breath. He'd stumbled through a good part of the Tenderloin, its borders marked by puddles of vomit and piss stains in the alleyways, kicking at the occasional crumpled sheet of newsprint that skittered ahead of the wind and wrapped itself around his legs. Broken bottles littered the gutters, and the analytical part of him wondered what the winos were drinking these days.

Still Cisco? Still Wild Irish Rose?

He heard somebody clumping down the stairs behind the door and stepped reluctantly back onto the sidewalk, nervously glancing up and down the street. A few people closing up shop, a few others heading for the cheap restaurants that filled the area. Nobody was looking at him or had even noticed him.

But he knew that somebody was watching him as surely as he always knew when it was five minutes to five at the hospital and he'd diagnosed enough clogged arteries for the day.

"Spare change?"

The mumble startled him. As nervously alert as he was, he hadn't noticed the panhandler huddled under the streetlight. He shook his head and hurried past, only half hearing the muttered "Fuck you" that floated after him.

*He'd walked over to Macy's from the Hyatt, finding protective coloring in the crowds on the street and among the shoppers crowding the aisles of kitchen accessories in Macy's basement. There had been a group of schoolkids singing Christmas carols at the bottom of the escalator, and any thoughts of violence at the hands of strangers had faded. It was probably the season; almost everybody was uptight at Christmas.*

*He'd been casually inspecting some stoneware—with his two boys earning their allowance by doing the dishes, the attrition rate among the cereal bowls had been fierce—when he thought he saw somebody staring at him from the center aisle.*

*He'd almost knocked over a serving platter when he jerked around. But there had been nobody there except some harried housewives and bored husbands browsing among the automatic breadmakers and the copper-bottomed pans.*

*From then on, it had been all downhill. There was some-*thing *in the basement and it was after him.*

*Panicked, he'd pushed his way to the escalator and a moment later was on the street, the chill night air seeping beneath his coat and turning his sweaty shirt clammy. He'd managed a shambling run down Geary for half a dozen blocks, then north on Larkin, looking over his shoulder every five steps and cursing to himself because he never saw anybody following him though he knew damned well somebody was stalking him on the open street.*

The pause in the doorway had given him a little time to calm down. He should call the restaurant—it was almost six and Mitch and Artie and the others would be there by now. He could catch a cab or maybe somebody could pick him up.

Or maybe he should just call the cops. Tell them his name was Dr. Lawrence Shea, that he was a law-abiding citizen and he was being followed by somebody he didn't know for reasons he didn't know. He'd probably sound like a drunk or an idiot or maybe both, but it was better than running.

There was a phone in its plastic hood next to an alleyway and he hurried over to it, fumbled in his pocket for some coins, heard them drop, and frantically dialed. The restaurant first and then 911.

It took a moment before he realized there was no dial tone, that the armored cord on the handset was swinging free where somebody had yanked it out. He stared at the dangling cord for a moment, ignoring the sweat that trickled down his forehead and into his eyes.

*Sweet Jesus. . . .*

He stood there, holding the phone, refusing to move. He'd make them come to him, make them show themselves.

As soon as he thought it, his heart started beating wildly and his chest felt as if somebody had him in a bear hug. The shirt bunched up in his armpits started soaking up sweat like a bath towel. Medically, he knew he was probably having a panic attack, but he couldn't forget those patients who had dropped dead with no previous history of heart disease. He was a doctor; he was aware of the symptoms, but it didn't make any difference. His nerves had tightened up until they were stiff enough to squeak and he was sure he could feel the beginning of chest pains.

He slammed the handset back into its cradle and fled up Larkin, grateful when the heaviness in his chest suddenly eased and his heartbeat slowed. Once he glimpsed himself in the window of a secondhand-magazine store, his face framed by ancient copies of *The Saturday Evening Post* and *Look.* A frightened man in his middle forties, just beginning to go to fat, with thinning brown hair, pale face, eyes sunken and terrified, lips pulled away from clenched teeth.

It was the wrong season of the year, he thought: It was Christmas and he was wearing a Halloween mask.

He realized it had been a mistake to leave the holiday crowds downtown, that he would have been much safer there than in the seedy area around Larkin and Post. Nobody was buying Christmas presents at the porno stores or massage parlors, and few people were enjoying a holiday dinner at the Thai or Vietnamese restaurants that dotted the neighborhood.

He'd head back to Union Square. He could lose himself in the crowds; nothing would happen to him surrounded by shoppers.

He turned to hurry south down Larkin and once again his heart tumbled into an erratic, rapid beating. He blindly turned and ran back north, indifferent to the young Asian kids who watched wide-eyed before they ducked out of his way. He tried to force himself to calm down, to think logically about who might be following him and what they might want.

It never occurred to him that he was being herded.

**It was getting darker** now and the streets were emptying quickly, people chased indoors by the cold and the start of a chill drizzle. Shea could feel his legs trembling, his muscles giving out, and knew he couldn't run much farther. He was out of shape: he'd never followed the advice he'd given his patients to stop smoking and exercise more.

He could slip into a restaurant. He'd be safer among people, but the moment the idea crossed his mind he felt a brief spasm in his chest and knew if he tried to hide among the crowds he risked having his heart speed up again. He was still too panicked to realize he had finally been run to ground.

Then it struck him that if he couldn't run, perhaps he could hide. Someplace dark where nobody could see him. He ran for another block, finally cutting into an alley where he crouched down on the far side of some steps leading to a loading dock. He was sobbing with fright and fatigue and frantically trying to control his breath so his loud gasps for air wouldn't give him away. He waited.

Nothing.

Nobody had followed him into the alley. The only sounds were those of rats rooting around in the garbage cans behind the back of a restaurant thirty feet away. He was calmer now but still anxious to find a

place to hide. He strained his eyes searching the alleyway, which was dimly lit by small bulbs overhanging the
back doors of cafés and warehouses.

On the other side of the cracked concrete, a few
yards from where he crouched, a huge plywood shipping crate sagged against a brick wall. He waited a long
moment, watching the street, then scrambled over.
The crate was lying on its side, the lid at the far end
propped open a foot or so, and he squeezed in.

He was feeling more like himself by the moment and
guessed that whoever it was who had been tailing him
had either given up or lost him. He'd just started to
relax when he felt the short hairs rise on the back of
his neck. He wasn't sitting on wood; he was squatting
on something that felt like remnants of carpet, while
another strip of carpeting partly covered the opening
he'd just squeezed through.

And he wasn't alone.

He fumbled for his key-chain flashlight and waved it
around the interior. He was right: dirty carpeting covered the bottom of the crate, while at the other end
there was a bedroll in one of the corners and a blue
plastic recycling box upended to serve as a table. Sitting a few feet away, bundled up in two scarves and a
filthy overcoat, a weather-beaten old man with a three-
day beard and bleary eyes stared at him. He looked
sixty, maybe more, with a face of tanned leather,
clumps of gray stubble sprouting from hedgerows of
wrinkles.

Reality, Shea thought. Not pleasant but something
he could see and touch, a situation he could handle.

"I'm sorry," he mumbled, "I didn't mean . . ."

He let the sentence dribble away, noticing for the
first time the bottle by the man's side. Shea crawled
over and waved the flashlight in front of his eyes. The
pupils responded sluggishly; the old drunk had passed
out with his eyes half open, one of the army of homeless clogging the arteries of the city. You saw them all

over downtown and even in the outlying areas, pan-handling by ATMs and squatting outside restaurants and any other place that might attract tourists, rattling their coffee-takeout cups with a few coins in the bottom. At night, some sought refuge in the city shelters while others found it in doorways or packing crates.

Shea was nearly himself now, managing to light a cigarette with hands that trembled only slightly. He forced himself to try to figure out why he'd become so panicked. Something vaguely felt but never seen had spooked him, and his imagination had run away with him. His emotions must have created a feedback loop so every time he thought somebody was following him, his reactions had become more extreme. The fear of being hunted had become a self-fulfilling prophecy.

Mitch was the psychiatrist in the Club; he could explain the mechanics of it.

But for right now, he would stay where he was. He was out of the cold and the drizzle, and his host wasn't about to complain. He propped up the tiny flashlight on the recycling box so the glow in the crate made it seem almost cozy. He'd wait until he got a grip on his nerves, find a working phone someplace, and call the restaurant—everybody would still be there. It had been an odd occurrence and it would be a while before he forgave himself for panicking but—

He felt the sweat dampen his forehead again. He'd been staring at the old man, vaguely aware that something was wrong but too preoccupied with his own problems to give it much thought.

Sometime during the last few minutes the poor bastard had stopped breathing.

Shea crawled forward a few feet and felt his neck, right under the jaw by the carotid artery. No pulse. It couldn't have been very long: he would have sworn the man was alive when he'd first noticed him. But the ravages of chronic alcoholism, acute intoxication, the cold—it happened.

He struggled to get out of his coat, his own breathing ragged and uneven. Cramped quarters for CPR, but he'd give it a try. Jesus, nobody was ever going to believe this.

He suddenly froze, his arms half in and half out of his coat. Once again he had the feeling of a *presence* nearby, the same thing he had felt in Macy's basement. This time it was right outside the packing crate. Something was standing by the crate, knowing he was there, knowing he was hiding. . . .

*frightened, monkey?*

The whispery voice came from *inside* the crate, not outside. Dry, raspy, old, but very clear, with no slurring. A part of him—that very small part that wasn't terrified—noted that the words didn't sound threatening or contemptuous, they merely sounded—descriptive.

"Who, who . . ." he bleated. His voice drained away. He was afraid for a moment that he was going to lose control of his bladder, and then, of course, he did. The old man opposite him, bundled up in his ragged scarves and filthy coat, was talking to him. And that was impossible—he was dead. Or maybe he'd missed the old man's pulse, that had to be it. But there had been no flicker of life in the half-closed eyes at all.

*who did you tell. . . .*

This time Shea saw the old man's lips move. His heart might have stopped, but brain death could still take a few minutes longer. Which meant that somehow somebody was using the old drunk's corpse like a ventriloquist would use a dummy, using him while his neurons could still fire and before his muscles grew stiff.

"Tell what?" Shea gasped at the dead man. "What do you want?" He was too frightened even to feel embarrassed about his soaked pants.

*you took notes. . . . you must have—you're the type . . .*

Shea shook his head, wanting to deny everything.

"I don't know what you're talking about—"

*you're lying . . . but you don't know you're lying . . .*

Somewhere a back door banged open and Shea could hear the rattle of garbage cans. Then: "Hey, you—you there by crate. What the hell you hang around back here for?"

A sudden sense of consternation and regret.

Another whisper.

*good-bye, monkey. . . .*

There was a feeling of withdrawal, and the old man slumped forward. Shea stared at him, then reached out with a shaking hand and once again checked the carotid artery in his neck. He hadn't been mistaken. No pulse. Dead.

He sat there for minutes, afraid to move, afraid to leave, afraid even to touch the old man for another try at CPR. His mind was spinning, wondering what the hell had cornered him and what it had wanted. The revelation was slow in coming, and when it did, it left him in shock. *Sweet Jesus,* he thought once again. He rocked back and forth, his arms wrapped around his chest for protection against his own fears and the suddenly biting cold. It was half a minute before he became aware of something scratching at the strip of carpeting that covered the entrance of the crate.

He turned just in time to throw up his hands to protect his face but not his throat, and his screams never made it past his teeth. He fought in the gloom as best he could, but he was too frightened and too weak and there were three of them tearing at him. They were large and ferocious, and he didn't struggle very long at all. As a doctor he knew it was easy to die. He was mildly surprised at just *how* easy. His last thought was a half-formed, wistful longing for Cathy and James and Andy and a sudden conviction that he had been followed because he had something somebody else wanted.

But he hadn't thought about it soon enough, so nobody had been able to pick his brain and discover where he'd left it.

# CHAPTER 1

**It was Artie's favorite** dream.

He was lying on a grassy plain, naked, staring at the billowy white clouds slowly vaulting past in the blue sky overhead. It was warm, and a breeze stroked his chest and fingered the tangled hair that fell over his shoulders. He lifted his head slightly to stare at the mountains in the distance, their outlines fuzzed by a slight haze, then let it fall back. Without turning to look, he knew there were several caves a stone's throw behind him and that the plain in front ran forever.

It was so pleasant that he didn't want to move; he just wanted to lie there feeling the rough blades of grass against his back and buttocks and stare up at the sky, his mind a blank. He sensed others there as well, but he didn't bother looking around to see who they were. Most of all, he was aware of the overpowering scent of flowers. Thousands of them. Out of the corner of his eye he could see them spotted in the grass, little clumps of purples and reds and yellows and pinks.

A gorgeous summer day and he was very young and the warmth of the sun was arousing but he didn't care. It was a lucid dream, the kind where in the dream you know that you're dreaming. Some of his friends who were into meditation said they had a lot of dreams like that but this was the only one that Artie Banks had ever had. The dream probably meant something but he was afraid that if he ever found out, he'd never dream it again. In the dream, he had no idea where he was, but it didn't matter. All that mattered was the warmth and the sky and the smell of the flowers and his own unashamed arousal.

There were birds wheeling overhead, which was something new, and they were calling to one another, making noises that sounded like distant chimes. Then the scene wavered and grew faint around the edges and a voice was saying *". . . an accident on the Bay Bridge just west of the incline has blocked two lanes and traffic is backed up . . ."*

The dream vanished and Artie yawned and fumbled for the clock radio on the bedstand. Why did he always dream it around morning? Why not earlier, so he could spend some time in it, find out who the others were and where he was? He shrugged. What the hell, it was a kid's dream. He was getting too old for early morning erections.

He swung his feet over the side of the bed and yawned again. He ran his fingers through his hair and his tongue around the inside of his mouth, then glanced over to where Susan was usually huddled deep within the covers. She wasn't there. He stared at the rumpled blankets, his mind still fogged with sleep. Then he remembered that today was the day she was leaving for Willow. Her mother had called late last night with the news that her father wasn't doing well. Susan had wanted to take Mark with her but he had begged off—he still had a few days of school before Christmas break. Artie had offered to drive up later if things got worse, and that's where they'd left it. Susan had looked unhappy, but Artie felt relieved. He had never gotten along with her parents; her father was openly hostile and even small talk was a chore.

He fell back into bed and rolled over so he could

feel Susan's lingering warmth, smell her familiar scent, and rub his body across the still warm sheets. Why did she have to be leaving on the morning of his dream? The dream was an aphrodisiac, and afterward, as in the dream itself, he was without shame.

Susan, of course, was *always* without shame. After fifteen years of marriage he considered that pretty remarkable, but he wasn't about to complain. Susan sometimes seemed a little remote to him, more than a little puzzling and sometimes difficult to understand.

But not in bed. *Never* in bed.

He stretched and got up, suddenly aware of the smells of coffee and toast and the chirping of the microwave indicating the bacon was done. Time for a quick shower and breakfast before Susan vanished for three days.

He shuffled down the hall toward the bathroom, pausing outside Mark's room with his hand on the doorknob. A week ago when he'd entered without warning, Mark had stopped what he was doing to frown slightly and say, "I'm way past puberty, Artie— you ought to knock." What had bothered Artie more than anything else was Mark's total lack of embarrassment. But then, Artie had been embarrassed enough for both of them.

He rapped on the door, then smiled wryly and rattled the doorknob. "Your mother's about to leave, Mark, but you can still catch her for breakfast."

A muffled voice. "Be right there, Artie. Give me a minute."

Call me Ishmael, Artie thought sarcastically. What the hell was wrong with "Dad"? Or maybe it was just a phase kids went through, a way of leveling the playing field between their parents and themselves. He listened for a moment to the creaking of the bed and pictured Mark muscling himself over the side and into his wheelchair.

As usual, the image hurt. The accident had been . . .

how long ago? Five years? When Mark was twelve? Susan had been driving and she and Mark had been sideswiped by a drunk. Thankfully, Susan hadn't been hurt, but Mark had been partially paralyzed from the waist down. Susan had found a specialist and some feeling had been restored—the morning he'd walked in on Mark had been proof of that—but Mark had used a wheelchair ever since.

Artie had always felt guilty about it. He'd married Susan when Mark was two, but he and the boy had had difficulty bonding and he'd always felt that every bad thing that happened to Mark was partly his fault.

He pushed into the john, shivering when his bare feet touched the cold tile, and turned on the hot water. What was happening to him? Half the time he was grateful for his family, the other half he was depressed by it. More accurately, maybe it was a growing sense of inadequacy, a feeling that he wasn't living up to their expectations—hell, to *his* expectations.

He angrily turned the shower knob to Cold, jumping at the sudden spray of chilly water. It was strictly the shits to wake up from his dream and then slip into his usual morning depression. More than likely it was the weather, not Mark or Susan—the seemingly constant overcast and drizzle that was winter in San Francisco was enough to depress anybody.

**"So what did Larry** have to say?"

It had been in the back of Artie's head all morning but he hadn't *really* thought about it until Susan mentioned it.

"He didn't come. They missed you, by the way."

Susan was leaning back in her chair, cradling her cup of coffee and taking little sips while she talked.

"How come Larry never showed?"

Artie felt faintly irritated—not at her, at Larry. "Beats me. We phoned his house but got the answering machine. He was probably called to Kaiser on an emergency."

Susan finished her coffee and walked over to put her cup in the sink. There were days when she was just a housewife, Artie thought, fighting forty and watching her diet and dismayed by the occasional gray hair. But this morning wasn't one of them. She was dressed in a casual beige suit, light brown hair gathered close around her head, and wearing just a hint of makeup. How old did she look? Thirty, maybe? And how the hell did she do it? Or was it all in the eye of the beholder? She was a little on the heavy side—zaftig, she joked—but he never noticed unless he was looking at her critically, and he seldom did that.

"Cathy should have been home, or one of the boys."

"Probably Christmas shopping."

It sounded like he was making excuses for Larry, when the truth was that he was worried—a little—and annoyed—a lot. Larry might have been called to the hospital, but he knew they were meeting at Soriano's and he could have phoned. Should have phoned.

Mark reached for another slice of wheat toast and ladled on the strawberry jam.

"What was he going to talk about?"

He was still in his shorts and T-shirt, and Artie felt both pride and pity. He had been lucky with Susan and Mark. With Susan because she was bright and beautiful—and tenured in the psychology department at San Francisco State, he thought gratefully; taking care of Mark had been horrendously expensive and even though her parents helped, her income and contacts had been invaluable. It had been Susan who'd managed to enroll Mark in the private school for the disabled.

But he had been lucky with Mark, too, who was strong and healthy despite the paralysis. Artie stared at him. Mark was a good-looking kid, he realized with something of a shock. You saw them through acne and scabs and dirty hands and faces and "Don't slouch—keep your shoulders back," and then one day you were suddenly proud of the way they looked: a pale face framed by thick, black hair and eyebrows that almost met in the middle. A striking face and undeniably handsome, marred only, in Artie's view, by a small, ancient ring in his right ear that Susan had given him as a family heirloom—all the style, Mark had gleefully claimed. He was strongly muscled above the waist and even though he couldn't walk, his legs looked normal. He was stocky for a seventeen-year-old, and therapy had kept the flesh from withering. Remarkably, Mark had never let it get him down. And from the number of phone calls he got, he had to be one of the most popular students in his school.

Mark looked embarrassed. "What're you staring at?"

"Nothing," Artie lied.

"So what was he going to talk about?"

Mark was all wide-eyed with anticipation and Artie felt annoyed. Mark was putting him on, as he frequently did lately, constantly feigning surprise at whatever he did or said: the not-so-subtle war between the generations, or maybe Mark was still getting back at Artie for having walked in on him.

"How long have I been going to meetings and telling you all about them later? Did you ever listen?" He was sorry immediately: Had he ever listened to his father when he was a teenager? "I don't know what he was going to talk about; that's the whole point of the Club. Each of us talks about the latest developments in his or her specialty—nobody knows the topic in advance." He went back to buttering a slice of toast and grumbled, "Eat your Cheerios."

Mark obligingly filled his bowl and dropped a glob of jam on top. Artie winced, then realized that at Mark's age it could just as easily have been peanut butter. Rebellion usually started at the breakfast table and ended in the bedroom, or was it the other way around?

"Odd sort of club."

"Not really. It's a modern version of the nineteenth-century French salon. Besides, it keeps me informed and"—he lowered his voice and intoned the slogan of KXAM—"information is our business."

Mark looked blank and Artie sighed. "It's a joke, son."

The gulf between the generations. It first showed up in their senses of humor. Mark thought Artie's jokes were lame, and what cracked Mark up usually left Artie shaking his head. Each generation had to have its own music, its own movies, its own humor. Well, hell, when was the last time he'd laughed at Bob Hope, his father's favorite comedian? Or Milton Berle? And was either one still alive? His own favorites had been Chevy Chase and Bill Murray; Mark's were Jim Carrey and Robin Williams.

"Gotta run," Susan said, pushing away from the table. "And so do you."

She bent down to peck Mark on the cheek, who gave her a quick hug in return. "Give Grandma and Grandpa my love."

Artie felt a brief twinge of jealousy. Mother and son. They seemed to have more in common with each other than they had with him. In his next incarnation he'd make sure he married a woman who had a daughter as well.

He walked Susan to her car, holding her a shade too tightly and deep-kissing her before she got in.

She smiled. "Your dream again?"

"Yeah. Sorry you have to leave so soon."

"So am I, but Mom asked me to try and get there in time for supper. I've left their new number on the phone pad if you have to get in touch."

"You got the presents?"

"They're in the trunk. Don't forget to call Larry—Cathy said they were thinking about having friends over Christmas Day."

Larry. Again, he'd almost forgotten.

"Soon as I get back in the house." He pulled his shirt tighter around his shoulders. "Christ, it's freezing out here."

"Take care of Mark. I know it's a bad time of the year to take off, but Dad . . ." Then, oddly serious: "You mean a lot to me, Artie."

He half shrugged, half shivered. "I love you, too, baby. Be careful on the freeway—there're places where the tule fog can get pretty thick."

She put the car in gear and Artie watched the old green Volvo roll down Noe toward Market and the freeway entrance. It was a bad day to go anyplace. Overcast, chilly, a fine drizzle in the air. Worst of all, the city itself had lost the magic it used to have on cold, rainy days. San Francisco hadn't been Baghdad by the Bay for years now. It was dirty and damp, run-down at the heels—the old girl had certainly seen better days. The signs of the times were the graffiti spray-painted on decaying wooden walls, the army of homeless with their in-your-face panhandling, and the fat old bag lady he'd seen the day before relieving herself over a sewer grating.

The world's going to hell in a handbasket. That's what his father used to say. He'd been thinking about it for weeks now, unable to get the phrase out of his mind. What was frightening was that thirty years from now, *these* would probably be "the good old days." Pack up and move to Portland or Seattle, that's what they ought to do. Or maybe Tucson, where the sun shines even in the winter, so they say.

At the bottom of the hill, the Volvo turned right and disappeared into the traffic on Market Street. Artie stood there a moment, watching where it had vanished with a deep sense of affection. When Susan said he meant a lot to her, he knew the emotions went far deeper than the words. But when was the last time she had said she loved him? Or had she ever? She must have, but he couldn't remember when. He'd always considered Susan a shade too good for him, and in the back of his mind was the fear that someday she would think so, too. He needed reassurance, but she had never offered any. She wasn't entirely to blame, of course—he'd never asked. And then, as he frequently did when he thought about Susan, he felt guilty. She might not be a saint, but as far as he was concerned, she was above reproach. Meeting her at the Club had been the best thing that had ever happened to him. But he would give a lot to know if she felt the same way.

Some men's lives were wrapped up in their jobs. For him, his job was important, but first and last he was a family man. He would give his life for Mark and Susan but it wasn't the sort of thing you talked about, and he was never really sure they knew.

He shivered and started up the walk, then came to an abrupt halt, his senses taut as a bowstring. He could hear the soft creaking of the trees in the wind, feel the rough texture of the concrete beneath his slippers, even smell the faint odor where a cat had marked its territory.

He ignored the cold wind fingering his shirt and the chill drops spattering against his face. He turned to stare at the cars parked across the street and the bushes in front of the houses.

Odd feeling. Like somebody was out there watching him.

But there was nobody else around. Nobody was sitting in any of the cars along the curb. Nobody was picking up the morning paper where it had landed in the bushes. Nobody was watching him through slatted blinds in any of the neighbor's windows, at least that he could see.

He started to shiver uncontrollably and padded quickly back to the house.

Inside, Mark had dressed and packed his schoolbooks in his bag. He was waiting by the front door for the van that picked up the handicapped kids for the private school. One of Susan's contacts had recommended Bayview Academy to them, and it had been a godsend.

"Last few days before Christmas break, sport?"

"Yeah. Mom's gonna be gone for three days?"

"Maybe more. Your grandfather's not doing well and she may want to stay longer."

"Lots of chances for me to beat you at chess, then." Mark looked smug, reminding Artie that Mark was up on him by a dozen games. It was also an affirmation of the father-son bond, and for that, Artie was grateful.

Then the bus was honking outside and Mark opened the door and wheeled down the walk. Artie watched through the window as Mark maneuvered his chair onto the lift and was hoisted into the van. My fault, Artie thought. Maybe if I'd been driving, it wouldn't have happened. But he'd been engrossed in watching an episode of *Cheers* and Susan had offered to drive Mark home from the basketball game.

He was halfway through his second cup of coffee of the morning when he remembered Larry Shea and dialed Shea's office. No, Dr. Shea wasn't in yet. Did he want to leave a message?

When he called the Shea house, he got the answering machine.

Nobody picked up.

# CHAPTER 2

**Artie was late getting** to KXAM—a bus and a bottled-water truck had collided on Van Ness so he couldn't drive ahead, and the crush of traffic behind prevented him from driving around. He leaned on the horn for a long moment, then relaxed and stared through the rain-streaked windshield at the cars jammed around him. On the sidewalk, pedestrians were using their umbrellas as shields against the wind and the rain, which had become a downpour.

It didn't matter whether there was an accident or what season of the year it was. Every morning was gridlock, every street a clogged river of honking horns and bumper-to-bumper traffic. Why the hell did he and Susan still live here? The sunlit, whitewashed city of twenty years ago had long since turned a prison gray. What were the old lyrics? "Where have all the flowers gone?. . . ." The smiling hippies of two decades before had suffered a sea change into the alcoholic homeless, and "Spare change?" had become a mumbled threat.

He never used to have black moods, but lately it seemed like almost every day was a downer, though this time he had good reason: no Susan, the stress of Christmas, and the stinks and strains of city life.

What did he expect?

The traffic lurched forward a few feet and Artie concentrated on tweaking the gas pedal. He parked in the
outdoor lot behind the station and hurried through
the crowded newsroom to the little glass-walled cubicle
that was temporary headquarters for the documentary
unit. He was twenty minutes late for his nine-to-who-
knew-how-long shift and swore to himself. For the next
few weeks he would be wearing the hat of field pro-
ducer as well as newswriter, and after that maybe it
would be his regular assignment.

Connie Lee was waiting for him, leaning back in her
chair, hands wrapped around a container of coffee,
studying the newsroom outside. Connie would be the
on-camera reporter, track the segments, and do the
narration and the stand-ups when their series aired.
Her hair was loose around her shoulders with just a
hint of gray; her high cheekbones and neighbor-next-
door smile had been a staple of the evening news forever. On-screen, she came across as honest as Jane
Pauley or Diane Sawyer with all the other virtues close
behind. She wasn't "cute" enough to irritate any of the
women watching and was authoritative enough that
men paid attention when she covered politics or occasionally filled in on sports. Connie's "Q," her recog-
nizability rating, was off the charts.

She'd become a legend at the station when, just after
they'd hired her, she'd said flatly, "I don't do windows
and I don't do ethnic." Connie was the house cynic,
but she knew television inside and out, was one of Artie's best friends, and had the happy knack of being
able to make him laugh. These days, that was worth a
lot.

Connie's only fault—if you could call it that—was
her belief in tarot cards. Nobody kidded her about it—
they knew better. To Artie, it was like the one flaw that
made beautiful people truly beautiful: It was Connie's
one flaw and it made her perfect.

She nodded at him, a toothpick firmly clenched between her front teeth. "The new anchor's here. Take a look, then tell me why Hirschfield hired her."

Artie looked out at the newsroom, quickly sorting through the reporters and the newswriters hunched in front of their computers. She was the blonde sitting at the workstation nearest the anchor desk, nervously scanning a sheaf of notes she held in one hand while giving her hair a final brushing with the other. She was easy to look at but not pretty enough to be distracting. Her name was Adrienne Jantzen and that was all he knew about her.

"Because she's a good lay?"

Connie laughed. "You're a chauvinist pig, Banks. Besides, maybe she likes women."

"You wish." Artie studied Jantzen through the glass. She looked a little shy, but he was willing to bet that beneath it all she was cool, reserved, and hard as nails. Probably a lot like Susan when he'd first met her.

"They're starting her on the midmorning newsbreak," Connie continued, telling Artie something he'd already heard. "Flaherty's out with the flu."

"Another amateur from the Valley?"

"Don't think so—Hirschfield didn't offer to throw in bed and breakfast so I figure she must have something on the ball. And her Sacramento ratings were decent." She watched while Artie opened his briefcase and pulled out a yellow pad. "How'd your show-and-tell go last night?"

"Larry Shea didn't make it."

Connie looked surprised. "He get an emergency call from Kaiser?"

Artie shook his head. "He wasn't at the hospital last night and I couldn't raise him at home this morning." He thumbed through his notes, Shea temporarily forgotten. Connie balanced her own yellow pad on her knees and took out her ballpoint.

"Sounds strange to me." She glanced at her pad. "Got a working title?"

"Nothing I like. You?"

"Same. How's Susan?"

"She took off for three days to visit her folks, leaving the Christmas shopping to me." The moment he said it, it sounded like he was whining, and he felt embarrassed. "Not her fault—her father isn't well."

Connie half smiled. "Three days without Susan? You'll never make it."

"You go three days without Kris, see how you do."

"I'd do just fine, thank you." She put down her pen and started counting on her fingers. "Okay, the standard environmental disasters are cutting down the rain forests, global warming, melting of the polar ice caps, the hole in the ozone layer, the spotted owl—and then I have to switch over to the other hand. What do you want to include?"

"All of the above." Artie grimaced. "Jesus, even the sitcoms have covered them."

Connie frowned. "That makes a difference? C'mon, Artie, we've got four and a half minutes a night Monday through Friday right after New Year's plus a half-hour recap running as a special the following Saturday. That's a lot of airtime to fill, and we've only got a few weeks to finish the series. Easiest way to go is just update the material on hand, right?"

Artie groaned. "It's bad enough they canceled the series on the mayor, and then we get this thrown at us."

"Be positive—it'll look good on the old résumé."

"I've found a home here, Connie. I'm not looking."

She sounded enthusiastic about the idea of a series but not about the subject, and Artie guessed she would be on automatic for the duration. He started to scribble some notes, then suddenly glanced out at the crowded newsroom. He felt like he had when he was standing in his driveway that morning, all his senses at full alert. He could hear the faint murmur of newsroom conversation even through the heavy glass and smell the slight metallic tang to the filtered air inside their booth.

There was somebody out there who was watching him and Connie, but he hadn't the slightest idea who it was.

"Any new hires besides Jantzen?"

"Not that I know of . . ."

Her voice trailed off and she leaned forward, staring through the glass at the news set, where Jantzen was reading off the TelePrompTer.

"Listen—she's going to blow her lines."

Artie hastily turned up the volume on the cubicle's monitor.

". . . and UN peacekeeping troops were flown in to Mir-acle—that's Miravachi, Macedonia, a border town near Greece. . . ."

"Nice recovery," Artie murmured. "First-day jitters or somebody sabotaged the 'Prompter as a joke." Then he asked, curious, "You get that from the cards?"

She gave him a long look. "Get what?"

"That she was going to blow it."

"C'mon, Artie—after ten years? It's got nothing to do with the cards—it's reporter's intuition. Also woman's."

"Working title," Artie muttered, chewing on his ball-point.

Connie didn't answer for a long moment, then: "How about 'Death in the Mine Shaft.' "

Artie wasn't able to put his finger on it until later, but at that moment the cubicle suddenly seemed stuffy, almost stifling. For a minute he thought he was seeing double and it felt like his heart had skipped a beat. Just as quickly, the feeling passed. He glanced up, frowning. Connie looked pale, sweaty.

"You okay, kid?"

Uncertainly: "Yeah . . . I'm fine." Connie doodled on her pad for a moment. "So what do you think?"

"I don't get it."

"The goddamned canaries are dying, Artie." Connie
had recovered and now looked irritated. "You remember the canaries miners used to take down into the
shafts to detect coal gas? In this case, East Coast song-
birds. Loss of habitat, that sort of thing." Artie bent
over his pad and started writing. "Include the frogs as
well; they're in decline, too—and half the ones we find
are deformed. Something to do with a fungus. We'll
have to check it out, see if anybody's done something
similar—*Nova* or *National Geographic,* maybe we can
borrow some footage, give them credit." She snapped
her fingers. "Don't forget the fish. Too many fisher-
men coming back with empty boats. The Grand Banks
are being overfished, the salmon runs on the West
Coast are down. And the epidemic of skin cancer in
Australia because of the hole in the ozone layer . . ."

Artie would have sworn this wouldn't be her cup of
tea.

"You been boning up?"

She frowned. "Haven't you? You've known for three
days that we had this assignment."

His black mood suddenly returned. "Does anybody
really give a fuck, Connie?"

"About what?"

"About this crap. People have been crying that the
sky is falling ever since they looked up."

She cocked her head, her voice icy. "Have you been
listening to me, Banks? Or are you still mooning about
your wife?"

Low blow, Artie thought, wondering if she was serious. It wasn't like Connie. Not like Connie at all.

"You think it's a shit assignment, don't you, Banks?"
For the first time since Artie had known her, Connie
sounded hostile. "DBI—dull but important. It's going
to air the week after New Year's when nobody's watching and nobody's advertising, so you think we should
do a fluff piece. You think if Hirschfield thought it was

hot, he'd have scheduled it for the February sweeps when the ratings really count."

What the hell was bugging Connie? She was out of character, way out. Artie shrugged. "You could say that. Why did he even bother?"

"Because it's important, that's why—it doesn't matter when it airs." She swung her chair around to study the newsroom again. "It'll look good when it's time for license renewal, but over and above that . . ." Her voice faded away and she whispered, "It's important."

Artie concentrated on his notes. Connie was acting weird, and he was beginning to feel a little strange himself.

"So we tape five segments, one for each night," he said, trying to make peace with her. "Feature the most recent ecological update, then show what's being done to help. Have the Grub chase down the latest on EcoNet and the Internet."

"The Grub" was Jerry Gottlieb, the intern, smarter and fatter than anybody else on staff and the one who knew all there was to know about databases.

Connie had closed her eyes and was massaging her temples with her fingers. Artie looked at her, alarmed, then touched her on the shoulder.

"You really okay, Connie?" She was sure as hell fighting something. If she felt this bad, why had she come in at all? Nobody was going to thank her if they came down with what she had.

For just a moment, she seemed confused. "I'm fine. . . ." She shook her head and opened her eyes wide, focusing on the newsroom just beyond the glass. "We could do it that way," she said slowly, her voice stronger. "Play it by the numbers."

She turned back to Artie and waited. Artie searched her face for clues to what she wanted to hear, then gave up. Reading Connie was usually fairly easy, but not this time. Her facial muscles were rigid, the skin taut.

"You have something in mind?"

"Sure—tell them what they don't want to hear."

Artie stared.

"Which is what?"

"That we're breeding like flies in a garbage dump and all our ecology problems are really only one problem."

Connie was serious—she was *really* serious—she wasn't putting him on.

Artie fumbled for words. "That's old, that's really old—too many people, not enough food, starvation, wars for living space—"

She smiled tightly. "By George, I think he's got it!"

Artie crumpled the sheet from his yellow notepad and pegged it at the wastebasket. "Goddammit, Connie, nobody at all is going to watch if the series is a downer. And there's no reason why it should be. The more prosperous a nation becomes, the more its birthrate falls—"

She cut in, her voice curt. "That's bullshit. No matter how you slice it, there're going to be a lot more people and some Third World countries are going to be a lot more prosperous. You think they're going to be nice and tidy about their prosperity? We never were."

Artie couldn't believe it. Connie was lecturing him, as out of character as if she'd suddenly started combing her hair with her fingers. It wasn't just that the ground had suddenly shifted; he wasn't even sure he was standing on it anymore.

"China restricts births—"

"Come off it, Banks—the only Social Security for nine-tenths of the people in this world is their own kids. The more they have, the more to take care of them in their old age."

Connie wasn't looking at him; she was staring at somebody in the newsroom. But when Artie tried to follow her eyes, he couldn't figure out who she was looking at.

"They don't give you awards for playing it safe," she said harshly. "Or promotions, either."

Why the hell had he thought this assignment would be fun and games if he was working with Connie? Artie started to stuff his notes back into his briefcase, then hesitated. Connie couldn't be a complete bitch.

"So what's your hook? How you going to tease it?"

Connie's eyes were muddy and unfocused, as if she were staring at him from the bottom of a pool of dirty water. She was on something, she had to be. Had she ever been to Betty Ford? He couldn't remember.

"Imagine a lily pond . . . with one lily pad in it. The next day there are two lily pads and the day after that, four. In thirty days the pond is completely covered with lily pads and the rest of the life in the pond smothers— no sunlight, no oxygen. Question: At what point is the pond only half covered with lily pads?"

Artie sighed. "Let's get coffee. We'll come back to this afterward."

"At what point, Banks?"

"On the twenty-ninth day, goddammit! Satisfied?"

"That's right." She looked pleased. "On the twenty-eighth day it's only a quarter full and on the twenty-seventh, only an eighth. But by one of those days, it's going to be much too late to do anything about the growth of lily pads."

The picture she had drawn was oddly chilling. "Meaning what?"

"Meaning that any population that breeds out of control sooner or later crashes because it's used up its environment. It's happening right now—I figure we're in the twenty-seventh day."

**Artie could feel the** hairs rise on the back of his neck. He couldn't remember Connie ever getting on a soapbox about anything. Or maybe Hirschfield had put the fear of God into her on this assignment, but why Hirschfield hadn't spoken to him, Artie didn't know. Granted that Connie's take on the series could probably be done. Shots of crowds with a telescopic lens so it looked like everybody was standing on someone else's shoulders, stock footage of sick deer wobbling around Angel Island from when the deer population had exploded because there were no natural predators, immigration smuggling from China and Mexico and a dozen other countries.

It was doable.

If anybody wanted to do it.

"You want to win a Peabody," Connie said slowly, "you have to take risks."

"A little while ago you said it was a shit assignment."

"I didn't say that—I said you probably thought that. And you probably do." Connie's eyes were narrow, her face blank of any friendship at all. Right before Artie's eyes she had turned into the Dragon Lady. "How long have you been here, Banks?"

Artie felt his face grow red.

"What the fuck's going on, Connie? You know how long I've been here: a year and a half, give or take a few weeks."

"And before that you put in a dozen years on a suburban daily and before that you worked for a clipping service and before that you had long hair and wore tie-dyes and worked for a hippy-dippy little counterculture station in Berkeley and before that—you were in the service, right? Special Forces, hero type, a chest full of medals? And now you think you've been here long enough and you deserve a promotion and a raise."

Artie suddenly didn't give a shit—he didn't have to take this. It had been a lousy day ever since he'd left the house and now he'd been ambushed at work. And by one of his best friends.

"Damn straight. And if Hirschfield is unhappy with my work, he can tell me so in person."

Connie was sweating so much her blouse was sticking

to her bra. Her eyes kept darting to the newsroom beyond the glass.

"You come from a print background and you think television's easy, that it's beneath you. You start doing crappy work because you think crappy work is good enough to get by. 'They call TV a medium because it's rarely well done.' Some print maven probably made that one up."

Artie stood up and started stuffing his notepad and pencils into his briefcase. Connie was suddenly on her feet, plucking at his shirt, apologetic.

"I'm not saying you're doing lousy work, Artie—all I want you to do is think a little. Every assignment is worth your best shot. End of lecture. I'll buy lunch."

Artie shook off her hand.

"You're a fucking bitch, Connie."

There was a knock on the door of the booth and Jerry Gottlieb leaned around so they could see his face through the glass. He looked worried. Artie waved him in.

"You just got paged, Artie. Some cops want to talk to you. They're in the lobby."

Artie had a momentary vision of Susan on the road to Willow with the tule fog smothering the freeway.

He picked up his briefcase. "Right behind you, Jerry." Out of the corner of his eye, he could see a pale Connie sag back in her chair. Serve her right if she died at her desk.

He worried about Susan all the way to the lobby, but a part of his mind kept going back to Connie's lecture. Somewhere along the line, he must have fucked up. And Jesus, he needed the job; he was too old to hustle for a new one. Maybe Hirschfield had put Connie up to it, was giving Artie a warning before calling him in. Or maybe Connie was just trying to make it look like the program premise was all his idea, and if the ratings sucked the albatross would be around his neck.

Then he remembered the confused look on Connie's face at the end and felt a sudden chill slide down his spine. Connie had been trying to convince him of something and had tried to make her point by picking an argument. But all of it had been out of character for Connie—way out. When was it that she had started to sound like somebody else? Just after she'd guessed that Adrienne Jantzen was going to blow it?

"Mr. Banks?"

He had reached the lobby, where two cops were waiting for him. His mind immediately filled with visions of Susan in a wreck on I-5.

It came as a complete shock when the cops told him about Larry Shea.

# CHAPTER 3

**The room in the** city morgue had a tiled floor with a drain in the center, several waist-high stainless-steel tables covered with rubber sheeting, and against the far wall a bank of stainless-steel drawers. Sullivan, the older and more poker-faced of the two cops, checked the names and motioned to the attendant in blue scrubs, who pulled one of the drawers halfway out. Artie could feel the butterflies start fluttering in his stomach. He'd seen war victims in 'Nam but had never gotten used to it. Besides, that had been a lifetime ago.

The attendant folded back the sheet so the body was exposed down to the navel. Sullivan glanced at it impassively. "His wallet ID was for one Lawrence Shea, M.D. Can you confirm that?"

Artie forced himself to step closer and take a long look. It was Shea, all right—but just barely. The eyes were blank and staring, the hair matted with dried blood. The soft tissues around the mouth were gone, exposing the teeth, and both the jugular and carotid arteries in the neck had been torn. The rest of the face was hamburger.

"Yeah, it's Larry." A part of Artie was morbidly comparing the body in the drawer with the live Larry Shea, laughing and cracking jokes and full of off-color stories about the nurses and interns at Kaiser. Another part of him was numb with the sense of personal loss.

"You sure?"

Artie nodded. "Didn't Cathy . . . didn't his wife identify him?"

"We called her last night—helluva thing to have to tell her. She said she'd come right over but she never showed. We called again this morning and nobody answered. The Oakland police reported a neighbor said she'd seen Mrs. Shea and two boys leaving the house early the previous evening. One of the doctors who worked with him at the hospital should be down any minute, but we like to get more than one ID if we can."

Artie wondered why they'd called him and how they'd gotten his name, then forgot it when he took another look at the body. He felt like throwing up. The attendant covered what remained of Shea's face with the sheet and rolled the drawer back into the wall. It seemed like it was freezing cold in the room and Artie wanted to rub his hands together to warm them up; the two cops seemed oblivious to the chill or were making a point of not noticing it.

Sullivan took pity on him. "Coffee, Mr. Banks?"

Of the two officers, Sullivan seemed the more relaxed in his uniform. McNeal, younger and buffed, was still playing the role of a rookie. Both of them looked like they might have been extras on a TV cop show.

"Thanks—black." A moment later he buried his face in the steam from a paper cup, grateful that it killed the smells of death and disinfectant.

"He was found in an alley off Larkin, about eight o'clock last night," McNeal said. He straddled a wooden chair and leaned his elbows on the back. "Actually, he was found in a packing crate in the alley."

The details were going to be sickening, Artie thought. No way was he prepared for them, no way he could tell the police to stop.

"Somebody . . . dumped the body there?"

Sullivan interrupted before McNeal had a chance to answer. "Don't think so. His keys and a pocket flashlight were also in the box, ditto his wallet. So far as we know, nothing was missing." His eyes never left Artie's. "It was a crate big enough to hide in. It's possible he crawled in it to get away from his killers."

Artie looked up from his coffee, bewildered. Plural. How did they know that?

"He wasn't alone," Sullivan added. He had settled comfortably back in a chair a few feet away, his own cup of coffee on the tiled floor beside him. "Some homeless guy was in the crate with him. Apparently he was living in it, judging from the crap strewn around. He was dead too, but he wasn't torn up. Alcoholic. Probably died of natural causes."

"I don't get it," Artie said.

Sullivan shrugged but offered no explanations. "Any idea what Dr. Shea was doing in the Tenderloin that time of night?"

Artie shook his head. "We were all supposed to meet last night at eight, at Soriano's on Geary—"

Sullivan glanced over at McNeal.

"You know the place, Mike?"

"Yeah—good Italian, pricey. They got rooms in back for parties."

Sullivan turned back to Artie. "Who do you mean by 'we'?"

Artie took a big swallow of coffee and felt it burn all the way down. "We're members of a club. Larry was supposed to be the speaker that night."

McNeal, suddenly alert, said, "What kind of club, Mr. Banks?"

"We're all professional men—some women, too," Artie said slowly. "We meet every three weeks and talk about the latest in our different fields. I'm a television newswriter, Larry was a doctor, Mitch Levin is a psychiatrist—"

"Any idea what Dr. Shea was going to talk about?" Sullivan interrupted.

"Nobody ever knows; that's the point."

Sullivan and McNeal glanced at each other without expression. Sullivan cleared his throat.

"A couple of kids in the neighborhood said they saw Dr. Shea running north up Larkin. From their description, he was either on drugs, drunk, or running away from somebody. But there was nobody chasing him. That would have been around seven-thirty or so. One kid saw him duck into an alley about half a block south of the Century Theater. Sometime later a cook in a Thai restaurant went out in the alley to dump some garbage and saw a man standing by the crate. The cook asked what he was doing there and the man didn't answer, just walked away."

Sullivan finished his coffee and put the cup back down on the floor.

"It's well enough lit back there that the cook should have been able to make some identification, but he claimed he didn't get a good look. He sounded a little spooked—he was the one who found the body."

"Larry didn't drink," Artie said. "He didn't do drugs either."

Sullivan stared at him. "Any idea where his wife might have gone? We had the Oakland police check this morning. Nobody home, no sign of foul play."

Artie felt shock and then a sudden wave of fear. He shook his head.

McNeal had been teetering on the back two legs of his chair and now dropped to the floor and leaned forward.

"Dr. Shea didn't make any rounds in the Tenderloin, did he? Drop in on some of the down-and-outers? Maybe some of the prostitutes?"

Artie smothered a glare and shook his head. "He was a happily married man." He caught the look on McNeal's face and let his voice freeze. "Really."

Sullivan said, "Ever been in trouble with the law, Mr. Banks?"

Artie hadn't been expecting it, then realized he should have.

Stiffly: "No." And then he remembered. "Just kid stuff."

McNeal unfolded from his chair and said, "Would you come with us, Mr. Banks?"

Neither of them seemed very friendly now.

**The conference room had** a battered wooden table in the middle surrounded by a dozen folding chairs. A few feet away was a card table with a large coffee Thermos, a stack of paper cups, a small jar of Coffee-mate, and a bowl holding little blue packets of Equal. Artie guessed that the coroner and his assistants met here to discuss the bodies on the floor below.

The man in the rumpled business suit at the head of the table looked like he was a year this side of retirement. He had salt-and-pepper hair, a belly that pushed against the edge of the table, and looked vaguely familiar. He nodded at Artie to sit down and Artie judged him as curious, friendly, and professionally detached. There was a small ashtray in front of him, a straight-stemmed pipe resting in it.

McNeal had remained by the door. The suit glanced over at him, then back to Artie. "If you want any coffee, just signal officer McNeal."

His voice was familiar, too: heavy and whiskey rough, the result of too many doubles after a shift. When he talked, he flashed a mouthful of gold crowns, and it was only then that Artie recognized him.

The suit caught the sudden look of recognition and smiled. "My name's Matt Schuler. I'm a lieutenant of detectives. I used to be assigned to Park Station."

It had been a long time, and Schuler had changed a lot. He was a little pudgy now and Artie guessed he'd given up his workouts at the gym years ago. But then he was twenty pounds heavier himself and it wasn't all muscle, either.

Schuler glanced at some papers in front of him.

"Ordinarily I'd have you sign a statement—you can do that later—and I'd fill you in on the investigation and that would be that. Unless we had occasion to call you back. But you were a friend of Dr. Shea's and I thought we might talk about him a bit, try and figure out just what happened and why."

He was a lot smoother than he used to be, Artie thought. Experience counted for something after all.

"How'd you get my name?"

"We checked Dr. Shea's ID when they brought him in, phoned the hospital, and they gave us his schedule. He was on call and they knew he'd be at the restaurant. We checked with the manager and he said a group of you were having a meeting there. Apparently you've been meeting there for some years now; he remembered all your names without even checking the reservations list."

"The officers told me something of what happened," Artie said in a strained voice. "Larry was supposed to meet a group of us at the restaurant and he never showed. That's all I know."

Schuler leafed through some yellowing papers in front of him and Artie suddenly realized what they were and why the cops had asked if he had ever been in trouble with the law. Arrest records from when he had lived in the Haight.

"All of you have known each other for a long time," Schuler said thoughtfully. "Long before you started having your dinner meetings."

For Christ's sake, Artie thought bleakly, it had been more than twenty years ago.

Schuler took a pair of steel-rimmed reading glasses from his shirt pocket and centered them on his nose before picking up one of the records to read. It was all for show, Artie realized; Schuler had gone over them before he'd even walked into the room.

"We all do things when we're younger that we'd like to forget when we grow older." Schuler glanced at him over the top of his glasses. "I don't think you'd be up to climbing the towers of the Golden Gate Bridge today."

**It had been after** most of the hippies and the rock groups had left the Haight-Ashbury to the students and young singles. There had been a group of them who used to hang out at a coffee shop on Irving near Ninth, and one night they'd decided to form a club. You had to have been there, Artie thought wryly, and most of all you had to have been young and stupid.

That first night they'd voted for a group initiation and decided on doing something really daring: They'd climb the north tower of the Golden Gate Bridge. It had been a moonless night, the tower had been wreathed in fog, and at the top the wind had been chill and so strong it would have blown him off if he hadn't held on for dear life. He'd been scared shitless.

Mitch Levin had taken one look at the tower and immediately elected himself as lookout. He hadn't been a very good one. A driver in a passing car had spotted them and called the police. When they finally climbed down, the cops were waiting for them. The story had made the front page of the *San Francisco Chronicle* and the fine had been a hundred dollars each, a lot of money back then. All of them had framed the clipping—Artie's was somewhere on a shelf in the bedroom closet—and prevailed on their parents to pay the fines.

Schuler had been the arresting officer.

A month later they'd climbed the wall and paid a nocturnal visit to the San Francisco Zoo. The animals hadn't been happy to see them, and the uproar woke the neighborhood. That time they'd spent the weekend in jail in addition to paying a fine. After that, they scaled down their adventures and became more cautious. Or so Artie had heard. Two weeks after the animal act, he decided to do something positive about his education and joined the army; later, he heard that most of the others had done the same. It had been an education, but not quite the kind he'd been hoping for. He'd been in time for the last year of the war in 'Nam and still had nightmares about the three months spent in a Charlie prison camp before escaping.

Schuler was looking at him with a bemused smile on his face, probably remembering when they all had been a bunch of hippie kids and he had been the Establishment Pig. Christ, had they ever called him that?

"I've always wondered," Schuler said. "Why'd you call it the Suicide Club?"

"It was from a story by Robert Louis Stevenson. We started meeting in a coffee shop and the owner suggested it—I think he might have collected Stevenson. At the time, it seemed appropriate."

"I heard later that most of you wound up in Vietnam. Decorated—all of you, right?" There was a note of respect in Schuler's voice.

Artie nodded without saying anything. Schuler put down the yellowed forms and shifted gears.

"Do you know why Dr. Shea was in the Tenderloin?"

Artie shook his head. "No—he was supposed to meet us at the restaurant. He was the speaker for the night." Schuler looked curious and Artie explained what the Suicide Club had turned into.

"Any idea what he was going to talk about?"

"He'd phoned Susan—my wife—earlier in the afternoon and sounded excited about the meeting, but he didn't mention the topic." Schuler looked thoughtful and Artie asked, "Do you have any idea who did it?"

Schuler surprised him. "We have them in custody right now."

*Them.*

"I still don't understand why Dr. Shea was wandering around the Tenderloin. Your club doesn't have some kind of oddball ritual . . ." Schuler looked embarrassed for even suggesting it.

Artie stiffened. "We're a little old for that, Lieutenant."

"My apologies for asking. It's just that I suspect there are no straight answers to any of this."

"You said you have somebody in custody?" Artie tried to sound strictly professional. He was a long way from being a kid and he wanted to remind Schuler of that.

"Do you know where Shea's wife might have gone?" Schuler suddenly asked. "She was scheduled to come in last night to identify him. She didn't and when we called this morning, she didn't answer. We had the Oakland police check and she'd left, along with their two boys. Any idea where they went?"

"None at all," Artie said slowly. "You think she's . . ." His voice dribbled off.

Schuler shrugged. "The husband is dead and the wife has disappeared. It's impossible not to think there's a connection, but at the moment I don't know what it could be." He turned to McNeal. "Okay, bring 'em in, Mac."

Artie moved his arms slightly so his sweaty shirt wouldn't stick to him. He wondered how he would react to seeing the murderers of a good friend. Dispassionate? Or filled with rage and a desire to commit murder himself?

McNeal came back leading three dogs on leashes: two pit bulls and what looked like a collie-retriever mix. Artie stared. The three of them would be enough to take a man down, but it was still difficult to believe. They trotted behind McNeal, glancing curiously around the room and wagging their tails.

"You serious?"

Schuler lit his pipe and leaned back in his chair. "Ordinarily if dogs attack somebody, they're destroyed

almost immediately. These we're saving for evidence
until we locate the owners." He looked disapproving.
"People turn dogs loose in the city when they don't
want them anymore. Pit bulls are always bad news if
they've been trained to fight and then are abandoned
by their owners. Back in the good old days, we used to
have dogcatchers who took care of them. The city
doesn't have that kind of money now, and neither does
Animal Care and Control. So we wind up with packs
of feral dogs on our hands. The small ones die, get
run over, get killed by bigger dogs. Some of the larger
ones acquire street smarts—they avoid busy streets,
they learn to keep away from traps and poison. They
attack people's pets, sometimes young kids. This is the
first instance we know of where they've attacked an
adult male—and killed him." He shook his head. "Dr.
Shea was apparently hiding in the packing crate. He
would have been on his hands and knees—an invitation for feral dogs."

Schuler glanced down at a report in front of him
and read it aloud.

" 'Officers called to the scene found three blood-
stained dogs at 15 Olive Street'—they call it a street
but it's really an alley—'nosing around a packing crate.
They apparently attacked Dr. Shea in the crate and
were responsible for his death.' " He looked up. "We
still don't have a clue as to what Dr. Shea was doing
in the Tenderloin or why he was hiding in the crate."

Artie stared down at the dogs sniffing around his
shoes and the leg of the table. He had a sudden desire
to reach out and scratch the nearest one behind the
ears.

Then he noticed the matted hair and the rich dark
stains around its muzzle.

**Outside, Artie had just** flicked open his umbrella and stepped to the curb to hail a cab when somebody called, "Hey, Artie, over here!"

The group was huddled under an overhang, and he hurried over. Schuler must have interviewed them one by one and afterward they had waited to see who had been next and to compare notes.

Artie furled his umbrella and squeezed under the overhang with them. "What do we do, wait for Jenny and Lyle?"

Mary Robards looked impatient. "I'm getting soaked. If we're going to talk about it, let's go someplace."

Charlie Allen turned and started to waddle down the street. "Coffee shop's this way; spotted it driving over."

At the tiny restaurant with its faded beer signs and grease-stained walls, Artie ordered coffee, black, then hesitated and added a pastrami sandwich.

He glanced around the table. Hail, hail, the Suicide Club was now in session. Mary Robards, one of the few original women members who had stayed in the Club, now thirty pounds heavier and abrasively cynical. Schuler must have been surprised. The last time he'd seen her, Mary was a sweet-tempered eighteen with a bad complexion and a figure that wouldn't stop. Both had given her an attitude, one that had changed a lot when her sexy walk became a middle-aged waddle. She was an attorney now and considerably more self-assured; she also seemed more comfortable than the others with growing older.

Pudgy Charlie Allen looked sweaty and nervous and obviously guilty of something, but then he usually did. Charlie had been the bravest of them all; he'd always figured they were going to get caught anyway so what the hell. He now had two kids and was assistant city librarian for San Francisco Public—he was the only one Artie really envied, purely because he seemed the happiest.

Then there was Mitch Levin, his best friend and a regular racquetball partner he could always beat—the best kind. Tall, wiry, with a sharp nose and thin face that made you think of the old *Strand* drawings of Sherlock Holmes. A professional bachelor and man-about-town whom they all claimed to envy but whom nobody did. As always, Mitch was dressed to the nines but still managed to look at home in a south-of-Market grungy coffee shop, even with his steel-framed granny glasses. Mitch had a sharp mind and was somebody Artie always felt he could depend on. His only fault was that he had been a captain in 'Nam when Artie had been a sergeant, and Mitch had never quite forgotten it.

Artie lingered a moment at Dave Chandler, the leading man and director of Theater DuPre, making a production of ladling sugar into his coffee and stirring it with a plastic spoon. Whatever Dave did, he did it as if an audience were watching. Boyishly handsome, so the reviewers said, even in his midforties. What irritated Artie was that the reviewers were right; for Chandler, time seemed to have stood still. In real life, he had been cast against type: a man who was universally well liked and would give you the shirt off his back if only he had one. Scratch him behind his left ear and his right foot would twitch. Dave was an inoffensive guy but always on stage. To the best of Artie's knowledge, the real David Chandler had never stood up.

"Schuler's just as big a bastard as always," Mary said, grimacing at a trace of lipstick on her cup. "He didn't need all of us down here." She looked like everybody's mother, Artie thought—a great asset when she was trying to convince a jury. "Goddamned cold in there. At least they could have told us to keep our coats. . . ."

Her voice faded and they were all quiet for a moment, remembering the stainless-steel table and what Larry had looked like.

"Anybody talk to Larry yesterday?" As usual, Mitch had elected himself to chair the meeting.

"I had an appointment two days ago." Charlie Allen looked uncertain. "He talked about the meeting but he didn't say much." They all stared at him expectantly, and he shrugged. "Just a general physical—

prostate exam, that sort of thing. Pretty embarrassing when a friend does it."

"Thanks for sharing," Mitch said dryly. "Anybody know of any enemies Larry might have had?"

Artie certainly didn't; neither did the others. There was a long silence. Then Chandler said; "What about drugs?"

Mary stared at him. "Drugs?"

"Don't doctors have access?" Chandler said defensively. "Maybe somebody wanted him to write a prescription, badly. You call it—you know more about drug cases than I do."

"I doubt it," Mary sniffed.

Their food came and they fell silent again. Artie's pastrami-on-rye was better than he expected.

Mitch took several bites of his sandwich, then pushed it away. "Anybody have any ideas why Larry was in the Tenderloin?"

It sounded too much like McNeal, and Artie muttered, "He sure wasn't looking for a peep show."

Schuler had put his finger on something during their meeting, something that Mark had mentioned at home. Charlie Allen said it for him.

"Anybody know what Larry was going to talk about?"

Mary frowned. "Medicine's a big field; it could have been anything. I doubt that it would have been world-shaking. Last time it was his turn, he talked about the importance of aspirin in Western civ."

"I thought that one was pretty good," Chandler murmured. He concentrated on his hamburger, not meeting her eyes. Jesus, Artie thought, some antagonisms die hard. Twenty years ago, Chandler had been the only one in the Club whom Mary had turned down and he'd never forgiven her.

He teetered back in his chair. "Cathy talked to Susan a few days ago; said Larry was looking forward to their Christmas get-together."

Mary turned sarcastic. "Not exactly of crushing importance in a homicide, Artie."

There was another long silence, then Chandler offered, "I had lunch with him last week. He said he was working on an article for *Science*—sounded pretty enthusiastic."

Even Charlie Allen looked serious at that one, but it was too easy to draw a connection, Artie thought. The *Science* article and his talk, both about the same thing? Maybe.

"You tell Schuler?"

"I didn't think it was important." Chandler caught the expressions of the others and looked embarrassed. "Hell, I didn't know. Maybe it was. I'm not a cop."

Charlie Allen smothered a belch and pushed back from the table. "None of us are," he said regretfully. The undertone of sadness in his voice reminded Artie of Larry Shea and the body in the morgue and his own difficulties in making a connection between the two. Charlie had probably been Larry's best friend; the two had been a lot alike.

"Anybody think the dogs did it?" Chandler asked.

They looked at one another in sudden silence. Larry had been a palpable presence at the table, but they had gone out of their way to keep the conversation technical. Now Larry was upfront in their minds, the contrast between the memories of a laughing, very-much-alive Larry Shea and the ruin in the morgue stark and tragic.

Mary was the first to offer a professional opinion. "I think the wounds on Larry's face and throat would be consistent with an animal attack. But I don't think the dogs went after him out of the blue. I think . . . somebody was responsible."

Chandler nodded at Mary, taking advantage of a chance to make peace. "You're probably right."

Another moment of silence, then Mitch dabbed at his mouth with a paper napkin. "If Schuler comes up with more information and lets any of us know—"

"Not likely," Mary muttered. "I don't think he trusts any of us."

Artie signaled the waiter for the check and fished around in his pocket for his wallet. The only new information had been offered by Chandler, and it didn't seem like much on the face of it. But it was a shame they all hadn't been there. Jenny Morrison—quiet, beautiful, reserved—a dean's assistant at San Francisco State and Mary Robards' significant other, which nobody ever talked about. And Lyle Pace, a former star athlete never able to forget the one time he'd almost made the Olympics. Artie hadn't been close to either of them when they had joined. He still wasn't. But they might have had something to offer.

"The services," Charlie Allen said at the door. "What about the services for Larry?"

Mitch shrugged into his coat. "Cathy will probably make the arrangements." Then he added vaguely, "Or relatives. I'm sure Schuler's notified them."

Which meant that Schuler had told Mitch they hadn't been able to locate Cathy, but he hadn't told the others. Artie paid at the cash register, pulled his collar up around his neck, and stepped outside into the drizzle. These were sad circumstances but it was always good to see his friends—despite the fact that they had pretty much drifted apart over the years and it was only the Club meetings that kept most of them together.

He smiled to himself. It was tragic, but it was almost like it was the old Club again. Somebody had attacked one of their own, and suddenly it seemed like it was all for one and one for all, even with the backbiting. Unconditional loyalty was probably a tradition in every club.

Except something hadn't been right.

But he couldn't quite put his finger on it.

# CHAPTER 4

"**You want a lift,** Artie?" Mitch Levin was half in the door of his BMW. "C'mon, I'll drive you back to the station."

"Sure, why not." Artie ran his hand over the paint job before climbing in. Mitch had bought the car a month ago and had immediately driven over to show it off and let Artie drive them to Sonoma and back. Shrinking paid better than Artie thought, though Levin had a reputation for being a damned good psychiatrist.

They had driven in silence for several blocks when Mitch said, "I can't believe the dogs were feral. One of them was still wearing tags. Nobody abandons a dog with their name and address hanging from a tag around its neck."

Artie was only half listening. He'd have to call Susan that night and tell her the bad news.

"They tore a man apart, Mitch. They had to have been feral—savage dogs." As an afterthought he added, "They were probably runaways."

Mitch shook his head. "My old man used to raise dogs. These weren't runaways, unless they ran away in the last day or so. All of them looked like they had been groomed sometime within the past week. The cops certainly wouldn't have touched them—their coats are evidence."

Artie hadn't wanted to talk about it, but Mitch had already distanced himself from the tragedy and was looking at it like he had looked at cases in 'Nam. Questions and answers, investigations and interrogations. He'd liked doing it and he'd been good at it.

"I wonder what the hell Larry was doing in the Tenderloin."

"You can bet dollars to doughnuts Mary was right—somebody sicced the dogs on him."

Artie had a mental image of muggers with attack dogs. Not a bad idea, but not in this case.

"Trained dogs would be valuable, Mitch. They wouldn't have been abandoned. And you just said that one of them had a tag." Some of the day's depression resurfaced. "If somebody *had* sicced the dogs on him, why Larry?"

"Chandler probably came close. Larry was a doctor. He had a triplicate prescription pad so he could prescribe Class Two narcotics. I've had patients try to blackmail me for prescriptions and one or two who threatened violence." Mitch looked thoughtful. "I just can't believe the dogs went after Larry on their own."

How long had it been since he had been a staff sergeant and Mitch had been a captain in Intelligence? They had been close when they were kids in the Club; they had grown to depend on each other in 'Nam.

Which didn't mean they were qualified for this one, Artie thought. Stay the hell out of it.

Mitch suddenly pulled over to the curb. From the look on his face, Artie guessed he'd made up his mind. Mitch, Charlie, and Larry had buddied together when they were in the Club, and Mitch and Larry had gone to medical school together. Mitch wasn't going to let Larry's death lie, to just let the police handle it.

"Somebody had it in for him, Artie. Larry was in the Tenderloin because somebody wanted him to be there.

Either he was decoyed there or chased there and then killed there. Where the dogs fit in I'm not sure, but it wasn't accidental. The only motive I can think of is that his killers wanted drugs. You'd have to believe in the Easter Bunny to think Larry was involved in any kind of dealing, so they must have been after him for access—his prescription pad."

Mitch sounded unemotional, but Artie could sense the anger beneath.

"The only things we know for sure are that he never made it to the meeting and that he was killed in a Tenderloin alley. And that nobody knows what the hell he was going to talk about."

"Mary was right—Larry probably would have rattled on about some wonderful new advancements in medicine," Artie said quietly. "You know that—that's what he always talked about."

Mitch took a deep breath. "Any other ideas?"

"The cops said they contacted Cathy last night and she was going to come in and identify Larry. But she never showed, and when they called this morning, nobody was home. Maybe Cathy and the boys have returned from wherever they went. We could call them. . . ."

"Come on, Artie—you want to talk to them about Larry over the phone?"

"No, of course not." And then Artie thought, In for a dime, in for a dollar. "We could drive over there. I could call the station, tell them I won't be back this afternoon—not much of it left anyway."

Or better yet, not call in and let Connie stew for a while. Besides, he needed a cooling-off period before seeing her again.

Mitch punched a number on his cellular phone and left a message for his secretary to cancel all appointments. A few minutes later they were on the Oakland Bay Bridge heading into the blanket of winter smog that covered the East Bay. The steel beams of the lower deck flickered past, and Artie found his mind cycling back to the morgue and the bloody ruin that had once been Lawrence Shea. He agreed with Mitch: feral dogs were hard to believe. But why would anybody want to kill Larry? Money? He would have turned over his wallet without a fight. Drugs? Despite what Mitch had said, far-fetched. And why go to the trouble of setting him up in the Tenderloin?

Aside from war and crimes of passion, people were killed for only two reasons: either for what they had or for what they knew. And Artie couldn't think of anything that Larry had that somebody else might have wanted badly enough to kill for.

Which left the question, What had Larry known that might have made him dangerous to somebody else? Hell, he had been a doctor; medically speaking, he had known a lot about a lot of people.

"You still coming over for Christmas Eve dinner, Mitch?"

"Yeah—wouldn't miss it."

"Bring somebody if you like. Just let us know in advance."

"I'll do that."

It had been a standing invitation, but when Mitch came over, he always came by himself.

"We've got tickets to *A Christmas Carol* on the twenty-seventh—Mark doesn't want to go, and Chandler's playing the Ghost of Christmas Past."

"Chandler? Thanks heaps, Artie—but no thanks. He'll leave the scenery in shreds."

They were heading into the Oakland hills when Mitch said, "You know, you were really the ringleader."

Artie looked blank. "What do you mean?"

"The Club. It was your idea."

"No it wasn't. It was Dave Chandler's."

Mitch shook his head, half smiling. "It was your idea, Artie. You were the one who wanted to call it the Suicide Club."

Artie was only half listening.

"I thought it was Rob, the guy who ran the coffee shop."

There was a simpler explanation for Larry's death. He had wandered innocently into the Tenderloin and three stray dogs had attacked him and killed him in an alley. It came down to a choice between improbabilities. On one hand, motive and purpose. On the other, a sequence of random events—

"You sure, Mitch?"

"Absolutely."

**It was almost dusk** when Mitch parked half a block away from Shea's house in the hills, the BMW half hidden by the trees and the curving road. Artie looked at him in surprise. "What's up?"

"Just cautious. Supposedly the Oakland cops checked it out this morning. Don't know if they might still be around, so let's wait a minute."

Artie peered down at the house. There were no police cars parked in the driveway, no yellow tape was stretched across the entrance warning trespassers away from a crime scene. After a moment, they drove on up. Strings of Christmas-tree lights outlined the garage and the steps that led to the redwood balcony circling the house. The garage was open, Larry's Chrysler still parked inside. Cathy must have driven Larry to the BART station the previous morning, Artie thought. But her own Honda wasn't there.

There were no lights on in the house, and Artie figured the outside Christmas lights were on a timer.

"Nobody's home," Mitch murmured.

"No surprise. She's still away with the kids, then." Artie felt relieved; they'd be spared an hour of tears and reminiscences about Larry.

Mitch was already out of the car. "No sense sitting here freezing. Let's take a look."

They walked down the stairs to the porch and rang

the buzzer at the side door. There was the sound of chimes on the inside. Mitch waited a moment, then leaned against the buzzer again. Another long moment. No lights came on; there were no sounds of footsteps, no sounds of life.

"The glass doors overlooking the hillside," Artie muttered. "Larry never locks them."

They walked around to the front of the house that faced the ravine below. The hill was steep and clogged with brush and eucalyptus trees. Larry had been lucky; the fire of '91 had spared this particular glen.

There was a two-inch gap between the frame and the leading edge of the glass doors. Artie put his fingers inside and pulled back until one of the doors obligingly rolled open a few feet.

"Cathy? Andy?"

No answer, though Artie hardly expected any. It was twilight now, the moon full, the ravine below thick with shadows. The wind had also picked up, rustling through the eucalyptus leaves.

"Let me find the lights. . . ."

Artie heard Mitch feeling his way around the wall and then the lights flared on.

The living room was spacious, with the glass doors and huge picture windows fronting on the balcony and overlooking the woods below. A long oak table was flanked by a couch and several black leather recliners, all of them facing the windows. A writing table, chair, and floor lamp were in the far corner. A brick standalone fireplace blocked off the kitchen from the living room, while an entertainment center hugged the far wall. Two VCR tapes were on the floor in front of the television set: *Men In Black I* and *The Mask II*, the evening's entertainment for the boys. Bookcases lined the entry hall, and several shelves of CDs were half-hidden behind the large floor-standing speakers.

"Hey, Artie, in the kitchen."

There was an urgency in Mitch's voice and Artie

turned away from the view and hurried into the large kitchen. Cathy was a gadget nut with the latest in fridges and a glass-topped stove where spills could be wiped off with a damp cloth. Spice racks filled the wall over the prep counter and pots and pans dangled from hooks on an iron wheel suspended from the ceiling.

Mitch was standing by the round kitchen table. It had been set for three. The serving dishes in the middle were still partly filled with food: sweet potatoes, ham, and broccoli with a small wicker basket of what looked like sourdough bread. On all three dinner plates, the ham and the sweet potatoes had been partly eaten; on two of them, the broccoli lay untouched.

Apparently neither Andy nor James cared for broccoli, Artie thought. Mitch lifted a plastic carton of milk from the tabletop, then set it back down.

"Feel it, Artie."

The carton was warm, room temperature. Then Artie noticed the little things: the chairs that had been shoved away from the table, the container of now-liquid Dreyer's strawberry ice cream sitting on the counter. Cathy had probably put it out to soften by meal's end so it would be easier to serve. Susan did it all the time.

"From last night," he murmured.

Mitch nodded. "Looks like they left in the middle of the meal."

Artie glanced around the kitchen. No signs of a struggle, no signs of violence, no blood splashed around, all the knives still safely in the knife rack.

"They just got up and left?"

"Apparently," Mitch said. Almost to himself he muttered, "She must have been terrified." He picked up the milk carton to put back in the fridge, then paused with the refrigerator door open. "Hey, Artie, take a look."

On one of the shelves inside, several jars of jam were

lying on their sides, leaking their sticky contents onto the shelf below.

Mitch frowned. "Cathy's too neat—somebody looking for something?"

Artie shrugged. "Probably the kids." He started down a hallway. "The bedrooms are down here."

**The boys' bedrooms were** first, one on either side of the hall. They were typical rooms for ten- or twelve-year-old kids: bookcases cluttered with games and a few comic books, *Star Trek* posters on the walls, school T-shirts hanging on the inside knobs of the doors. In Andy's room—he was the oldest—a small Mac sat on a desk with a stack of video games to one side. Andy was a computer nut, junior grade, and a Little Leaguer, major.

Artie opened the closet door. Shirts, pants, jackets, and gym sweats hung haphazardly on hangers; Rollerblades and several pairs of scuffed Reeboks lay on the floor along with two piles of wadded-up underwear. There was a small suitcase in the corner. Artie hefted it. Empty.

Mitch called from James's room. "They didn't pack."

"Yeah, I know," Artie muttered. They had walked out without taking a damn thing with them.

The far end of the hall was the master bedroom. It was neat, the bed made up, the rug freshly vacuumed. A brief portrait of Cathy surfaced in Artie's mind. Trim, obsessively neat, compulsively friendly. Adored her kids, was probably more proud of Larry than in love with him. At parties he'd caught her glancing at Larry with a faraway look in her eyes and had wondered who she was thinking of. Not Larry, that was for sure. But she was a dutiful wife and he didn't want to look behind the curtain to see who might be hiding there. Cathy was Susan's best friend, and Larry had been one of his and he'd never wanted to know too much.

Artie glanced in the closet. He'd already guessed that Cathy hadn't packed anything either.

They hesitated a moment outside the closed bathroom door, then Artie turned the knob and abruptly pushed it open. Empty. One of the towels, the one featuring Batman, was bunched up on its rack. Andy's. Superman, next to it, was neatly hung, the edges carefully lined up. James took after his mother when it came to neatness. He was a skinny kid with thick glasses and his nose constantly in a book, so quiet you seldom knew he was around. When he reached his teens, he'd be another patient for Mitch.

The towels were soiled but dry; nobody had used them recently.

"So what now, Mitch?"

"His office—we probably should have searched it first."

"Mitch, what the hell are we looking for?"

Levin seemed completely dispassionate now, pure intelligence captain. "Anything and everything, Artie. Try and find out who saw him last."

The office was off to one side of the kitchen. It was small, no bigger than one of the boys' bedrooms, with bookcases overflowing with medical books, two four-drawer filing cabinets, a copier and a portable phone, plus an IBM clone and HP printer. And on the edge of the desk, a Rolodex, a leather-bound Daily Reminder, and half a dozen copies of *Science*, one of them opened to the contents page. Chandler was right— Larry had probably been working on an article.

Artie picked up the Daily Reminder and thumbed through it. Larry had stopped making entries in March. Most likely he kept an appointment calendar in the computer.

Mitch was ahead of him. He was sitting in front of the computer and had already opened the appointment file. He glanced at the screen a moment, then shrugged. "Nothing, didn't use it. Probably kept everything down at work."

Artie was watching over his shoulder. "See if he had any research files."

Mitch clicked the mouse on "Program Manager" and read down the directories, stopping at "Research/December." He double-clicked on the entry but no filenames appeared on the screen.

Artie looked over the desk, picked up a small box of floppies, flipped through them, and pulled out one with the same directory name. The diskette had a dozen filenames penciled on the label, starting with *Austin* and ending with *Talbot*.

He handed it to Mitch. "Try this—probably the backup. See if you can access 'Talbot.' "

Mitch inserted the diskette in the B drive, then clicked on the name of the directory. The screen read: *No files found.*

"It doesn't make sense," Artie murmured. "He wouldn't have made a backup if there was nothing to back up."

"Maybe somebody erased both it and the hard drive."

"So where does that leave us? We've no idea what Larry was working on or who he was seeing or what happened. We're back to square one."

Mitch shook his head. "Check out the desk."

Artie squatted down and inspected the desktop. A small clock radio by some shelving had been moved several inches, and Artie could see a light ridge of dust where it had been. Most likely Cathy and the boys had stayed out of the room and Larry hadn't been the type to do much in the way of cleaning—the desktop clutter was a sure indication of that. Why would anybody move the radio now? he wondered.

Then he saw the row of small boxes behind it, several of them out of alignment with the others. Somebody had checked out all the boxes of backup floppies, not just the one he'd picked up. They had been neat about it, but not too neat.

There was a lined yellow pad on the desk, a corner of it jutting over the ridge of dust where the radio had been. Somebody had moved it, too. He picked it up and squinted along the edge. The paper was smooth, no impressions at all. But there were sheets missing; he could see where they had been ripped out. Larry had probably written on it, but somebody had taken his notes and the few pages beneath.

Mitch clicked off the computer and leaned back in the chair, his face blank of expression. "You put it together yet?"

"You tell me."

"Cathy knew what Larry was working on—no way he wouldn't have talked to her about it. Whatever it was, it worried her. More than that, it frightened her—a lot. When the police called, she grabbed the kids and split. Right in the middle of the meal—no time to pack. She was out of here. Sometime later—maybe within minutes—she had a visitor who was looking for something. The house was empty, so her visitor went right to the office. He knew exactly what to look for, and it wasn't the family silver."

"Why *a* visitor?" Artie asked. "Why not several?"

"Just a hunch. Maybe there were more than one, but nothing indicates it. House is too clean—they would have left more traces."

"So what do we do now? We've no idea what Larry was doing or who he saw or what happened."

"You're right. Let's pack it in."

Mitch stood up and started for the door, Artie following. Then Artie snapped his fingers and headed back to the kitchen. "If you were married and you were looking for an appointment, you'd know the first place to check is the fridge."

The yellow Post-it was stuck to the front of the refrigerator, nestled between episodes of Doonesbury torn from the Sunday paper. A brief reminder to see a Dr. Paschelke of East Bay Medical Center, dated the day before the meeting. There were two numbers listed, followed by an *H* and an *O*. At the top of the tiny sheet were three red-inked stars. Important.

Mitch studied it for a moment. "You pick it, Artie—home or office?"

Artie glanced at his watch. It was still early in the evening.

"It's the Christmas season; he's probably working short hours—try home. Set up an appointment for tomorrow."

Mitch looked through the windows at the darkening shadows outside. "Whatever's going on, I have a hunch there's a time frame involved. Cathy ran the moment the police called her with the bad news. I'd feel better if we could see the doctor tonight, get it over with. He can't live too far away—the call's local."

He had a point, Artie thought. And they'd come this far—wrap it up tonight and he could concentrate on ecology and Connie tomorrow. If he wasn't home by six, Mark would assume he was working late and defrost a frozen meal for supper. He wouldn't be too disappointed; he lived on them.

Artie slipped into his coat and buttoned up while Mitch picked up the kitchen phone and started dialing. He was halfway through the entrance to the side door when he saw it. An old raincoat dangling from a hallway hook, flanked by jackets and scarves and several school caps hanging from other hooks.

Artie felt the folds of cloth. Bingo. A three-and-a-half-inch floppy disk in the right-hand pocket. There was no name on it but it was smudged with prints and was obviously a "traveler" diskette. Larry apparently took his homework to the office so he could work on it when he had an occasional few minutes of free time.

Artie slipped it in his coat, then snapped alert when he heard Mitch suddenly say, "Dr. Paschelke?"

Much to Artie's surprise, the doctor was in.

# CHAPTER 5

**Castro Valley was half** an hour from the Oakland hills in the daytime but closer to forty-five minutes during the evening rush hour with a light rain slicking the streets. Dr. Leonard Paschelke's home was hidden in a small grove of young redwoods a hundred feet off the road. His office was in the basement rec room and was a lot like the man himself: large, rumpled, and comfortable. Books lined the walls; a stack of well-thumbed medical journals held down a corner of his desk. The far end of the room was taken up with a cheap stereo system and an old TV set. The battered couch in front of it was half-filled with torn pillows and kids' toys. Paschelke shooed his two small daughters off the couch and sent them upstairs to keep their mother company in the kitchen. He turned off the TV and waved Artie and Mitch to take a seat, then waddled over to an easy chair and sank into it with a sigh.

"You said you wanted to talk to me about Larry." He added affectionately: "The son of a bitch in some kind of trouble?" Paschelke peered at them over the top of his thick glasses. "You said you were friends of his, right?"

They hadn't talked to Paschelke about Shea's death over the phone, and Artie was now sorry that they hadn't; it was going to be much more difficult face-to-face. He and Mitch looked mutely at each other, then Mitch told a simpler story about Shea being mugged and killed in the city and his wife and children having disappeared. He didn't go into detail about the dogs.

A fat, pale-faced man who nervously polished his glasses and rubbed his nose, Paschelke looked more mournful with every word. When Mitch had finished, he said in a husky voice, "We did our internship together. Good man, good doctor. We kept in touch. Sometimes I'd ask him to come over to East Bay Medical for a consultation."

"Outside of his wife and kids, you were probably the last one he knew who saw him alive," Artie said.

Paschelke blew on his lenses and attacked them with a dirty handkerchief for the third time. "Nobody knows where Cathy and the boys are?"

Artie shook his head. "They obviously went someplace, but there was no sign they had packed for it—their suitcases were still in the closet."

"I don't know what I can add . . ." Paschelke paused in midsentence, frowning. "You said Larry was going to give a talk at your meeting?"

Artie edged forward on the broken-down couch.

"Did Larry mention it to you?"

Paschelke looked from one to the other, suddenly cautious. "If he did, I'm not sure I'd remember."

Artie sank back, disappointed. Dry hole. Or maybe Larry had mentioned the meeting and the subject matter but Paschelke didn't want to talk about it. If he didn't, it must have been a hot topic between them. "Larry was a consultant for East Bay?"

"More for me than for East Bay." Paschelke squinted at Artie, the light from the desk lamp reflecting off his glasses. "You're not a medical man, are you?"

"TV newswriter," Artie said. "My job has nothing to do with Larry."

He could read the suspicion in Paschelke's face. Reporter, so be wary. Paschelke turned to Mitch.

"You're the psychiatrist?" Mitch started to fumble for his wallet and identification, but Paschelke held up a hand. "No, no, I believe you." He hesitated, then made up his mind to trust them. "I'm on staff at East Bay. They've got a twenty-four-hour trauma center and it gets pretty busy on the weekends. I'm usually on call in the ER—the interns call it the Knife and Gun Club because we get a lot of inner-city homicides. Also, freeways 580, 880, and 238 run close by, and if you get racked up on any of them, the East Bay ER is where they're going to take you."

He hoisted himself out of his chair and shuffled over to a small refrigerator in the back of the rec room. "You want a beer? Soda?"

Artie declined with thanks. Mitch asked for a beer and Paschelke returned with two cans of Miller, wiping the frosted tops against his pants.

"We were just trying to follow up on Larry's last day or two," Mitch said.

Paschelke popped open his can of beer and took a sip, then looked at Artie with renewed suspicion. "Anything I tell you, I don't want to see it on the evening news. Larry was the private type, and so am I."

"I was a friend of Larry's," Artie said simply. "That's why I'm here. You don't want to tell us anything, you don't have to."

Paschelke stared at him a moment longer, then nodded. "Banks . . . I think Larry mentioned you." Another sip of beer. "Anyway, three weeks ago last Friday there was a bad accident on 580 about one in the morning. Two high school kids high on beer and methamphetamine were driving an old forty-nine Merc—can you believe that? a classic car—and plowed right into this poor old bastard in his Saturn. The kids went through the windshield and it was slice-and-dice all over the freeway. No seat belts, no air bags, no nothing. . . . There wasn't anything we could do but pour them into buckets and notify their folks. They went straight to the coroner."

He was silent for a moment, concentrating on his can of beer.

"The old man in the Saturn was . . . something else. We did what we could for him but he was pretty badly busted up—died on the table." He sank back in his chair, his expression suddenly remote as he remembered the scene in the ER.

"You said the old man was 'something else,' " Mitch prompted, curious.

A snort. "Because he was something else, that's why. That's when I called Larry and asked him to come over and have a look-see, confirm what I thought I was seeing."

Artie was puzzled. "There must have been other doctors present."

"Always is. But not everybody sees the same thing . . . or is interested in seeing the same thing. Larry and I had worked together a number of times; we usually saw things the same way."

There was an edge to Mitch's voice. "You didn't call the police? Notify the relatives?"

Paschelke looked pained.

"I guess it's been a while since you did a rotation in an ER, Doctor. The police are usually first on the scene—they follow the ambulance crews to the hospital. They're the ones who go through the victim's pockets and the car, find the ID, and call the next of kin. They were right there with this one. I made my report and they went away. Nobody they could notify in this case. The car wasn't his. And he had no ID."

"No place of employment?" Artie asked, surprised.

"I told you. No ID, no nothing. The police went through what was left of his car with a fine-tooth comb. All they got was a name on a cleaner's tag on the inside of his coat. William Talbot. Just a name and a garment number, nothing more—no address or city for the cleaner, nothing. Only a tag the wearer had forgotten to remove. Not even sure that was his real name—what the hell, he could have borrowed the coat, I suppose. The police checked out the car. A rental but the name on the rental agreement didn't check out either. Perhaps his prints will, I don't know. The police will probably just log him in their files and hope someone reports him missing. Maybe somebody will, but I doubt it. Had to be a reason why there was no ID anywhere in the car."

Artie forgot about his long trip back to the city.

Talbot was the name on one of Larry's files.

**"Why did you call** in Larry?"

Paschelke crumpled the empty beer can in his fist. "Specifically? Condition of the body. Facially, Talbot looked like he was in his early sixties. Only thing was, his bones weren't old. We tried to set a few of them while he was on the table—I told you he was pretty broken up. A lot of compound fractures where the long bones protruded through the flesh." He shook his head, remembering. "A real mess."

"I don't understand about the bones," Artie said, frowning.

Paschelke leaned forward to explain, his expression almost professorial.

"Look, when you grow old, your bones get brittle, they lose calcium. If you exercise a lot, the deterioration is slower, but it's still there. What you can't change are the pads of cartilage at the ends of the bones that begin to thin out as you age. You're not as flexible anymore; you've got less connective tissue, less cushioning. The shafts of Talbot's long bones were thick with heavy ridges for the attachment of what were exceptionally powerful muscles. If I had to go by the bones, I would have said the man was a naturally very strong thirty-, thirty-five-year-old. One thing for sure: He was either a young man who'd been through a helluva lot or he was one damn healthy old fart. That's when I called up Larry and asked him to come over."

Mitch looked at him sharply. "Larry wasn't a specialist in orthopedics."

"That's not why I called him. Larry and I had worked together before; we were interested in the same things, medically speaking. In this case, the limits of human variability. Me, because as a surgeon I'm naturally curious. Larry, because he specialized in the circulatory system and, believe me, the anatomical variations can be enormous. Human variability is something all doctors are interested in, *have* to be interested in. It's a good part of what makes horse races in medicine. How much a person can differ physically in heart size, brain size, weight, height—that sort of thing—and still be within normal bounds. Strip down a pygmy and a tall Swede, have them stand side by side, and you'd be hard pressed to say they were of the same species."

He got up and waddled over to the fridge for another can of beer. When he came back, Mitch said, "So Larry came over. Then what?"

Paschelke looked uncomfortable. "The man was dead. He had no ID, no known relatives. You can't hold them in the morgue forever. If the body isn't claimed, it's turned over to the coroner and cremated or donated to a medical school. Larry came and took a look and we got curious. There was nobody to notify, no way we could hurt the man no matter what we did. So as the physician of record, I decided to do an autopsy."

Mitch raised his eyebrows. "And what did you find out?"

Paschelke held up his hand and started listing the findings on his fingers. "The arteries showed no signs whatever of atherosclerosis—they were what cardiologists call 'pipes.' Even when you're young, your arteries usually show some fat deposits. The heart was oversize, beyond what I'd call normal limits. I mean the entire heart, not just the left ventricle, which might be expected if the man had valve trouble or was suffering from heart failure. The arteries feeding the heart were very large and, as I said, very healthy. No way in the world he would ever have had a heart attack."

"What about the lungs?"

"Clean, much too clean even for those living in the country these days." The basement was cool but Paschelke had started to sweat. "The body didn't look— normal. To either of us. Larry took measurements, a lot of them, and inspected the other organs. No signs of deterioration in any of them—I'm talking about normal deterioration with age. If the man hadn't died, our guess was that he would have lived a lot longer than a healthy hundred."

He sank back in his chair, rolling the cold can of beer between his sweaty palms.

"And there was the accident itself. The kids were going the wrong way on a ramp. It should have been a head-on, both cars completely demolished. It didn't happen that way. Talbot reacted pretty fast—far faster than he should have been able to. According to the police, he almost made it, twisting the steering wheel to swerve out of the way. The kids clipped his Saturn at the rear and it rolled down an embankment. That's what did the damage, both to the car and the driver. Seat belt didn't help and, since the car was rolling sideways, neither did the air bag."

He lapsed into silence, concentrating on his can of beer.

"You think Larry was going to talk about this?" Artie asked. It was pretty morbid; he couldn't imagine Larry picking it as a topic.

"I told you Larry took measurements." Once again, Paschelke sounded uncertain of himself. "A lot of them. In anthropology, they call it cladistics, the science of measurements to determine what species a creature belongs to. The pygmy and our Swedish friend might not look much alike, but when you measure the shape of the skull and the way it sits on the spinal column, the teeth and the shape of the long bones and all of that, it's obvious they're members of the same species." He paused, remembering. "Larry got pretty excited."

"Why?" Artie asked, puzzled.

Paschelke looked embarrassed.

"He didn't think William Talbot was human."

"Jesus Christ, little green men," Mitch muttered.

Paschelke sat up in his chair, suddenly very formal. "I didn't say anything like that, Doctor. The man was genus *Homo,* there was no argument about that. But Larry didn't think he was *sapiens.* From what he told me about your meetings, I'd say yes, that's what he was going to talk about."

It was suddenly so quiet in the basement that Artie could hear the wind in the redwoods outside.

"What did you think?"

Paschelke looked uneasy. "I can't say as I came to any conclusions. The body certainly pushed the limits of human variability, but after you see a lot of bodies, you get reluctant to set limits. But I couldn't disagree with Larry on any of his findings. And the man's physical strength was certainly beyond the norm."

Mitch snorted and stood up, ready to leave. Artie pushed himself off the couch, thinking once again about the long trip home. He slipped into his coat and turned to say good-bye.

"What do you mean, his physical strength was beyond the norm? How could you tell?"

Paschelke shrugged. "Just that. Beyond the norm. William Talbot twisted the steering wheel to swerve out of the way of the Merc. He still had it in his hands when the police pulled him out." He looked up at them. "He twisted the damn wheel right off the steering column."

"Superman," Mitch sneered.

Paschelke was insulted.

"I didn't say that, either. Who knows what somebody can do in extremis? I know a man who once lifted a car off a friend pinned underneath. . . . Oh, I thought Talbot was human enough. At the high end of the bell curve, obviously, but human. It was Larry who thought he was . . . different."

"He could have taken a DNA sample," Mitch said coldly. "Satisfied his curiosity easily enough."

"He did, Dr. Levin," Paschelke said, just as cold. "Five milliliters of blood and a small tissue sample from the kidneys. But I doubt that he had time to have the tests performed before his . . . death."

It was dark and the drizzle had changed to a cold rain. Mitch turned up the heater and slowed the car, searching for the turnoff to the freeway.

"Did you believe all that crap?"

Artie stirred, half asleep.

"I'm no doctor, Mitch." After a moment's thought: "Maybe. If everything he said was true, it's the sort of thing that would've gotten Larry's water hot. I can see him going off the deep end about it."

"You think there's a connection?"

"Connection to what?"

"Between the man they autopsied and Larry getting killed in the Tenderloin."

Artie blinked the sleep from his eyes.

"That's some stretch." He suddenly wasn't sure. "Larry did the autopsy and wrote up his notes. The next night he's killed in the Tenderloin and his family disappears and his home is ransacked—carefully." He frowned. "I don't know. Because events happen in sequence doesn't necessarily mean there's a connection. Paschelke was with him. He knew as much as Larry did and he's still alive."

The roadside sign said another twenty miles to San Francisco.

"Larry believed the guy was something else, and Paschelke didn't. That might make a difference."

Artie was wide awake now. Despite the heater, it suddenly felt colder in the car.

"He didn't believe it until we stopped by and told him about Larry being killed. Maybe he's rethinking his position. There's a chance we didn't do him any favors asking him about it."

He thought about it a moment longer.

"Imagine there *is* a connection. Say somebody knew the old man was . . . different . . . and didn't want anybody else to know and went to extraordinary lengths to shut up the one man who did know and those he might have mentioned it to. But first he would have had to know that the driver was in an accident. Then he would have had to know that Larry had done the autopsy and made notes. After that, presumably, he followed Larry into the city, somehow sicced the dogs on him before he could talk to us at the meeting, and then went over to Oakland to kill the family or confiscate all the research—or erase it—or maybe both. Not to mention going through the fridge looking for little test tubes of DNA samples. That's a lot for one man to do in one night."

"Maybe he had help."

"Sure, Mitch, maybe it was all a secret experiment of some sort. Larry found out and so the government had to get rid of him. They sure chose a strange way of doing it."

"Larry's dead, Artie. Don't make jokes about it."

Artie felt irritated.

"What difference does it make if Talbot was . . . unusual? Who the hell cares? So the cops called Cathy and she freaked, grabbed the kids, and went to a friend's house or maybe a relative's. What would you expect her to do? At the very least she'd be looking for comfort and somebody to help handle the kids. What's so surprising that the diskette was erased and the hard drive was fucked up? The office was probably forbidden to the kids, which meant it was a huge attraction for them. So they played with the computer when nobody was around and they screwed it up. They wouldn't have been the first kids to do that."

"You're trying too hard," Mitch said quietly. And after a few miles more: "I guess I just can't believe Larry's dead. I don't want to believe that was him on the table." He changed the subject. "What about the diskette you found in his lab coat?"

Artie had forgotten about it. "You saw me?"

" 'The Shadow knows'—there was a mirror by the side door so Cathy could see who was coming."

"I'll give the diskette to the intern down at work to print out. Maybe it's nothing, maybe it's Larry's notes— we'll find out. We ought to think about services for Larry. His parents are dead, but I know he had a brother or a cousin back East. And we should contact Cathy's relatives. . . ."

"The ones she went to visit last night without even packing?" Mitch shook his head. "Sorry, Artie, promise."

Artie wasn't sleepy anymore and was sorry that he wasn't. In his mind's eye he kept seeing Larry crouched in the packing crate, trying to fight off three feral dogs.

"Paschelke was something else—to coin a phrase," Mitch mused.

Artie didn't answer. He had closed his eyes, but much as he wanted to, he couldn't doze off.

" 'I'm a victim of soicumstance,' " Levin suddenly said, chuckling.

Artie opened one eye.

"Too easy, Mitch. That's Curly."

Artie picked up his car in the KXAM lot; he didn't bother checking to see if Connie was working late. He'd see her in the morning and that would be too soon.

It was a little after ten when he got home. Mark had fallen asleep on the couch, a *Friends* rerun on the TV set. Artie didn't wake him but went to the kitchen and ate half a bowl of cereal, then dumped the rest in the sink and walked out on the back porch. The rain had let up and it didn't feel quite so cold.

He leaned his elbows on the railing and stared out over the city. They were on a hill, the porch three stories above Noe Street. It was a great view, one of the things that had decided him and Susan on buying the house. They had bought it in the early eighties and gotten it cheap. It was worth a lot more now—retirement money when the time came.

On the street below, a few young men were slogging through the drizzle to the bars around Castro and Market. Lonely people, he thought, everybody by themselves, almost nobody walking in pairs. They'd sit in a bar, get loaded, and pick up somebody at closing time so they wouldn't have to spend the night alone.

He stared more intently at the sidewalk. Somebody was watching him from the street below, he thought, annoyed. Then the annoyance slipped easily from his mind and he went back to staring out over the city. It was one lousy time for Susan to go up north. Nobody should be alone on the holidays; nobody should have to be alone anytime. Too many people looked forward to going to work simply because they were surrounded by people they knew, then went home to TV dinners and their one reliable friend, the Tube.

To a part of Artie, it suddenly seemed like the air was alive with electricity. There were little crosscurrents of wind and whispers in the night. But most of him ignored the wind and the whispers and the tentative plucking at his mind, the twinges in the air around him.

Then a murmur in his mind, a bubble of thought.
*that's right . . . one fucking, depressing life . . .*

A part of Artie was suddenly frantic.

There was a flutter of wings a few feet above him, and he looked up to watch a gull wheeling by in the rainy night. If you had to settle for living, that would be the life he'd settle for. Just flap his wings and fly.

Only a faint sigh this time, a subtle urging.

*go ahead . . . try it . . .*

He wasn't aware of climbing to the top of the railing that circled the porch and teetering on the edge, his arms outstretched. One step, he thought. One step off the railing to catch a rising air current and then he'd soar over the city like the gull.

"Dad!"

Somebody grabbed him around the waist and the next thing he knew he was lying on the redwood deck of the porch, his face bruised and bleeding from smashing into the wooden planking. Mark was holding him, his T-shirt clinging limply to his chest, his hair plastered over his face from the rain. He must have lunged for Artie from his wheelchair, which was still in the doorway.

For a long moment Artie couldn't even think. It was raining and he was wet and cold, though there seemed to be less electricity in the air. Just the wind and the rustle of the leaves and, somewhere in the night around him, a vague sense of surprise and disappointment.

"What? What the hell—"

"God*damm* it, Artie, you were standing on the railing! You were going to jump!"

Artie twisted around to stare at the railing. When had he made up his mind to go over? Or what had made it up for him?

He shivered. Larry had died because he'd found out something he shouldn't have.

Now he knew part of what Larry had known and if it hadn't been for Mark, he'd be dead too.

Which didn't make any sense at all, because he
didn't know enough about the dead driver of the Saturn to believe or disbelieve—
Anything.

# CHAPTER 6

"This will hurt a little," Mark said. He'd wheeled his chair over to the sink and filled a basin with cold water, grabbed a washrag, and turned back to the kitchen table, where Artie was huddled in a chair clutching a cup of coffee. Mark soaked the rag in the water and wrung it out. "Lean back—I'll wipe away the blood and pull out any splinters."

It hurt like hell, but Artie held his head still and let Mark mop his face. He could feel Mark's hands tremble. After a minute, Mark asked in a strained voice, "What happened out there?"

Mark was frightened, Artie thought. Afraid of what he'd just seen, afraid of *him*. He was probably convinced his father was losing it. What the hell did he tell Mark? Or did he tell him anything?

"I was staring out over the city and—Jesus, be careful with the goddamned rag!"

"Sorry."

"I was staring out at the city and I was feeling depressed—" He stopped. It was coming out lame and weak and sounded more like an admission than he wanted it to be.

Mark didn't meet Artie's eyes. "You . . . can get

help," he said, picking his words, not sure what was appropriate.

Artie took a deep breath. "I wasn't so depressed I wanted to go off the railing, for Christ's sake." He was talking to Mark like they were equals, something of a novel sensation, though it had to happen sometime. He picked up a dish towel and dabbed at his wet face. The towel came away streaked with blood, but he wasn't bleeding too badly; no need to go to Emergency.

Mark rolled over to the sink to rinse out the washrag. "I knew you were going through a downer the last few days." He was trying very hard to sound adult.

"Somebody was watching me from the street," Artie said slowly. "They . . . got inside my head." He started to shake with reaction.

Mark stared at him.

"What do you mean?"

Artie thought of telling him everything that had happened at the office when Connie had been off the wall, and then what Paschelke had told him and Mitch. But it was going to be tough enough trying to explain his sudden desire to imitate a seagull. He changed the subject.

"Larry Shea was killed last night. He was in the Tenderloin and a pack of dogs got him. Feral dogs."

Mark was shocked, the expressions fleeing across his face like shadows.

"You can read about it in the morning paper," Artie said. He got up from the chair, grimacing at the sudden pain. He'd twisted his leg when Mark had pulled him back from the railing and it hurt to walk. He limped over to the sliding doors that opened onto the rear porch. Mark wheeled after him, alarmed.

"What the hell you going to do?"

"I want to see if they're still out there. I'll be on guard this time." He wondered if it would do any good even if he was.

It took all the courage he had to step back onto the porch and walk to the railing. But the evening was still, the rain a steady drizzle, the wind a quiet murmur in the trees. Artie shivered. Somewhere down the block a dog barked and then there was nothing but the small noises of the night. There was no sense of anybody on the street below, no feeling of being watched, no feeling of *something* slipping into his mind.

When he came back in, Mark wheeled over to the doors and locked them. "We're in deep shit, aren't we?"

"I may be, Mark—you aren't." He wondered if that was completely true. "I don't know." Artie suddenly ached with exhaustion. "Honest to God, I don't know what the hell's happening." It was true, but it was an admission and he was ashamed because it made him sound weak in front of Mark.

Mark put a pot of coffee on the stove. "Sleep on the couch. I'll take the first watch." His voice was calmer now, his hand steadier when he lifted the pot.

"Against what?" Artie asked sarcastically.

Mark rolled to the desk and rummaged around in the bottom drawer where Artie kept his old army automatic. It had been special issue for Intelligence, small and easy to conceal, the grandfather of the Saturday night specials that soon followed. Not good for long range, deadly at short. "Neither of us knows, do we?" It was a brave, smart-ass answer and oddly cheering. Mark was sounding more like himself. And besides, he was right. Mark took out a magazine from another drawer. He loaded the gun quickly, efficiently.

"I told you never to go into the desk," Artie said, surprised not so much that Mark knew where the gun was but at the obvious familiarity with which he handled it.

Mark hesitated. "You want me to put it back?"

"Hell, no."

Artie stumbled over to the living room couch, only

half aware when Mark spread the afghan over him. There was a lot of his mother in the boy, Artie thought, and right at the moment he was desperately grateful, though a sense of shame lingered. Mark was protecting him, not the other way around, and that wasn't the way it was supposed to be.

So much for a terrifying night, Artie thought, slipping off. The hard questions would come the next day, and he didn't know how he was going to answer them. Or if he wanted to.

**In the morning, they** ate in silence. Artie's face hurt when he chewed, and he'd passed on shaving. Mark hunched over his bowl of cereal, not looking at him.

"You don't want to tell me anything more?"

"Not at the moment, sport." Mark was at the age where you first realize your parents have feet of clay, but there was no need to hurry the process. He wouldn't be able to make sense of the truth, even if he was told it. On the other hand, if he asked a specific question, Artie knew he couldn't lie to him.

"You going to call Mom?"

"Yeah. Find out how your grandfather is. And when your mother's going to come home." Christ, he wanted to talk to Susan so bad it hurt. He pushed aside his cup of coffee. No time like the present.

Five minutes later, he sat back down at the table and poured himself some more coffee. Mark had been watching him like a hawk, picking up on his end of the conversation and trying to fill in his mother's end.

"She's not coming back, is she?"

"Not right away. Your grandfather's doing worse; she's going to have to stay. She wants you to fly to Eureka as soon as possible. She'll meet you there and drive you to Willow. She was pretty insistent."

Mark went back to chasing the last Cheerio around the bottom of the bowl. "What about you?"

"This weekend. I'll take some sick leave. I'm working on a project with Connie Lee, but she can carry it for a few days."

Mark nodded. "I'll go up with you. There're two more days of school left and I want to finish. If you can wait until the weekend, so can I."

Susan had been definite about that—she wanted Mark up there now. She hadn't been nearly so definite about *him*.

"Your mother wants you today, sport."

Mark's face set. "I'll go up with you," he repeated.

He should make him go, Artie thought grimly. He'd told Susan about Larry Shea's death without going into any of the details, but she'd sensed something in his voice. After fifteen years, she could read him all too well. She knew something was going on and she wanted Mark out of there.

Another milestone, Artie thought. When your son develops a mind of his own and he's too big and too determined for you to use either force or argument.

"Suit yourself. We'll drive up on the weekend." Then, casually, "Stick around the house after school tonight." Mark was popular; his friends from school were always driving over to pick him up. "And stay away from the porch."

Mark hesitated and Artie would have bet he was going to say "I can take care of myself." He probably wanted to, but they both knew he couldn't.

"Sure, Artie."

After the school van had left, Artie packed his briefcase for work. Touching, Artie thought. Mark had wanted to stay because he was worried about him. But not nearly as much as he was worried about Mark. He hesitated at the door, then turned and walked back to the living room, taking the automatic from the drawer where Mark had put it and slipping it into his pocket. From now on there would be very few places he would go without it.

On the way out he wondered if he should call Susan back, tell her that Mark would be coming up with him on the weekend. But that would be a long conversation, and right at the moment he wasn't up to it. He'd call that night.

He got the car out of the garage, pausing a moment before getting in. There wasn't the same presence he'd felt the night before. There was no electricity in the air, nobody trying to open his head like they might open an oyster.

But *something* was out there.

Something very watchful.

Something very still.

"Hey, Jerry, catch."

Jerry Gottlieb plucked the floppy out of the air and glanced at it. "No name—mysterioso, right? What do you want me to do with it?"

Artie shucked out of his coat and threw it over his shoulder. "Print it out. Everything that's on it."

Jerry groaned. "One-point-four megs—that could be close to eight hundred pages."

Artie made a guess. "It's not full—maybe thirty, forty pages at best."

"You got it, but don't bug me for a while." Gottlieb disappeared down the hallway to his own cubbyhole, which was jammed with printers and computer gear. Artie headed for the glass booth, where he could see Connie already at the desk, thumbing through some pages.

"You're ten minutes late, Banks." She said it with a smile, but Artie didn't smile back and Connie looked uncomfortable. "I'm joking, Artie—just trying to make up for things."

Artie hung his coat on a hook and pulled over a chair. "I hope you're going to try harder than that." An image of a seagull fluttered through his mind and he felt some of his anger evaporate. He had a very good idea of what Connie had gone through yesterday.

"So just what happened?" he asked, deliberately trying to keep his voice bland.

A light coating of sweat covered Connie's forehead. "It's getting hard to remember, Artie. I was talking to you and then . . . it was like somebody else was using my mouth and my tongue. I swear to God, it wasn't me."

"Somebody else," Artie repeated, feigning skepticism.

"It sounds nuts, I know." Connie nodded toward the newsroom on the other side of the glass and shivered. "I thought . . . I don't know what I thought. I talked with Security to find out if we had any visitors. The usual messengers and such and then one guy who signed in from our ad agency. Nobody checked—who would? I called the agency and they'd never heard of him."

"What'd he look like?"

She shrugged. "The guard didn't remember anything. Just a guy in a coat. Not skinny, not fat, not tall, not short. Had hair, don't ask what color. He signed out shortly after you left."

"Nobody else saw a stranger in the newsroom?"

"Nobody I talked to." She shivered again. "Fucking creepy . . . Look, Artie, it wasn't me. I swear to God."

Artie got out his own pad of paper. There was nothing he could do, not until the Grub came back with the printout. And there was still the series. Probably a saving grace, take their minds off everything that had happened.

Connie shivered for the last time and penciled something on her tablet. "I think I know how to go with it. Extinctions."

Artie looked up, suspicious. Connie shook her head, her expression gray. "It's still me." She cleared her throat. "Extinctions," she repeated.

"What about them?"

She hunched forward over the desk, as if she were about to confide a secret. "Whole species are dying, Artie, and more of them are endangered. More extinctions are happening now than since the dinosaurs vanished. There've been five big extinctions before this—this is the sixth." She hesitated a moment, trying to read the expression on his face, then continued, a little defensive. "People are the cause; there're too many of us. Nobody's covered it except the science shows. And it gives us an overall view."

Even though Connie sounded like the old Connie, it still wasn't quite her, Artie thought. The old Connie would go for the immediate: the spotted owl, the whatever-you-call-it frog. Not for the philosophy of it, not for the big picture. She usually went for the little things that could give the viewer a perspective on the whole. Like the image of a child rooting around in a Dumpster for a feature on hunger among the homeless.

"You *have* been boning up, haven't you, Connie?"

She looked blank. "I don't follow you."

"When did you first think of 'extinctions'?"

She put her pad down on the table and looked out at the newsroom. "When I was talking to you yesterday," she said slowly. "I was going to bring it up but you were getting angry and I didn't want to push it." She turned back to Artie. "But whether I thought of it or . . . somebody gave me the idea, I thought it was worth following up on. So I had the Grub search the Internet."

Her voice started to trail off and Artie looked at her sharply. Connie was preoccupied with the idea. Normal enough.

"They're dying out there, Artie. Four thousand plants, five thousand animals at fifty to a hundred times the expected rate. Shit, we're not fishing these days, we're sifting the sea with filament nets. We don't catch many dolphins anymore but that's because so few are out there—"

"Throw your pad over, Connie. Let's see what you've got."

He was halfway through her notes when Jerry Gottlieb knocked on the door and opened it. "The assignment desk says to get your ass over there, Connie—we've got a breaker." He stood to one side to let her out, then handed Artie a sheaf of paper with a heavy binder clip at the top. "You were off by thirty pages, Artie—came to seventy-three, single-spaced."

Artie casually riffled through the pages. Text and diagrams and formulas, very little straightforward exposition—so far as he could see. It wasn't easy to read—gaps in a lot of the lines, pages with no paragraphing, type characters he'd never seen before.

"What the hell's wrong with it, Jerry?"

"Some sort of oddball format. When I get a chance tomorrow, I'll go back in and try and clean up the disk, print out a decent copy."

"You read it?"

Jerry shrugged. "I didn't get very far. The first few pages were grisly and after that, the writer lost me. What's your interest in it?"

"Favor for a friend of mine."

Jerry looked offended. "Always willing to help a friend of a friend, Artie. But don't ever make it a friend of a friend of a friend."

"So I owe you one."

Just before closing the door, Jerry turned, frowning. "That was bullshit about your friend, right? If you want it deciphered, I'd try one of the anthropologists at the science museum in the park—they're more user-friendly than the ones at UC Berkeley."

Artie raised an eyebrow.

"Then you read it through?"

"Are you kidding? It was hard to read and I only

understood every fifth word anyway—your secret's safe with me."

After he'd left, Artie spread the pages out in front of him and glanced through them. The details of the accident, sketches and photographs that Shea must have scanned in, were just as grisly as the Grub had said. Then there were lists of measurements and descriptions of how the skull set on the spinal column, complete dental charts—and comparison charts of just how the knee bone connected to the thigh bone, he thought irreverently, not only in Talbot but in a list of controls. Measurements of bone thickness, the size and shape of the teeth, the thickness of the orbital ridges . . .

And all of it harder than usual to read.

The Grub had made a good suggestion: take the printout to the Academy of Sciences in Golden Gate Park and let a professional guess at what Shea had been up to. Artie juggled the pages back into a neat stack and slipped them into a heavy envelope. He'd call the museum and make an appointment for later that morning, see what he could come up with for a bribe. It would have to be a hefty one to get anybody to try to puzzle out this mess.

A slight movement in the newsroom outside caught his eye and he turned. He had a vague memory of a brightly colored silk scarf and searched for it. Adrienne Jantzen—she'd been watching him. Now her head was down and she was busy at her computer, probably writing notes for the noon news. Attractive woman, he thought, then felt a sudden flush of guilt. Jesus, real macho.

He dialed the museum and a Dr. Richard Hall said he'd be glad to see him. Especially if Artie could help out with publicity for their new exhibit.

**Golden Gate Park was** an upper, even in the cold and the drizzle. The Academy of Sciences had been a favorite hangout when Artie was a kid. A planetarium, an aquarium, and halls full of stuffed animals all rolled into one. Plus a bookstore where you could buy books about dinosaurs and kits you could put together to make your own pterodactyl and a restaurant in the basement that served hamburgers that weren't as tasty as McDonald's but were probably better for you.

The director's office was hidden behind a gallery they were renovating for a new exhibit—according to the sign, it would be the world's first virtual reality diorama. The walls were blank. In the middle were a dozen cubicles with a chair in each, a computer workstation and a VR helmet and gloves hanging on hooks. Not very inviting, Artie thought, but then they weren't finished. Paint some dinosaurs on the walls, add some sound effects, and it would pull in the kids.

"Mr. Banks?"

The man was younger than Artie had been expecting. Short and muscular, kinky black hair in a modified Afro, horn-rimmed glasses, light brown skin, and teeth so white they made his smile seem bigger than it was.

He held out his hand. "Richard Hall, assistant curator." Artie shook it and was led into a cramped office. Hall motioned to the chair on the other side of an ancient wooden desk. "You said over the phone you were willing to do an article on Visions of the Past— that's what we're going to call the room outside—and you also wanted a favor. Quid pro quo?"

Artie started to apologize and Hall waved it away. "We could use the publicity—though the room won't be open for another month—and I've got some free time on my hands. So. What can I do for you?"

Artie opened the envelope and shoved the papers across the table. The work of a doctor friend, he said, who'd recently died. Apparently research on a body he'd autopsied, but Artie hadn't the slightest idea what it was about except it had something do with anthropology. . . . He let his voice trail away and looked at Hall expectantly.

Hall picked up the pages and thumbed them quickly with a slight frown. "It's readable, but just barely. What's wrong with your computer?"

Artie looked apologetic. "The technician said the copy was in an oddball format. He's going to clean up the disk tomorrow, but time's important."

"You're a relative, I take it?"

"Close friend." Artie hesitated, then added that the information was connected with the estate and if he could have some idea today—

Hall sighed. "If they're paying for it, they're seldom in a hurry. If they get it for free, they want it the day before yesterday." He grinned. "Okay. A feature story when we open the room. Deal?"

Artie thought about it a moment, then nodded as if the decision were a hard one to make. Hall pointed to the room outside. "The first booth is set up to go— you might as well try it out while I go through this stuff. The software's already in the machine—just put on the helmet and gloves, turn the computer on, and you're all set. The full program runs about an hour. When we're up and operating we'll slice it into five-minute segments—just about the attention span of kids these days."

In the Visions of the Past room, the cubicle setup looked as simple as Hall had said. Artie fumbled with the gloves a moment, slipped on the helmet with the virtual reality goggles and headphones, and flicked the computer's On switch.

**The scene was blurry** at first, taking a few seconds to swim into focus. Artie gasped. He was back in his dream, lying on the hillside, naked except for a piece of hide tied around his waist. White clouds floated slowly overhead and he could even smell the faint fragrance of the wildflowers. How the hell could they program odors? Or was he imagining the smells that would naturally go with the scenery?

There was a buzz of conversation in the air and he rolled to his knees, then stood up and turned to the caves behind him. Gathered in front were maybe twenty members of the Tribe, mostly young adults with half a dozen kids plus a middle-aged giant of a man with a dirty white beard. Just coming out of one of the caves was an old woman of forty winters, half supported by her young daughter. The kids were naked, the adults not wearing anything more than he was. A piece of hide around their waist, nothing binding the breasts. A husky-looking group, all of them with tangled hair and several with livid scars and limps, including the white-bearded giant.

He knew them all, Artie thought with wonder. Purple Flower, Deep Wood, Soft Skin, Clear Stream—the old woman, White Beard. He knew the kids even better; he was only a little older than they. Few of them had been named yet because so many, like Little Fox, died early.

White Beard grunted at him and he had a sudden mental image of a small pile of chipped rocks. The image faded and he scurried back into the cave and picked up a rush bag filled with a dozen flints. He was the most proficient in the Tribe at making scrapers and cutters, and he was responsible for them. They were moving to another set of caves and they couldn't afford to leave anything behind, least of all the flints.

He came out in the bright sunshine blinking. Deep Wood laughed at him and he laughed back and pegged a stone at his feet. White Beard scolded him again, and the Tribe got in a ragged line and started off down the path that wound along the side of the stream. It was time to move on; game was getting scarce and the berry bushes had been pretty well picked over. The new caves were closer to bigger game, which both excited and frightened him. A lot of meat for the effort, but you had to get in close to kill the larger animals and it could cost you your life.

He looked back only once, to glance at the spot where Little Fox had been given to the Spirit of the Flames the previous evening, after coughing for the last time. When they reached the riverbank, Clear Stream scattered the ashes from a leather pouch and Little Fox was returned to the Mother of Waters.

Artie shivered, then concentrated on Soft Skin walking in front of him, admiring the sway of her ample hips and imagining them both in a dark corner of the cave. She picked up on his thoughts and emphasized the swing of her hips even more. He grinned, delighted. Then Tall Tree noticed his arousal poking out from under his strip of hide and hooted and the rest of the Tribe turned and laughed. He reddened and resolved to get Tall Tree alone when they reached the new caves and teach him some manners.

It was a warm day and they'd broken once for a rest when Clear Stream noticed some new berry bushes still full with fruit. Shadows were just beginning to appear when they picked up their few belongings and continued on, their lips and fingers now dyed a deep purple. Cliffs were starting to rise along both banks of the stream and Artie noticed animal tracks breaking off from the path to lead down to the water. Game would be plentiful; White Beard had made a wise choice.

The path had narrowed, the cliffs rising to Artie's right. They were maybe twenty feet high, their shadows almost reaching to the water. But it was still warm, even in the shadows, with no wind—a beautiful day.

The attack came without warning. There were shouts from the cliffs above, and some Flat Faces appeared at the top to heave rocks down at them. The Tribe scattered along the pathway, some of them already clutching broken arms and showing leg wounds. Artie noted with amazement that Tall Tree had fallen to the ground, moaning, a stick jutting from his back.

White Beard whirled his club above his head and let it go. There was a scream from above and one of their attackers tumbled down to the path. Then a dozen of the Flat Faces were swarming down on them, either climbing across the rock face or sliding down on vines they'd thrown over the edge.

The Tribe managed to get together in a group with the cliff at their backs and clubbed down two more of the attackers. Suddenly one of them, who had been shouting commands in a language that seemed far more complex than White Beard's grunts, stepped forward, holding up his hands and smiling. The Flat Faces withdrew down the path and the leader came up to White Beard, still smiling and this time speaking in their own tongue, though he wasn't very good at it. They could go in peace if they left their flints behind.

White Beard nodded at Artie, who stepped forward with his rush bag. Then he stopped, alarmed. Around a curve in the path ahead he could see more of the enemy sliding down their vines. They were trapped now, Flat Faces in front and behind. Their leader in his speaking had been ... had been what? Artie couldn't think of a word for it.

The leader noticed his expression and sprang back while the others leaped toward them, thrusting with their sticks and clubbing those in front. Two of them clung to White Beard, stabbing at him. He went down, his throat cut. Artie was horrified. There might be nobody left to make a pile of twigs and branches and place White Beard and his favorite club on it as an offering to the Spirit of the Flames.

Deep Wood had floundered into the stream, which was now rapidly turning red, splashing frantically toward the other side. He almost made it before a stick cut into his side and he fell, holding his wound with both hands and screaming. Ahead of Artie, Soft Skin had been knocked to the ground, scratching at the Flat Face on top of her who'd torn away her strip of hide.

He hit her in the head with a rock and she suddenly lay still, but he didn't get off. Clear Stream was already dead, lying alongside the path, blood oozing from her mouth, her eyes blank.

Artie was the only one left standing now, bleeding from a dozen different wounds and screaming because of the pictures that kept flashing through his head and then fading and going black. In his mind he saw the death of every member of the Tribe while all around him he could hear the screams of the children and the cries of the injured. Then two of the Flat Faces grabbed him and threw him on his belly in the dirt, kneeling on his arms while they spread his legs apart and stripped away his bit of hide. He was filled with sudden fear because he knew they were going to use him the same way they had used Soft Skin. He tried to twist away but the one on top grabbed his hair and yanked his head up while the other held a cutter to his throat.

He was forced to watch while they slaughtered everybody, including the young children; he couldn't even move his head to look away. The cries were dying down now and soon the air was filled with silence and there were no more images flitting through his mind. He knew the Flat Faces were the enemy and he wanted to kill them all, but then he suddenly felt ashamed because compared to the members of the Tribe he thought they were . . . beautiful.

Just before his throat was cut he realized with horror that they were treating the Tribe like animals. Everybody's throat had now been slashed or their heads crushed by rocks, and the Flat Faces were hard at work with the cutters and scrapers they had taken from his rush bag.

They were butchering the Tribe for meat.

# CHAPTER 7

**"You all right?"**

Hall had shaken him lightly by the shoulder and Artie gingerly took off the helmet and the gloves. It was difficult to come back to reality, and he was afraid for a moment that he was going to be sick.

"You're pale as a ghost," Hall said, worried. "Too much for you? Some people get vertigo with the VR glasses."

Artie got to his feet, holding on to the top of the chair for support. "You're not going to show this to kids, are you?"

Hall looked surprised. "Why not? I think it's pretty effective. The kids'll love it when the pterodactyl zooms down at them. We're doing another one with a fight between a seismosaurus and a tyrannosaurus—one's from the Lower Cretaceous and the other from the Upper, but at least they're both North American, and anyway, I think we should be allowed some license."

"That's not what I saw," Artie said slowly.

Hall frowned and stepped around him to pull the diskette out of the drive. "Sure it is—see, it's marked."

Artie glanced at the typed label and mumbled, "What the hell . . ."

Hall was already back in his office, calling to Artie over his shoulder, "Let's do it; I've got an appointment."

Artie's mind was still thick with images of White Beard and Soft Skin and the feel of the stone cutter against his throat.

"I take it your friend wasn't the practical-joker type," Hall said, flipping through the pages of research in front of him. "Or was he?"

"I didn't see anything funny in there," Artie said curtly. He was looking at Hall through a haze of time that was only slowly beginning to drift away. Right then, Soft Skin and Deep Wood were more real to him than the anthropologist.

"No, of course not." Hall leaned back in his chair, uncertain how to begin. "If everything here is accurate, then I can understand why he was writing a paper about the deceased—a couple of references to *Science* in here. But I think this is one of those times when believing has to also be seeing. No scientist would take Dr. Shea's research at its face value without being able to see the subject he was writing about."

"You're losing me," Artie said.

Hall looked uneasy.

"According to Dr. Shea's research, the man in the accident wasn't human." He hesitated. "Let me rephrase that. He was but he wasn't. Human variability is enormous but"—he thumbed the pages again—"the statistics are here for anybody who wants to read them. Following Dr. Shea's figures, William Talbot wasn't human—not in the way we ordinarily define human."

"So what was he?"

Hall waved his hand at the papers, frowning. He was silent for a moment, obviously reluctant to comment.

"Your doctor friend was trying to prove that William Talbot was a modern descendant of a different species, one that dates back maybe hundreds of thousands of years. Dr. Shea was convinced he was right and thought he had the measurements to prove it."

Artie stared. It was one thing for Paschelke to say that Talbot had been different—radically different. It was quite another for Hall to say it.

"You're telling me that Larry autopsied a caveman."

Hall looked sour.

"Jesus, I hate that term. It's like the 'missing link.' I'm not talking about primitives, movie monsters running around in hair suits. I'm talking about the *descendant* of a species. You and I are descendants of an archaic human species called Cro-Magnon and we're not exactly primitives. I don't think Dr. Shea autopsied a primitive man."

"The only other species I know of is Neanderthals," Artie said, puzzled.

Hall sighed. "Neanderthal is safely extinct, Mr. Banks. So is *Homo erectus,* which some anthropologists think might have coexisted as well—primitive men have really been coming out of the woodwork lately. But Dr. Shea's measurements wouldn't support any theory that primitive men are still running around today."

"A descendant of another species," Artie said slowly.

Hall nodded. "That's right. A totally different species. One different from us and definitely from Neanderthal or *Homo erectus.* And that's just flat-out impossible."

"You keep coming back to cavemen," Artie said, uncomfortable.

Hall looked impatient. " 'Caveman' carries a lot of baggage with it. When I'm giving lectures to little kids, I use the terms 'Old People' and 'New People.' We're the New People, the late arrivals."

Artie pointed at the papers. "If Larry was right, that Talbot was different from us, then he would stand out in a crowd, wouldn't he?"

"I don't think so. From the photographs, facially Talbot was fairly average looking, your typical male of sixty or so. Even if you stripped him down, you wouldn't notice much out of the ordinary unless you were a doctor or an expert on anatomy—" He broke off. "You don't know much about this, do you?"

Artie shook his head. "That's why I'm here."

Hall glanced at the wall clock. "I'll make it brief. When we mention cavemen, we usually think of the classic type of Western Europe, the ones with the barrel chests and the short limbs and broad noses—adaptations to glacial conditions of Europe at the time. You can see the same sort of adaptation in modern Eskimos. There might even have been several varieties of the Old People—we'll call Dr. Shea's species that. Others might have lived around the Mediterranean and could have been a racial variation. More gracile—more slender, more graceful, more like us, if you will, adaptations to a gentler climate. Dr. Shea suggests all of that in his notes; he apparently thought Talbot was one of their descendants."

He frowned at Artie. "You getting this?"

Artie still felt numb from the images of the slaughter.

"Yeah. They weren't human."

Hall looked bemused. "They might have been more 'human' than we were at the time. They could have buried their dead with ceremony, signs of a primitive religion. Placed grave goods in with the burials—favorite weapons, toys if it was a child, things like that. They needn't have been 'inhuman' at all. They might have known about medicinal plants, might have taken care of the elderly and others who might have been sick or crippled. They wouldn't necessarily have left them on a hillside to die. We know that Neanderthals, for example, did all of that."

Artie managed a smile.

"That's a lot of might-haves. Now you're the one who's doing the speculation."

Hall shrugged. "You didn't read all of Dr. Shea's notes, did you? I'm just repeating the speculations he made."

"But you don't believe them."

"I told you. The idea is impossible."

"Why?"

"There's no proof. The simple fact is that any competitors to *Homo sapiens* died off thirty-five thousand years ago. We're the descendants of the only species that survived. We find the remains of Cro-Magnons, our own ancestors, and God knows we find plenty of remains of Neanderthals and a few recent ones of *Homo erectus* on the island of Java. But that's it. No mysterious other species, Mr. Banks. They left no bones behind at all, and without them there's no reason to believe they ever existed. We can account for all the bones in the bone bank."

Memories of the scorched spot where the Tribe had built a funeral pyre for Little Fox flashed through Artie's mind.

"They've found a lot of Neanderthal remains," he said slowly. "Why?"

Hall was beginning to look bored.

"Primarily because they buried their dead, usually in caves. Frequently with ceremony, indicating some sort of religion." He paused. "In a lot of ways they were much like us, Mr. Banks. They even had brains as large or larger. Maybe your Dr. Shea's Old People did too. Whether they were wired up the same way, who knows? But they're all gone now, one with history."

Artie shook his head. "What if the Old People had a different religion? What if they cremated their dead and scattered the ashes over running water? Then they would have left no remains, no bones, right?"

Hall laughed. "You're persistent, Banks. Granting that cremation dates back to prehistory—if that was the case, then you're absolutely right. They could have vanished without much of a trace. But your Dr. Shea doesn't suggest that, which puts you one up on him."

"They could have interbred."

Hall shrugged. "Who knows? To put it inelegantly, Mr. Banks, bones don't fuck. If they existed at all, your Old People might have interbred with the New People—us—and their genes lost in the larger gene pool. If they were a truly separate species, the offspring would have been sterile, 'mules.' But chances are if they were a separate species they would have been marginalized and just died out. Pushed out of their hunting grounds, outbred, that sort of thing. Simple competition would have done them in and modern man would have replaced them."

" 'Replaced,' " Artie repeated, remembering his hour in the virtual reality room. "You're being polite."

"Not really." Hall stood up and straightened his necktie, getting ready to leave. "There were probably some things your Old People weren't very good at. Some experts think that the real edge *Homo sapiens* had over other species was language. If the larynx of Dr. Shea's Old People was high up in the throat like it is in babies—they have to be able to breathe and swallow at the same time—they would have had a lot of difficulty. Lower down gives you a larger resonating chamber—you can make many different kinds of sounds. But the larynx is soft tissue and would never have survived, even if your Old People left some bones behind."

Hall took a moment to fumble out his keys. "The point is, if they weren't very good at language, that would have put them at a survival disadvantage with a group that was good at it—namely us."

"How?" Artie asked.

"It's obvious. Language is good for instruction, telling people how to make things. It's good for giving commands. With language you can have a verbal history, you can pass on information. . . ."

"You can lie with it," Artie muttered. The fight by the river was very vivid.

Hall looked startled, then changed the subject.

"They might not have been as good as *Homo sapiens* at hunting. For example, if they didn't have spears they could throw from a distance, everything would have been close up and dangerous." He shuffled the sheaf of papers back into its envelope, then hesitated. "You mind if I keep this until tomorrow? I'd like to go over it again tonight."

Jerry still had the diskette, Artie thought. He could print out another copy anytime. "Sure, I'll pick it up in the afternoon." He pushed back his chair. "You mentioned competition. Like competition for patches of forest that had berries and nuts, for hunting grounds with lots of game? Which might have led to warfare between the Old People and the New? Maybe they were killed off—early genocide. Same thing as being replaced, right?" The image of the slaughter was still flickering in his memory.

Hall's smile was patronizing. "Some anthropologists think it's a possibility, but you'd have to show me the killing fields. There's no evidence of any pitched battles with any other human species, or even any skirmishes, though there aren't enough bones lying around to prove it one way or the other. In Europe your Old People probably shared the same living space with *Homo sapiens* for thousands of years, the same in the Levant. My guess is they would have got along. But then thirty-five thousand years ago, something happened. Nobody knows what."

He suddenly sounded doubtful. "Maybe they didn't get along so well after that." He slipped into his coat, motioned Artie out, and locked the door behind him.

"What do you think about Talbot?" Artie asked. "You think he could be one of the Old People?"

"You mean like he was the son of a mother and father, both of whom were Old People? My God, no—

of course not. You'd be talking different species then. Your doctor friend got carried away."

"But say he was," Artie persisted.

Hall looked pained; he was getting tired of humoring him. "If he was, then that means there must be more of them out there, doesn't it? And if there are, my guess is they certainly wouldn't want anybody to know about them."

"Why not?"

"It's inbred in humans—we hate anybody who's different," Hall said dryly. "We don't treat other races very well. I wonder how we'd react to another species living among us?" He frowned. "Mr. Banks, we're all there is. I'm sorry your doctor friend wasted so much of his time. Neanderthals died out thirty-five thousand years ago and there's absolutely no evidence that any other species besides them and *Homo sapiens* and possibly a few examples of *Homo erectus* existed back then. Dr. Shea's theory is a little like the old saw about if we had some ham we'd have ham and eggs if we had some eggs. In this case, there's no ham, there's no eggs, and there's no other species. I'm sorry about that—I'd be fascinated if there were."

He glanced at his watch, said "Shit!" and half ran toward the main display rooms, taking a hard right around a display case holding a saber-toothed cat and almost running into a teenager with his face pressed against the glass.

Artie started to follow him, then hesitated at the first cubicle. He slid into the chair and put on the helmet and gloves, then flicked the switch. There was no warm-up period; he was suddenly sitting in the middle of what looked like a computer game. Better than Sega, better than Sony, and it was a *great* pterodactyl, but it had none of the sense of reality of the hour he'd spent trudging along a riverbank with the Tribe. What he'd seen that first time was beyond the capabilities of any computer he could think of. There had been the feel of wind, there had been smells, there had been . . . blood.

The images suddenly flooded back, and once again he was on his belly in the dirt with the cutter pressed against his neck, watching a two-year-old boy being held over the river while his throat was cut.

Artie tore off the helmet.

He was definitely going to be sick.

Artie managed to make it to the washroom before losing his breakfast, then soaked some paper towels in cold water and washed his face. It was midmorning; Connie would probably still be on assignment. He wasn't ready to go back to the station yet, in any event. He went out to the parking lot and sat in his car, the radio tuned to the twenty-four-hour news station, a white-noise background for his own thinking. The Tribe was at the far edge of his memory now, and Mark was much more center stage. Maybe he should have called in sick, stayed home with Mark. But what the hell—he'd told Mark not to go out after returning from school. He'd be okay.

". . . *Castro Valley. The doctor and his family . . .*"

Artie had a sudden premonition and turned up the volume.

". . . *apparently were murdered before the house was set on fire. The suspect is in custody at the scene. The Paschelke family was well respected in the community . . .*"

Connie's breaker, had to be. It was the middle of the day and traffic was light; he could be there in maybe half an hour. Artie fumbled his cellular phone out of the glove compartment. He'd call the station and then phone Mitch, have him meet him there as soon as possible. Find out what had happened. This time they had the maniac who'd done it, though he definitely wouldn't be your ordinary murderer.

**The drizzle had stopped,** leaving little droplets of water glistening on the needles of the pine trees.

It was chilly but the sun was out, and Artie guessed it would be warm by midafternoon. The town itself was idyllic, the kind you found on picture-postcard racks in drugstores. Not the proper setting for a brutal murder.

He could smell wet ashes two blocks away, then spotted the reeking heap of blackened timbers just beyond the line of trees that bordered the street. The ambulances had left but the fire trucks were still there, and several police cars. Mitch was watching Connie interview a fire captain.

"You're fast," Artie said. "I just called—"

"I had the radio on between patients and heard the first news flash an hour ago. Thought you might show up."

Artie showed his press pass to a curious cop, and he and Mitch walked over to the ruins. The cameraman was taping Connie's interview, the charred remains of the house in the background.

The house had been set back into a hill, so the rec room had actually been on the first floor. Artie could make out the few sofa spring-coils that marked where the couch had been and the half-melted bulk of the small refrigerator. A singed page from one of Paschelke's medical journals fluttered past and Artie grabbed it. Atenolol for arrythmias, "King of the Beta-Blockers."

He inspected the ruins a moment longer, then drifted over with Mitch to hear Connie's interview.

". . . the intruder apparently broke a window at the back—"

The fire captain was a big man with a mustache flecked with gray and rivulets of dirty sweat that had dried on his cheeks and neck. He was soot-smudged and tired, barely managing to tolerate Connie.

"We found Mrs. Paschelke in the bedroom. Dr. Paschelke and his two daughters were sitting on the couch in the rec room. Apparently they had fallen asleep watching TV."

"They had been"—Connie paused, professionally aware of the audience that would be watching the six-o'clock news—"murdered before the fire started?"

The fire captain nodded, knowing what she wanted. "Their throats were cut. Apparently the killer caught Mrs. Paschelke first, then the doctor and the little girls. All of them were probably asleep when he entered— no signs of any struggle."

"Robbery the motive?"

"Hard to tell. I don't think the police found anything on the guy they picked up. A neighbor phoned in the fire at the first sight of the flames." He sounded puzzled. "I don't know why the suspect hung around; he should have been long gone."

"Dumb," Mitch murmured to Artie. "Too dumb."

Artie spotted a figure huddled in the backseat of one of the police cars. "Let's ask him."

They walked over and peered in the closed windows, then a policeman came over to shoo them away. Artie flashed his press card again, but the cop ignored it. "Sorry, fellas, we've got to book him first. He'll be arraigned this afternoon or tomorrow morning. We'll have a statement then."

Artie had gotten a good look. A bewildered, skinny little man bundled up in dirty pants and a scarf and a worn overcoat two sizes too large. Salvation Army issue— the uniform you wore when you slept in hallways and pushed around a grocery cart with everything you owned in it.

"Some poor homeless bastard who hung around the town," the cop offered. "A few of the neighbors recognized him—he usually got to the recycle boxes an hour before the scavenger guys showed up, grabbed all the bundled newspapers and the bottles worth a refund. Probably how he lived."

"How'd he start the fire?"

"Would you believe it? Booze. The firemen said they could smell it, even over the stink of the ashes. Christ knows *he* smelled of it when we picked him up."

Artie glanced over again at the figure in the backseat of the patrol car. The man was pounding on the closed windows and shouting at them, a frantic look in his eyes. Artie couldn't make out the words.

Mitch said, "He's saying that he knew the two little girls, that he wouldn't have hurt them."

"You read lips?"

Mitch nodded and Artie walked away, embarrassed by the little man's pleading. At his car, Mitch asked, "Did he look like he was drunk to you?"

"Not really—but he's had time to sober up. Think he did it?"

"Do you?"

"Of course not—the devil made him do it." Artie caught Mitch's frown as he slipped into the driver's seat.

"I'm not being funny, Mitch. I'm serious."

# CHAPTER 8

**Connie would get back** to the office before he did, but she'd be tied up most of the afternoon editing the story. Artie figured he had plenty of time to do what Hall had suggested: if seeing was believing, then he ought to see just what William Talbot had looked like. He was no expert but he might be able to glean something.

East Bay Medical Center was only a mile or so from Dr. Paschelke's home and, like the doctor's house, was nestled in among the redwoods. The nurses at the front desk were friendly; the doctor he was eventually referred to was less so.

An elderly Dr. Frank Lassiter, thin and dignified and smelling very faintly of aftershave and strong disinfectant, obviously resented anybody from the media. Artie guessed that sometime in the past he'd paid a heavy price for being misquoted.

Lassiter thumbed Artie's press pass, studied it, then dropped it on his desk and leaned back in his chair, his hands behind his head. "So how can I help you, Mr. Banks?"

"The front desk said you were a colleague of Dr. Paschelke's."

"I'm a senior partner in his medical group." Only

the tiniest flicker told Artie that Lassiter had suddenly become more guarded than before. "The police have already been here. I couldn't tell them much of anything except how sorry I was. Apparently the world's going to hell in a Safeway grocery cart." He was cool, distant, and Artie couldn't tell whether he was genuinely sorry or not. He was the opposite of Paschelke; there wasn't much chance the two had gotten along. Paschelke had been a beer and barbecue man; Lassiter would prefer poached salmon and a German white.

"You worked with Dr. Paschelke in the ER?"

Lassiter nodded. "I've worked in the ER from time to time." Then, abruptly, he added, "Why the hell are you here, Banks? My time is valuable; I imagine yours is as well."

"I was a friend of Larry Shea's; he used to work with Dr. Paschelke too."

Lassiter relented. "Affable man. Two of a kind, I'd say."

Which meant that Lassiter had nothing bad to say about them but nothing good, either.

"They worked together on an accident victim," Artie said slowly, watching for any sudden change of expression. "The victim was a man in his sixties named Talbot."

Lassiter studied his fingernails.

"I remember the man. Drs. Shea and Paschelke performed an autopsy on him. I didn't approve." He looked up. "I thought it was unnecessary. They should have waited a few more days, see if any relatives showed up. There was the danger of litigation if they had disapproved. In short, I thought they were a little too eager."

"Did you inspect the body yourself?"

Lassiter shrugged. "Shea wanted to point some things out to me one day. I was busy; I had other matters to attend to. I wasn't particularly interested." He made a show of glancing at his watch.

"What sort of things?" Artie asked.

Lassiter was running out of patience.

"I'm a doctor. I deal with the living, not the dead. I'm experienced in autopsies and postmortems, but I'll be the first to admit there are others more knowledgeable in the field than I. And more interested."

"But you did take a look," Artie persisted.

For the second time there was a small flash of expression.

"I thought they were wasting their time on an unethical procedure. They really should have talked to an anthropologist, not a fellow doctor. I told them that."

It was going to be a contest between him and Lassiter over how little the doctor would tell him.

"Why an anthropologist, Doctor? What was it you saw that made you recommend one?"

"I thought they were letting their fantasies run away with them. A good anthropologist would have brought them down to earth." Lassiter stood up. "Look, Mr. Banks, this conversation could go on forever and I'm a busy man—"

"I'd like to see the body."

Lassiter looked startled. "You're not a relative—it's against regulations. Even if it weren't, it's not possible."

Artie misread him. "Perhaps another doctor who has more time?"

"The family claimed the body this morning," Lassiter said, now bored with the whole conversation. "And that *is* all I know. I never saw them, I never signed the release papers. The nursing supervisor took care of all of that."

Artie stared at him. What family? Aside from the name, there had been no ID for Talbot, no family to notify.

The supervisor wasn't very helpful at all.

"We got a call that the mortuary had come to pick up the body. I countersigned the receipt and filed it and arranged for the showing of the body to the family.

A younger brother and a woman, maybe a little older. A cousin, I believe she said. From Mr. Talbot's hometown in Illinois." The nurse smiled slightly. "A suburb of Chicago, Evanston. I had an old boyfriend who came from there."

"You didn't check them out?" Artie asked.

Like Lassiter, she was suddenly less friendly.

"They arrived right behind the mortuary van and had already made arrangements with an airline for shipping the body out. I didn't see any reason to hold them up." She read Artie's dissatisfaction in his face. "I'm not a policeman, Mr. Banks," she said stiffly. "They had ID; everything seemed to be in order."

And the medical center didn't have to foot the bill of a cheap cremation. Artie flipped open his wallet to his press card. "Do you have a phone or an address for them?"

She pursed her mouth, hesitated, then opened a file on her desk and scribbled some information on a piece of paper and slid it across the counter.

"That's their address. We definitely don't give out phone numbers and I probably shouldn't give you that."

Artie stopped at a public phone in the lobby and got the number from Information, then dropped in enough change to connect him to Evanston. The voice at the other end of the line was suspicious and curt and, surprisingly, without an Illinois twang. There was little that the voice would say about the late William Talbot except that they planned to cremate him tomorrow and scatter his ashes over Lake Michigan.

When he hung up, Artie's hand was shaking. Case closed, he thought.

Larry was dead and Talbot's body would be returned to the Mother of Waters.

The only people left who were suspicious of anything at all were he and Mitch.

. . .

**It was the middle** of the afternoon by the time Artie got back to the city. There was no sense in going to the office; Connie would be in the editing room getting the Castro Valley tape ready for the six-o'clock news. If he needed to grab a few hours for Christmas shopping, now was the time. He wanted to be home when Mark got there.

It was chilly for a San Francisco afternoon, cloudy and overcast, the temperature probably in the high thirties—damned cold for the Bay Area. The TV weathermen would call it unseasonal and blame it on the jet stream dropping down from Alaska. At least it wasn't the pineapple express, which picked up moisture in the mid-Pacific and dropped it by the bucketful along the coast and on the Sierras.

Macy's was jammed with shoppers, but he managed to get a ski sweater for Mark and a silver serving tray for Susan. Expensive, but a nice piece of work. He spent ten minutes admiring the displays in store windows, then walked back to Union Square and the underground garage. There was an ice-skating rink at one end of the square and Artie pushed through the crowd of spectators to catch a glimpse of the skaters.

"They've only had this for a couple of years—a few more and it'll be tradition."

The husky, pleasant voice belonged to a man about his own size and age, though Artie wasn't sure, what with his collar turned up and a woolen navy watch cap pulled down over his ears.

"Just like Rockefeller Center in New York," Artie said. "We've got a Christmas tree, too, maybe even bigger." San Francisco, the only city in the world with Christmas tree envy.

He concentrated on the skaters in the center of the rink. There were little kids pushing tentatively along on their blades and taking an occasional pratfall, and a covey of teenagers flashing around the edges of the enclosure showing off for the crowd and each other, trying figure eights and an occasional leap, usually badly. A solitary old man glided sedately through the swirl of other skaters around him.

Not a bad time of year, Artie thought. Skaters, fresh air, the municipal Christmas tree—if he didn't watch out, the spirit of the season would get to him yet. All he really needed was for Susan to be home. And for Larry to be at the other end of the phone line.

"The afternoons are sponsored," Watch Cap said. "This time, it's the AIDS Foundation. Poor bastards, something like seventeen thousand dead in the city and thousands more to go."

Artie knew the stats by heart; he'd lost enough friends to the disease. But right then he didn't want to think about it and spoil a pleasant afternoon.

Watch Cap wasn't about to take silence for an answer. "Not like Ebola, though. Now there's a disease for you—no cure and it's wiping out half of Africa. Or take Rift Valley TB—"

"I've lost friends," Artie interrupted. "I don't want to talk about diseases with strangers."

"Pardon me for living, fella." There was no anger in the voice, just a mild amusement, which annoyed Artie even more. His black mood returned in a flash and he swore quietly to himself. He started to edge away, trying to protect his packages from the crowd around him. He didn't have to fucking listen to this.

Watch Cap suddenly grabbed his arm.

"Catch the old man—can you believe that?"

Artie automatically turned back to the ice. It took a few seconds to spot the figure in the middle of the rink. He was doing jumps and turns with a grace Artie hadn't seen outside of competition or TV specials. Some visiting professional, probably. Then the skater flashed by fairly close to him.

He was better than good, Artie thought, astonished. At seventy, the old man was miraculous. Artie watched him intently, the crowd laughing and applauding every time he leaped into the air. A triple axel, and then another . . . The applause and the laughter died and the crowd was suddenly silent. What the old man was doing was impossible.

Not more than a dozen feet away, the skater folded his arms close to his chest and spun on his skates. He slowed, threw out his arms, and stopped, staring straight at Artie. The expression on his face was one of confusion and terror. A moment later, he slumped to the ice.

Heart attack, Artie thought. Had to be. No man his age could have done what he'd done without his muscles and joints freezing up, without his heart giving out.

Artie felt the cold sweats start then. It couldn't have been a senior citizen's idea to try to imitate Brian Boitano or Scott Hamilton. And it probably hadn't been a homeless man's idea to slit the throats of the Paschelke family and then burn down their house. And he doubted that it was the original intent of a roving pack of runaway dogs in the Tenderloin to tear the throat out of Larry Shea.

Nor had it been his idea the night before to play at being a seagull and soar over the city from the railing of a porch three stories above Noe Street.

He shivered. Last night *something* had put him on as easily as putting on its socks. He had thought what it had wanted him to think, had done what it had wanted him to do. So had the terror-stricken old man on the ice, so had the homeless arsonist, so had the dogs in the Tenderloin.

Larry Shea had been killed by a pack of dogs, Paschelke and his family had been murdered by a homeless drunk, the old man out for a lark on the skating rink had probably died of a heart attack, and if Mark hadn't stopped me, Artie thought, I would have been a suicide.

All of them had been murder by proxy.

Or would have been if he'd launched himself off the back porch. And the only connection was Larry Shea's research. Except that the old man didn't fit.

But, of course, he did. The murderer had been showing off. For his benefit.

Artie suddenly turned around. Watch Cap, the man whose face he'd never really seen, whose voice he hadn't recognized at the time but that now seemed oddly familiar, a voice he'd heard someplace before— was gone.

It was six o'clock when Artie got home, and Mark wasn't back from school yet. He started to fix supper, then gave up and called up the House of Chen for takeout. Chinese from the House of Chen was second only to a Haystack pizza on Mark's scorecard of Good Things to Eat.

Artie made himself a cup of coffee and tried to remember Shea's notes—he'd have the Grub make another copy for him in the morning. But he knew Larry had been convinced he had autopsied a descendant of a . . . caveman. Artie half smiled. He preferred Hall's term. One of the Old People. It sounded a little more mysterious but also more acceptable. And Hall hadn't believed it in any event.

But *he* did, Artie thought. Talbot had been a member of another species that shared the planet with them. And that species would do anything to remain hidden. Murder? Sure. What would happen if people knew about them? *Something* had shown him just what had happened thirty-five thousand years ago. For an hour he had been a member of the Tribe; he had been one of the Old People. But the Tribe had been ambushed, slaughtered to the last man, woman, and child, and then butchered. Could it happen again? On a bigger scale?

Why not?

*Homo sapiens* wasn't about to share its world.

Artie got out a scratch pad and started listing points he wanted to remember, wishing to God he'd taken a course in anthro in college. Comparisons of William Talbot to . . . what? Shea would have drawn his control group from his own patients. But Larry's graphs and charts had been Greek to Artie. All he knew was what he remembered from what Paschelke had told him and what he had gathered from his interview with Hall. Talbot had shown great strength in extremis. So might anybody. Heavy bones, thick pads of cartilage for a man his age . . .

If Hall was right and Larry had been full of shit, maybe it was because Talbot had been a health nut, watching his diet and working out regularly.

The other things that Hall had said—the Old People in many ways could have been just as advanced as the New People. If anything, they could have been more "human" in some respects. And what if they'd had bigger brains? What would they have used them for? And finally, they might not have been as good hunters as the New People.

But certainly good enough.

Artie thought of the last scene with the Tribe, of the butchering. Could you call it cannibalism if it was another species? He vaguely remembered a photograph he'd seen in *National Geographic* of an African native roasting a too-human-looking monkey. The resemblance hadn't bothered the native—after all, the monkey had been another species.

Hall had been right on one score. The Old People would probably go to any length to remain hidden. Even to committing murder. It would never be traced back to them because the police would be fed the suspect who'd actually held the knife or fired the shot, or it would be a suicide, or "death from natural causes," or simply an accident.

And they were after *him*, Artie thought. He knew more than anybody else about Shea's research. Larry was dead and so was Paschelke, and he wouldn't bet a dime on Hall's life, even if the man hadn't believed the research he'd read. When it came to himself, they'd missed once—Mark had saved him then—but they'd try again. And sooner or later, they'd succeed.

Unless he got to them first.

The doorbell rang and Artie answered. He gave the delivery boy a two-dollar tip, walked back to the kitchen, and cleared the notes off the table. He got out several plates and the silver, then glanced at his watch.

Seven-thirty. Mark still wasn't home.

Goddammit, Mark knew they had an answering machine. If he wasn't coming straight home, he should have phoned and left a message. He always had before.

Artie called one of Mark's friends, a neighborhood kid who went to the same school and caught the same van. No, a friend had driven Mark right home—he hadn't stayed behind at school. When? About four-thirty, right after phys ed and a dozen laps in the pool.

Artie sat there, staring at the wall, the containers of chicken lo mein and moo shu pork untouched, his mind a blank. Then he spotted it out of the corner of his eye, the closet door off the kitchen—ajar. He got up very quietly and walked over to it, yanked it open, and stood there while a chill started in his chest and settled in the pit of his stomach.

Mark's wheelchair, neatly folded up and pushed against the back of the closet. He couldn't possibly have gone anyplace without it.

Artie searched the house then, even doing frantic, stupid things like looking under beds, sick to death that he would find a body someplace.

Nothing.

At nine o'clock, he called up Susan.

*"I'm sorry, that number is out of service. . . ."*

Twenty-four hours, Artie thought. It would be twenty-four hours before he could report either one as missing. The police would ask if he'd called all of Mark's friends, if he'd checked with the school, if he'd talked with the van driver. Sure, they could understand his worries about Mark, but he wouldn't be the first parent who'd sweated it out all for nothing. As for Susan, there were winter storms in northern California, nothing unusual about it. During the winter the phones went out all the time.

But Artie knew beyond a shadow of a doubt that Mark, at least, wasn't coming back.

# CHAPTER 9

By three in the morning Artie had called every friend of Mark's for whom he had a phone number, checked in with the police—who sounded sympathetic but not very helpful, and questioned the neighbors on both sides of Noe and Twentieth Streets who might have seen or heard something.

He finally crashed on the living room couch, the windows and doors locked and a brown-painted, seventy-pound plaster elephant placed by the front door where anybody trying to enter would knock it over. The automatic was on the floor beside the couch, fully loaded. He slept only fitfully and when he woke at six, he called Mitch. A helluva time to be calling and Mitch had been sound asleep, but when Artie told him about Mark, he was instantly alert. He would be over as soon he could get there. Give him, say, half an hour.

Mitch lived across town—he rented a small house on Telegraph Hill—but there wouldn't be much traffic this early. And Christ, Artie thought, he desperately needed somebody he could talk to.

He went into the kitchen and made coffee, then called Susan again and got the same message he had the night before. He took in the morning paper and skimmed it, skipping the political and foreign news to read the small stories at the bottom of the inside pages of the second section where the paper chronicled the deaths of the petty criminals and the poor who lived in the rabbit warrens of the city, people whose names you forgot the moment you read them and people with no names at all.

Nobody fitting Mark's description was among them.

Mitch showed up ten minutes after Artie had finished the paper and was staring through the kitchen window at a city half hidden in morning mist, his mind fogged with a sense of helplessness. Mitch hadn't shaved and his coat still smelled faintly of wet wood ashes. He poured himself a cup of coffee and sat in silence at the table, waiting for Artie to begin.

Artie told him about Mark's failure to return home and his own failure when he tried to contact Susan.

When he'd finished, Mitch said quietly, "Mark's seventeen, almost a legal adult."

Artie shook his head in frustration. "How the hell can he go anyplace without his chair?"

"Maybe he didn't need it. You said Susan wanted him up in Willow. If one of his instructors at school found that out, he probably told Mark to get his ass up there and make up the school time after the holidays. So a friend took him to the airport, helped him board, and Mark gave him the keys to drop the chair back here. Susan would've had one waiting at the other end."

Artie sipped at his coffee, not meeting Mitch's eyes. "Try and be helpful, for Christ's sake."

Mitch shrugged. "Okay, we'll check again with the cops this afternoon and remind them that Mark's missing. They'll contact the hospitals, his description will go out to all the beat cops to watch for him. They'll log him in as a runaway and wait for something to turn up. He's too old for them to put his picture on a milk carton or for your neighbors to hang yellow ribbons on their fences."

"Violence—" Artie started.

"I doubt it," Mitch interrupted. "He wouldn't have gone with anybody but a friend."

But somebody could have taken him away by force, Artie thought. He tried to block thinking about that possibility and concentrated on his coffee.

Mitch said gently, "Any friction, Artie? Any arguments with him? Anything that would make him run away? Any girlfriend who would shove him into her van and light out for a week of romance in Palm Springs?"

"There was no friction," Artie said finally. "If anything, I wanted to be more of a father. And I wanted him to be more of a son."

Mitch looked uncomfortable. "Chances are Mark will call within the next day or so; runaways usually do. A better guess is that he's with Susan up north and she doesn't know you're stewing down here. She'll contact you when the phones come back on line—probably complaining because you didn't insist he pack an extra pair of underwear."

"What's he going to do for money?"

"You ever give him a credit card?"

He'd forgotten. "Yeah, for his last birthday."

"Then we can trace him through the card."

Artie started to make another pot of coffee while Mitch watched him, an almost clinical look on his face. "You said you talked with some anthropologist at the museum?"

Mitch was trying to get Artie's mind off Mark. It took an effort.

"A Richard Hall. The Grub printed out the floppy and I took Hall the printout. Paschelke was right—Larry didn't think Talbot was human and he had a lot of measurements to prove it."

Mitch looked away, staring through the glass doors of the porch at the streets below. "Jesus Christ, our caveman again."

"The Old People, Hall called them," Artie said dryly.

"He didn't believe it either. Said seeing might be believing so I went to the med center to see the body for myself. The relatives had already claimed it—I told you. Larry and Paschelke tried to convince one of Paschelke's colleagues and he didn't buy it any more than Hall did."

Mitch studied him for a moment.

"But you did." Artie nodded. "Why?"

How could he tell Mitch about his dream? About the Tribe? No more than he could have told him about Watch Cap or his almost suicide off the back porch. He remembered the look on Mark's face when he'd told him about Larry and what had happened on the porch, how he'd felt. Mark had been frightened; he hadn't understood. Would Mark have left because of that? He didn't know; he hoped not. But he couldn't think of any other reason. Except, of course, the obvious one. That somebody had Mark and might be willing to trade him for Shea's diskette and printout.

"No particular reason."

Mitch sighed. "Jesus, Artie, I'm your best friend and you're not willing to level with me." He opened the door of the refrigerator and started rummaging around. "What do we have for breakfast? Chinese . . . Chinese is good. No cold pizza, but you can't have everything. Leftover potato salad—not the season for it but that's good, too. . . ."

He found a plate and started serving himself. Artie stared at the mounds of food, wondering what the hell seemed strange. He knocked Mitch's arm away when he started to spoon out the potato salad.

"What's wrong?"

"Susan didn't make that. I never saw it before."

"Didn't make what? The potato salad?"

"She doesn't care for it. Neither does Mark."

Mitch stuck his finger in the salad to taste it. Artie grabbed his hand. "Don't do it."

Mitch frowned. "Come on, Artie, maybe a neighbor

brought it over. Maybe it was on sale—why the hell else would it be in the fridge?"

Artie shook his head. "She wouldn't have bought it; no neighbor would have brought it over."

Mitch shrugged, wiped his hand on a paper towel, and pushed the plate away. "You're being paranoid but—Got a plastic sandwich bag?" Artie found him one and Mitch spooned some of the salad into it, then sealed it. "A friend of mine's a chemist—he can test it. If it turns out like you obviously think it will, then you're in deep shit, buddy. Somebody wants you dead."

"You're the one who was going to eat it," Artie said.

"Right. But it was meant for you. . . . Exactly what was it that Hall said about the Old People?"

"That they didn't exist—and if they did, they died out thirty-five thousand years ago. If any modern versions are around today, Hall thought they'd go to any lengths to keep us from knowing about them. Larry knew about them and Paschelke knew everything that Larry did. And now so do I." He hesitated. "And so do you."

"Larry was killed by a pack of feral dogs," Mitch said slowly, "and some homeless nut did in the Paschelke family."

"Yeah, sure."

Mitch shrugged. "Okay, I see the connection you're trying to make. I sure as hell don't know how they'd work it, but maybe the important thing at the moment is how you feel about it."

Artie was puzzled. "I don't follow you."

Levin slipped into his professional role. "Remember when you returned from 'Nam? Besides having served in my unit, you were one of the first patients I worked with—though not for long; you really didn't need that much help."

"Post-traumatic stress syndrome," Artie said carefully. "One of the souvenirs I brought back with me." The war was a long time ago; he hadn't thought about it for years.

"You said you hated the war, Artie. Your problem was that you really didn't, and you were deeply ashamed because you didn't. You didn't like killing people, you didn't like the idea of death, but just the same . . . it was the ultimate test of whatever it was that was *you*, and you finally admitted you had never felt more alive. You said you felt like a hunter in the middle of the hunting season."

"I wasn't proud of it," Artie said stiffly. "What's your point?"

"Just a thought, Artie. Something has scared you shitless, but if I were that something, I think I'd be afraid of you."

**By the time Artie** got to work, Connie had already loaded the desk with a dozen books and what looked like a hundred pages of computer printout. She held up a finger when he came in, finished the page she was reading, then looked up.

"Top of the morning, Artie—" Then: "What the hell happened? You look like shit."

Artie leaned his umbrella against the wall and struggled out of his coat. "Mark took off last night. I've no idea where to."

"So call the police."

"I already did. They said they'd check with the hospitals and have the beat cops watch for him. They think he might just have split—it's a little difficult to call a seventeen-year-old a runaway."

"He's still a minor and he's handicapped, for God's sake!"

"I can't prove he didn't leave willingly."

"A kid in a wheelchair shouldn't be that hard to find."

"He didn't take it with him," Artie said dryly. "Which

means he's sitting in a car someplace or in somebody's house."

She struggled with it a moment, then gave up. "I don't know what to say, Artie. You want to take the day off, I'll cover for you with Hirschfield."

Artie didn't want to talk about it; it hurt too much.

"I've done everything I can, Connie." He pointed at the books. "What's up?"

"Research for the series." She looked relieved at the change in subject. "I've been doing my homework."

Artie looked at some of the titles, then thumbed the stack of computer printouts. Greenpeace apparently had a Web site.

"Anything interesting?"

"All of it—but depressing as hell. You read all the time about the ozone layer and then it becomes old news and you lose interest. But this winter it's thinned by half over Greenland, Scandinavia, and western Siberia. That's the worst it's been. Serious stuff."

"Wrong season for a suntan," Artie joked, then waited for Connie to come back with a snapper for his first and probably only yuck of the day.

She stared at him, sober-faced. "Not funny, Artie. The ultraviolet stands a good chance of frying the plankton in the Arctic ocean. That's the bottom of the food chain. No plankton, no krill, and pretty soon no fish, no seals, no sea lions, no whales."

Artie pulled out his yellow pad. "The world's going to hell," he muttered.

Connie slid one of the printouts across the table. "That's only the beginning of the bad news. Most of the forests will be gone within fifty years, ditto the animals that depend on them."

Artie read a few paragraphs.

"We're not going to do a once-over-lightly, are we?"

She looked offended. "Hell, no. Not when we've got a chance to make a difference."

The last time Artie had heard the phrase was fifteen

years before, when he had dropped four hundred on an est seminar—the seminar assistants had chirped it like a mantra. Connie still wasn't Connie, he thought clinically, but it was more subtle this time, less confrontational.

Artie waved at the books. "That's a lot to absorb for the series."

Connie had gone back to reading. "Meaning am I going to be the one who's stuck with the research? Probably—but I don't mind. Really."

"Believe me, Connie, I didn't plan—"

"Hey, it's not my kid who's gone AWOL."

Artie's phone suddenly started ringing and he picked up. A confused Richard Hall asked why he'd changed his mind and taken the printout with him. Artie denied it and Hall was silent for a moment, then said he'd talked to the secretary for the department, who claimed that Artie had returned and told her he'd left the manuscript behind in Hall's locked office and that he needed it. She'd checked his ID, then sent a guard back with him.

"It wasn't me," Artie said slowly.

Hall now sounded angry. Both the secretary and the guard had given a detailed description, down to the clothes Artie had been wearing. It didn't matter a rat's ass to him if Artie wanted to keep the printout, he just didn't want to be jerked around.

"I'll be right over," Artie said and hung up. Connie was staring at him, puzzled, and Artie shook his head, annoyed. He had no idea what was going on, but somebody had passed himself off as him and apparently they had been damned convincing. He'd have the Grub print out two more copies, one for him and another one for Hall.

Jerry glanced up when he entered the computer cubbyhole, his expression sour. "Last time I do you any favors, Banks. You and your fucking mystery diskette . . ."

Artie felt the first chill of premonition. "What's wrong?"

"Virus, fella. I loaded it into the computer and opened the file to start cleaning it up and everything blew up in my face. It wiped my hard drive plus the main memory and then erased itself. Suicide virus. Nobody was ever supposed to look at it—your friend probably thought anybody wanting to snoop would not only check it on-screen, they would also print it out directly. What you got yesterday is all you're gonna get." He took a diskette off the worktable and flipped it at Artie. "Here you go, a Frisbee for midgets." He took a breath. "You have any idea what management's going to do to me? Only it's not going to be my ass, Banks—it's going to be yours."

**Hall wasn't very friendly.** As soon as Artie showed up, he rang for the guard. "Fred, you know Mr. Banks, right? He was the one you let into my office yesterday."

The pudgy guard glanced at Artie, started to answer, then leaned closer. "I . . . don't think I know this gentleman, Dr. Hall. But I checked the man's ID yesterday—"

"Thanks, Fred."

Hall steered Artie back to his office.

"My apologies—to be honest, I don't know what the hell is going on." He wasn't the type actually to wring his hands, Artie thought, but he was doing a good job of it verbally. Hall managed a weak smile and tried to make a joke of it. "Maybe it was somebody from the *Journal of Forensic Pathology*—they would have had a field day with Dr. Shea's notes."

He closed his office door, settled himself in his chair, and motioned Artie to the other one.

"I'm sorry, I really am." Then, tentatively, "You understand that the Academy of Sciences can't be held responsible—"

Artie waved it aside. "Not your fault."

"You still have the original computer diskette, right?"

"Not anymore. A technician at work tried to print out two more copies and a virus on the diskette erased everything in the computer, including itself. He called it a suicide virus."

"There are no other copies?"

"I don't know of any."

Hall looked worried. "That doesn't make any sense— why would anybody want to erase the diskette? Or steal the printout?"

It made perfect sense to Artie. "Because of the information. Either they wanted it or they didn't want other people to have it."

Hall shook his head. "You steal facts; you don't steal speculation. Speculation is cheap."

"Maybe they thought they *were* stealing facts," Artie suggested.

The anthropologist studied him for a long moment. "You believe Dr. Shea, don't you? You think descendants of his Old People exist—right now, today."

"That's right."

Artie was mildly surprised at his own answer. Hall had put into words what he had been mulling over in the back of his mind ever since his first meeting with Paschelke. Since then, he had come very close to suicide and—probably—almost been poisoned. If a modern version of the Old People existed, then they were doing exactly what Hall had predicted: their very best to keep any knowledge of their existence secret. Any skepticism *he* had had about their existence had vanished after his hour with the Tribe.

Except you'd think they'd be trying to make him more skeptical, not less. The only explanation that made any sense was that the right hand didn't know what the left was doing.

Hall looked disappointed. "Then you're withholding

information. You've made your decision based on something other than Dr. Shea's notes."

"You must have an opinion," Artie said stiffly.

"There's absolutely no proof that Dr. Shea's Old People ever existed, Mr. Banks. I told you that yesterday. Anything other than that is fantasy."

"If their descendants *did* exist," Artie persisted, "how would they differ from us today?"

Hall obviously didn't know whether to humor him or throw him out, then decided he owed Artie something for the loss of the printout.

"I couldn't tell you. All I can do is speculate about a species that never existed." He looked sour. "Since *we* exist, I suppose it's fair to speculate on any differences that there might have been."

"Yesterday you told me they might have been better than *Homo sapiens* in some respects," Artie said.

"Different, not better. 'Better' implies judgment, and we don't know enough to make one. They might have been humane, they might have taken care of their injured and their sick. They might have had ritual burials—or, as you suggested, cremations—indicating some sort of religion. They might have been good tool-makers, though toward the end they probably copied the tools and weapons that *sapiens* had. Again, a lot of might-have-beens."

"But they couldn't talk, right?"

Hall frowned. "How the hell would we know that? Admitted that most of my colleagues think it was language that enabled *sapiens* to make their big leap forward, culturally speaking. Your Old People might have had language too, but if they did, I doubt they could use it nearly as well."

"Then they probably couldn't sing," Artie mused, surprised at how wistful he sounded. "They had no music."

Hall looked intrigued in spite of himself. "Modern man is the only one of the hominids that makes music.

I don't know of any chimps or gorillas that even come close. My guess is that if your Old People had music at all, it was a simple, percussive variety."

"Language would have been the key difference, then?"

"It would have been back then." Hall leaned toward him across the desk. "What we're doing right now—talking to each other—is an amazingly complex process. Language is much more than just naming things or passing along information. With it we can deal in concepts, things that have happened in the past, things that might happen in the future. We can talk about things that we can't see, that we can't touch. Consider the complexities of modern physics and then consider that we deal with all of them through language, either spoken or written. And all of it comes down to our ability to say *ay, eee, eye, oh,* and *you.* Pretty remarkable when you think about it. Then listen to opera sometime—say some tenor with the range of a Tagliavini—and think of all those sounds coming from that tube of flesh called a larynx, a simple voice box."

"Then language is one way the Old People could have been different from *sapiens,*" Artie said slowly. "There might have been others."

Hall smiled; he was on a roll.

"Let me count the ways. . . . The most obvious one is art. We can trace cave art back more than twenty thousand years. Fantastic images of animals drawn in charcoal, yellow ocher, and red hematite on cave walls in France. Many of the drawings would do credit to any modern artist. My guess is your Old People wouldn't have had art, Mr. Banks. Maybe they had body ornamentation, but there's no way of knowing. I don't think they would have been able to draw pictures, or decorate their tools or weapons. Maybe they strung beads or made necklaces, though it's more likely they would have traded for them. We know for sure that Cro-Magnons—archaic *Homo sapiens*—made necklaces."

Art and language, Artie thought. They were probably joined at the hip, anthropologically speaking, though he wasn't sure how. And there was always the possibility that the Old People didn't have language and art because they had something else as good . . . or better.

"And then something happened thirty-five thousand years ago."

"That's right. A tremendous explosion of creativity by *Homo sapiens*. For a hundred thousand years or more, nothing. Then, all of a sudden, language, art, and prodigious advances in tool and weapon making, everything from needles to spears. They made outdoor habitations of hide and wood, even huts of mammoth tusks and bones—they probably hunted the mammoth to extinction to get them."

Artie could believe that. "No wars, no conflict between *Homo sapiens* and any other group?"

Hall shrugged. "There's no indication of that; there aren't enough bones showing battle wounds or anything like it. Sure, there might have been some skirmishes. *Sapiens* probably penetrated into northern Europe from the Levant, following the migratory paths of the reindeer. Undoubtedly any other group would have hunted them as well. There could have been some localized conflicts, but nothing approaching war or genocide. That's tabloid thinking."

"The Old People disappeared, just like that?" Artie said.

Hall looked exasperated. "Mr. Banks, I'm debating with you as if the species existed. It didn't. But if it did, 'just like that' might have been over a period of at least several thousand years. *Homo sapiens* would have been more successful as a hunter, more innovative in making tools and weapons. If they hunted the same prey, *sapiens* would have won out. Your Old People would have been forced to shift their hunting grounds into areas that were relatively barren."

"Where they probably starved to death."

"Whatever."

"Lions and hyenas hunt the same prey," Artie said thoughtfully. "Neither one has disappeared."

"Apples and oranges." Hall's smile was the one Artie guessed he reserved for amateurs. "But we haven't considered breeding itself. If your Old People lived in a cold, inhospitable climate, then their gestation period might have been closer to twelve months than nine to give the baby a better chance of survival. With his shorter gestation period, *sapiens* could have simply outbred them."

"By producing babies not as well equipped to survive?" Artie shook his head in disbelief. "You're implying that if *sapiens* produced more children, then the Old People necessarily had to produce fewer, that the countryside could only support so many. But that would have depended on population, and I don't think anybody knows what population pressures were back then."

Hall suddenly smiled.

"You're picking on me, Banks. I'm only telling you what the theories are. Ask me again five years from now and I'll probably have a whole different set of them. But one thing for sure: When *Homo sapiens* invented agriculture ten thousand years ago, that was the name of the game. They settled down into villages, farmed for their food, domesticated cattle and pigs, organized trade routes, the whole bit. Once they could raise all the food they needed on the back forty instead of having to forage for nuts and berries, then there really was a population explosion."

Artie glanced at his watch. "Look, I've taken up enough of your time. I appreciate it."

"It's been fun. Buy you lunch—?" Hall looked at him questioningly.

Artie grinned. "Just 'Artie.' My car or yours?"

Hall shook his head. "Let's try the de Young Café, the other side of the music concourse—it's one of the best-kept secrets in town. Strictly high-class—cream of carrot soup and chocolate mousse if you want it, real San Francisco."

Artie promptly forgot his nostalgia for the hot dogs and hamburgers downstairs. He hadn't known the art museum had an upscale cafeteria.

They were almost to the front doors when a guard tapped Artie on the arm. "You Arthur Banks?" Artie nodded and he said, "Phone call for you at the Information Desk."

"Ask a docent for directions to the café," Hall called over his shoulder. He disappeared into the drizzle outside. Artie went back to the Information Desk and picked up the phone. "Hello, this is Banks." There was a click and then a dial tone.

He was still holding the phone, puzzled, when he heard a *pop-pop-pop* out front. A moment later, a woman started to scream. Artie stood frozen for a moment, then dashed for the doors.

Hall lay facedown on the concrete, his blood running slowly down the steps. The back of his head was a matted mixture of black, gray, and red. Artie felt numb with shock. 'Nam suddenly seemed very close— he remembered all too clearly friends who had been shot in the face, shattering their features and turning the back of their head into a muddy no-man's-land of blood and brains and hair.

He wished he'd gotten to know Hall better. He seemed a nice enough guy.

And that made it like 'Nam in still another way. People you'd grown close to over the months and then suddenly they were gone. They became just names on a casualty list or, worse, you stumbled across their mangled bodies half buried in the mud. After a while you grew numb; you couldn't cry anymore, you couldn't even grieve. You just walled off your memories of them in your mind. Larry Shea had been one of his best friends, Paschelke a friendly family doctor, the old man at the skating rink for whom he'd felt a brief burst of pity a stranger. Now Hall, and the only obit he could think of was: Nice Enough Guy.

The six-o'clock news would call it a drive-by shooting, a drug deal gone sour. Hall had been the right color to hang that one on him. And when the cops searched Hall's house they'd probably find a bag of crack someplace where his wife might have dusted two days before but not the night before, when something watching had seen them go out for dinner or to a movie and then slipped into their house.

Hall's sudden offer of lunch—what had suggested it to him? And if it hadn't been for the phone call, whoever had shot Hall would have gotten two for the price of one: the sophisticated crack dealer using his job at the museum as a cover, and the courageous KXAM reporter investigating a tip about him.

That somebody was trying to kill him wasn't exactly news, Artie thought.

That somebody was trying to save his ass was.

# CHAPTER 10

Artie watched while the police cordoned off the steps of the museum and pushed back the sight-seers, pleased that they had been this close to tragedy but that it hadn't involved them. Two of the women were weeping, and Artie guessed they had been co-workers of Hall's.

There was nothing more to see—but that wasn't quite true. Artie inspected the faces in the crowd again. There was whoever had shot Hall and had come back to see how good a job they had done. Say somebody like Watch Cap who, for all Artie knew, was searching the crowd looking for him.

He started back to his car. The crime scene investigators and police photographers would show up any minute, and Schuler would wonder what the hell he was doing there. He glanced at the body once more. A spot on the six-o'clock news, a tragedy for Hall's family, and momentary curiosity on the part of the kids who came to the anthropology wing and wondered what had happened to the nice Mr. Hall who had always been so patient with answers to their questions.

Artie sat in his car for a long moment, then drove out of the park to Lincoln Way. Mitch had been wrong, he thought. He didn't like war, never had. He certainly didn't like this one. Larry, Paschelke, Hall, the old man in the park—all innocent bystanders in a conflict he didn't quite understand, whose participants he'd never met. Or at least didn't think he had, with the possible exception of Watch Cap.

Then there was Mark. He couldn't believe that Mark had just decided to leave, without any warning whatsoever. Had Mark gone up to see Susan? Maybe. He'd told Mark his mother wanted him up there. Mark knew his grandfather was doing badly—his going would have made sense.

Except he didn't believe it. Mark sometimes seemed remote; probably all teenagers did to their parents. But he would have left a note, would have called, would never have thought, Fuck you, hurray for me, and split. He knew Mark better than that.

Or thought he did.

Mitch didn't think there had been violence, but he wasn't sure of that, either. If *something* had slipped into Mark's head, he could have ended up doing anything it wanted or going anyplace it wanted him to. There were different levels of violence.

But what would have been the point? To hold Mark hostage for the return of Larry's research diskette? He had never gotten a call, there had been no note slipped under the door. Mark had vanished into thin air, with no indication of violence, no indication of abduction. And someone, *something*, had taken the diskette anyway.

He still hadn't been able to get hold of Susan, even though the operator assured him the lines were open—and always had been. She should have called him in any event, would certainly have phoned if Mark had shown up at the Eureka airport and called her in Willow to say he was there.

His world was slowly going to hell. His family had disappeared and something or somebody wanted him dead, as Mitch had put it. And he had no face to put to the somebody or something except the photographs that Larry had taken of a sixty-year-old man who seemed younger than he should have been and who had died after an automobile accident on 580 late on a Saturday night. Artie had looked at the photos in Larry's research a dozen times and could remember nothing about the man except that he'd seemed so ordinary—nobody you would have looked at twice.

The sun had come out and the drizzle had stopped, but Artie didn't notice either one. He had braked for a ten-year-old battered Mustang that cut in front of him, and his sudden surge of anger had blanked out the slight feeling of fingers plucking at his mind more subtly than they had done several nights before. For Artie the sky still seemed just as gray, the mist still condensing and running down his windshield in rivulets.

The car that had cut in front of him had swerved back into the outer lane and was now crowding him over toward the curb. Artie leaned on his horn and glanced over to look at the driver. Long brown hair, street kid, early twenties at best. The type Artie had come to hate for what they were doing to the city he loved. The kid turned toward him at the same time and flipped him off. Artie couldn't read lips but he knew what he was saying: "Get off the street, old man!"

They were on Kezar Drive now, then hit the light and turned onto Oak Street, paralleling the Panhandle. Artie twisted the wheel a little to the right and for a moment sparks flew from their fenders. He could feel his lips curl away from his teeth. Just like in the movies. Then his car jumped the curb and he hit the brakes to avoid a tree. The kid cut in front and stopped, jerked open the door of his car, and bolted out holding a tire iron.

Artie yanked open his own door, his hand on the automatic in his pocket. He had no clear idea of where he was or exactly what he was going to do, but he was mad enough to kill, his rage as thick as cotton in his head.

The kid came at him swinging the tire iron and screaming, "What the hell, you old bastard, you don't own the road!"

Suddenly a car directly behind Artie's turned out and raced on past. In his head Artie sensed bemused frustration, and then something cold as ice water slid into his mind and his anger faded. He glanced around, noticing with surprise the cloudless sky and the brilliant green of the Panhandle on his left, drops of water glistening jewel-like on the grass.

He turned to the kid and gaped. A student type with glasses, an inoffensive skinny nineteen, his face pale with fright. He stood there looking at the tire iron in his hand, shaking and trying frantically to piece together what had just happened.

"I don't know what the hell got into me, man— honest to Christ, I don't know! You all right, man? I didn't mean to cut in like that!"

A few minutes more and the fight would have escalated, Artie thought. He could have killed the kid, *would* have killed him. And if he'd tried to drive away, there were plenty of people around who would have gotten his license number. When the cops caught up with him it was more than an even-money bet that one of them would have shot him for resisting arrest.

Artie sat down on the curb, holding his head in his hands. "It's all right—anybody can lose control of a car. It happens." Especially if they had help.

The kid looked embarrassed. "Shit, my insurance has lapsed."

His own car was almost as old as the kid's, Artie thought. Why get the cops and the insurance companies into it?"

"Forget it."

The incident was a reminder, Artie thought, as if he needed one.

Four times now, he'd been lucky.

He couldn't count on being lucky the fifth time.

What the hell was going on? Something had it in for him, and sooner or later they'd kill him and it would look like an accident or like it was all his own fault.

**Artie pulled into a** gas station and had the attendant fill his tank while he called Mitch on his cell phone. He got the answering machine, nobody at home. Office hours, noon to five—he could never keep it straight. He called the office and got a worried secretary. Mitch hadn't shown or called in, and she'd already had to cancel one appointment. No, she had no idea where he might be.

Artie held the phone for a minute after the line went dead. Mitch never failed to show for work, or if he couldn't make it, he never failed to cancel well in advance. An accident or . . .

Artie gunned the car and took off. He wasn't the only one who knew too much. Mitch knew almost as much as he did.

There wasn't much parking at the top of Telegraph Hill, and he left his car in a neighbor's driveway with the motor running. The door to Mitch's small cottage was locked, and Artie fumbled out his key ring and searched frantically for Mitch's key, a leftover from when Mitch had gone on vacation and asked him to look in on his cat and feed her.

The inside of the small cottage was quiet. A living room, bedroom, bath, and kitchen, all decorated like a Cape Cod cottage. The small office in one corner of the living room, pale blue chintz curtains by windows overlooking the bay, driftwood furniture and maple antiques, braided-wool space rugs over polished wood-plank floors. The hill itself could have been transposed from New England, with wooden walks leading off to the various cottages. It was a perfect bachelor's hideaway.

Mitch was stretched out on the kitchen floor, bleeding from a scalp wound where he'd hit his head on the table when he fell.

"Mitch!"

Levin was out cold, a half-empty bottle of scotch on the tiled sink ledge. Artie knelt down to feel his pulse. It was then he noticed the glass that had rolled beneath a chair and a small bottle of prescription pills. Valium—half the small yellow tablets were spilled on the linoleum. Bad combination if Mitch had taken them with the scotch, and he apparently had.

Artie lunged for the phone. The ambulance was there sooner than he thought possible, and he rode in the back while the attendant fixed an oxygen mask to Mitch's face and monitored his slow and laborious breathing.

At the hospital they pumped his stomach, but it was a good two hours in the emergency room before they let Artie in to see a pale Mitch, sitting on the side of his bed.

"You okay?"

"Yeah, I am now. It wasn't much of a lunch, but they took all of it. It'll be a week before I'm hungry again."

"What the hell happened?"

Mitch stared out the hospital window at the gray winter sky. There was a slight sheen of sweat on his forehead but his voice was steady enough. Only his eyes gave away how jumpy he really was.

"After I left you this morning, I went home. Looked over some patient folders and poured myself a drink before going to work. Two fingers of scotch, a few cubes, and half a bottle of five-milligram Valiums."

Mitch said it casually and Artie wasn't sure he'd heard right. "I don't get it."

Mitch sounded as if he couldn't quite bring himself to believe it either.

"A neighbor came over to bitch about my cat digging in her flower bed and when she left, I decided to make myself a quick drink before going to work. I knew what I was doing, Artie. I just didn't believe there was anything strange or dangerous about it."

Mitch struggled to keep his voice calm.

"I started to come out of it when I felt myself falling. Something just drained out of my head, like you'd pulled a plug. Something had been inside my mind and I didn't even know it. . . ."

After a long moment of silence, Artie said, "It's a strange feeling. You suddenly realize somebody's been pushing your buttons but you have no idea what it was. Or who."

Mitch looked at him in surprise.

"When? For you?"

"When I came home from seeing Paschelke that first time. I went out on my back porch and climbed up on the railing. I wanted to fly. I thought it was perfectly normal, too. Three stories down to solid concrete, Mitch." He didn't mention Mark; he didn't want to start talking about him again.

"You should have told me."

"Would you have believed me?"

"Not then. I sure would now."

A nurse looked in, disapproving, then pulled the curtains and left.

"Do you know how they do it?" Artie asked.

Mitch seemed more himself now, his voice calmer, his eyes less jumpy. He was still pasty-faced but that would clear up with a decent meal—whenever he felt like eating, which probably wouldn't be for a while.

"I've got my ideas. They're probably no better than yours."

"I don't have any at all." Artie hesitated. "I don't understand how anybody can manipulate my mind, Mitch. I just don't."

He sounded like a small boy asking his father for reassurance and felt like two-thirds of an idiot. It was Mitch who had almost died, not him.

Mitch glanced at the white curtains drawn around the bed and lowered his voice.

"Forget about free will, Artie—you don't have any. Physically speaking, you're an electrochemical machine. Especially your brain. The neurons fire, an electrical impulse travels along a nerve, and you think a thought or move your arm. If you were small enough to crawl inside somebody's head, you'd probably see little sparkles of light when their neurons fired. And like most electrical devices, your brain generates waves. You broadcast them and you receive them, too."

He leaned back against the pillows. For a moment, Artie thought Mitch was going to be sick, then he realized Mitch was probably so empty he couldn't even vomit green bile.

"We talk about it all the time, Artie. We feel the 'electricity' in the crowd when we're at a football game. You can feel the 'electricity' of a mob if you get caught up in one. And your mind can be taken over by that mob, Artie. You can end up going along with whatever the mob wants you to do, even if you don't really want to. The mob is doing your thinking for you."

"One on one," Artie objected, keeping his voice down. "We can't do it one on one."

Mitch managed a weak smile. "I read about it in the psychology newsletters all the time—talk to any biofeedback expert about your brain's alpha, beta, and theta waves. A few years back, the air force gave Stanford a grant to link computers with brain waves—they wanted to teach pilots how to fly planes with them. And I've seen demonstrations where the participants played Pong on a computer by controlling the ball with their minds. It's the next frontier, Artie."

"There's got to be an electrical connection," Artie said, unbelieving. "There's got to be a wire, some mechanical link."

Mitch shook his head.

"I told you, Artie, we broadcast. And we receive. How

many times have you picked up the phone to call somebody and there they are, on the other end of the line?
Or when somebody knows exactly what you're going
to say a split second before you say it?"

Artie's memories of balancing on the porch railing,
arms outstretched, the wind tugging at his hair, were
suddenly very vivid.

"I'm sorry, Mitch—maybe I just don't want to think
that somebody can make me do something by thinking
at me."

Mitch looked away. "I can't blame you. I don't like
to think that I did what I did this morning. We like to
think the mind is truly private, that it's even more personal than our bodies. It's *us*, it's peculiarly our own,
we operate it. But think of the last time you were
'drunk out of your mind,' or you were high on pot or
had swallowed a tab of acid. Sure, it's ancient history.
But we did it. We own our own minds, Artie, but we
abdicate that ownership often enough. And all of us
are susceptible to suggestion. With us, it's verbal. With
something else, it's what we might consider a stray
thought. It's a wild talent—one that we don't have. But
something sure as hell does. Was it your idea to climb
up on the porch railing?"

The nurse was back, pulling aside the curtains and
looking at both of them suspiciously. Mitch peeled off
the hospital gown and started to slip into his street
clothes, ignoring the nurse's objections. "Let's get the
hell out of here."

"Will they let you go?"

"They won't like it, but I'll sign myself out."

When Mitch had finished dressing, Artie said,
"Where to?"

"You pick it."

It was one of Charlie Allen's days off, Artie thought.
They could talk in his living room while Charlie put-
tered around with his computers and took on all com-
ers in his Librarians Anonymous chat room.

They'd be in a friend's house.

And they'd be safe.

**Charlie Allen was glad** to see them, greeting them at the door dressed in a ratty bathrobe. "Come on in, guys—Franny's downtown, she'll be out most of the afternoon. And it's the last day of school for the kids; they won't be home until three so we got the house to ourselves. Want some lunch?" He didn't wait for an answer but swept into the kitchen and started pulling bread and luncheon meat out of the refrigerator. "There's some ice cream in the freezer, help yourselves—and I don't mind if I do."

He loaded up a cereal bowl with several scoops of strawberry and squirted chocolate sauce over the top. "What's up? You sounded pretty vague over the phone."

Artie wasn't very hungry. He dropped some deli ham on a single slice of unbuttered rye and folded it over. "We wanted to borrow your library for maybe an hour—talk over some business. We needed a place where it would be quiet and we wouldn't be disturbed." He took a breath. "So we thought of you."

Allen looked puzzled, turning from one to the other. "What's wrong with your places? Not that I mind— it's great to see you."

"You were midway between," Mitch said, as if the answer made a lot of sense.

Artie watched Charlie turn it over in his mind and thought to himself, Jesus, what a lame idea. Charlie must think they were a little nuts.

"Okay, my casa is your casa—feel free." Allen led the way to the living room that doubled as a library, separated from the rest of the house by glass French doors. "Make yourselves at home."

"Thanks," Artie mumbled, "appreciate it." He passed a bookcase on his right when he entered, then suddenly paused. He'd been to Charlie's home dozens of times. He'd also walked past the same bookcase filled with its rows of little black notebooks at least twenty times and never really noticed them before. This time he did. Each notebook carried a neat red plastic label on the spine: SUICIDE CLUB. There was a book for every year since they'd started the Club when they were kids, sometimes two or three books to the year.

He waved at the shelves. "What gives, Charlie?"

Allen shrugged. "You guys elected me secretary way back when and I guess I never stopped." He looked embarrassed. "Call it a hobby. I probably know things about you guys that you forgot years ago."

Hero worship, Artie thought. Charlie had had a bad case of it back then and had never gotten over it. He was suddenly as embarrassed as Charlie was. "Have to look at them sometime—bring back memories."

"For you, any time." Allen waddled back toward his office, closing the French doors behind him.

"Strange guy," Artie muttered after he'd left.

Mitch shrugged. "Don't knock him, Artie. He's a generous, friendly slob, and we're charismatic. Neither of us can help it—and please don't take me seriously." He leaned back on the couch. Behind his steel-framed lenses his eyes were a bright ice-blue and he seemed a little remote, a little cold—the way Artie remembered him from the times they'd served together in 'Nam. "We haven't been using our heads. Who knew Larry was coming over to the city?"

Artie thought for a moment. "The people he worked with at Kaiser. The people at the restaurant—they took the reservations, they knew all of us would be there or were planning on being there."

"Who else?"

"All of us, of course—all the members of the Club."

"You're leaving somebody out."

"Anybody they might have talked to," Artie said slowly. "And maybe some of the kids."

"Who knew what he was going to talk about?"

"Probably only Cathy. Larry was writing an article, he wanted to go public with his findings. Maybe Cathy was apprehensive, maybe like Hall she figured that if there were one there had to be others and considering Talbot's lack of ID, they probably didn't want anybody to find them."

"You're giving her a lot of credit."

"She's nobody's dummy, Mitch. And she would have worried about the family. When the cops called with news of Larry's murder, it confirmed her fears and she grabbed the kids and ran."

"Who else?"

"I don't know." Artie frowned. "Paschelke didn't know about the meeting, though he must have known Larry was writing an article."

"You're not thinking, Artie. Would Cathy have kept Larry's research to herself or would she have confided in a close friend?"

Artie shrugged. "I suppose it would have been natural if she'd confided in a friend. Especially if she were scared. But Susan never mentioned it—she would have if Cathy had talked to her."

"I wasn't thinking of Susan. If Cathy had talked to her, Susan probably would have talked to you. Which leaves the other members. One of them didn't want the rest of the Club members knowing about Larry's research and definitely didn't want *Science* printing it. Which means the prime suspect is whoever Cathy made the mistake of confiding in. The danger for her is that she might not realize it."

"That's just a theory," Artie objected.

"You got a better one?"

Artie felt like a slow study. "Find Cathy, then, and maybe we've found our man. Or woman."

Mitch shook his head. "You're never going to find her, Artie. Or the kids. My guess is they've been dead for days." He was silent for a moment, thinking. "What did Talbot look like? You saw Larry's photos of the body."

"Ordinary. Nobody you'd look at twice."

"So what we've got is a group of people living among us who really aren't 'us,' who will kill to keep their existence a secret. All we know is that they can fuck with our minds and you'd never notice them in a crowd. Short of an autopsy, like Larry did on Talbot, there's no way of knowing who they are."

Artie thought about it. "You're driving at something."

"The obvious, Artie. The largest group of suspects are the members of the Club, or those related to the members. That means one of us, perhaps more than one, may not be who we've always thought he was. That for all the length of time that we've known him—or her—for them it's been a game of Let's Pretend. Worst of all, they're not human. Not human the way we're human. If Larry Shea was right, they're a different species."

Artie felt the small hairs stir on the back of his neck.

"So how does it affect us—you and me? Give me an example."

Mitch smiled. "I told you a cock-and-bull story at the hospital and you believed every word of it. You didn't doubt me for a moment."

Artie had the automatic out without even thinking. Jesus Christ, he'd walked right into it.

"You're my best friend, Mitch," he said slowly, "but if I were you, I wouldn't move." The gun was rock steady in his hand.

Mitch didn't even look surprised. "What I told you in the ER was true," he said dryly, "but you asked for an example and I gave you one. This is exactly how it affects us. And I could turn it around. How do I know that you're really you—somebody I've known for half my life? Because you're my friend? The ones who really screw you are your friends, not your enemies. You can watch out for your enemies." He smiled bleakly. "You could have lied about the porch railing bit. How do I know it's true? I wasn't there. You could have spent the last few days trying to sound me out for what I believe—or don't believe."

Artie sat there in silence, staring at him, the automatic never wavering. "Then that's a problem, isn't it?"

Mitch looked disgusted. "For Christ's sake, Artie, put it away. It goes off, you lose a friend and gain a murder rap."

There was a knock on the French doors and Allen opened them. Artie made the gun disappear before Allen had a chance to see it.

"If you guys are still hungry, there's some leftover potato salad—it's Franny's specialty." He caught the sudden shock on their faces and looked offended. "Hey, if you don't like it, that's fine—don't blame me for trying to be a good host."

Artie and Mitch listened to him shuffle back to the kitchen before speaking. Artie was sweating. He had to go to the bathroom, bad. Innocent, innocuous Charlie Allen. Why not?

Mitch shook his head.

"Relax, Artie—he's okay."

"Based on what?" Artie jerked a thumb at the notebooks in the bookcase. "He said he probably knows more about us than we do about ourselves. And he certainly knows more about Larry Shea than we ever did. He was close to Larry; if Cathy was going to confide in anybody about what Larry was working on, it could easily have been Charlie."

Mitch stood up and reached for his coat. "And there's always the chance that we're paranoid."

Outside, Artie shivered—it had turned chilly and gray again. Charlie had been miffed when they'd left so suddenly, but he'd get over it. All they had wanted was to get out of the house as quickly as possible.

Mitch stopped at his car and turned to Artie. "You're a good friend, Artie—one of my best."

"Yeah," Artie said, trying hard to sound convincing, "same here."

They looked at each other, each a little awkward, and then Mitch said, "Don't forget, Artie—you're the only one who saw Larry's research and is still alive." Artie nodded. "And I'm the only one you talked to about it, right? And I'm still alive. We've both had plenty of opportunity and we're still around. We both know the other is safe."

"Right," Artie said, still dubious.

Mitch blinked nervously behind his granny glasses.

"We're going to have to trust each other, Artie. We're the only ones we know for sure who know too much."

Artie nodded in agreement and got in his car.

Mitch was right: They were going to have to trust each other. But Jesus, right then he wasn't willing to trust anybody.

And he was sure Mitch wasn't willing either.

**He got home and** called the station, then went through a ritual of locking all the doors and windows and pulling down the shades and turning the lights low, keeping to the center of the rooms so his shadow wouldn't show on the window blinds. It was only after he finished his TV dinner of macaroni and cheese that he noticed the blinking red light on the answering machine.

*"Artie? Susan. It's noon, Wednesday. Please call me at the following number—haven't heard from you."*

That wasn't right. He had tried to get her two days running. He hastily dialed the number.

"Where have you been, Susan? I've been calling—"

"I'm at the hospital." A slight pause. "Dad's dying. . . ."

He had expected it but it was still a shock. "I'm sorry, Susan."

Her voice became sharper. "Where's Mark? I thought I asked you to send him up here—please try to get him on the next plane."

His throat suddenly felt very dry. He told her that Mark had disappeared, that he'd filed a missing persons report with the police but with no luck so far, that he'd tried to phone her—

Her voice turned frantic. "You've got to find him, Artie!"

"Can you come back?"

"I can't—I told you, Dad's dying. Find him, Artie! Please, you've got to find him!"

"Sure, Susan," he mumbled. "Sure, I'll do my best."

And then she had to go and he sat there holding the phone and all he could think of for a moment was that she had wanted Mark up there—she'd never mentioned him. Her father was dying and she'd lost her son, and he hated himself because what he'd thought of first was that she hadn't pleaded for him to come up.

Which made sense, because if he went up there, who would be left behind to look for Mark? And he sure as hell couldn't help her father.

He wore his heart on his sleeve, he thought. He had for fifteen years.

# CHAPTER 11

**Bayview Academy was located** just off of Skyline Drive in Oakland, a pleasant ten acres that seemed a jumble of eucalyptus trees at first until Artie got a few hundred feet off the drive and saw the main building and the athletic grounds behind it. Beyond the track-and-field area the ground sloped sharply down to the bay and a view of San Francisco on the other side, partially hidden by tendrils of fog.

He had seen the school five years before, when he and Susan had first enrolled Mark there, but the ivy had grown since then. Now the redbrick buildings of Bayview Academy would look right at home in upstate New York or in some small town in Vermont.

Scott Fleming, the headmaster, was cordial enough, affable but careful to maintain a certain reserve as a protective barrier between himself and the parents of his students. He had been about to take his afternoon stroll around the grounds and invited Artie along. He looked in his early sixties, a small and somewhat placid man, thin and wiry. His hair was gray, and with his woolen jacket and thick scarf trailing behind him in the breeze, all Artie could think of was Mr. Chips. He even had a faintly English accent to go with his appearance.

Artie remembered when he'd first met Fleming and the headmaster had filled him in on the history of the academy.

"We were founded in the middle forties, just after the Second World War. Mr. Elias Putnam had his only boy come back badly wounded—he had lost a leg and the use of his right hand—and Putnam became interested in the plight of the crippled while overseeing the rehabilitation of his son."

" 'Crippled,' " Artie had repeated. He hadn't been sure he liked the sound of it. He had always considered Mark handicapped, not crippled.

"The students here are crippled, Mr. Banks," Fleming had said quietly. "We could use the phrase 'physically disadvantaged' but I'm afraid that being politically correct wouldn't help our students at all. They're crippled. We deliberately use the word and with usage, the word itself is defused. It's not the word, it's the baggage that goes along with it. The students are certainly going to hear the word on the outside; better they get used to hearing it at Bayview."

They were at the back of the building now, looking out over the track and the small baseball field. It was late in the afternoon and turning colder; Artie envied Fleming his thick woolen sweater. He waved at the diamond and the cinder track.

"I can't imagine those would get much use."

Fleming raised an eyebrow. "Physical activity is more difficult than it would be with ordinary boys and girls of the same age, but then they're not competing with ordinary boys and girls—they're competing with each other." He wrapped his arms around his chest for warmth. "There's not much to see beyond this, might as well start back. We can have some coffee in my office if you'd like."

They detoured through the gymnasium and Artie watched a wheelchair basketball game in progress, then found himself distracted by a muscular sixteen-year-old climbing a rope to the ceiling, using only his arms.

"He can't walk," Fleming offered. "Nerve degeneration in his legs. But he's an ace gymnast and the star of our wheelchair basketball games—I've seen him sink one from the middle of the floor."

They had started for the exit when Fleming called to a student, his right arm hanging limply at his side, who was picking up towels from the benches. "Collins, I'll be in my office with Mr. Banks. When you finish, I'd appreciate two containers of coffee from the cafeteria. Tell Mrs. Deveny it's for me."

He glanced at Artie. "I've cream and sugar in the office, if you use it."

"Black," Artie said offhand. Collins had caught his eye and they stared at each other for a second. Sturdy kid, reddish hair, probably looked young for his age—more pretty than handsome, in a homely sort of way. The type of face where all the flaws made for an agreeable whole; the tough Irish kid who looked angelic as an altar boy.

In the office, Fleming relaxed in the black leather chair behind his desk and stared thoughtfully at Artie.

"Over the phone, you said Mark had disappeared. We thought he was sick and you had just forgotten to notify us."

Artie shook his head. "He vanished two days ago— he never came home from school. I called some of his friends; they said he'd done a few laps in the pool and then a friend had given him a lift home. Apparently he left again shortly afterward. No way he could have left by himself; his chair was still there."

Fleming nodded. "After you called, I did some checking here. Collins was the student who drove him home; you can talk to him later."

Artie wasn't sure how to approach what was on his mind. "I was wondering . . ." His voice trailed off.

Fleming didn't help. "Yes, Mr. Banks?" His face was impassive.

"I was wondering if . . . if Mark has any girlfriends. That sounds funny—I'm his father, I should know. I'm sure he would have brought any home but he never has and I was curious—"

"He's popular," Fleming interrupted shortly. "I would say he has his share of female friends. He's a very outgoing young man."

There was a knock on the door and Collins came in clutching a tray in his left hand with two sealed containers of coffee.

"Thank you, Collins. Stand by outside for a bit; I think Mr. Banks would like to talk to you."

Again, the brief spark of something in Collins' eyes, and then he was gone.

"You were saying, Mr. Banks?"

"How deep do the relationships go, Mr. Fleming? There's probably no way I would know—but you might."

Fleming looked puzzled.

"I'm not sure I follow you."

He was beating around the bush, Artie thought. But he didn't have all day and neither did Fleming.

"Sexually," he said bluntly. "I keep wondering if some girl . . . woman . . . might have gotten Mark to run off with her, say, for a week in Palm Springs or maybe Las Vegas."

Fleming looked amused. "I rather think it would have been a mutual decision, not the young lady's alone. But frankly, sexual activity isn't something we monitor, Mr. Banks. On campus, certainly. Off campus, it's none of our business." He paused. "You've never worked with crippled children, have you? As a counselor or anything like that?"

Artie shook his head.

"Being crippled creates a rapport among the students, Mr. Banks. It's a very strong one; they feel very close. You don't have the usual dating rituals you find in most high schools. Friends aren't chosen on the basis of beauty or physical prowess. They're very open with each other, they're very honest. To be truthful about it, I suspect our students are more sexually active than most. For one thing, to have sex at all usually requires close cooperation between them. The feelings of closeness and cooperation are already there, and I know they have great compassion for each other. I imagine that sexual activity is not far behind."

"And what do you do when students get pregnant?"

"They usually inform their parents—we don't have to. Pregnancy is uncommon, but when it happens it may interest you to know they invariably choose to keep the child."

"Mark—"

Fleming held up his hand.

"That's about all I can tell you. Mark is a very popular boy, it's my observation that he's much in demand. I'm somewhat surprised you aren't aware of that. I suppose his mother probably is; a lot of fathers seem to be remote from their sons. Too bad, but then I don't know the circumstances of your family life."

Artie felt his face color. "I don't see where—"

"Collins is waiting for you, Mr. Banks. It's the last day of school and I think he would like to go home."

It was a dismissal, but that wasn't what hurt. He'd been accused of being remote when it came to his son, and Fleming was probably right. Only he had blamed it on Mark when he should have been blaming it on himself.

**Collins was waiting for** him just outside the door. He sized up Artie quickly, then said, "If you want more coffee, the cafeteria's still open." Artie followed him down the hallway, then caught himself watching Collins closely. Stocky build and athletic, his right arm useless but not withered. Physical therapy had to be a

good part of their phys ed routine. But the kid walked
with the same sort of confidence that Artie had noticed
in Mark the last few years. Not cock-of-the-walk, but
very confident in who he was.

They took a table in a corner of the almost deserted
cafeteria and Artie sipped at his coffee and studied
Collins over the edge of his cup.

"You gave Mark a lift home Tuesday night?"

Collins nodded, a faint curiosity in his deep-set eyes
as he watched Artie in turn. "We left here at three-
thirty and got to your house about ten after four. Traffic on the bridge was pretty light. I helped Mark get in
his chair and he rolled up the walk and that was it."

"Any reason why Mark might have left the house
again later? Anybody coming to pick him up?"

Collins shrugged. "He didn't mention any."

How the hell did you discuss sex with a seventeen-
year-old? Artie wondered.

"Any girlfriends who might have showed up after you
left?"

"Was he fucking anybody?" Collins asked coldly. "Is
that what you want to know?" There was more than
just belligerence in his voice; there was something else
as well.

"He's been missing for two days," Artie said coldly.
"He's handicapped"—he couldn't bring himself to use
the word *crippled*—"and I don't think he could go anyplace by himself. Somebody had to help him."

Collins took pity on him. "He has a lot of girlfriends," he said, but once again something was hidden. "If he didn't . . . sleep with them, I'd figure he was
a fool. And he's no fool. He might have had a date for
later that evening; he acted like it but I didn't ask.
There's a senior woman who likes him a lot. They're
close."

"He gets around," Artie said bitterly, more because
he hadn't really known about it than because of any
bias against teenage promiscuity.

"More than I do," Collins said coolly.

"His mother's desperate," Artie said, pleading. "And so am I. Who is she? We'd like to find out if she and Mark went . . . somewhere."

Collins stood up; he wasn't about to be a snitch. "I'm sorry. I've told you everything I can. Mark can take care of himself. I wouldn't worry about him."

He was halfway across the cafeteria when he suddenly stopped and came back. He reached in his left pocket, took out Mark's earring, and put it on the table.

"We were wrestling in the gym earlier that day and this fell off. I found it on the mat the next morning. If Mark doesn't come back, then I guess you should have it."

Artie took the small piece of stone and what looked like worked silver, wrapped it carefully in a napkin, and dropped it in his shirt pocket. He glanced up at Collins to thank him for it, then realized with sudden shock that it wasn't a bad case of hero worship Collins had for Mark; it was something else.

"Mark didn't drop this—he gave it to you, didn't he?"

For a moment Collins looked like he was going to deny it, then shrugged, his face suddenly drawn. Whatever memory he had obviously hurt. "It was a consolation prize," he said quietly. "He said we would always be friends."

Collins got a few feet away, then turned back once again.

"Mark is still my best friend, Mr. Banks. He was generous with me—I've no complaint."

Artie stared after him, not quite sure what he should think. He didn't know what, if anything, had happened between Mark and Collins, but Collins had called Mark generous and the earring had been an heirloom. Mark hadn't given it away lightly. Artie felt like he had when he'd walked in on Mark that one morning.

Mark was way past puberty and besides, it wasn't any of his business.

**It was eight in** the evening. Artie sat alone in his car, the lights and radio off, the engine silent. He had put on two sweaters and the heaviest jacket he had and he was still cold. The Avenues in San Francisco were on rolling dunes west of the hills and nearest the ocean so they caught the brunt of the fog and the winds off the Pacific. When it was sunny in the Mission and the Castro, you could usually count on the Avenues being fogged in and chilly.

Tonight the fog had rolled in late in the afternoon and now blanketed the entire city. But he would bet the Avenues were still colder and clammier than the rest of the town. He shivered and hunkered down lower in his seat, watching the pink stuccoed house a few doors up at the corner of Ulloa and Thirtieth. It was a two-story affair with a huge garage beneath and surrounded by stubby little palm trees and rows of potted cactus plants on the front steps. Big house: Lyle Pace couldn't be doing too badly.

All Artie knew about stakeouts was what he'd seen in the movies, but they never let you know how the characters kept from feeling foolish—or guilty. He was going to spy on one of his friends and, once again, he wasn't even sure what he was looking for. Something out of the ordinary, something that didn't jibe with their character as he knew it. That was vague as hell, but presumably he would know what he was looking for when he saw it.

Or would he? His black mood was back in force and he reached for the key to start the engine. Enough of this bullshit.

But Larry Shea lying gray and torn in the morgue hadn't been bullshit, and neither had Hall, crumpled on the steps of the museum, his heart pumping his life's blood over the concrete. And it hadn't been bullshit when he'd stood on the railing of his porch about to plunge to the sidewalk three stories below.

He folded his arms and settled back in his seat, once more concentrating on the house on the corner. He'd been there half an hour now but nobody had come or gone and there were no lights on. Lyle obviously wasn't home, though Artie doubted he was out of town. He was manager of the Market Street Copeland's, and sporting goods were a popular item for Christmas. Maybe he had taken Anya, his live-in girlfriend, out to the movies or a holiday dinner.

Lyle Pace, one of the last members to join the Club. Artie had never gotten to know him well—a few months after Lyle had drifted into the coffee shop, Artie had enlisted. Lyle had followed a little later, but their paths had never crossed in 'Nam. After Lyle was discharged he'd enrolled in State and picked up a degree in psychology. Jenny Morrison, who'd dated him briefly back then, said he had never been more than a C student.

Lyle had been planning to work for the City but it hadn't panned out—like most things in his life. At State he'd been on the wrestling team and at one time had hopes of going to the Olympics, but he never even made the qualifying rounds. He'd had a three-year failed marriage, and then he'd drifted away from everybody. He'd surfaced again two years ago and showed up at a meeting—who'd brought him? Jenny?—and everybody had been glad to see him, but they knew they were dealing with damaged goods and had kept their distance. Artie had felt guilty about that. He should have extended himself more.

Lyle wasn't the star athlete he had once been. Now he was thicker in the middle, with a faint sag to the shoulders. Not especially handsome as a kid, a lot less so now. Broken nose, bushy black eyebrows, eyes that were too small and too bright, a face badly used by time. On the other hand, he had a way with women.

Anya was exotic, a statuesque brunette ten years Lyle's junior with an executive position at Bank of America. What the hell had Lyle used for bait?

He'd picked Lyle for his first stakeout not because he knew so much about him but because he knew so little. He'd gotten over his paranoia about Charlie and Mitch—almost—and that hadn't left a whole lot of possibilities. Lyle had been first on the list of those who remained.

Artie scrunched around in his seat, trying to find a more comfortable position, then froze at a sudden tapping on the passenger-side window. He glanced over, thought *Shit!*, and rolled down the glass.

"Recognized your car from down the street," Lyle said cheerfully. "What the hell you sitting out here for?"

Artie fought his sense of shock, suddenly feeling like he was back in 'Nam and had stumbled into an ambush. Then once again the sense of unreality hit him and he felt faintly ashamed. He had never really tried to be Lyle's friend and now here he was compounding his guilt by spying on him.

"Waiting for you, Lyle. I just got here, you weren't home, and I thought I'd give you a few minutes to show up—glad I did."

"I was taking Fritzi for a walk." The rottweiler had put her paws on the edge of the window and was giving him a wait-and-see look, probably hoping he would be good for a biscuit or two. "Come on in. Anya's visiting relatives in San Jose so we've got the house to ourselves."

Artie climbed out and locked the car.

Everything was perfectly normal.

Why had he thought it would be otherwise?

The kitchen was clean and open, the dinnerware in the glass-front cupboards a pleasant delft blue pattern, no dishes in the sink, the linoleum floor freshly waxed, floral curtains over the windows. A woman's touch, Artie thought; a little too frilly for Lyle.

Lyle filled the dog's water bowl, then put on a pot of coffee. "You want to see the house?"

Lyle might not be the huge success in life he had wanted to be, but he was obviously far from down and out. If he wanted to show off or brag a little, he had the right.

"Sure, Lyle—sorry I haven't dropped in before."

"Really, Artie?"

The tour was cursory—nobody ever showed you their bedroom or the john. You usually saw only the rooms that were deliberately on display: the office, the library, the living room, the rec room if they had one. Lyle's office didn't amount to much, but the den in the basement was impressive. A bookcase full of CDs, a component music system that must have cost a fortune, a big-screen TV. Managing Copeland's obviously paid well, though Anya's salary undoubtedly helped.

Artie ran his hand over one of the shelves of CDs. "You must have spent a mint on these."

Lyle shrugged. "We all spend more than we should on our hobbies, right? And if you think that's something, you should see Mary's—she could set up her own store. Big on books, too, mostly poetry—didn't expect that, either."

Artie was surprised.

"You must be the first one in the Club that Mary ever invited over."

"Who said anything about being invited? I went over to see Jenny when Mary wasn't home."

Artie floundered for a moment. "You and Jenny—"

"—were a number before Mary cut in, remember? When I came back to town, I thought I'd look her up and try and fan the embers when the wicked witch was away. I never believed that lesbian shit. I thought she might at least be a switch hitter. When Jenny opened the door, I just walked in. Jenny wouldn't have any of it—she and Mary were for real—but I got a good look at the house. Nice decor if you care for turn-of-the-century."

He turned and switched on the light in a workout room just off the den. The room was small but laid out for efficiency. A NordicTrack machine and then several free-weight setups. A workout bench with two metal uprights holding a bar that was loaded with at least two and a quarter for bench presses. Lyle might have seemed like he was out of shape, but if he actually lifted those weights it was obvious he wasn't.

They returned to the kitchen and Lyle poured out two cups of coffee, then teetered back in a kitchen chair, looking at Artie with an expression that was vaguely unfriendly.

"Why did you come to see me, Artie? I mean, all of a sudden like? I've been going to meetings almost a year this time around and you're the first member who's dropped over. I thought for sure Larry or Charlie might, but they never did. You guys are friendly enough at meetings, but otherwise it's like I don't exist. You've got me pegged as a loser, right? And you decided to keep your distance because you were afraid it might be catching."

He'd never liked Lyle, Artie remembered, and now he knew why.

"You disappeared for eight years, Lyle. I don't remember you saying good-bye to anybody."

Lyle shrugged. "Okay, you've got a point. I should have."

It was difficult to keep it casual, not to take offense.

"It's kind of hard to pick up where you left off."

"Mea culpa, Artie." Lyle got up to fill his cup and gestured with the pot. "You want some more? Drink enough, you'll have to sleep in the bathtub tonight."

Artie shook his head. "One will do me."

"So why *did* you come over, Artie? And don't tell me it was because you were in the neighborhood."

If Lyle was Lyle, then he had a right to be pissed. If he was . . . something else, then they were fencing. In either case, he was going to have to fake it. He wanted out of there, badly, but there was no way he could up and leave. Not right then.

There was a box of dog biscuits on the table and he shook one out for Fritzi to cover his nervousness. She was very dainty in taking it from his hand, her hindquarters wriggling as she tried to wag her docked tail, and Artie remembered the three dogs in Schuler's office and how friendly they'd been. It took an effort not to shiver.

"When you first joined the Club, I wasn't around long enough to really get to know you. When you came back, it was difficult to start all over again. Most of us are married and have families, and it's natural to stick with old friends. It's not so easy to make new ones when you get older, Lyle. So none of us volunteered. I felt bad about that, and since this is the Christmas season, I thought I'd drop by. Once here, I came down with cold feet and sat out in the car. I was afraid if you were home and I rang the bell, you'd tell me to get lost. You would have had every right to."

He meant it all. Every word of it. And he hoped, desperately, that Lyle believed him.

Lyle softened slightly. "Apology accepted, Artie. But to be honest, I don't know what the hell we've got in common to talk about."

"Larry . . ." Artie let his voice trail off, but there was no reaction on Lyle's part. He changed the subject. "It was something of a shock meeting Schuler again. He dredged up old times, at least for me. I imagine he did the same for you."

Lyle relaxed even more. "A real prick. He told me about the time he busted you guys. He busted me once and kept me in a jail for a week, said he didn't like my attitude."

And that was it for a good forty-five minutes, until

Artie yawned and said if he were going to sleep in the bathtub, he'd better get started. It had been all old times, nothing about Larry's murder or Mark's disappearance. And toward the end, the nostalgic mood had worn rather thin.

Once outside in his car, Artie realized his shirt was sticking to him—he had sweated up a storm. Fritzi had even refused to come over when he offered her a third biscuit, probably because he smelled bad. But one minor mystery had been solved. Nobody had written Lyle off because he had failed at some time in the past. The reason was simpler than that: They didn't like him because he wasn't very likable.

Artie chose an indirect route on the way home, one nobody could have expected him to take to get from the Avenues to Noe and Twentieth. He was paranoid, he realized, but Jesus, who could blame him? The only time Lyle had struck him as real was when he'd let his hurt feelings surface at the very beginning.

And there had been all the other things that hadn't rung true, the little things. Lyle's workout room. What was Lyle now? Middle to late forties, like the rest of them? He looked like a schlump, but he was benchpressing two and a quarter and the schedule pasted on the wall wasn't for casual workouts. He was stronger than he looked. But why the hell did he keep it hidden? At his age and in that shape, you'd think he'd be wearing tailored shirts and Italian suits to show it off.

Jesus, Mitch was right. The only thing he had to fear was paranoia itself. Anything he'd wanted to know about Lyle, he could probably have asked and Lyle would have told him. So Lyle was vain about his build and doing his damnedest to recapture the days when he'd yearned for the Olympics. What else was new?

But something had stuck in his mind.

Something about Mary Robards.

Mary was reclusive; nobody had ever been invited to her house. Ever. But Lyle had stormed his way in. He'd seen the inside of the house and commented on her extensive collection of CDs, enough to stock a store. Lyle had been right when he'd mentioned that everybody spent too much on their hobbies. They seldom kept quiet about them, though; hobbies were what you talked about when the conversation was on life support.

Mary had never mentioned her passion for music, and he never would have guessed her interest in poetry. But it was hardly strange for a lawyer to love the language.

Things started to swim into focus then and Artie felt like he'd just fallen into a pond of ice water. They couldn't sing, he'd told Hall when they had been discussing the Old People. *They had no music. . . .* And Hall had said they had little in the way of language.

There was an element of pathos about it, Artie thought. The descendants of the Old People probably loved the symphony; they probably went to the opera as often as they could, as well as to plays and poetry readings and probably art shows.

And if they collected anything at all, it was probably CDs and paintings.

And maybe chapbooks of poetry.

# CHAPTER 12

**Once home, Artie checked** in with the police. There was nothing new on Mark—no runaways or young victims of violence who fit his description. Connie Lee was working late at KXAM and sounded a little plaintive when she asked Artie if he'd be in for work the following day. Artie assured her that he would; the rest of the conversation was devoted to Connie's growing belief that the world was going to hell.

Mitch's answering machine was on; he apparently wasn't home. For a few minutes Artie's mind was filled with possible scenarios of what might have happened to Mitch, then he forced himself to stop thinking about them. Things were scary enough without his imagination adding fuel to the flames.

He called Susan but there was no answer. She was at the hospital, he thought, and debated calling her there, then decided against it. He had nothing more he could tell her about Mark.

He slept fitfully and awoke the next morning with a splitting headache. He sat on the edge of his bed for a good five minutes, massaging his temples and trying not to think about what he was going to do that morning. He'd have to call Connie's voice mail and tell her he was going to be in late; there was no helping it.

He read the paper starting with the comics and ending with the front page, then dialed Mary Robards after nine. She was usually at her law office early—if she answered at home, he'd simply hang up.

Again, an answering machine.

He ate a quick breakfast of orange juice and oatmeal, then pocketed the automatic and drove over to the Potrero Hill section of town. Mary lived on Connecticut Street in a white clapboard house that seemed small from the front but extended back almost the full length of the lot. It was a large enough house for her and Jenny to have separate offices—neither one of them would feel cramped. The only drawback was that there was no garage tucked underneath. The house itself was on a hill that sloped away toward the back and Artie guessed that the first floor was set back into the hill. The floor that fronted on the street was actually the top floor.

Artie parked and watched for a few minutes. There was no movement behind the curtains and there were no cars parked on the street that he recognized as belonging to either Mary or Jenny. He glanced at his watch, then quietly got out of the car. Mary had cats, that much he knew, but she didn't care for dogs—"Dirty animals, always humping your leg and fouling the sidewalks." Mary had said the house had been painted that fall and it looked it. Certainly pretty enough from the front, the landscaping carefully groomed. That was Mary's one hobby that he knew of: gardening.

Artie spent a moment rehearsing a story to tell Mary in case he had miscalculated and she was home, then rang the bell. A minute of panic before he relaxed. Nobody had answered the door. He tried the knob—locked—and guessed there was a dead bolt on the inside. He stood there a moment, shivering in the cold, thinking about Mary. Serious, almost grim—and forgetful. She wouldn't rely on her memory when it came to taking along her keys when she left the house. She'd even joked about the time she'd locked herself out.

Artie lifted the mat—nothing—and glanced around the small front porch. The usual leaves that had blown into the corners, plus a half-empty bag of potting soil almost hidden in the shadows. He felt underneath it, found the key, and a moment later was inside the house. Heavy curtains and drapes kept out most of the sun and Artie stood for a moment in the gloom, listening. Nothing.

He took a breath and started exploring. The street floor was laid out like a railroad flat, with all the rooms opening off a long hallway that ran along one side of the house. A large living room in front with windows looking out on the street, then a dining room, and finally the bedroom with a kitchen opposite and a sunporch in back. The bathroom was across from the dining room just after a few steps that led down to a landing. Then more steps from the landing to . . . what? Probably offices and a family room downstairs, cut into the slope of the hill.

It was a turn-of-the-century atmosphere inside the house. Mary and Jenny had restored the interior, letting the outside of the house blend with the others on the block. Thick, heavy drapes and lacework curtains, dark oak furniture—probably all antiques. Area rugs carpeted the light oak flooring. The walls of the living room were covered with prints of famous paintings, all of them realistic, almost illustrative. Winslow Homer, Sargent, Gainsborough, Wyeth, Alma-Tadema, Eakins, Pyle, and a St. John of a cave girl being threatened by a saber-toothed cat. A lot of it kitsch, all of it romantic realism.

In the dining room, the table had a linen cloth spread over it and was set for two with antique dinnerware, obviously for show. The dining table and the setting went with the framed 1906 copy of the *Oakland Tribune,* the headlines about the San Francisco earth-

quake, that hung among the print gallery on one of
the dining room walls. It was a room reserved for small
dinner parties, Artie decided—Mary and Jenny probably ate most of their meals in the kitchen.

There was only one bedroom. Against the far wall
was a king-sized four-poster with goose down pillows
and a comforter that had probably won a prize in a
county fair a century before. Large closets and two oak
chests of drawers, one for each of them. Artie opened
the bathroom door, then quickly closed it. The cat box
by the toilet was overdue for changing.

He almost expected to find a woodstove in the
kitchen, but when it came to cooking, Mary had the
same taste for the modern as Cathy Shea, salted with
a few antiques. Heavy cast-iron frying pans hung from
wall hooks and an ancient butcher block squatted next
to the sink. The surface was concave from usage but
Artie guessed that Mary kept it mostly—again—for
show.

Show for whom? He didn't know anybody in the
Club who had ever been there with the exception of
Lyle, and he had hardly been a guest.

Artie walked quietly to the head of the stairs. There
were no windows downstairs and the stairwell was pitch
black. He couldn't find the light switch and fished
around in his pocket for his cigarette lighter and
flicked it on. He felt his way down the stairs, catching
glimpses of more paintings in the faint glow from the
lighter. Opening off the stairwell at the bottom were
two offices—one somewhat spartan with a large poster
of San Francisco on the wall, a plain, uncluttered desk,
a single filing cabinet, and a computer table. Jenny's.

The other office was larger, with a bank of four filing
cabinets and several large bookcases filled with law
books. Mary's hideaway from her office downtown. A
more ornate desk with two telephones on it, a fax machine, and another computer workstation. And on one
corner of the desk, a large color photograph of Jenny,

which must have been taken when they had first met. She wasn't a bad-looking woman now; she had been drop-dead gorgeous back then.

The room that lay beyond was the one Artie was most interested in. It was a huge recreation room with a conversation pit lined with black leather pillows around the rim. One wall was covered with more paintings, most of them prints of the Impressionists. The only exceptions were some Maxfield Parrish prints in thin black frames—covers from some old magazines. The far end of the room was taken up with an elaborate surround sound system.

The left wall held Mary's CD collection, one that made Lyle's seem tiny. Thousands of jewel boxes lined shelves that ran from the floor to the ceiling and extended from one end of the room to the other. Artie walked over and waved his lighter along the shelving. There were no instrumentals—all the CDs were voice. Popular, classical, operatic, jazz . . .

The opposite wall was taken up with bookcases, and Artie guessed they were filled with first editions. Mary probably hadn't been selective; he suspected she had everybody from Hemingway to Eliot to Ginsberg.

Such little things as art and music and poetry to give her away.

Artie never heard the creaking of the stairs, never heard anybody walking down them. The first he knew he was no longer alone was when the overhead track lights flashed on, blinding him. He dropped the lighter and the gun was in his hand without his even thinking. Then he had sense enough to freeze.

"You're a clever species," a voice behind him said. "Too clever by half."

**Artie stood still another** few seconds, then said, "I'd like to turn around."

"Please do," Mary Robards said. "I don't want to talk to your back all day." Her voice was heavy, gravelly. She was dressed in black with a looping strand of pearls. Your stereotypical old-fashioned matron, the perfect image of the motherly lawyer for the defense. To complete the picture she was holding a huge black cat with a splash of stiff white fur around its muzzle. A tom that Mary must have had for years.

"Congratulations, Artie—you've discovered the real me." She nodded toward the conversation pit. "We'll be more comfortable over there if you want to talk, and I assume you do." She turned her back on him and walked over to the pit. "And put away the cannon; you're the only one who's armed."

Artie sat gingerly on one of the leather cushions, hunching forward with his elbows on his knees. He was face-to-face with the enemy—and the enemy turned out to be a plump, middle-aged woman whom he considered his friend and whom he had once slept with when they both were younger. An enemy who wore reading glasses and held a basketful of knitting in her lap, her cat curled up next to her.

"You were waiting for me?"

"You paid a visit to Lyle last night; I guessed I would be next on your list."

Artie felt the first prickle of sweat.

"You're good—I never knew I was being followed."

She shook her head and pulled out a row of stitches, frowning. "Nothing so time-consuming. Lyle called Jenny after you left; they're still friends, he's closer to her than other members of the Club. I'll give him one thing—he's a game loser once he knows he's really lost."

To Artie, it sounded like a confirmation of what he'd suspected.

"Lyle's one of you?"

"Perhaps. But that's for you to find out, Artie. For your own protection, I'd certainly try to find out soon if I were you."

Artie could guess but asked anyway. "Why so important?"

She took a sip from a water glass on the coffee table in front of her. Vodka, Artie thought, or more likely gin. She'd been a drinker all her life but he'd never suspected she hit the bottle that early in the day; she was probably smart enough to limit herself to a glass in the morning and a martini in the evening. Who was it who said that as you grew older you didn't give up your vices, they gave you up?

"He could be a Hound, you know."

"Hound?" Artie felt lost.

"One of our soldiers, if you like. Or think of the children's game, Hare-and-Hounds, with the hounds out to catch the hare. Or the hound in *The Hound of the Baskervilles*. Better yet, the poem by Thompson. 'I fled Him, down the nights and down the days; I fled Him, down the arches of the years. . . .' It's one of my favorites—'The Hound of Heaven'—but I think 'Hound from Hell' is more appropriate in this case." She smiled slightly. "I never knew, Artie—Do you like poetry? Your species has a way with words, I'll grant that." And then, deadly serious: "You're the hare, Artie. I think you've already met the Hound."

It was hard for Artie to think of her as one of the Old People. His mind kept slipping back to when he'd first met her. She'd had a peasant's stocky body and there had been occasions when he'd delighted in it. But there had also been a remoteness about her that he never understood until she and Jenny became a couple. He hadn't accepted that until much later.

"You're toying with me, aren't you, Mary?"

"Of course. I'm hardly going to point the finger at anybody; you wouldn't respect me if I did." Her voice was sarcastic.

"Did Lyle murder Larry Shea?"

She shrugged. Artie had always thought Mary and Larry Shea had been close friends. It didn't seem to matter to her now and it was obvious it never had.

"I don't know who our Hounds are, Artie. What we don't know, we can't tell. If I suspected, I would never ask and they would never say. Some Hound, maybe Lyle—if he is one. For all I know, he's *Homo sap*, just like you."

She chucked her cat under the chin one more time, then set it on the floor. It ran for the shadows in a far corner of the room and disappeared.

The house was made for entertaining, but nobody Artie knew had ever been there—or had admitted to it. She obviously had a different circle of friends from those in the Club, friends with whom she could let her hair down, friends with whom she could dispense with the act. Friends just like her.

"Who are you people, Mary?"

She didn't look at him but concentrated on her knitting, holding up a length of scarf that seemed a bizarre collection of colors—she had no sense of the artistic at all, Artie thought. But she wasn't fat, she didn't have a dowager's hump, and when she held up the scarf the flesh didn't hang in loose folds from her upper arms. Like Lyle, she was probably in damned good shape but kept it hidden under flowing dresses.

"Come on, Artie, you already know—we're the meek who were supposed to inherit the earth. Until your species came along. And that's not quite accurate, either. Did you know we managed to coexist for thousands of years?" She grimaced. "Then thirty-five thousand years ago nature gave you too many talents all at once. It was like giving an ape an arsenal of assault rifles and teaching him how to use them. Maybe it was a mutation, maybe it was a gene for violence—that's something your scientists ought to look into. But the problem isn't who *we* are, the problem is who *you* are." She shook her head in mock dismay. "You always want to know how other species differ from you, not how you might differ from them, unless all the differences are on the plus side."

"One of you killed Dr. Hall," Artie accused.

She took another sip from the glass and studied him, her eyes a crystalline blue in a remarkably unlined face.

"All I know about it is what I read in the papers, Artie. You apparently went to Hall and showed him Shea's research. Not very kind of you in the long run. You're as responsible for what happened to him as the Hound, whoever he is."

"And Paschelke?"

"Same thing."

She seemed friendly enough on the surface, but beneath it Mary struck him as being as alien as somebody from another planet. Artie kept trying to think of common ground, of points of rapport. She was willing to talk but he didn't know where to start asking questions. In 'Nam he'd sat in on interrogations with Mitch where the languages differed, but here it was the mind-set itself—and something more. Different species, he thought uneasily. How the hell *would* they talk to each other?

"You said that we're different from you."

She looked disapproving.

"Oh, you're different all right, in a way you don't suspect. Most of your anthropologists know it but they'll never tell you. You're a fluke of nature, a flawed species, Artie. Only a part of you is rational. The other part is mad as a hatter—as a species, you're committable."

Artie felt uncomfortable.

"That's a pretty harsh judgment."

"Is it? For starters, you breed uncontrollably, you war constantly, and you've made the world into a pigpen. Worst of all, you take no responsibility—you excuse yourselves by saying that somehow it's all part of God's grand design. I've got news for you, Artie. God sometimes makes mistakes, and you're one of them."

Artie remembered balancing on the railing of his balcony and the subtle urgings that had bubbled up in his head. He hadn't known what to call it then; he didn't now.

"You can read minds?"

She cocked her head, frowning.

"Don't be silly—nobody can read minds. We can't press a button on your mental computer and watch the words scroll up on a screen. We can see images in each other's minds and we can project them if you're receptive, that's all. It's like the Rhine experiments: The subjects weren't asked to identify words, they were asked to identify images. Many of your own children can do it when they're two years old. They mostly lose the ability as they grow older." She pointed to her glass. "You want something to drink?"

He might think about getting roaring drunk later on. But if Mitch was right, he knew he could never afford to lose control of his mind again.

"I'm fine. I didn't know that about kids."

"You should. When you're growing up, what's the one ability you always wished you had? To know what somebody else is thinking, right? When you're a teenager, it's 'will she or won't she' and how much you'd give if only you knew. To be able to glimpse an image of you and her together, to know that that's what she's thinking about. Wouldn't you have liked to be able to do that, Artie? You lose that ability early, but you never get over wishing you had it back."

"That must have given you a big advantage over your enemies."

For a fleeting moment she looked sad. "We could see pictures in other people's minds. It was useful on the hunt. And racial memories were our history books. A simple talent, but you more than made up for your lack of it."

Artie couldn't understand why she was telling him

as much as she was. She had to be doing it for a reason, but he didn't have a clue what it might be.

"How?"

She put down the knitting and took another sip from her glass.

"Didn't your professor Hall explain the possibilities? Your species could make a far wider variety of sounds than we could, and eventually it led to language. We didn't need to describe what we saw in words. For much the same reason, we didn't need art. You needed both and you ran with them. And then you were clever enough to substitute paintings for mental images, the one talent we had that you envied."

She twisted her head to glance at the wall of CDs and books behind her.

"Nature not only made you handsome, it gave you language and music and art and you did wonders with all of them. From a personal viewpoint, I'm very glad that you did. I can't carry a tune—few of us can—and I couldn't draw a recognizable stick figure if you paid me. But it was a Faustian bargain, Banks. Nature also made you the most homicidal species the planet has ever seen."

She suddenly turned accusing.

"Your species learned to lie with language, Artie. Lying was a concept that was foreign to us; you can't lie very well with images. We believed you during truces, in battles, in negotiations—and by the time we understood you were lying, we were almost gone."

Artie tried in vain to see in her face the Mary Robards he'd once known, but that Mary had vanished for good. They had been lovers briefly and then friends for how long? Twenty years? Now she'd taken off the mask she had worn for so long and beneath it was the face of a stranger. It was like a death in the family.

"Language—that was your key to winning the world, Artie. Then you trumped it and organized the sounds you made into words you could carve in stone or print on paper. Remarkable! You could do with print the same things you could do with your voice. You didn't need racial memories; you could leave printed books behind. And you could lie with them just as easily as you could with the spoken word."

"You're afraid of us," Artie accused.

She looked surprised. "If you were us, wouldn't you be? What do you think would happen if everybody knew about us? How soon would it take your governments to launch the greatest pogrom the world has ever seen?"

He already knew the answer to that one; once again the memory of the Tribe was fresh in his mind.

"You're experts at genocide," she continued, her voice now heavy with anger. "It's in your blood. The genocides of the Second World War—"

"Committed by the Nazis—"

"Oh? And since then it's been the Hutus trying to exterminate the Tutsis, all those loser tribes in the Sudan killing each other off, the Serbs slaughtering the Muslims— That was another genocide where the murderers did their jobs with enthusiasm, an evening's entertainment! And remember 'Nam, remember My Lai?"

"Thousands died on both sides," Artie said angrily.

Mary's smile was sardonic.

"So what's your point, Artie? You want to go back to Tasmania a hundred and fifty years ago when the early settlers shot the natives for sport and exterminated an entire race?"

She resumed knitting, the needles flashing savagely.

"Or try your eden of Tahiti where warring tribes nailed children to their captive mothers with spears and drilled holes in the heads of other prisoners so they could be strung together like beads on a string. Consider the Turks and the Armenians or the Mayans, whose population dropped ninety-five percent in fifty years because of wars of extermination. Better yet, read your own Bible—"

"That's the dark side," Artie interrupted, desperate. She sounded exasperated.

"My God, Artie, you think there's a bright side? Look at your history books. They're nothing but a recital of battles won and battles lost with the victors sitting atop a mound of skulls at the end! And the generals who engineered the slaughters become your heroes! What was it your General Grant said? That he could walk across the battlefield at Shiloh stepping on the bodies of the dead without his feet ever touching the ground?"

She drained what was left in her glass, hesitated, then refilled it from a bottle beneath the table.

"You should read your morning paper more often, Artie. Your species is monstrous when it comes to hypocrisy: you keep telling yourselves how much you prize human life when it's obvious there's nothing you value less. You love violence, you adore it. Three hundred years ago you even treated guns like works of art, decorating them with intricate carvings and inlaying them with mother-of-pearl. It's a wonder you're not doing the same thing with the stocks of AK-47s today. For all I know, maybe you are."

Mary turned colder now, her face masking her emotions. "History is a two-way street, Artie. You want to know what you were like in the distant past, look at what you are today. You're the same murderous species now that you were thirty-five thousand years ago. You exterminated the Neanderthals and then you went after us. You wanted our hunting grounds and our foraging areas, and the simplest way to get them was to kill us—men, women, children, babes in arms. And it was so easy! We looked different from you, so you could identify and kill us on sight. We were the 'other' and because we were, you didn't need an excuse."

Artie remembered the slaughter on the riverbank

and turned away, sick. "You're still here, Mary," he said in a low voice.

"There were two groups of us. Those of us who lived in northern Europe were big nosed, heavy browed, stumpy people who had adapted to the cold. We were tribal, we tended to stay in the same areas, so we didn't get any images about what was happening until it was too late. We became the ogres of fairy tales, the hairy, ugly people who lived in the woods. It was open season on us and within a few thousand years we were gone."

Artie could see no trace of the primitive in her.

"You look no different from us."

Mary turned back to her knitting, her voice sad.

"I said there were two groups of us. The tribes who lived in southern Europe, around the Mediterranean, looked more like *Homo sapiens*. It was survival of the fittest, Artie, and the fittest were those of us who looked and spoke the most like you. Children who were throwbacks were killed by their parents for fear they would cast suspicion on their families. We were selected out by our environment and *you* were that environment, as selective as the glaciers or the veldt. We ended up breeding according to your specifications. We adapted to *you*; we had to."

"You interbred—"

"God, yes, we interbred, Artie—there was mating and there were offspring. But we were a different species, it was like donkeys mating with horses, where the offspring are mules, sterile. Since lives were short, there were few grandparents around to become suspicious. As a species, we survived through arranged marriages. It's an honorable practice; it just goes back much farther than you think."

Artie remembered the few times he had watched her in court. She was as passionate then as she was now. Except then it was a calculated passion and now it was spontaneous.

"Why are you telling me all this, Mary?"

This time her smile made his skin crawl.

"*We* were the species in a direct line of succession from ancient man. You came out of nowhere, a quantum leap in potential, and you looked like nothing that had gone before. You were flat-faced, relatively lightly built, comparatively hairless with well-shaped heads . . . an elegant species. And thirty-five thousand years ago you stole our world." She held the scarf up to check her stitches, the mismatched colors jittering in the light. "We want it back, Artie."

Once again, Artie wasn't sure what to say.

"What are you going to do?"

"That's the second question. The first is what are *you* going to do."

She wasn't making sense. "I don't understand."

Her voice was very calm, deliberate.

"You're going to exterminate yourselves, Artie. You don't stand a prayer of lasting another hundred years. For a while we thought all we had to do was wait."

Artie stood up. The feel of the small gun in his pocket was comforting.

"Larry and Dr. Paschelke and Richard Hall aren't examples of waiting."

Her expression was somber.

"Our original plan was simple: Stay hidden until all of you died in wars or starved to death in a habitat you had ruined beyond saving. Unfortunately, it's our habitat as well. In the meantime our chances of being discovered have grown immeasurably. Medicine has become more sophisticated, there are physicals for work and for the military—you're only a few years away from having DNA data included on everybody's birth certificate. You'd be shocked when you came to us. And we can't foresee accidents and autopsies like Talbot's. Shea was a curious doctor. There'll be others. We can't afford to wait any longer, Artie—we want you gone. Now."

"And you're going to use the Hounds as weapons."

She shrugged, as if somehow they didn't involve her. "They're a loose cannon, a wild card. I don't know what they plan or who they are, but even if I knew, I wouldn't try to stop them." She paused. "We breed them like you breed pit bulls. They're dangerous, Artie. But you know that."

He would give a lot for the old Mary, Artie thought. The former lover whom he could talk to about his problems at work, his problems with raising Mark. How did a Muslim and a Serb, who might have been lifelong friends, talk to each other now?

"Why did you join the Club, Mary?"

She took another small sip from her glass.

"You sweated testosterone, you and the others. And you were courageous, adventurous. More than any military academy, the Club was a natural breeding ground for your own Hounds. You proved it when all of you went to 'Nam and came back decorated. You were brave, you were resourceful—we knew you would be and we were curious about you, about what made you tick. So several of us joined to find out."

"I didn't enjoy 'Nam," Artie said somberly. "I didn't enjoy war."

She shook her head. "I don't say you enjoyed killing people. But you enjoyed war, you enjoyed the hunt. You're ashamed of that now."

She sounded like Mitch, Artie thought with sudden anger. He knew what he was ashamed of and he knew what he was proud of.

"You could have talked me out of what I suspected when I came here, Mary. I thought it was going to be a wild goose chase."

She looked surprised.

"Does it really make any difference what I say? You have no proof of anything; all you have are fantasies. We claimed Talbot's body, your printout of Shea's diskette is gone, so is the diskette itself. And everybody who's read Shea's research is dead."

He remembered Shea and Paschelke and Hall, and for the first time he accepted Mary as a complete stranger—one who would probably consider it a victory when he was dead as well.

"Except me."

"Except you." She shook her head. "But nobody in authority is going to believe you. For everything that's happened, there's a reasonable answer."

"You've told me too much, Mary. You've played the traitor. Your own Hounds will be after you now."

She raised an eyebrow. "Traitor? Hardly. Call it a favor for a friend. Someday you might have to make a judgment based on what I've told you. And that's . . . important. But in any event, we don't kill each other like your species does. Incidentally, don't bother coming over here again. Jenny and I will be away on vacation."

Artie paused by the stairwell. It would probably be his last chance to ask a question that had bothered him for years. "Why you and Jenny, Mary?"

There was a flicker of tenderness on her face. "I mated outside of gender and outside of species, Artie. Jenny needed somebody to take care of her and I needed somebody to take care of. She was beautiful and I was lucky. It worked out."

Mark had been in the back of his mind ever since coming over. He had nothing to lose by asking about him now.

"Mark disappeared three days ago. You know he's handicapped, he has to use a wheelchair to get around. He couldn't have gone anyplace without help. I'm worried your people might have taken him."

He was pleading with her, gambling on any feelings that might still exist between them, and for a moment he thought she looked concerned.

"I'm sure none of us have him but I don't really know."

Artie heard a car drive up outside and started up the

steps. It was time to leave; more than time.

Behind him, Mary said softly, "Artie?"

He turned.

"I'd like to help you but I can't." She hesitated. "I probably wouldn't, even if I could."

What surprised him was the sorrow in her voice when she said it.

# CHAPTER 13

"**I thought I was** going to have to ask Accounting to mail you your check," Connie said. "Anything more on Mark?"

"I made a few phone calls trying to track down a possible girlfriend he might have left with. Either everybody's keeping silent out of loyalty or, more likely, nobody wants to get involved. He's underage and if she was over eighteen, then she probably broke the law and goddammit—"

Connie held up her hand. "Not being cruel, Artie, but the cops aren't going to get their water hot about a seventeen-year-old boy and a nineteen-year-old girl running off to Palm Springs or wherever for a little fun in the sun. If she were older, they might look into it, but only for a snicker or two."

Artie sagged into his chair and watched the bustle outside in the newsroom. "When do you stop being a parent, Connie? When do you decide to let them go out on their own?"

She looked sympathetic. "One, you never stop. And two, you don't do the deciding—they do. And please don't ask me how I handle Elizabeth and John. I don't. And it's not because they're adopted."

"I don't understand Mark," Artie said, his voice close to despair.

"You only think you don't. Wait a few years and when you talk to him, you'll be talking to a duplicate of yourself."

Artie glanced at the clock. Late afternoon. He'd spent more time at Mary's than he'd thought. She'd scared the crap out of him and he'd called Levin right after he had left. Mitch had been out of the office but he'd try him at home that night, tell him what Mary had said and scare the crap out of him, too.

The desk was still piled high with printouts and books and half a dozen tape cassettes. Artie thumbed through a stack: the Grub must be spending all his time searching the Internet and Nexis.

"You're going to have to bring me up to speed, Connie."

"Sure." She said it offhand and continued staring through the glass at the newsroom outside.

Artie watched for a second, worried, then figured Connie was herself, though it was the first time Artie had seen her in a blue funk.

"Earth to Connie Lee, Earth—"

"Sorry, Artie." She rubbed at her face and blinked open her eyes. "What'd you want to know?"

No jokes and funny stories today, Artie thought. "You're still you, right?"

She frowned. "Yeah," she said uncertainly, "we had an argument or something. I'd forgotten all about that."

Artie shrugged. "It doesn't matter." The Old People were keeping one step ahead of him.

Connie thumbed through a stack of reports. "To be honest, Artie, I'm sorry as shit I ever got involved in this. You read enough of these and after a while you begin to think you've got a ringside seat at the end of the world. It's all around us, nobody's doing anything about it, and you feel like you're barreling toward the edge of the cliff at full speed. Maybe we won't go over in my lifetime, but we sure as hell will in my kids'."

Artie was suddenly all attention. What was it Mary had said? They didn't stand a prayer of lasting another hundred years?

"What was such a downer?"

She waved a hand at the clutter on the desk. "For Christ's sake—everything! What do you want to start with? The shrinking penises of alligators in Florida? Declining sperm counts and growing sterility in human males? There's some argument about that, but in light of everything else, I wouldn't bet against it—the optimists are probably whistling in the dark. And on top of that, we can include the vanishing glaciers in Alaska and the Alps, the shrinking Arctic ice cap, the increasing failure of antibiotics, and the sudden increase in infectious diseases. . . . Or maybe just man's inhumanity to man, the social meltdown in Africa. . . ."

Connie was sounding like a *Homo sapiens* version of Mary Robards, but it was suddenly more involved than that. Who had thought up the series in the first place—and why? And why give him the assignment? It would have been a great research assignment for the Grub; Jerry knew all about the environment.

Artie stood up and covered the papers on the table with his arms. "We're just reporting it, Connie, and that's doing a lot. Go home and recycle, hope for the best, and live your life. So your kids are going to have big problems. So did you. So did your old man and his old man. Your great-granddaddy helped build the Southern Pacific and he was one of the lucky ones who lived through it. If you could ask him, he wouldn't think we have it so bad."

Connie sank back in her chair. "Okay, you win. But it's hard not to take it seriously."

"Didn't say you shouldn't—just keep it in perspective."

Sweetness and light and it was all lies, Artie thought.

When it came to going over the cliff, if they didn't jump, they'd be pushed. But what the hell would an astronomer do if he spotted a comet heading right for the Earth and knew there was nothing that could be done? Put out a press release and have millions die in the resulting panic, or shut the hell up and let people enjoy whatever few months or weeks they had left?

Then there was a sudden stray thought that he knew wasn't his, a mere nibble at his consciousness.

*no . . .*

And a sense of deep disagreement.

**Artie turned away from** the glass and started pawing through the printouts. Anything to look busy to anybody watching. And to hide his lips as he talked to Connie.

Somebody had just given themselves away.

"Connie, three days ago you talked to Security about possible visitors. Do you remember what they said?"

She looked at him blankly.

"Why the hell would I talk to Security? About what?"

"Forget it." Artie went back to fumbling with the papers on the desk, then after a few minutes picked up the phone and dialed the ad agency that did the station's self-promotion commercials. Connie was engrossed in one of the printouts; she wasn't listening.

The agency remembered Ms. Lee's call. No, they had no record of any of their messengers going over to the station. It had been a busy day. Right. All their messengers were out that day. Very busy. Did they ever use a professional messenger service when they were jammed? Yes, of course. Yes, she'd check which one.

The record was in another file. Deluxe Downtown Messengers. They had sent someone over. A quick delivery and pickup. A kid named Watson, James Watson. Artie called and got a complete description, and this time the guard remembered him. A skinny kid, black hair. He'd only been there a few minutes, a hasty in-and-out.

The messenger hadn't been there long enough, Artie thought slowly. It had to have been someone on the news floor who'd slipped into Connie's mind so easily. But if Mary was right, Connie had to have been receptive. And there was only one person she had noticed. Adrienne Jantzen, just as she was about to fuck up reading the 'Prompter.

Artie refrained from looking out on the floor. One quick glance and he knew he'd tip somebody off. But Jantzen had already given herself away. She'd looked toward their glassed-in cubicle several times. She was nervous. Was she a friend of Mary's? He'd seen her pick up the phone once and then look around the newsroom, her eyes lingering for just a second on the cubicle. She wasn't a Hound; they would never have made that mistake. But ten to one she'd been to a party at Mary's more than once.

"You haven't been keeping me up to date on Adrienne, Connie. How's she working out?"

Connie didn't look up. "Fine, I guess. She covered a five-alarmer in San Bruno around lunchtime, came back and wrote it up this afternoon for the six-o'clock. She's probably hanging around to watch it. Catch it yourself and make up your own mind."

"She dating anyone?"

"Got me—I hear she's a loner."

He'd bet on it. Artie glanced at his watch. About five-thirty; the station execs, the advertising and business staffs and the dayside reporters would be leaving soon. By six-fifteen or six-thirty the parking lot should be almost deserted.

He pushed away the papers, closed his briefcase, and yawned. "Time to hit it, Connie. See you tomorrow."

She looked at him over the top of her glasses, disapproving.

"How about making it a full day, Artie? I'm doing all the damned work here."

"You love it, Connie."

"Yeah, right. We're doing a series on the end of the world and it's a barrel of laughs. Make it in early tomorrow—we'll share a giggle or two."

Artie gave her a thumbs-up and headed out to the parking lot, behind the little outdoor plaza where the brown-baggers usually ate their lunch when the weather was decent. It was dark—the pole light had burned out the week before—and he felt his way across the flagstones past the little metal tables and the wire wicker chairs and the white plaster statue of Pan mottled with a year's worth of pigeon droppings. The parking lot was just beyond, only a few cars bellying up to the yellow line that separated the lot from the small luncheon plaza.

It wasn't hard to find Adrienne's car. In the darkness he could just make out the bumper sticker that said I LOVE SACRAMENTO with a big heart for "Love"—the standard imitation of the "I Love New York" poster. Artie checked his watch. Six o'clock on the button. The fire would be the top of the news, which meant that Jantzen should be coming out of the back door within ten minutes if she were going to leave right afterward.

He dropped his briefcase in his own car, then stood in the shadows one car away from Adrienne's Taurus. He concentrated on blending in with the dark, not thinking of anything at all. He had started to shiver in the chilly night air when she finally came out, pulling on her gloves as she walked. He'd always seen her sitting down; he hadn't been around enough this week to catch her at lunch or even walking around the news floor. She was there when he arrived and was still there when he left, always sitting at her desk, always working. He'd never even seen her go to the can. Which meant that every minute he was there, she was there. He'd

been under constant surveillance and she had probably "seen" every word he spoke.

Her heels made little staccato clicking noises on the
flagstones and Artie caught his breath, clutching the
automatic in his pocket for reassurance. He watched
as she stopped by her Taurus and fished around in her
bag for the keys. Attractive woman. Not too tall, not
what you would call willowy. Pretty but solid.

He stepped out from behind the nearby car. She
heard the slight noise and looked up, her hand going
to her throat. "You scared the life out of me!" And then
immediate suspicion and anger: "Strange meeting you
down here, Mr. Banks—hiding in the parking lot."

All the time her eyes were darting nervously around
to see if he was alone. He couldn't quite believe the
sudden fear, the apparent relief, and then the anger.
It was all appropriate, but all it meant was that she was
a good actress, that she knew why he was there.

"The lily pad was your idea, wasn't it?" he said, adding, "You're using Connie like a puppet, aren't you?"

She laughed.

"I haven't the slightest idea what you're talking
about. I hardly know Miss Lee, but I have great respect
for her."

She was still glancing nervously around the lot,
which struck Artie as odd—she knew he was by himself.

She looked desperate. "I was trying to help—"

The expression on her face suddenly shifted to one
of fear and then went slack. Artie guessed immediately
what was wrong, but it was already too late to do anything about it. It was a setup and he'd walked right
into it. They knew he'd follow her sooner or later, and
tonight she had been delayed just long enough so the
lot would be deserted.

She caught the look of awareness on his face and
exploded. Her knee jutted through the folds of his
coat and caught him in the groin and he doubled up
at the same time she screamed.

He caught her foot and twisted, and she almost went down, then chopped at the back of his neck. She was strong, surprisingly so. Talbot had been strong too, according to Paschelke. Suddenly a different comparison occurred to him: the old man at the skating rink doing the impossible. But it hadn't been him. And it wasn't just her.

He'd gotten over his distaste for fighting women in 'Nam and now he backhanded her in the face. All he'd wanted was to ask questions, to try to start a dialogue. But Mary obviously had been the exception, not the rule. She *could* talk; Adrienne couldn't.

Her nails left his cheek bloody and then his heart started doing double time, thumping so wildly it felt like it was going to jump out of his chest.

*try and scream, monkey. . . .*

Something else was in the lot and Adrienne had become a mere extension of it, like a hand puppet. The same something that had stage-managed the whole affair. And now it was trying to get a grip on him. For a moment his heart felt like it was going to explode and he had to remind himself that the last time he'd had a physical, the doctor had made a point of telling him he never had to worry about a heart attack—

She suddenly caught him in the throat with the side of her hand. He couldn't scream now if he wanted to; he couldn't make a sound.

*thought you would be better . . .*

She threw him against the side of a car just as he was trying to fumble out the automatic. He realized with sudden shock that he had lost his peripheral vision, that his sight was dimming and within a second or two he'd be blind. He was fighting for his life and he was losing.

He was struggling in total blackness now, knowing where she was only by her scent and her breathing and the sudden puffs of warm air between them. It was like it had been in 'Nam when he'd been ambushed at night. He'd learned how to fight in the dark then and hadn't forgotten how. Then she had her fingers on his throat, her nails pressing into his windpipe, and he grasped his hands together and thrust them up to break her grip.

She whispered in his ear, "You're an asshole," but he wasn't sure it was really her. She drove her elbow into his ribs and he went down, the gun he'd never gotten to use flying from his coat pocket. He was helpless, crumpled against a car wheel, curled into a ball, his arms over his face to protect it from the stiletto heels of her shoes.

There was a pause and a sense of surprise in the air around him and the feeling that somebody else was in the parking lot. Artie was suddenly terrified more than he already was. He had stumbled into a whole group of them.

*what . . .*

He heard Adrienne get into her Taurus and gun the motor, then squeal toward the exit.

A snarl of rage in his mind.

*next time, monkey . . .*

His sight returned abruptly. He was sitting on the ground near the flagstone plaza, his back against a pickup, blood covering his face and the front of his coat. How the hell long had it been? And where the hell were *they*? There had been two of them, he was sure of that. He moved slightly, groaning with the effort, and glanced toward the rear door of the station. The clouds had parted just enough for the moon to peep through. Pan's face was staring down at him, its plaster lips curled in a smirk.

"Jesus Christ, Artie, what the hell happened to you?" Levin was leaning over him, reaching for his hand to help him up. "You look like you got hit by a truck."

He didn't want to admit whom he had lost to, but he knew he was going to have to tell Mitch everything. Most importantly what Mary had told him and why.

He went cold thinking how fortunate it was for Mitch to show up right then, for Mitch to save his life.

"I got your call when I checked in with the office," Mitch said, pulling him to his feet. "I came over as soon as I could break free."

And just in time, Artie thought. He must have seen something; he must have seen Adrienne and the other two.

"I guess I got here a minute too late," Mitch said.

And that was funny as hell because without even meaning to, Mitch was reading his mind.

**They sat in Artie's** car, the heater turned on, and Artie dabbed at the blood on his face with his handkerchief and filled Mitch in on everything Mary had told him. But the only enemy he had seen so far was a heavyset, matronly woman for whom he had once had a thing and a woman news reporter who had tried to kill him in the station parking lot. He told Mitch about the deadly game of Hare-and-Hounds with himself and Mitch and the others as hares and out there, somewhere, the unseen Hound.

After he had finished, Mitch fished out a cigarette and reached for the car lighter, then thought better of it.

"You don't believe me," Artie said.

"Two days ago I almost swallowed half a bottle of Valium and two fingers of lousy scotch. Why shouldn't I believe you?" Mitch glanced out the window at the parking lot, searching for figures in the shadows. "But there's no proof of anything. All you know is what Mary told you."

"You must have seen something when you drove in."

"I told you—I didn't see a damned thing. You were sitting on the ground looking like you wanted to puke your guts out and there was a lot of blood." He hesitated. "You sure you don't want to go to Emergency?"

"We'd probably never get there," Artie said bitterly.

"And if we did, how could we be sure the doctor was who he claimed he was? Goddammit, there were two of them besides Adrienne, I could *feel* them!"

Mitch was silent for a moment. "I almost got hit by your lady friend's car barreling out of here and there you were. That's all I saw, Artie."

"We could go to the government," Artie said sullenly, and the moment he said it he regretted it. If Mary was right about who her people were, then she was also right about genocide. What would happen when you really couldn't tell friend from foe? It wouldn't be like the Serbs and the Muslims or the Tutsis and the Hutus, who'd known each other all their lives. In this case you didn't know who was who; your next-door neighbor could be the enemy, the guy who sat next to you at the office. It would start with suspicion and accusation and end up with . . . what? Burning people at the stake?

"We've got nothing to take to them, Artie. We don't have the diskette, we don't have the printout, all we have is Mary's crazy story. We believe it, but who the hell else would?"

Artie's ribs ached, but most of all he felt angry and embarrassed. He had been handled so easily. Not alone by Adrienne but by . . . somebody else. He could have been killed, probably would have been if Mitch hadn't showed up. And Adrienne would have said that she'd been attacked in the parking lot, that he'd come on to her the last day or so and she'd turned him down.

Behind his granny glasses, Mitch's eyes were bright and speculative.

"Who knows besides us, Artie?"

"Cathy Shea and whoever killed Larry—or had Larry killed. And Paschelke and Hall and they're dead as well."

"Somebody else believes, somebody else knows. And that somebody is somebody we know."

"Hardly anybody ever really keeps a secret," Artie

said after a moment. "Larry probably talked to Cathy. He might also have talked to ten or twenty other people that we never heard of. He couldn't have kept it to himself. Christ, people even talk in their sleep."

Mitch shook his head. "Sorry, Artie, I don't agree. He had too much riding on this one. Larry wouldn't have wanted to share it with anybody. It might have made his reputation." He looked at Artie, taking in his battered face again. "If you don't want to spend the night alone, you can bunk over at my place."

Artie had a sudden image of himself alone in the house without Susan working in the kitchen or Mark studying in his room, the music turned up loud. He'd be alone . . . and he'd be vulnerable. Somehow he'd forget and walk out on his balcony and the next morning they'd find him splattered on the sidewalk below.

But worst of all, he'd be alone.

"I'd be putting you out."

"Big deal."

**It was quiet on** Telegraph Hill, Mitch's small cottage peaceful. Mitch gave him sheets and blankets for the couch, plus a monogrammed towel and washrag. Artie stripped to his shorts and started placing the contents of his shirt pocket on the coffee table. Mark's earring was still wrapped in its napkin, and he unfolded it and held the ring in his hand for a moment.

Mitch noticed it and said, "Can I see that?"

Artie gave him the ring. "It belongs to Mark—gift from Susan. Family heirloom, I guess."

Mitch turned it over in the light.

"Looks Mayan. Let me borrow it for a day. I'd like a friend of mine to take a look at it."

"Go ahead. Just don't lose it. Mark would never forgive me." He reached for the phone on the table. "Mind if I make a call?"

There were no messages on his answering machine at home. Artie called the new number Susan had given him and a tape recorder repeated that the line had been disconnected. It didn't say when and there was no forwarding number. Artie dialed Information and asked for the number of the hospital in Willow and was startled when she said there was no hospital but she would connect him to the only medical clinic in town. Artie felt the sweat start when the puzzled voice at the other end of the line told him Susan's father wasn't there, that he never had been.

He was still sitting there holding the phone when Mitch walked through on his way to the kitchen.

"What's wrong?"

"Susan's gone."

"I thought you said she was in Willow, that her father was in the hospital there?"

"That's what she told me. He isn't, never was."

Mitch stared, not understanding.

"Susan's not in Willow." Artie was suddenly afraid his voice was going to break. "I don't think she ever went there."

# CHAPTER 14

**Artie lay on the** couch staring out at the darkness through the front windows. It was a chill night with no overcast and the stars were bright, the moon a thin crescent above the streetlight at the top of the Filbert Street steps. By his watch it was almost two in the morning and he hadn't slept a wink; he was still sore and bruised from his fight with Adrienne. Mitch had knocked off about fifteen minutes after hitting the sack, he could tell by the snoring.

Not a worry in the world, Artie thought with envy. But then, in 'Nam Mitch had the reputation for being able to sleep through even the worst of the shelling.

Vietnam . . .

If he had to choose being here and being there, he wasn't sure which he would pick. You never knew who the enemy was over there: the little old lady hoeing her garden, the waiter at your table when you went to Saigon for R&R, the whore you slept with . . . You didn't know who the enemy might be here, either, but in both cases you knew what the enemy wanted. They wanted you out.

What the hell were the Old People planning? They were sure as hell plotting something. But he had only seen two of the enemy. There must be . . . what? Hundreds of them in the city? He probably ran into them every day and had no idea who they really were. They were in deep cover, had to be. It would cost them their lives and the lives of their families and friends if anybody found them out. It would probably cost the lives of their entire species except for a few who would end up in jails or zoos. And that was a lousy thing to think. My country, right or wrong. Who'd said that? Stephen Decatur? Patrick Henry?

He turned his pillow over and fluffed it for the twentieth time, then lay there trying to make up his mind whether to hit the john or get a drink of water. Telegraph Hill was quiet at night—at least during the middle of the week when the kids weren't cruising around Coit Tower—much more so than the Castro. When he and Susan had first moved to Noe Street, it was partying every night until two in the morning. It had slacked off some since, but hardly completely.

Susan ....

He'd tried to wall her off in his mind; it hurt too much to think about her. She'd walked out on him, with Mark due to follow—except, for the moment, Mark apparently had other plans. He'd call the bank in the morning and see how much money Susan had taken with her. Walking out on him was the one thing he'd always dreaded, was always afraid that she might do. But he'd also thought she would discuss it in advance.

Try to forget it—for the moment. Too much of his world had collapsed all at once and there was little he could do about any of it.

Mitch ...

Mitch had gotten to the station's outdoor parking lot just in time. Another few minutes and he would have been a dead man. It was hard to think it was coincidence but like Mitch said, you had to trust somebody. Everybody he met now would be suspect, from the postman to the taxi driver to the waitress at Welcome Home, where he sometimes ate breakfast.

Or would they congregate in the professions? Like they said most hairdressers and actors were supposed to be gay? Bullshit, but maybe most of the Old People were professors or accountants or . . . psychiatrists like Mitch or lawyers like Mary. All of them would be great ways of getting to know the enemy.

There was a rustle in the shrubbery outside and Artie suddenly tensed, waiting for the plucking at his mind, the little thoughts that weren't his, the suggestion to slash his wrists or swallow a can of Drano.

There was something out there, he knew it for sure, and then he slowly relaxed. Jesus, he was dreaming; he had finally slipped off. A lucid dream in which you know you're dreaming, like the first one he'd ever had about the Tribe when Susan was in bed with him. He turned and glanced around at the shadowy outlines of the furniture in the room. Everything seemed slightly fuzzy and out of focus, like you might expect in a dream. And he didn't feel a chill just beyond the margin of the blankets. If anything, it was almost a cocoonlike feeling of warmth and safety.

But why just lie there—why not walk around in it? He sat up and slowly started to put on his clothes, taking care not to make any noise. Which was silly—how could he wake up Mitch in a dream? He started to struggle into his shoes, then gave up and slipped his feet into the fancy leather slippers Mitch had lent him.

He let himself out, closing the door quietly behind him. He floated up the wooden steps to Montgomery, then left past the little corner grocery store and down the hill to Broadway. There weren't many people on the street and those few he passed were silent, huddled in their coats against the chill. The advantage of a dream, Artie thought: You didn't feel cold, you didn't feel heat. He'd put on his coat but hadn't buttoned it; he didn't feel the need to.

There was an all-night hamburger joint on Broadway

and he stopped to stare through the windows. The night people were out in full force, the stools by the counter almost filled. Artie grinned to himself. Why not? When was the last time he'd had a burger and fries in a dream? He pushed in through the door and found himself a vacant stool.

An old man in dirty white pants and T-shirt with a stub of a pencil behind his ear moved down the counter taking orders. He stopped in front of Artie and mouthed something at him. Artie couldn't hear a word he was saying but made a guess and ordered a double cheeseburger with fries and a Coke.

A man sat down next to Artie and leaned over to pick up a menu.

"What would you do with us, Banks?"

He was big, heavyset, but Artie couldn't quite make out his features. They were blurry, like almost everything else in his dream.

"You're the first person I can hear," Artie said, marveling.

The big man nodded.

"You can only hear the Old People. You've listened to *sapiens* long enough, it's time you listened to us. Like I said, what would you do with us?"

Artie stared at him blankly.

"What do you mean?"

The big man frowned.

"Put us in concentration camps? Feed us to the ovens?"

Artie suddenly wanted to wake up.

"We don't put people in concentration camps."

"Sure you do. You did once before."

It took Artie a moment to remember. He changed the subject. "What do you do? For a living."

"Construction. Dry wall, like the character used to do on *Roseanne*. How about yourself?"

"Newswriter for KXAM." Artie concentrated on his cheeseburger.

"You're ruining the world," the big man said, reaching for the napkin dispenser. "Did you know there's a sanitarium near Krakow, Poland, that has its patients sleep underground in salt mines because the air outside is so polluted?"

"You're an eco-nut," Artie said.

"Everybody talks about the weather and now you're doing something about it," the big man said. He stood up to go to the cash register. "It's your world. But it's ours, too."

The busboy came up to clear away the plates.

"The customer's always right," he said to Artie. "I mean the other one." He disappeared with his tray of dirty dishes into the kitchen.

Artie frowned and stared around the inside of the diner. Some faces he could make out, others were fuzzy and blurred. Deep cover, he thought. The Old People were all in deep cover. But Jesus, there were a lot of them. Maybe they all worked at night.

For a moment, outside the diner, he couldn't get his bearings. Which way back to Montgomery? There was a blurry-faced cop sitting in a patrol car on the corner and Artie drifted over to ask directions.

"They used helicopter gunships to kill the hippos in Mozambique," the cop said. "Carved the teeth and sold them for decorations in Asia."

Artie stared.

"Which way to Montgomery Street?" he asked.

"You can travel for miles in Mozambique today and not see anything larger than a bird." The cop jerked a thumb behind him. "Montgomery's that way."

Artie started back up the hill. There was a strip joint still open on the corner, the barker, a skinny, middle-aged man in a checkered sport coat, lounging out in front having a cigarette.

"Too bad about the frogs," he said.

Artie turned. "What?"

"The frogs," the barker repeated. "Billions of them.

If the ultraviolet didn't get them the pollution probably did—they use their skin to exchange oxygen and
carbon dioxide, you know. The air's going to kill you,
too. Eventually." He took a final drag on his cigarette
and ground the butt beneath his heel.

"Which way's Montgomery?" Artie asked.

"Bet you didn't know when fisheries net sharks with
other fish they cut the fins off and dump the live sharks
back in the ocean. The fins are worth ten bucks a
pound for soup. Montgomery's next street up."

Artie tried to fix the barker's features in his mind
and couldn't. His face was a blur, a hint of pocked
cheeks, a suggestion of deep-set eyes and a nose that
might have been broken, and that was it. Deep cover.

Artie turned toward Montgomery. At the corner, a
cab slowed and the woman driver cranked down the
window. "Need a lift, buddy?"

"I'm just going to the Filbert steps," Artie said, then
hesitated. Another one; he could hear her but couldn't
quite make out her face.

"I'll take you, on me. Hop in."

Artie climbed in and the cabbie drove up Montgomery in silence.

"You're too quiet," Artie said after a minute. "I
thought you'd be an eco-fanatic, too."

"You're a self-endangered species," she said casually.
"Why waste my breath?"

Artie let himself back into the house and closed the
door quietly behind him. He took off his clothes and
slipped between the blankets on the couch, surprised
to realize that he was suddenly freezing cold and the
blankets were a welcome patch of warmth. Something
wasn't right, and then the thought drifted out of his
mind and he could sense his breathing becoming deep
and regular.

He wasn't aware at all of the first tendrils of smoke
that drifted in from the back of the house.

.        .        .

It was the sound of the fire engines that finally woke him. He coughed for a minute, then was suddenly wide awake. Somebody was hammering at the front door, shouting, and there were sounds of several men around in back. Mitch burst out of the bedroom, bleary-eyed, struggling into his bathrobe and fumbling with his glasses.

"What the hell's going on—Oh, Christ, fire!" He ran toward the rear of the cottage while Artie opened the front door. Several firemen crowded in lugging a hose, and one of them shouted, "Get your clothes and get out!" Artie could hear another engine drive up. Outside, he could see the lights turning on in the other cottages that lined the steps.

An hour later it was all over. Smoke damage and the wooden steps out back were the main casualties. One of Mitch's neighbors had seen the first flames and turned in the alarm. He thought he'd seen somebody at the back of the cottage but the fire chief had shrugged and said it was probably raccoons chewing on one of the hoses to the outdoor propane tank. Fast response time had saved the house. They probably had the fastest in the Bay Area, he said, otherwise the whole city would have burned down a dozen times. San Francisco had the highest percentage of wooden houses in the country this side of Baltimore.

After they'd left, Mitch made some coffee and he and Artie sat in the kitchen and stared at each other.

"I've never had raccoons before, Artie."

"It was two for the price of one, Mitch. Too good for them to pass up."

"What the hell do we do? Sleep in hotel lobbies?"

"Maybe." Artie got up to pour himself another cup. "It's getting personal," Mitch said, thoughtful.

Artie raised an eyebrow. "The scotch and the Valium weren't personal enough? They want you dead too, you know."

Mitch looked frustrated. "The trouble is, neither one

of us can prove a goddamned thing." He was quiet for a moment, the lines in his face gradually smoothing out. "It's a process of elimination, Artie. Mary and Jenny have left town, or so Mary said, right? Apparently she didn't want to be around for the kill. Charlie's not involved—at least we don't think he is."

"*You* don't think he is," Artie said. "I'm not so sure."

"Which leaves Lyle Pace—"

Artie shook his head. "Not Lyle. I saw him the other night; if he'd wanted to do me damage, he had plenty of opportunity."

Mitch didn't look convinced. "You were in the wrong place at the wrong time. What excuse could Pace offer if something happened to you in his own home? Even Schuler wouldn't believe him, no matter what the story."

"Dave Chandler," Artie said, turning the thought over in his head. Dave, the airhead of the Club. Nice guy, innocuous, deep cover at its very best. "Or maybe Cathy Shea. She's the one we know for sure who knew too much."

Mitch sipped at his coffee. "Not Cathy. She was home at the time Larry was killed. I'm not saying she couldn't be connected in some way, but she could hardly have killed Larry herself, even if she had wanted to. No time."

"Which leaves Chandler," Artie repeated.

"So what do we do? Both of us stop by to see him? He'd probably have difficulty handling two of us at the same time."

"Contact Schuler—"

Mitch looked disgusted. "And tell him what?" He tore open another pack of sweetener and dumped it in his coffee. "Is Chandler close to anybody?"

Artie thought for a moment. "Yes and no. He's close to everybody and close to nobody. Closer when we were younger and he was the class cutup and everybody's friend. The act got tired when we grew older.

Dave never changed. But you know all that."

"So when do we pay him a visit?"

"Tomorrow? After work? I've got to check and see how much Susan left in the bank accounts. And put in a full day's work—Connie's beginning to bitch and I can't blame her."

Mitch yawned. "It's close to six—you want to hit the sack again? I could set the alarm for eight."

The thought was attractive but Artie was already wide awake.

"I'll just show up for work early. Surprise the hell out of Connie."

He finished dressing and folded up the couch and rearranged the pillows on top, piling the used sheets and pillowcase at the other end.

He was about to put the slippers on top, then held them for a moment in his hands, feeling slightly dizzy: the shiny patent-leather slippers that Mitch had lent him, probably a present from somebody. Nordstrom's finest pair, maybe a hundred dollars, two hundred a pop—

—were now water-stained and covered with mud.

He'd had growing suspicions that it hadn't been a dream at all, and now he knew for sure.

Somebody had just given him a guided tour behind enemy lines.

# CHAPTER 15

**The streets were quiet,** the parking lot at KXAM almost empty. The attendant opened one eye when Artie drove up, then yawned and nodded off again. A moment later Artie was in his newsroom cubicle, staring dull-eyed at the plastic container of black coffee he'd bought on the trip in. Jesus, there were days God should have just deleted from the calendar, and this was one of them.

He dialed the Bank of America twenty-four-hour hot line and waited for voice mail to give him a number he could punch to ask for his balance.

Susan had taken exactly half of the almost five thousand in their savings account. She'd taken something like four hundred and fifty in cash from the checking. Again, exactly half.

She wasn't coming back. The next time he'd hear from her it would be through her lawyer.

She apparently hadn't used any of their credit cards, and Artie doubted that she would. She hadn't wanted him to find her, that was obvious. She wouldn't leave any tracks. Did she take any clothing? He'd check when he got home. She could have loaded up her car the day before, when he was at work. No way he would have thought of checking at the time.

Susan.

*Aw, Christ . . .*

It hit him then and for a moment he was afraid he was going to cry, something he hadn't done since he was fifteen and True Love had waltzed out of his life on the arm of the high school diving champ. His father had been sympathetic, his mother much less so.

"Women will break your heart all your life, Arthur. You're the thin-skinned type. Better get used to it now."

He never had gotten used to it and knew he never would, though he doubted there would be a successor to Susan.

Was Mark with her? Not right then, but had he known where she was going? Probably. He'd catch up with his mother later, after his own Christmas vacation.

What hurt Artie most was that he knew Mark as little as he knew Susan. Both of them apparently had been willing to stick it to him.

But he couldn't even be angry about it. Somehow it was his fault, though in what way he hadn't the foggiest idea. He'd been faithful; he hadn't cheated—had never even thought of it. He would have given his life for both of them, but that was an abstract that couldn't compare to a bigger house, a larger paycheck, a member of management—whatever the tangibles were by which success was measured these days.

He knew he was feeling sorry for himself and wallowed in it, only gradually acknowledging that something far more important was going on than his marriage coming apart at the seams. He was in the middle of an underground struggle that nobody knew about, and his very knowledge of it meant that sooner or later somebody was going to try to kill him again and probably succeed.

Susan and Mark hadn't left him at the worst of times; they had left him at the best of times. He should be damned glad that they had left when they did, that they were out of it and didn't run the risk of ending up like Paschelke's wife and kids.

"You're in early, Artie—first time I can remember you ever paying any attention to something I said." Connie hung her coat and umbrella on one of the back wall hooks, then glanced out at the newsroom. "I still think we ought to do our own morning show rather than pick up the feed from the network. We can do happy talk with the best of them—" She caught the haggard expression on his face. "Susan left you, didn't she?"

"How'd you know?"

"That expression on a married man's face goes with either death or separation. She walk out?"

Artie nodded. "She took half the money and split."

"Only half? Merry Christmas, Artie, you got off cheap." She suddenly looked apologetic. "Forgive the cynicism. I'm sorry, I really am. Anything I can do, just ask."

He shook his head. "I'll hear from her lawyer and we'll go from there. In the meantime, we've still got the series, right?"

"Right." Connie looked relieved. "I had the Grub pull some tape from the files and I wrote a preliminary script—give us an idea of where we're going with it. We might as well call in Jerry and go over it."

"Hirschfield's not bitching because I haven't been around?"

"I said you were out doing research."

"I owe you."

"Big-time, Banks."

When Jerry squeezed into the cubicle, Connie passed around copies of the script. Artie studied his. Connie, as he suspected she would, had done a better than excellent job. On the right of the page were Connie's narration and verbatims of the sound bites they would use; on the left were time codes and notes on the B-roll, the various pieces of field and file tape and stock footage they would use to "cover" the audio.

She had covered pretty much what he thought she would. Changing weather patterns, melting glaciers, rising sea levels . . . The Netherlands would catch it, so would Bangladesh and island nations like the Marshalls.

"You right about thirty thousand vanishing species, Connie?"

She nodded. "That's per *year*, Artie—and it's probably on the low side. Me, I'll miss the tigers."

After they had finished the script, Jerry shook his head. "Anybody who watches this is going to go out and slash their wrists. I don't think you guys know what you're doing."

Connie pointed at the door. "Scat, Jerry." After he had left, she said, "I figure we could interview some scientist on camera for an overview of what's happening. It would be a long interview, but we could cover some parts with video. Be a change from staring at me most of the time."

Adrienne had planted the seeds, and in Connie they were growing into a forest.

"You think Hirschfield is going to schedule that?"

"Why wouldn't he?"

"Because it's the world's worst downer, that's why. Five minutes into that and you'll be able to hear them changing channels all the way down to San Jose. We're not the *New York Times* of the air, Connie—leave that to PBS. We'll have to make it interesting and light with just enough real stuff to impress the FCC in case some citizens' group challenges our license. That's what the hell Hirschfield wants." He shrugged. "Feel free to disagree. If you're confident with it, show it to Hirschfield yourself."

"I thought you of all people would back me up."

"I will—after we lighten it up."

She leaned back in her chair.

"I wanted to do another segment, but I didn't think

we could get away with it. Social meltdown, kids murdering kids. The kids over in England who stoned the four-year-old and placed the body on the railroad track and the six-year-old over here who almost beat a baby to death in his crib."

"That's not ecology."

"I'm not so sure. You seen the studies on rat behavior when they get overcrowded?" She rubbed her forehead. "You still got coffee in that cup?"

"It's probably cold."

"Doesn't matter—I can use the caffeine." He shoved over the container and she sipped at it, looking drained and listless. Adrienne had pushed Connie over the edge.

"How much time you been putting in on it?" He hesitated, apologetic. "I know I haven't been as much help as I should."

"It wouldn't have mattered. The last few days I've been going at it for twelve, fourteen hours a day. . . ." She waved a hand helplessly at the printouts and magazine articles and books that covered the desktop. "There's too much of it; there's no end to it."

"The trick in doing research is knowing when to stop," Artie said. "You taught me that when I came here."

Connie stood up and walked over to the window, glanced out at the newsroom, then turned around to lean against the glass. Artie felt embarrassed. He had never seen her look so vulnerable before.

"It's an end-of-the-world story, Artie. We make a few gains here and there, but then they're lost in the disasters."

He managed a smile. "Hey, c'mon, you're supposed to be the perky one."

"Yeah, right. Boy, was that a long time ago."

His phone rang and Artie picked up. At first he couldn't make out the voice, a slurred combination of lisp and grunt as if the caller had a serious speech impediment or a throat wound. "Say again?" This time he got it: a desperate Dave Chandler who needed to see somebody. He sounded in pain, and an alarmed Artie suggested an ambulance. Chandler said no, he'd just come from the hospital, he needed somebody to talk to.

Sure, Artie said slowly, he'd get there as soon as possible. Yeah, he knew he was a prince.

He hung up and dialed Mitch. No way was he going over alone—he needed backup. Mitch came on the line and they agreed to meet outside Chandler's apartment in the Marina. And yes, it might be smart to be armed.

Connie had been watching him and when he hung up said, "You're off again, right? Something about Mark?"

"Not this time. A friend—needs help apparently. Couldn't talk straight. I've no idea what's wrong. Sorry, Connie."

Artie was almost out the door when Connie suddenly said, "I've had this strange feeling lately, Artie. Like all of us are at the tail end of the third act and pretty soon the curtain's going to fall and the play will be over. And I've no idea at all what's going to happen to us next. I even read the cards about it."

"And?"

"All the cards were bad."

She was feeling the same way he'd felt for a month, Artie thought. But he didn't need anybody else's troubles to add to his own. Chandler was spinning a web and he was about to walk into it.

Or maybe, once again, he was just being paranoid.

**It was late in** the afternoon and the sun was already starting to dip behind the hills of the Presidio. It was hell finding a parking place, and when he finally found one and got to the whitewashed stucco building where Chandler lived, Mitch was waiting for him.

"I didn't buzz—thought I'd wait until you showed."

"Lousy parking."

Mitch pressed the buzzer, waited a minute, then pressed it again.

*"Who is it?"*

It was a strange voice, as if its owner had difficulty talking. It didn't sound like Chandler at all. The few times Artie had been over, Dave usually answered with some clever line from a play or a movie—"I'm Dave Chandler and I coulda been a contendah! Who are you?"

Mitch leaned closer to the intercom.

"Artie and Mitch, Dave."

The buzzer sounded and they pushed the door open. It was dark inside, no hall light. A voice at the top of the stairs mumbled, "Come on up," in the same combination of lisp and grunt. Artie looked at Mitch and muttered, "Think it's a setup?"

Mitch shrugged. "We'll never know down here."

Artie felt for the automatic nestled in his pocket and started up the stairs. At the top, a voice said, "I'm in the office, in back." Mitch found a wall switch and turned on the hall light and the voice became almost hysterical. "Turn it down! It's on a dimmer."

The long hallway was lined with framed theater posters and the occasional signed photograph: *To Dave, with love—Sharon* or *For Dave, I'll never forget you— Brad.* At least Chandler was nondenominational, Artie thought.

The office in back was large and equipped like a small theater with a row of upholstered fold-up seats facing a fifty-inch rear-projection TV flanked by large, floor-standing speakers. Chandler had had the room soundproofed years ago so he could show films late at night without the neighbors complaining. An old-time popcorn machine was in one corner, while in the other was a small desk and filing cabinet and an easy chair with an ottoman. The windows had been covered with black drapes, and the only light in the room came from a small red bulb above the door.

Chandler's party room, not as cool as it must have been fifteen years ago. Artie wondered how many hours Chandler spent watching old movies in the dark.

The figure in the easy chair moved and mumbled, "Thanks for coming," and Artie almost yanked out his gun. It sounded like Chandler but it didn't sound like Chandler, and it didn't look much like him. Just a dark shape in the oversized chair.

There was the sound of a small tug on a pull chain and the floor lamp by Chandler's chair came on. Artie caught his breath. It was Chandler all right, but he recognized him more by his standard uniform of chinos, loafers, and light blue woolen sweater than by his face.

He couldn't make out Chandler's features at all; some kind of white ointment covered his face like a mask with small holes for his eyes.

Artie said, "What the hell happened, Dave?"

Chandler leaned forward in his chair, taking a moment to catch his breath. It obviously hurt to talk. "The other night at the theater—Theater DuPre—I was in the dressing room putting on a makeup base and five minutes after I got it on, it started to burn. I wiped it off and then I guess I went nuts. The cast called an ambulance"—he tried to grimace but it was clearly agony—"a little late."

Chandler took a towel from the desktop and wiped off the ointment from part of his face. Beneath it, the skin was pink and seamed with red furrows. Artie thought it looked like a lightly plowed field.

"The doctors said it could have killed me if it had been poisonous. They got me to the emergency room just in time; it might have burned right through the flesh. They told me there'll definitely be scarring." Chandler's voice was pushing hysteria. "Who the hell would do that? Put whatever they did in the base? They knew it was mine—they knew it was my personal kit!"

Nobody was going to envy him anymore for looking like the youngest member of the Club. And no way was anybody going to cast him in the occasional TV or movie role when they shot locally. Not unless they were doing a *Nightmare on Elm Street* segment.

"Who would do something like that?" Chandler asked again, his voice breaking. "Christ, I can't even cry, it's too painful. . . ."

Artie didn't know what to say. Mitch said, "I know some plastic surgeons, Dave—the best there are."

"My insurance," Chandler mumbled. "I don't know what it will cover. It wasn't an accident—somebody did it deliberately."

Next to castrating him, it was probably the worst thing anybody could have done to Chandler, Artie thought—to any actor, but especially to one whose face had been his fortune, if only a small one.

"I wouldn't worry about the cost," Mitch said, trying his best to be reassuring. "We'll figure out something. The surgeons work out of St. Mary's and there's probably some fund someplace that they can tap."

"Thanks," Chandler said. It took a moment for him to control his voice, and Artie could make out several tears trickling down through the ointment. It probably hurt Chandler like hell.

"Anything else we can do?" Artie offered tentatively. "We'll drop by as often as we can."

Chandler turned away and there was a long pause. It must be torture to want to rub your eyes and be unable to because you knew it would hurt so much. Artie touched him lightly on the shoulder.

"Appreciate it," Chandler said and reached up and squeezed his hand.

They stayed for a while and talked, mostly about Chandler's past "triumphs" in the theater, and then left when it became apparent that it hurt Chandler to talk much.

Outside in the chill night air, Mitch murmured, "And a Merry Christmas to you, too."

"Who would have done it?" Artie asked.

Mitch shrugged. "Who knows? There's nobody who doesn't have enemies. Maybe an ex-lover, maybe somebody who wanted a part and Dave wouldn't give it to him. Or her."

"You don't think it was connected with Larry?"

"I didn't say that. After we saw Schuler and met in that south-of-Market diner, Chandler said he'd had lunch with Larry, that Larry had told him he was working on an article for *Science*."

"He never said Larry told him what it was about."

"Maybe Larry did and it was over his head so he forgot about it."

"Dave seldom remembers anything that isn't about Dave."

"Not kind, Artie—and it looks like somebody at that table would have disagreed with you. Somebody evidently thought Larry had told Dave something. It's a wonder the poor bastard's still alive."

"Sorry about the comment," Artie muttered. "We've joked about Dave for so many years it's become habit." He started back to his car, then suddenly turned.

"Mitch? If we eliminate Dave, that means we've eliminated everybody."

"Yeah, I know. Which means we've eliminated nobody."

# CHAPTER 16

**The Marriott near the** Moscone Center was big, expensive, and fireproof. Artie was convinced somebody would have to splash gasoline around their room to set it ablaze. Hotel security seemed to be good, though any Hound could get around it if he or she wanted. But at first glimpse it was safer than either his house or Mitch's Telegraph Hill cottage.

Mitch turned on the television set and they channel-surfed until the six-o'clock news. The usual depressing local coverage and a foreign affairs segment that wasn't much better. Another mini-uprising in what was left of Yugoslavia, a network story on the Russian mafia, and another on a standoff in the mid-Pacific between a Greenpeace boat and a Japanese whaling ship, plus there were eighty more dead in Africa from Rift Valley TB.

Locally, a suburban father had been shot by his son because he'd had a date and been refused the family car, and there was a fire in a Tenderloin hotel, one transient dead of smoke inhalation, fifty evacuated . . .

"The *National Enquirer* of the Air," Mitch muttered at the half-hour break. "No wonder I end up prescribing so much Prozac."

" 'If it bleeds, it leads,' " Artie quoted. " 'If it's fire, play it higher.' But you missed the biggest story, and most of the rest of the hour will be devoted to it, with the sports wrap at the end."

"So what was the biggest story?"

"Barring wars and plane accidents, what it always is: the weather. You're so used to it being the mainstay of the nightly news, you don't even notice. The Tenderloin fire wasn't much more than a teaser and they didn't waste much airtime on the father-and-son bit before they switched to a live feed from a mountain road impassable because of snow. It never rains, Mitch, it pours; and if it snows, it's a blizzard. If it isn't, you better make it one or, trust me, your ratings go into the toilet."

"I'm glad it's your job and not mine," Mitch muttered. He picked up the phone and Artie looked at him, alarmed.

"What the hell are you doing?"

"Letting my answering service know where I am—sometimes I get late-night calls from patients."

Artie took the phone out of his hand and replaced it in its cradle. "*They* already know your phone number—it's probably been tapped for the last three days. You want to let them know where we are?"

"You're telling me they're all over out there?" Then he added soberly, "Of course they are."

"They're not just Mary and Adrienne and whoever killed Larry," Artie said. "They're not a group or a gang, they're a *species*. They're all around. And there's no way of telling who they are."

"You're paranoid," Mitch said.

"You better be paranoid too, Mitch. You'll live longer."

There was a knock on the door, and a voice outside said, "Housekeeping."

Artie muttered, "You get it," and stood just out of sight in the bathroom, the automatic in his hand.

Mitch opened the door to the limit of the chain.

"Yes?"

A slightly muffled voice: "Housekeeping—I forget some towels when I clean room earlier."

Mitch stuck his hand through the opening. "I'll take them."

He closed the door and bolted it. "One maid, Hispanic. Late thirties. Probably an illegal."

Artie shrugged. "So?"

"Christ, Artie, just check the towels."

A moment later Artie called from the john, "We were shy a set of hand and bath towels."

"So I was right. No way she could have known we were going to check in. You're paranoid."

**They had been in** bed by eleven, but Artie was still wide awake. Mitch wasn't snoring, which meant he was wide awake as well.

"It's not a small conspiracy," Artie said into the dark. "First there was Larry Shea and the Hound, and then it became Larry and the Hound and Paschelke and Hall and you and me and probably Cathy. The circle keeps getting larger."

"You can deduct Larry and Hall and Paschelke," Mitch said.

"And add Mary and probably Jenny and maybe Lyle and just maybe Charlie Allen. And God knows who else."

"It's getting risky," Mitch said. "For *them.*" After a moment: "You keep saying it's a conspiracy, that it involves a lot of people. But where's the organization? Who's running it? There's got to be some sort of organization."

Artie thought about it, feeling increasingly uncomfortable.

"Mary said that the Old People are tribal. Maybe there is no central organization. Maybe everybody more or less knows what to do without somebody telling them."

"Which is what?"

Artie gave a mental shrug. "Stay hidden. Stay under-cover. Wait."

Mitch was starting to doze off.

"Strange sort of organization."

"It's like some ethnic groups, Mitch. There's usually little in the way of national organization but at the lo-cal level, depending on the city, it's something else."

Mitch sounded irritated at not being left alone to sleep.

"There's a difference. We don't know who the Old People are. And the potential for violence is there when you don't know who the enemy is. It would be a chance for terrorism on a gigantic scale. We live in a technological society: one person could throw a mon-key wrench into it and bring it all down."

It wouldn't take a massive organization, Artie thought. Maybe it would be more like whatever orga-nization the IRA had in Ireland.

"Cathy Shea," he said into the darkness. "What do you remember about Cathy, Mitch?"

Silence for a moment.

"Maiden name, Cathy Deutsch. I think she joined the Club about the same time I did. She dropped out when she got married and had kids. A looker, but then they all were back then."

"Everybody's handsome and everybody's pretty when you're in your early twenties," Artie said.

"Thanks for reminding me I'm getting older, Artie."

"Did you ever ball her?"

"Jesus Christ, you're talking about Larry's wife. She's an old married woman now. She's got two kids."

"I'm talking about twenty years ago. I'm not asking if you laid Larry's wife—I'm asking if you slept with Cathy Deutsch."

"I thought everybody made it with Cathy. . . . You want to know how she was, right?"

"Sure."

Mitch laughed quietly.

"We were all young and we were all horny; I doubt that any of us lasted longer than five minutes with her. I think we stripped down; I nuzzled her breasts a couple of times, she touched my prick once, and then it was all over and I told everybody how great she was afterward. By the looks I got from the other women, she said the same about me. I've been in her debt ever since."

Artie was starting to drift off again when he had another thought.

"Lyle and Jenny," he said aloud in the dark.

He sensed that Mitch was suddenly wide awake.

"Why do you ask?"

"Because it's still going on."

He could hear Mitch moving around in the other bed and suddenly the lamp on the bed table came on.

"You never told me that."

"I told you I'd seen Lyle the night before I went over to Mary's. He dropped in to hit on Jenny when Mary wasn't home. Nothing happened, they're still good friends, according to Mary."

"They were a number twenty years ago, you remember."

"He's got a new lady—Anya."

"I've met her." Mitch yawned and turned out the light. "Exotic."

"So why is Lyle still interested in Jenny? I mean—you know, after twenty years."

"Nobody forgets first love, Artie. Doesn't matter how old you get, given the chance you'll still try to breathe life into the embers if only to make sure they're out."

"Would Jenny have talked? She must know a lot."

Mitch was silent, thinking about it.

"I don't think she'd ever betray Mary intentionally. But she might drop a stitch here and there and, before you knew it, the whole scarf would be unraveled. She might have ended up saying more than she thought she did."

Artie tossed it around in his mind. If Lyle wasn't one of the Old People, then he could be in real danger. If he and Mitch had thought of the possibility, somebody else could have thought of it as well. Maybe Jenny was smart enough not to drop any stitches, but the possibility of it endangered Lyle as much as the reality.

And there was somebody else they hadn't considered.

"What about Charlie Allen and Franny?"

There was no answer. Artie listened for a moment, heard the faint sounds of snoring, and turned over on his side to go to sleep. There was no sense of anything or anybody outside the windows—there couldn't be, they were twenty stories up—and no sense of anybody standing outside their door.

How long had it been since he'd had a good night's sleep?

It was eight o'clock when Artie rolled out of bed. Mitch had already showered and shaved and was staring out the window, waiting for him. It had started to rain again, the drops pelting against the glass. It was going to be a damp and dismal Christmas, Artie thought. Both Susan and Mark gone . . . Bad timing. Like most of his life lately.

"Downstairs or room service?" Mitch asked when he had finished dressing.

"Downstairs—less chance of somebody messing with the food."

It was nine o'clock when they finished breakfast. Mitch gave his credit card to the waiter, then pushed slightly back in his chair and turned to Artie.

"So who's it going to be? Charlie Allen, to ask him what he remembers about Cathy and any bright ideas where she could be? Or Lyle, to ask him what Jenny might have said at one time or another."

"Lyle," Artie said at last. "I don't think anybody

would be after Charlie; he wouldn't have any direct information. Lyle might."

"See him at work?"

Artie shook his head. "It's the Christmas season—he's probably working his tail off. Call him and try and see him tonight."

Mitch stood up. "Be right back."

Artie was halfway through his second cup of coffee when Mitch returned, looking concerned. "Called the store, they said he hadn't come in yet—that he was usually there at eight. They were apologetic—he's never late. So I called him at home. No Lyle."

"Try Anya?"

"You know what she does? I don't, I only met her once and I got the impression she didn't do much of anything."

"She works at BofA. Lyle said she was visiting relatives in San Jose but maybe she's back by now."

Mitch sipped his coffee in silence until the waiter brought back his credit card. He tucked it away in his wallet. "Let's go check out his house."

**Ten o'clock on a** windy, rainy day in San Francisco. The neighborhood around Thirtieth and Ulloa was deserted, the only person on the street a mailman working his way slowly up the block.

"You want to watch for a while?" Artie asked.

Mitch shook his head. "What for? There's not going to be anybody coming and going. And all we want to do is ask him a few questions."

"Without giving the game away," Artie said. "And we're depending on Lyle being . . . Lyle."

"Big gamble." Mitch got out of the car and Artie tagged along after him, standing at the bottom of the steps while he rang the doorbell. There was no answer. Mitch tried again, then out of impulse tried the door itself. It opened easily; it wasn't locked.

"Cute," Mitch said. "It's deliberate, Artie, a signature.

If anybody was here, they've come and gone and we're supposed to know it."

He pulled on a pair of surgeon's gloves and Artie followed suit. It would make it difficult handling the automatic, but they wouldn't leave any prints if they touched something in the house. And he could pray he didn't have to use the gun.

The house was quiet, the kitchen area clean. Dishes had been washed from the previous night's supper and were in the drainer on the sink. Two plates, two cups, two sets of silverware—Anya had returned from San Jose, had probably cooked the meal.

But nothing had been set out for breakfast. There was no carton of milk slowly growing warm on the table, no butter slumping in its dish, no half-filled bowls of cereal or frying pan crusted with egg.

The bedroom was deserted. The bed hadn't been slept in, the towels in the bathroom were dry and neatly hung on their racks.

"That's a three- to four-hour window," Mitch said quietly. "After supper but before bedtime."

"Window for what?" Artie asked.

"We know they ate supper here. If they'd gone to a movie, they would have returned sometime before midnight or shortly afterward. Maybe they went out of town, but like you said, Lyle is manager at Copeland's and this is one of their busiest seasons; he wouldn't have left in the middle of it. My guess is they're still here." There was a ripple of excitement beneath the calm in his voice. "I think they're dead, Artie. The reason we had such a peaceful night last night is because they probably didn't."

They found Fritzi first, at the bottom of the stairs to the basement. The rottweiler was balled up in a corner, its eyes glazed. Both hind legs were broken, and it looked like its chest had been crushed.

Mitch knelt and ran his fingers lightly over the body. "Maybe muscle contractions could do this, but they'd have to be stronger than anything I know of."

Artie knew.

Lyle was in the exercise room, lying flat on his work-out bench, the barbell with its load of two hundred and twenty-five pounds on his chest where it had fallen and crushed his rib cage. His workout shirt was soaked in blood, and it took a moment for Artie to spot the several holes in his chest. He stared in silence for a long moment, once again feeling a wave of guilt. It really hadn't been one for all and all for one—ever. That had been a happy bit of hypocrisy on his part. Would he have liked Lyle any more if he had known him better? Probably not. He was a valued member of the Club when they were younger, but that was because he could score a lid whenever you wanted one. Nobody had really been close to him. He had been too aggressive, too brash, and while they all liked what the vintner sold, nobody had cared much for the vintner himself. None of them had been perceptive enough to realize that Lyle probably knew it and resented it and had used them as much as they had used him, though Jenny might have guessed.

"He was shot while he was working out," Mitch said. "When he would have been helpless."

"Any idea who shot him?"

"My guess is Anya. Ten to one her body's around here someplace."

They found her in Lyle's office, slumped in the big, black leather chair behind his desk. She had put a gun to her head and blown blood and brains all over the books in the bookcase behind her. Artie felt sick and had to force himself to be as clinical as Mitch. She was dressed in a black see-through nightgown that Artie had absolutely no desire to see through. Lyle had taken her to one club meeting and Artie remembered the faint surge of lust that all the men had felt, the momentary envy of Lyle. God, that was another thing to feel guilty about.

Artie glanced around the floor, frowning. "Where's the gun?"

"Not near her—at the instant of death she probably threw it across the room, again because of involuntary muscular contractions. Not the same as Fritzi's, though."

Artie found it near the door. Mitch picked it up with a pencil through the trigger guard and dropped it on the desk. There was a smear of red on the barrel and Artie bent down for a closer look, then jerked his head back. Lipstick.

Mitch studied the papers on the desk, then pushed one over to Artie with the eraser end of a pencil.

"She left a note."

Artie glanced over the first few lines, then read them more carefully. She had been faithful to him but she knew Lyle was cheating on her and that after everything he had promised her, he deserved to die. After she had shot him, she had realized she couldn't live without him, that life would be empty for her . . .

Soap-opera time.

"I didn't know her very well," Artie said when he had finished. "From the few times I met her, I got the impression that it was an open relationship—that she wasn't the jealous type."

Mitch looked dubious. "Maybe she wasn't, maybe she was. She probably got a phone call that set her off and a few minutes later I suspect somebody was around to help her build up a jealous head of steam. Cut and dried, Artie. The police will have the weapon, they'll have the motive, and there's nobody left alive to contradict her suicide note."

It had been the pattern all along, Artie thought. Plausible, open-and-shut, no loose ends. No real reason to investigate anything.

"Do you believe that letter, Mitch?"

"Of course not. But it doesn't matter. I don't think the police will look very far."

Artie let his breath out, realizing for the first time how long he had been holding it. "Should we call them?"

Mitch shook his head.

"Somebody from Copeland's will show up looking for Lyle. We'll leave the door unlocked, just like we found it. If we call in the police, Schuler will be all over us. What do you want to tell him?"

"Nothing," Artie said.

"Neither do I."

Mitch hooked the gun with the pencil again and placed it back on the floor in the same position where it had fallen. They made sure nobody was around, then left the house. Once in his car, Mitch picked up the cellular phone and started dialing.

Artie looked at him, surprised. "Change your mind?"

"Calling the office. Getting my messages. Life goes on, Artie." He listened for a few minutes, then snapped it off and turned to Artie, a bemused look on his face. "Got the report back from the chemist on the potato salad."

Artie had almost forgotten about it.

"What did he find?"

"Red herring, Artie—better check with your neighbors as to who went out of their way to do Susan a favor. The only thing wrong with it was too much Miracle Whip."

# CHAPTER 17

**Artie sat at his** desk going over Connie's script and jotting down notes. It was an uneasy balance between documentary and propaganda, and Connie had fallen off the high wire. It was a matter of emphasis more than anything else. The world was as dark as you cared to paint it, and Connie had deliberately chosen a black palette. And yet . . .

He scribbled another note, then tore the pages from his notepad, crumpled them up, and tossed them in the wastebasket. The problem was not that she was right or wrong—he knew she was right—but how the hell did you sell it? People would watch the bad news only if you told them somebody was doing something about it, that there was progress, that the water was safer to drink, the air safer to breathe, and a number 50 sunblock would take care of the hole in the ozone layer.

"Did you hear anything from Mark?" Connie had come up behind him and was looking over his shoulder at the script.

It took an effort to keep from jumping.

"Don't do that, Connie—I'm not in the best of moods. And no, I haven't heard anything from Mark." He wished to hell she hadn't asked. He had tried to wall it off in his mind and had almost succeeded. "I called the cops this morning—they don't know anything. They're not too excited about it."

"Susan?"

"Called our lawyer. He hasn't heard from her. She'll undoubtedly want her own lawyer anyway." He waved at the pages of the script spread out on the desk. "I was wrong: It needs work but it's honest and it's something people need to know. Trying to market it will be something else. Our ratings will suck—we'll only hold the PBS crowd—but what the hell, we'll have done our bit. As you put it, maybe we'll make a difference, and God forgive me the cliché."

Mary would be proud of him, wherever she was. Then he wondered if she would even see it.

For one of the few times he could remember, Connie leaned back in her chair and lit a cigarette. "I'm afraid we've got a problem."

Artie couldn't possibly think of any problem more serious than those he already had.

"Like what? We can always cut it if we have to, juggle sequences to make it more linear. . . ."

"I'm talking about Adrienne—who turns out to have been a prize bitch."

He looked at her, suddenly wary. "What about her?"

"You may have noticed she wasn't here yesterday. She didn't come in today. We called, nobody home. I sent Jerry over to check her apartment, expecting God knows what. The apartment was clean. She wasn't there and neither was anything else. No furniture, no dishes, no rugs, no books, no nothing. Jerry talked to the landlord and it seems she moved in with a futon and a hot plate and a telephone and that was it. That woman really traveled light."

"Surprise," Artie muttered. Which was no surprise at all. After the fight in the parking lot, nobody was ever going to see Adrienne again. "Anything else?"

"Oh, yes. I went over her résumé. She claimed she'd

gotten her bachelor's in communications at Mc-Murphy University in some little town in Nebraska. It doesn't exist. I called previous stations where she said she'd worked. Half of those don't exist either, and the other half never heard of her."

"She *did* work in Sacramento, right?" Artie sensed where all of this was going and wasn't sure he wanted to hear it.

"Right. But the news director who hired her left three months ago and seems to have disappeared. He didn't leave a forwarding address."

Artie definitely didn't want to hear it. "So? What do we do now?"

"You haven't asked me what her last assignment was."

He already knew. "Let me guess."

"You've got it—she was working on a series about the environment. I asked if anybody had seen her tape and they had so I asked them to describe it."

"And ours is the same as hers."

"Down to the same exact examples. Cookie-cutter time." She shook her head. "How the hell is that possible?"

Artie knew how it was possible: Adrienne had orchestrated the series from the very beginning. And how many other Adriennes were scattered about the country, all of them pushing the same special?

He felt as if somebody had just opened up a window and a cold draft had blown in. There were the Hounds and the bystanders like Mary, and now a different branch of the Old People. One devoted to a last-ditch effort to convince *Homo sapiens* of the errors of its ways. In one sense, not dangerous. A lot of people would agree with them. But it was an indication that there *was* a conspiracy, and it might be more tightly organized than he'd thought.

"I don't know, Connie. I haven't the foggiest. Did you talk to Hirschfield about her?"

"He said he was shocked. I'm not so sure. I checked and it turns out he'd interviewed her for only about five minutes and decided the station couldn't get along without her. Maybe he banged her after all."

Artie waved at the pages on the desk.

"Did you show this to him?"

"This morning, before you came in."

"And?"

"He loved it. He thought it was great."

Artie suddenly realized he had to go to the bathroom, bad. Maybe not all the Old People were lawyers or Hounds or TV news reporters after all. Maybe some of them were news directors.

Connie shook her head in disbelief.

"What the hell's going on, Artie? There's no way in the world two different people could think this much alike. Adrienne and I never had a conversation all the time she was here; we barely nodded to each other when we passed in the hallway. I always considered her an ice queen."

"So let's change the script."

Connie snuffed out her cigarette. "You're right. She's good, we're better."

They worked on the script for the next few hours, rearranging segments and rewriting Connie's voice-over. Adrienne's Sacramento tape was being held for the same after-the-holidays doldrums. Theirs had to be different, which meant drastic shifting and cutting. It was two in the afternoon before Connie called a break.

"You want lunch, Artie? My treat."

He shook his head. "Go finish your Christmas shopping while you're at it. I'm going to grab a cameraman and go to the zoo."

"What for?"

"The zoo's part of a nationwide cooperative breeding program to preserve endangered species. Some species you can only find in zoos nowadays—they've disappeared completely from the wild. A lot of the specimens we've got—here, in the San Diego, the Brookfield and the Berlin Zoos, and a couple of dozen others around the world—are all there are; there ain't no more."

She looked surprised. "How come you know all this?"

"The Grub knows everything, Connie. I had him print me out a list of the different endangered species; it's as thick as a small phone directory."

He was slipping into his raincoat when Connie said, "Artie? I hear they've got a Siberian tiger out there— shoot some tape of it for me, will you? I'm kind of fond of tigers."

**It was after three** by the time they got to the zoo and the daylight was already fading. It was cloudy and misting by the ocean; they wouldn't be able to shoot outside for much more than an hour and Artie wasn't sure whatever they got would be usable; the zoo had insisted they not shine lights on the animals. But at least it would serve as a guide if they had to come back another day.

Almost all the big cats were inside, and Artie watched while the cameraman shot tape of them moving around inside the large cages, then angled for what might be used as a head shot. The King of Beasts, with the background out of focus behind him, looking majestic. It was humid and, as usual in the cat house, it stank. After ten minutes Artie was ready for fresh air, even if it was chilly.

The Siberian tiger was in a special outdoor display, a large moat and high iron fence separating it from the curious spectators. It would make for better tape if it were spring and there were dozens of people around staring and pointing. As it was, the only people there besides himself were a middle-aged woman in a heavy cloth coat with the collar up around her ears and a teenager with a colorful scarf half wrapped around his face, the ends trailing in the stiff breeze.

They were a good ten feet apart, obviously not a family group; not much in the way of human interest when it came to an interview.

Artie watched the tiger for a few minutes, letting the cameraman shoot as much tape as he wanted. It was a gift from the Cincinnati Zoo, and Artie wondered what they'd gotten in return. A dozen buffalo? Maybe a couple of Kodiak bears—that might be more fitting for a zoo in the heartland. But if he were a zookeeper and had to choose between them, he'd pick the tiger, a good five hundred pounds with long, pale fur and sheer grace to its movements.

How many were left in the world now? he wondered. Less than five hundred, at best? Less than fifty? Connie would make a copy of the tape for her home library and her kids would show it to their kids and by that time wild Siberian tigers would be long gone, a fading memory along with their original habitat, probably destined to be a collection of resort towns, fancy hotels, and upscale restaurants in a distant, crowded future. The tigers would be nothing more than photographs in encyclopedias and "Mammals of the Twentieth Century," or creatures captured for a moment in time on scratchy videotape. With luck some natural history museums would have animatronic versions, and a few zoos would be desperately trying to breed them back.

Connie would have an odd sort of memento. Or maybe memorial, and that might be a line he should use.

Artie squinted at the sky. Not much more than half an hour of light left; they'd have to come back in the morning or preferably on a day when it was sunny.

He walked into the Primate Discovery Center, the new monkey house, stopping at a small cage complete with waterfall, rocks, and trees. The plaque on the railing identified the monkeys as macaques, the most widely ranging primate genus outside of man. You could find them in almost every country in Africa and Asia, from Morocco to the Philippines.

There were three white-faced monkeys inside the enclosure, all lined up behind the glass, staring at him. Artie stared back, feeling vaguely uneasy. There was rope netting inside the cage on which they could swing and climb: why the hell weren't they? He moved on to another cage to stare at more monkeys staring back. He was the only visitor on a chill and windy day and apparently the prime attraction.

He shivered and went back outside, stopping at the small island of rocks surrounded by a deep moat that was home to the chimpanzees. How long ago was it that several of the chimps had escaped from the island and scared the hell out of a dozen housewives who reported prowlers in the backyard? Years now—it had been a different, low-tech zoo back then.

He leaned against the railing and watched the few chimps shivering on top of the pile of artificial rocks, searching for any scraps of food they might have missed earlier in the day. One patriarch with graying fur sat at the edge of the moat and glared back at him.

A moment in time, Artie thought. A moat, five million years, and less than two percent of encoded genes separated them. How surprised the chimp's ancestors must have been when they saw the first primitive hominids venture out of the forest, creatures not that much different from themselves but swaying awkwardly from side to side as they tried to walk upright on two legs. Larger heads, flatter faces, and less fur. Ugly creatures who didn't have sense enough to stay in the forest where they at least had a chance of escaping the big cats and the other predators.

And how shocked a similar patriarch and his fellow chimps must have been to see the hominids make fires outside their caves to keep them safe during the long night. Artie imagined the years rolling past and the upright creatures becoming taller and heavier, shedding more of their hair while their heads grew ever larger and their faces flatter and their noses more defined. About the same time something curious must have started to appear in their eyes, something that frightened that early patriarch when he first saw it. Something that made it difficult for him to look the new creatures in the eyes for any length of time before he had to drop his own.

That patriarch was undoubtedly familiar with tools; he probably used sticks that he thrust into termite mounds and pulled out with a dozen juicy termites sticking to it. And he probably knew how to use logs and rocks to crack nuts and how to drive away predators by throwing rocks at them from the safety of a tree limb. But the new creatures did something else with the stones: They struck them together and used the chips that cracked off to cut meat and clean bloody skins so they could wrap them around their waists to take the place of the hair they no longer had.

That ancient ape might even have tried to imitate them and struck two rocks together and watched the sparks fly, but that was all that happened. There was probably a dim thought in the back of his mind that perhaps the other creatures used different rocks, but it was a difficult thought to grab hold of and he probably couldn't tell the difference between the rocks anyway.

He must have been afraid of this strange animal and the curious things it did, more afraid than he was of the big cats or the protowolves that hunted in packs. The new creature was more dangerous than all of them.

Artie smiled at the old chimp staring back at him. He was probably very much like that patriarch of long ago. Now he was too old and too slow to fight for mates and most likely considered himself fortunate to be in a zoo where old age might be a problem but not survival itself, and where the zoo veterinarian gave him odd-tasting stuff to ward off the chills he occasionally felt and where the keepers might save a particularly juicy piece of meat for him that was easy to eat because he had long since lost most of his teeth.

*he might trade it all for a real forest, monkey. . . .*

Artie suddenly felt sweaty and frightened. He glanced quickly around. There was nobody there, at least nobody he could see. He was alone in the middle of an almost deserted zoo and suddenly imagined all the cage doors swinging open to leave the animals free to roam the walks and buildings. What better place to be hunted than in a zoo?

*take another look. . . .*

Artie turned back to the island and caught his breath. The old chimp had disappeared and in its place was a naked man sitting on his haunches at the moat's edge, his eyes dull and only casually curious. It took a moment before Artie realized he was looking at himself.

*your future home, monkey . . .*

Artie waited, but there was nothing more in his mind than the sound of raucous laughter. It faded and he was looking at the elderly chimp again, slowly scratching itself and turning away from the fence to amble back to the center of the island. The middle-aged woman—probably a schoolteacher—and the teenager were now at the far side of the enclosure, staring at the little group on the rocks.

It was almost dusk now and all he wanted to get the hell out of there. He'd sent the cameraman over to the Primate Center to get some close-ups of some of the monkeys on Jerry's list of endangered species, but it was time to go; he didn't dare stay longer. Connie would want to know just what they had shot, but he'd draw up a list for her back at the office. At least she'd be pleased with the tiger.

Besides, he had more important things to think about than a television series. He'd try Susan's phone

number once again, hoping against hope that the dis-
connect message had been a mistake. She might even
have called him; she'd have to sooner or later. And
maybe Mark had checked in.

Wishful thinking, but that was all that was left to him.

He was suffering from terminal frustration, Artie
thought. He was in the middle of a conspiracy that
nobody but him and Mitch even realized existed, and
if he tried to tell somebody, they'd think he was nuts.
He had to try to stay alive and find his family—and
work on the series as if nothing was happening around
him.

He glanced at his watch. He'd check again with the
police, then he'd call Mitch and they'd pay Charlie
Allen a visit. Charlie knew everything about everybody.

Maybe he even knew where Cathy Shea was hiding.

"**Anything I can get** you guys? More coffee,
soda, some cake? Franny made a chocolate one for the
kids—it was Nathan's birthday today and chocolate's
his favorite."

Artie settled back on the living room sofa and shot
a glance at Mitch in the big easy chair, concentrating
on his coffee and trying to ignore Charlie Allen over-
doing his role as host.

"We were thinking about Larry and Cathy," Artie
said. "You were closer to Larry than we were. We wondered if there was anything you remembered about
him that might be relevant."

Charlie looked confused. "Relevant to what? His
murder? I told Schuler everything I knew. It wasn't
much—no more than you guys know." He cut into his
slice of cake. "Somebody cut him down in the city and
I've no idea why. He was a sweetheart; he didn't have
any enemies."

"What about Cathy?" Mitch asked.

"What about her?" Charlie washed down a bite of
cake with a sip of coffee and leaned back in the chair

by his desk, the inner man temporarily satisfied. "Cathy was a goddamned saint, if you ask me. Took care of Larry and the kids like nobody else, believe me."

Franny was almost a shadow in the room, filling their coffee cups and murmuring offers of more cake, then sitting on the edge of the chair by the doorway, ready to fly into the kitchen at the slightest indication of hunger or thirst.

"Cathy have relatives here in town? Anyplace where she might have gone with the kids?" Mitch was doing his best to cut to the chase.

Charlie shook his head. "Nobody in the Bay Area, not that I know of. A cousin in San Luis Obispo, another in Seattle. Think she was an only kid—both parents died in a car accident about ten years ago."

"Any close friends?" Mitch asked.

"Aside from everybody associated with the Club? Hell, I don't know. Probably the parents of some of her kids' school friends—I think she was active in the PTA."

"Any lovers?" Mitch asked it as if it were the most natural question in the world.

Charlie looked from one to the other, frowning. "Something going on that I don't know about? Why do you want to know stuff like that?"

He was irritated more by the idea that he might have been left out of the loop than by anything else. Mitch tried to soothe him.

"We're just trying to figure out where she might have gone. She's the only one who might have some information that could lead to Larry's killer."

Charlie concentrated on his cake. "That was one happy marriage, Mitch. She idolized Larry."

It was Artie who caught Franny's expression, the slightly sour look of disapproval that fled across her face to disappear into the rolls of happy fat that framed it.

"What do you think, Franny?"

She looked surprised and faintly annoyed at being caught out. "Oh, I agree with Charlie. Completely. She was very committed to her family. But . . ." She let it dangle out there, a worm on a conversational hook.

Mitch leaned forward in his chair, looking at her over the top of his glasses, clinically curious. "But what, Franny?"

A wave of the hand. "Nothing, really."

She wanted it teased out of her, Artie thought. She wanted to be encouraged to damn with faint praise and vomit twenty years of resentment all over the living room floor. Franny had been a member of the Club when it started, then had married Charlie early on and vanished into her family. She would still show up at occasional parties, though never at meetings. She hadn't cared for the other women in the Club and never bothered to hide her opinion that they were all a bunch of elitists.

Charlie stared at her in surprised silence and Mitch and Artie let the silence grow. Franny turned to her husband.

"Come on, Charlie. You remember how Cathy used to flirt with every man who came to our parties? She toned it down after she got married, but she still did it."

The jealousy flickered in her eyes like flames while she glanced from one to another searching for encouragement that wasn't there. She shrugged and began to backpedal. "It really wasn't anything serious. I suspect most of you weren't aware of it at all. But the other women were."

He *had* been aware of it, Artie thought, though he never would have called it flirting. Cathy was the type of woman whom men found easy to talk to, even to confide in. She didn't represent a threat to any happy marriage, but if you were in an unhappy one, you would have been drawn to her. Not that anything would have happened. Cathy drank too much at parties and she liked to kiss all the men good night and sometimes the kisses were really sloppy, depending on how much she'd had to drink. If you couldn't avoid it, you made a joke of it. Larry never noticed, or he'd spent so many years deliberately not noticing that he'd become genuinely oblivious to it.

The typical suburban housewife's night out: You knew instinctively when to avoid her at the door and nobody held it against her afterward. It rated the same as Charlie's occasional belch at the dinner table.

Franny was up and busy with the coffeepot to cover her own embarrassment. "I'm sure she never meant anything by it."

"No, I'm sure she didn't," Mitch murmured. Charlie looked slightly put out and Artie made a big thing about changing his mind over the cake. Give Franny a chance to excel at the things she was good at, rather than regretting that she hadn't been the belle of the ball like Cathy.

But still, there was something there.

When Franny had left the room on a mercy errand to get more cake, Artie said tactfully; "Anything you can remember about the early years with Cathy . . ." If there was anything to be found, it would be early on. There wouldn't be many surprises in the later years.

Charlie waved at the shelf of notebooks about the Club. "Hell, it's all in there. You're free to look through them."

"I wouldn't know where to begin."

"I'll flip through the early ones and pick out those that include anything about her. I don't remember much, but there may be something. Tell you what— I'll put those copies aside and take them down to the library. You can pick them up there."

If Charlie pulled more than a dozen, it would take longer than one night to go through them, Artie thought. But any information on Cathy's background might be useful.

He forced himself to eat another slice of cake and sit through half an hour more of start-and-stop conversation with an unhappy Franny sitting silent and sullen in the corner. Then Mitch yawned and Artie muttered something about early-morning work on the series.

Outside, on the porch, Charlie closed the door firmly behind him, looked faintly uneasy, and coughed. Mitch tried to anticipate him.

"I don't blame Franny, I can see—"

Charlie said, "It's not about Franny. She's a little on the jealous side, always has been. I take it as a compliment. It's about Nathan."

Nathan was the eight-year-old boy, Artie remembered. Quiet kid, a little on the chubby side, like his father.

Mitch was all professional calm. "Something wrong, Charlie?"

Allen took a breath. "He's been playing with matches."

"Normal enough, nothing serious. Just talk to him—"

"I have. Three times now. We had to call the fire department the last time. He started a fire in the basement—two of them, actually: a pile of rags soaked in kerosene beneath the bottom of the stairs, another by the water heater and the gas line. The firemen said they were very . . . workmanlike."

"You sure it was Nathan?"

Charlie was looking progressively more unhappy. "We caught him a couple of times before, in the kitchen and in his own room. Little fires, easy to put out. But the firemen said we found these just in time."

Artie could feel the hair stir on the nape of his neck. Nathan hadn't thought of it all by himself. He'd had help. If the house had gone up and Charlie and the family with it, somehow Nathan would have survived and confessed and once again it would have been murder by proxy.

But why Charlie? He didn't know a damned thing.

Mitch clapped Charlie on the back and said briskly, "Call me at the office tomorrow—we'll make an appointment for the boy."

The consummate professional, Artie thought with a trace of irritation. Levin was friend and clinician, but seldom both at the same time.

# CHAPTER 18

**They spent that night** at the Ritz-Carlton on Stockton and Artie dimly remembered taking an est seminar in the building. What had it looked like back then? He couldn't remember and there was little about the building now to remind him; the renovation·had been very thorough.

"A little rich for my blood, Mitch."

Mitch loosened his tie and dropped his coat on a chair.

"I wouldn't worry about it. We're getting it for half— the manager's a former patient of mine."

Artie ran his fingers over the pillow; both beds had already been turned down.

"You're ethically challenged, Mitch, but I accept."

"I said 'former,' Artie. I try to discourage it, but sometimes you end up sounding like you're being un-friendly. If I were still counseling him, I would have rejected it automatically." He pulled the curtains; there wasn't much of a view: Chinatown and the towers of the business district. "If we're going to have to hide out, might as well do it in style. He recommended room service, by the way—offered to put it on his tab."

The alarm bells started ringing in Artie's head. "How well do you know him?"

"Well enough not to worry."

Would Mitch trust his friend with his life? Artie wondered. But that was a little like asking how far he and Connie would trust Hirschfield. The station manager seemed reliable, but that's where the crunch came. You really couldn't be sure of anybody. Mitch ought to know that. It wasn't a case of better-the-people-you-knew-than-the-people-you-didn't-know. It didn't matter if you knew them or not; the only thing safe to assume was that you didn't know them. Not really.

"What did you think of Franny?"

Mitch was leafing through the room-service menu and didn't bother looking up.

"Aside from the fact that she's a bitch? I felt sorry for her—she's been holding it in all these years and tonight was the first chance she had to vent. She's not going to be a happy woman to live with for the next few days. Charlie didn't give her any support at all."

"Maybe he made it with Cathy Deutsch, too." It was still hard for him to connect the sexy Cathy Deutsch of his youth with suburban housewife Cathy Shea, Larry's widow and mother of two young boys. Artie yawned and stretched out on his bed, flicking on the TV with the remote but keeping the sound low. "What about Nathan?"

"He was set up. I'll get the kid alone and ask him why he did it and I'll be lucky if he even knows what I'm talking about."

"And the two times before last?"

"Normal playing around. Ordinarily he'd forget all about it. Our Hound picked it up from the kid's mind and saw a way he could use it."

Artie was halfway through a baked potato with the works and a small filet when he remembered the question that had worried him at Charlie Allen's house.

"Why would Charlie be in danger? He never saw Larry's research."

Mitch wiped his mouth and took a sip of chardonnay. "Think, Artie: Why did we go to see Charlie in the first place?"

Levin was playing the role of intelligence officer talking down to a subordinate, and Artie resented it. Mitch had been a top interrogator in 'Nam, and on more than one occasion Artie had looked on with a mix of admiration and horror as Mitch worked on a prisoner. At such times he'd had to struggle to remain friends with Mitch, to remind himself that it was war and a lot of lives depended on Mitch's skill.

"Come on, Mitch—to find out about Cathy Shea."

"Because we think she knows something that would shed some light on Larry's murder, right? Because she probably knew what Larry was working on, knew that he intended to publish it. Because she was the last one we personally know who saw Larry alive. She may know who our Hound is, Artie, might even have been friends with him—or her—at one time without realizing it. And Charlie Allen knows more about all of us than we do about ourselves—I'm willing to take his word on that. Poor Charlie has his memories and his diaries and could very well know too much—or know where to look for it. He probably doesn't give a damn, but that's beside the point."

He couldn't deny that Levin had a good sense of summary, Artie thought, but he resented having to play Dr. Watson to Mitch's Holmes. He set the trays and dirty dishes out in the hallway, then double-locked the door and stripped to his shorts for bed. He channel-surfed for a few minutes, then tossed the remote over to Mitch. He started to doze, the aftermath of a good meal, and made a mental note to tell Mitch to thank his friend.

Mitch finally flicked off the tube and Artie was alone in the darkness, thinking of Mark and Susan and what they might be doing now. He was sitting on his ass waiting for Susan to call him, and that was a mistake.

He should try to find out where she had gone, talk it out in person . . .

There was no noise at all in the room except for the murmur of the ventilation system and the muffled sounds of the city outside. With the drapes drawn, it was pitch black and Artie let his mind drift, then turned over and tugged on the blanket to cover his ear. The one mystery story that had left an indelible impression on him when he was a kid was one where the murderer killed his victims by pouring hot lead into their ears while they slept.

He'd never forgotten it.

**The cold was numbing** just beyond the mouth of the cave and the small night fire that Deep Wood was tending. The spirits of the dead were twinkling in the evening sky, and as Artie watched, he saw one of them flash across the blackness and disappear just over the trees that lined the other side of the river. One of the spirits returning to the earth to be reborn as who knew what? One of the giant bears that lived deep in the forest, maybe a beaver, maybe even a wolf.

He remembered the wolves that came around and watched him from just outside the ring of firelight, their eyes gleaming in the dark. He imagined that the spirits of the dead were looking at him through the eyes of the wolves, and when he told White Beard what he thought, the chief had nodded wisely and said, of course that was so.

There was one particular wolf who came quite often to sit just beyond the firelight, a huge male with a dirty white coat and black splotches on its muzzle. It stared at him with intelligent eyes, and lately Artie had taken to throwing it small pieces of meat, which it would grab out of midair. Artie wondered how close he could get to it without it biting him. There was a dim picture in the back of his head of the wolf standing where he was in the mouth of the cave, howling whenever danger approached and being rewarded with more chunks of meat.

But that was a foolish thought. Why would any animal from the forest want to protect them? It could get all the meat it wanted on its own.

The wind had picked up strength now and was howling through the branches of the trees and making the fire spirits dance as they ate the twigs and leaves Deep Wood fed them. Deep Wood was afraid of the dark, and Artie caught images in his mind of monsters hiding in the gloom, ready to pounce on him. They were marvelously inventive monsters and Artie felt an occasional flicker of fear himself, then shrugged it off.

White Beard had said the reindeer would be passing through in two more risings of the sun and they had already picked out where they would drive them, a small cliff with a thirty-foot drop, but not so steep that members of the Tribe couldn't scramble down the face and butcher their dead or crippled prey. There would be no problem in preserving the meat. They'd stack it outside the cave, away from the fire, and it would keep frozen until the sun lingered longer in the sky and the blue and yellow flowers dotted the valleys again. They would, of course, have to mount guard to keep away the wolves and the big cats.

White Beard had warned that the Flat Faces might follow the reindeer and if they did, then the hunt would be very dangerous. There were enough reindeer to feed many tribes but the Flat Faces acted as if the reindeer belonged to them, though Artie couldn't imagine the Flat Faces eating them all.

He shivered and wrapped his furs tighter around his chest, letting the fire keep his backside warm. The furs reminded him of what Clear Stream had gotten from one of the Flat Faces she met fishing in a small river nearby.

The Flat Face had shown some interest in a cutter she had and traded her several very thin strips of hide and a slender length of bone with a point at one end and a hole at the other. You forced the point through two furs, then pushed one of the thin strips through the hole. When you pulled on the bone the thin strip slid through both furs and you could tie them together. Clear Stream had demonstrated on the skins that Artie wore, tying together several pieces so they wouldn't fall off his shoulders. The Flat Faces had been good for something after all.

He shifted around so he was standing in front of the fire and could feel the warmth on his face and hands. It was a cloudless night, the sun's pale companion just a hand's-width above the top of the trees. It was almost time to wake Tall Tree to take over guarding the cave mouth and keep Deep Wood from falling asleep despite his fearsome monsters.

But first he wanted to spend a little more time staring up into the night sky and wondering how the spirits traveled to the inky blackness overhead after their ashes had been returned to the Mother of Waters. But it must be easy for them; there were so many up there.

He yawned and moved closer to the fire, shivering. The wind had shifted once again, blowing off the huge river of ice that crept through the mountains two marches away. He was puzzled why White Beard insisted the Tribe live here, when they had all heard of pleasant meadows where the sun traveled higher in the sky and stayed there longer.

It was more marches away than they could count, White Beard had said. And none of the other Tribe members seemed anxious to leave, to make a journey to places they had never seen but had only heard about and that might hold unimaginable dangers.

There was a sudden hooting in the forest across the river and Artie tensed. White Beard had warned that the Flat Faces constantly watched them, that sometimes when it was dark and they heard hooting it was actually the Flat Faces talking to one another.

But there was no more noise, only the crackling of the fire and the usual sounds of the forest. Artie turned and walked to the corner of the cave where Tall Tree was sleeping and kicked him in the rump. It took two more kicks before he was awake and stumbling toward the cave entrance.

Artie watched for a moment to make sure he didn't go back to his furs, then crept to his side of the cave, his mind alive with the dream images from those around him. Some were fighting off bears and wolves as they slept; others, especially those of the boys, were exciting in a different way. He crawled under his own sleeping furs, stiffening for a moment when he felt somebody else there. He recognized Soft Skin by her smell and pulled her closer to him, cursing the thin strips of hide that knotted the skins around his chest and waist. But it took only seconds to slip out of them and a moment later he felt her breath upon his face. He sighed with pleasure and let his hands dance over her breasts and slide down her stomach and between her legs.

It was very good to be alive, he thought. The spirits were watching overhead, the fire was blazing at the mouth of the cave, he had a full belly, and the hunt would begin as soon as the sun awoke. Soft Skin was moving steadily beneath him now and he could feel his own excitement build.

Somewhere in the cave a baby cried and Artie could hear the shushing sound of its mother. He could feel the rough surface of the cave floor beneath the furs and smell the air thick with the odors of a hundred meals and the assorted stinks of the other members of the Tribe. Just beyond the cavern's mouth he knew there were creatures who could tear him in two or delight in eating him while he was still alive.

But if he lived twice as many winters as White Beard had, he knew life would never be much better than it was right then.

"**Let's go, Artie.**" Somebody was shaking him by the shoulder, and it took a moment for Artie to wake up. Another visit with the Tribe, but this time no killing, no slaughter by the river's edge. It had been much more like the dreams he used to have with Susan beside him in bed, then he realized that Soft Skin had been far too real and his shorts were sticking to him. Jesus, that hadn't happened to him since he'd been a kid.

Susan had been gone for . . . how long now?

Mitch was already dressed and pacing nervously by the window.

"What's up?"

"We're going to have to get out of here. Right now, no time for breakfast."

Artie sat on the edge of the bed, blinking the sleep out of his eyes and feeling sudden alarm growing inside.

"Why the hurry?"

"I checked my calls—Schuler phoned in at seventhirty. He wants to see both of us as soon as possible."

"They found Pace and Anya?"

Mitch shook his head. "Don't think so. Said he'd meet us at an address in the Upper Haight."

"You ask him what about?"

"He wouldn't say. Said he'd call Charlie Allen and Chandler later."

Schuler had to know that he'd been present when Professor Hall had been shot, but since he'd mentioned contacting Allen and Chandler, this couldn't be about that.

"No Mary and Jenny?"

"I thought you'd told me they were leaving town? Schuler didn't mention either one, and I assumed he'd already tried to call them."

Artie vaguely missed the warmth and energy of Soft Skin; it was hard to adjust to the real world.

"You sure it was Schuler?"

Mitch searched the bureau drawer for the phone book and leafed through it. He grabbed the phone and dialed, asked for Schuler and got confirmation.

"Sorry, Artie, I should've checked. Let's go—we'll take my car."

Schuler was waiting for them outside a combination redbrick and stucco three-story on Woodland. The house was already cordoned off with yellow police tapes. Schuler was leaning against a police car holding a plastic container of coffee in his hands.

"Sorry to get you two up so early. Allen and Chandler both said they'd be down a little later, though Chandler didn't sound very happy about it."

Artie could understand why. Chandler had looked like hell in his dimly lit office; he'd look frightening in daylight.

Mitch said, "What happened?"

Schuler nodded at the house. "Homicide. Neighbors saw a light go on in the upper bedroom about two in the morning—then screaming half an hour later that abruptly cut off. Apparently two kids started in then, but they were choked off within seconds. Literally, as it turned out. The uniforms got here too late to do anybody any good."

Artie couldn't think of anybody he knew who lived in the Upper Haight, not since his hippie days. But Schuler must have had a good reason to call them down to identify the bodies.

Mitch asked the obvious. "Anybody we know?"

Schuler hesitated. "I know what her ID says. You'll have to tell me if it matches. One woman, two kids. Apparently she was house-sitting for the owners. They're up in Tahoe for the holidays; got hold of them half an hour ago but they can't make it back until this afternoon."

Artie glanced at Mitch, who nodded slightly. They both knew who it was without asking.

. . .

**Cathy Shea was in** the bedroom, naked on the bed, a torn pillowcase knotted around her throat. Her face was purple with blood; there was no expression in her bulging eyes. She was a larger woman than Artie remembered, then he realized that personality can add to or diminish the size of a person. Cathy had never struck him as very big in life. Quiet, basically insecure, sexy when she was drunk, though it always struck him as more of a parody than a reality. All he could think of was that he would have to tell Susan and when he did, she'd come apart. For himself, he was numb. Maybe tomorrow he would feel something. Right then, he felt cold, professional. She had kept the house neat as a pin, had loved her kids, had dutifully supported her husband, had been a good friend to her friends . . .

It was a crappy epitaph.

She had struggled, and her hands were bloody where her nails had scraped flesh. The coroner's assistants were still taking photographs and measurements. Schuler watched the expression on Artie's face, then asked, "Mrs. Shea, right?"

Artie nodded.

"We found an ID in the purse in the john. Didn't guarantee it was her, but ninety-nine percent sure. Time of death—maybe two in the morning. What you see is what you get; she was strangled."

"Raped?" Mitch asked.

Schuler didn't answer but started downstairs. "The two boys were in the living room; they were camping out on a futon. Must have been fun for a while."

It was harder for Artie to look at them than it had been Cathy. Both were sprawled on the futon, presumably in the same position they were in when they had died. Both wore shorts, now soiled and smelling. The aftermath of death. Andy's face was contorted and Artie guessed he had fought. His head had been bashed in by a table lamp, which was now lying nearby, its base covered with blood and pale blond hair. James, the youngest and thinnest, looked almost peaceful. He had probably been suffocated by the pillow next to him, his skinny arms spread out like the arms of a crucifix.

They'd been spoiled rotten. They'd also been full of life and mischief. For the first time Artie thought he was going to break down.

"Why?"

"They probably saw whoever it was. It's even possible it was somebody they knew."

"Breaking and entering?"

Again, Schuler didn't answer.

"We've got prints—a lot of them. One of the neighbors saw somebody leave the house and run down the street toward Golden Gate Park. We're rousting all the homeless encampments, checking IDs and possessions, that sort of thing. They might have lifted something on the way out, something that won't go with their usual collections of tin cans and bottles."

The cops would find something, Artie thought. He'd make book on it. Once again, murder by proxy.

**In the kitchen** a tired Schuler sprawled in one of the chairs by a large distressed-oak table, and motioned them to take two of the others. "You guys want some coffee? I can send one of the uniforms down to McDonald's. I could use some more—I've been up a long time."

Artie nodded and Mitch said "Thanks." They sat around the table in silence while Schuler jotted notations in a small notebook.

"Curious, isn't it? A few days ago the doctor was killed, his wife disappears, and here we are again wondering who the hell did it. And—tell me if I'm wrong—both you guys have a pretty good idea who. Right?"

Artie shifted uneasily in his chair.

"We can prove where we were—"

Schuler looked disgusted. "Nobody said you were suspects. I'm just saying you know something I don't and I wish to hell you'd tell me."

"Was she raped?" Mitch asked again.

Schuler considered it. "That's a hard question to answer. Did she have sex before she was strangled? The pathologist says so. Was it consensual? Probably. Neighbors saw lights go on in the upper bedroom maybe twenty, thirty minutes before they heard any screaming. There were no signs of breaking and entering. Whoever it was, she let them in."

"A friend," Mitch said.

"You don't let strangers in at two in the morning. A personal friend, maybe a friend of the family."

"Not a friend of Larry's, that's for sure," Artie murmured.

Mitch looked thoughtful. "Maybe more than one."

"Oh?" Schuler sounded sarcastic. "Tell me why."

"The kids. She was killed first so they must have been awake—they heard her screaming. They could have run or cried for help themselves, unless somebody was holding them."

"Or her screams could have woken them up, they ran up the stairs to help her, and met the murderer on the way down. He could have grabbed them both and thrown them back on the futon. They started screaming right after she stopped. Probably died seconds later."

"How many were seen running to the park?"

"Only one, but the witness could have been wrong." A policeman walked in with a sack of muffins and half a dozen coffees along with tiny plastic creamers and little packets of sugar. Schuler shoved several containers of coffee toward Mitch and Artie.

"How well did the two of you know Mrs. Shea?"

Artie was deliberately vague. "Well enough—she was a member of the Club, that's where she met Larry.

We've known her for more than twenty years. My wife, Susan, and Cathy were good friends."

"I understand your wife and son have disappeared too, Banks."

Artie flushed. "It's divorce time, Lieutenant. I imagine I'll hear from her lawyer before I hear from her."

"My sympathies," Schuler said dryly. Then: "I gather neither of you two found anything of importance in the Shea home."

Artie looked surprised; Mitch kept his face blank.

"The neighbors." Schuler sighed. "The eyes and ears of the world. The Oakland police called us. A woman one house over got your license number but nothing was missing, so I didn't figure there was any hurry questioning you about it. Happens all the time. Friends of the deceased, angry about the murder, decide to do some investigating of their own. Granted that the two of you were better equipped to do that than most."

There was silence, then Mitch said, "I don't think there's much we can tell you, Lieutenant."

Schuler nodded and took a sip of coffee, jotted something more in his notebook, and shoved it back in his pocket.

"I might have done the same if I were you. But you were operating under a handicap. One, you were friends of Dr. Shea's, which means you probably weren't objective to begin with. Two, you didn't have the authority so you couldn't approach those who might have been in a position to tell you something: the people who lived next door and across the street."

"I assume the Oakland police questioned them," Mitch said. His voice was curt, and Artie guessed he resented Schuler for implying incompetence on his part. As a military investigator, Mitch had been top flight and proud of it.

"That's right, Doctor. I asked for copies of their records and they were kind enough to turn them over to me."

"And?"

Schuler shrugged.

"Apparently Mrs. Shea was one hot lady. Dr. Shea was buried in his work; he was blind to it. My guess is that the rest of you knew it but who the hell wants to tell the husband, who isn't going to believe it in any event but will hate whoever tells him? She had visitors when the kids were at school. There aren't many pool boys in Oakland, but there are enough delivery men familiar with the lonely-housewife syndrome. Probably a fringe benefit of working the Oakland hills."

"Some of us knew it," Mitch said. "There wasn't much to be gained by blowing the whistle."

"You might be right, Doctor. And then again, you might not. We've got one dead lady and two dead kids. Maybe blowing the whistle would have been the kindest thing in the long run."

Schuler looked from one to the other.

"I'm willing to listen to any ideas either one of you might have."

Artie didn't say anything. Mitch said, "You must have some of your own, Lieutenant."

Schuler looked disappointed. "I was hoping this would be a conversation, not a monologue. My take is Mrs. Shea hears about her husband's murder and she figures she's in danger too, so she runs, so frightened she doesn't pack anything at all. She doesn't tell a soul where she's hiding. Barring any evidence to the contrary, I think somebody tracked her down, somebody she was glad to see, because she let him in the house of her own free will. Maybe she got tired of being alone after a few days and called him. If I had to go further, I'd guess the lady was in love but hadn't been about to leave her husband and fight for the kids. Men have mistresses on the side. She had a boyfriend stashed away. But sometime in that half hour she figured out that he wasn't just a terrific bed partner after all, that he'd had something to do with her husband's murder.

Maybe she confronted him with it, more likely it was a slip of the tongue, or maybe he just suspected she knew. But that was all it took."

Schuler helped himself to a muffin and took another sip of coffee. "What bothers me is that I think I'm right—and I'm not right. That there's a lot more to it than that but I haven't the slightest clue as to what. I still don't know what she was running from, what frightened her so badly. You two care to help me out?"

They were silent for a moment, then Artie said, "Did you check out the dogs that killed Larry?"

"Two of them were strays, the third—the one with the tags—had been reported missing two days before. Owner was some old guy about to retire from the Health Department. Claimed Fido wouldn't hurt a flea."

Schuler stood up, capping his container of coffee to take with him.

"Tomorrow I think I would like to talk to both of you some more about the Suicide Club. Dangerous club to belong to—the members keep dying like flies. Maybe you can tell me something about Lyle Pace and Anya Robbins. A friend of his at Copeland's stopped by Lyle's home last night to see if he was okay; he hadn't showed for work, didn't answer his phone."

He stared at them for a long moment. "I would like to think I surprised you, but somehow I'm not sure I have. And maybe you can fill me in on Professor Hall, Banks. Ten o'clock sound all right by you?" He didn't wait for an answer. "Fine. See you then."

On the sidewalk outside, a few neighbors had started to gather, whispering among themselves and watching the coroner's men wheel out the bodies.

Schuler opened the door to his car, then paused to glance back at Artie and Mitch. Schuler's face looked drawn and tired, and it occurred to Artie that Schuler was thinning down, becoming frail, that he must be close to retirement.

"I'm getting too old for this. The wife and I have a vacation cottage up in Victoria and I think it's time we put our feet to the fire and let the world take care of itself." He looked depressed. "You probably write obits for your station, Banks. How long do you give the world? Fifty years? Twenty?"

Just before the car pulled away from the curb, he cranked down the window to say, "If I were you guys, I'd watch my back." A thoughtful look, then, "Take care of yourselves."

The scary part, Artie thought, was that he wasn't just being polite.

# CHAPTER 19

**They had breakfast at** a small restaurant on Haight Street, sitting in the back, half hidden by a magazine and paperback-book rack. The fried eggs were passable, the bacon cold and greasy, the orange juice fresh frozen.

But Artie could have been eating hay and he wouldn't have complained. "Schuler's no dummy," he said at last.

Mitch dug into a jar of grape jam to spread on his toast, then gave up and shoved his plate away. "Never said he was. He was just in a better position to know some things about Cathy Shea than we were. He was right—we were too close to Larry and we didn't have the authority to interview the neighborhood. But we still know a lot more than he does."

"I wish to hell I didn't," Artie muttered.

"Probably wouldn't make much difference. We knew Larry—that's the major sin. Our homicidal Hound would have assumed Larry told us everything in any event and things would have happened just as they did."

"Professor Hall might still be alive."

"Paschelke would still have been killed—and so would Lyle."

The coffee was enough to gag on, but Artie drained half his cup.

"So what's next on the agenda? Cathy's a closed book—there's nothing she can tell us."

Mitch pulled several bills from his wallet and dropped them on the table. "Right in one sense, wrong in another. She was good friends with whoever killed her and there's a good chance he's mentioned in Charlie's diaries."

Artie dug in his pocket for some coins as a tip. "The only thing that's wrong with that is apparently she was good friends with almost everybody."

Mitch's smile was bleak. "Except you."

"Except me," Artie agreed.

"When you get around to the diaries all you have to do is pick out the right boyfriend, Artie." Out on the street, Mitch asked, "When are you going to get them from Charlie?"

"He said he'd call me at work so I could drop over to the library after hours."

Mitch leaned against a newspaper box and flipped open his cellular phone. "I'll help you run through them when I get back to the hotel." He looked apologetic. "I've got to check my messages and tell Linda I'll be in today—I've postponed too many sessions already."

He concentrated on his phone, punching in his code for message retrieval. A few nods—Artie assumed that patients had called in to make appointments or cancel them. Then Mitch's face suddenly became starched and flat of emotion. He glanced at Artie, then turned away. He punched in another number, looked again at Artie to see if he was listening, then held the phone so it was partly muffled by his coat. Artie could hear what he was saying but not the other half of the conversation. The only thing that gave Mitch away was his eyes, blinking furiously behind his granny glasses as they always did when he was excited.

Artie was insulted at first, then curious. What the hell? Mitch listened intently to the voice message he was getting, glanced again at Artie after the voice stopped, then punched in still another number.

Artie kept his own face blank and looked away, making a show of giving him some privacy. What was going on? Mitch had obviously received his messages, then punched in for a repeat of one of them, and now presumably was calling the caller back.

Mitch made his connection, then said in a soft voice, "Stu? Levin. Don't want to talk about it now, just repeat the date." A moment of tense silence. Then: "Got it. Yeah, unbelievable."

He clicked off and slipped the phone back in his pocket.

Artie looked at him, ready to be sympathetic.

"Bad news?"

"You could say that." Then a failed attempt at a smile. "Just business."

It was business that had something to do with him, Artie thought. He'd stake his life on it. Mitch suddenly seemed remote, a hundred miles away.

"I've got to meet somebody, Artie—you can get back to the hotel okay?"

"I'll grab a cab, go right to work. You sure you're all right?"

"I'm fine." But when Mitch looked at him, it was with the eyes of a stranger sizing up somebody he had met for the first time.

"See you at the hotel tonight?" Artie asked, suddenly tentative.

For a moment Mitch seemed surprised, then nodded. "Yeah, sure." He started up the street to his car. He didn't look back.

Artie stared after him. He had known Mitch Levin almost all his life, but inside of a few minutes it suddenly seemed like he didn't know him at all.

· · ·

"**I've changed it a** lot," Connie said nervously. "Jim and I had to go ahead without you—sorry about that, Artie, but Hirschfield wants it sooner rather than later."

"Have I made Hirschfield's shit list yet?"

She shook her head. "Not yet—but close."

She looked worn out, Artie thought—she must have shed five pounds in the last few days.

"You stayed here and worked on it all night?" He felt a brief twinge of guilt, then realized there was no way he could have helped her any more than he had.

"Not quite—we were here until three in an editing booth. Most of the audio track and sound bites are laid down and Jim started covering it with B-roll."

Jim Austin was their star editor, and he and Connie had been friends from the day she'd started working at KXAM.

"What's the standard, Connie? A bottle of Chivas?"

She gave him a long look. "Beam—and make it half a case. We took him away from his family at Christmastime."

He pulled a stool over in front of the monitor, sitting close to Connie, who had balanced her yellow notepad on her knees. Jerry asked, "Ready?" and, when she nodded, started the tape rolling.

It was more of a PBS opener than Artie had figured Connie would use. Stock tape of lush forests of oak and pine with eagles flashing through blue skies, tumbling rivers with salmon leaping over rocks, grasslands spreading as far as the eye could see with a herd of buffalo on the distant horizon. Eden, Artie thought. Then the camera dipped for a view of an Asian forest and a tiger padded into the frame, highlighted for a moment against a patch of waving grass. It looked overwhelmingly majestic. Then a dissolve into the field tape they had shot of the Siberian tiger the day before, pacing back and forth in its tiny enclosure of weeds and artificial rocks.

And finally a shop in some unknown Chinatown with a shelf of mounted tiger's paws, tins of something unknown but with the logo of a tiger on it—dried gall bladder? Powdered tiger's blood? Aphrodisiacs of some sort? And in the back of the shop, draped over a small mound of boxes, a tiger's skin, its teeth bared in a taxidermist's idea of a snarl, muted by the poorly painted plastic buttons that served as eyes.

The skin could have come from the same tiger they had seen a few seconds earlier.

"I'm not sure about this title setup," Connie murmured in his ear.

On the monitor was an animated version of an artist's palette with splotches of brilliant paints: greens and blues and reds and yellows and purples and pinks. Then an animated brush started mixing the colors, slowly at first, then speeding up into a flurry of motion. The different splashes of pigment were swirled into various tints and shades, which gradually lost any sense of purity and merged into a brown that covered the palette and then the entire screen. The title "World Without End?" was reversed out on the muddy background.

All the brilliant colors at the start had been reduced to a shit brown, Artie thought. The analogy was obvious: a pristine world that had been reduced to . . . what?

"We took it from the opening of a Disney cartoon," Connie said in a low whisper. "We can do a variation if we can't get permission."

Artie was fascinated by the images on the tube. She had taken the assignment and run with it; he'd been egotistical to think she had needed his help at all.

Now the screen was filled with portraits of various animals while Connie narrated the names of the endangered species: the Siberian tiger—fewer than five hundred remaining in the wild; the Florida panther—thirty to fifty; the black-footed ferret—less than five hundred; the red wolf—fewer than three hundred; the ocelot—a hundred. . . .

Her voice faded into a chroma-key shot with Connie standing in front of what would have been the weather map, only with the zoo footage rolling behind her while she explained the "sixth extinction": the thirty thousand officially threatened species, including more than five hundred mammals, almost a thousand each of birds and fishes, more than twenty-five thousand plants.

Species went extinct all the time due to natural causes, she continued. But this time the culprit wasn't nature; it was man. Take Mozambique, where a dozen different armies had used everything from assault rifles to helicopters to slaughter the animals. The white rhinoceros was now extinct, only a few black rhinos were left, the elephant population had fallen by ninety percent.

The image behind her now changed to a large commercial fishing boat, pulling in nets and dumping the day's catch on the deck. The situation was no better in the oceans, where overfishing was gradually emptying the waters. Bluefin tuna in the Western Atlantic was down by ninety percent and due to drop farther—it was selling for three hundred and fifty dollars a pound in popular sashimi restaurants in Tokyo.

Overfishing had gotten so bad that Canada had shut down its fishery in the Grand Banks of Newfoundland, throwing forty thousand people out of work. Poaching inside its two-hundred-mile coastal limits had already led to shooting with Canada firing on and boarding a Spanish fishing trawler; Icelandic fishing ships and Norwegian patrol boats had exchanged gunfire. Were these the first shots in the coming wars over the spoils of the sea? And inland, streams where fish had once been so plentiful early explorers claimed you could cross the water by walking on their backs were now so polluted they ran brown and empty.

Few fish caught within coastal waters were suitable for eating, the on-screen Connie said in the wrap-up.

Jerry stopped the tape after the end of the segment.

"How long did it run, Jerry?"

"Under five minutes—four forty-two. It's still a little over."

Connie frowned. "We'll have to take the time out of the final segment." She looked at Artie. "So? What do you think?"

Artie was impressed. "You did a great job—so did Jim."

"It gets better. Okay, Jerry."

The second segment was titled "Garbage World" and opened with squirrels gathering acorns at the bottom of an ancient oak, then panned to a stream a hundred feet away where the banks were spattered with rusting cans and empty bottles while the water was iridescent with oil and toxics spewing from a waste pipe jutting out from one of the sandy banks. Finally, shots of women washing clothing in the Ganges, a river that had "died of detergent."

A stand-up with Connie talking about a consumer society while she wandered through the aisles of a Costco packed to the ceiling with electronics and household furnishings, racks of clothing, pallets of detergent and twelve-packs of soda and beer, refrigerator cases filled with TV dinners and frozen chicken parts, and a meat department with ground beef in five-pound packages and steaks a dozen to the plastic tray. "And it all comes packaged," Connie said.

Jerry stopped the tape again. Connie turned to Artie and asked, "You want to take a break?"

Artie's coffee was cold but he didn't care.

"Let's go through the whole thing—after that I'll go home and kill myself."

**Half an hour later** the tape finished and Gottlieb ejected the cassette.

"Thanks a heap, Jerry." Connie left for their glassed-in cubicle overlooking the newsroom, Artie trailing after her in silence. They sat and watched the activity outside for a minute or two, then Connie said, "Okay, tell me what's wrong with it. I already know it can be polished."

"I think it's a great piece of work," Artie said. "Also, depressing as shit."

Connie nodded. "You read an article here and an article there, the newspapers run stories, once in a while you see a review of a book about it or watch a PBS special. But you don't read or see them all at the same time—you don't add them up. It's easier to worry about your next raise, your heartburn, what the kids are doing to each other after dark and what about a curfew. You feel you can do something about those. This kind of stuff just makes you feel . . . helpless. What the hell, you don't fish, you don't farm, you recycle and hope the problems will go away."

"Hirschfield seen the tape?"

She dumped some sugar in her cold coffee and stirred it with the cap of her pen.

"You hit the one bright spot. He loved the script, he loves this more—thinks he can get the network to carry it in six weeks or so, after the February sweeps. Hell, they've got nothing else important scheduled then."

Maybe it was their one last chance to change things before the Hounds of Hell came up with something really final, Artie thought.

Connie was studying him. "You don't think it's my cup of tea, do you?"

Artie looked at her in surprise. "The series? I can't think of anybody who could have done it better."

"You really mean it?"

"If I didn't think so, I wouldn't say so."

She looked away. "Thanks, Artie. A lot." Then: "I'm thinking of doing one on Russia."

"Why Russia?"

Jerry knocked on the door and came in with a cardboard tray and two containers of hot coffee.

Connie took one, glanced at it, and said "No cream?" in mock dismay. Jerry muttered "Jesus" and left, Connie's "Thanks" floating after him. She took a gulp. "The Russians are like the deer on Angel Island: they're crashing. But almost all we ever hear about are the politics and the crime. They destroyed themselves twenty years ago and they've been walking around ever since not knowing they're dead."

Artie felt uneasy. "I don't follow you."

"Terminal poisoning of their own environment. Almost all of the major rivers are polluted, and they've dammed the ones that fed the Aral Sea so they could use the water for irrigation; now the Aral is maybe half its former size and dying. They even have salt storms that blow off the crusted shores. It was fish versus cotton, and the planners in Moscow chose cotton because it paid better. They've dumped nuclear wastes into rivers and the sea, there's pollution from leaking pipes in the older oil fields, heavy metals have contaminated the countryside around smelters. . . . It's hurting, badly. The average life span of Russian men has dropped from sixty-five to fifty-eight. . . ."

Artie didn't want to hear any more.

"Connie, get the hell out of here."

She grimaced. "I'll be okay. But the next time I do a special, maybe it should be one on soccer moms. What I'm going to do right now is go home, curl up on the couch with half a gallon of eggnog, and get smashed. Let Kris take care of me for a change. She'll bitch but she'll love the novelty."

Artie turned to leave and behind him Connie said, "You got a call earlier. A Charlie Allen at the library. Said he had some books for you."

"Thanks—I'll pick them up." He slipped out of the door, leaving Connie to her demons.

# CHAPTER 20

**It was dark when** Artie left the station, the air cold and misting. Lately when he'd been getting up in the morning, he could see frost on the railings of his back porch. How cold was it now, high thirties? Maybe tonight it would even snow; there had been a dusting of it on Mount Tam a few mornings ago. He'd called for a cab before leaving the office and waited ten minutes behind the bulletproof glass of the front lobby until it showed up.

"We'll be closing in fifteen minutes," the library guard warned. People were already streaming out the doors, on their way to the Muni or BART.

Artie showed his press card. "Charles Allen?"

The guard consulted a printed listing on his desk. "Main Library Administration—that's on five. Elevators are across the rotunda on the Fulton Street side."

Artie started across the granite floor, stopping for a moment in the middle to glance up at the skylight six floors overhead with the staircases circling beneath it. The rotunda and its skylight were the architectural center of the building; the different reading rooms and cultural centers led off the staircases on each floor. A teenager a dozen feet away, his back to him, was also staring up at the skylight; he'd probably just signed off the Internet and was getting ready to go home and had stopped to look up at what he'd heard so much about. There wasn't much to see now—too dark—but during the day the sunshine streaming through the massive skylight illuminated the whole interior of the building.

Supposedly it was the first step to the electronic library, though Artie would have been happier with fewer computers and more books. There was something about the feel of paper and cloth that a computer screen could never replace.

"Hi, Artie. Come on in and close the door."

Charlie's office was hidden behind the stacks across from the rotunda. It was just big enough for a desk, a spare chair, a coat rack, a bookcase, and the ubiquitous computer. Charlie finished what he was working on and powered down.

Artie asked the obvious: "Working late?"

"Not this time of year—most everybody's doing their last-minute shopping. We get some young kids in the audio/visual center and some of the winos for the warmth, but that's about it." Allen locked his fingers behind his head and leaned back in his chair, yawned, then opened his eyes wide and stared at him. The stare of a too-curious man, Artie thought, with misgiving.

"Artie, what's going on?" Allen sounded plaintive and a little angry.

Artie tried to look surprised. "You tell me."

Charlie shoved the afternoon paper across the desk. Artie picked it up, afraid for a moment that Cathy had made the headlines.

"First Larry, then Lyle and his lady. Lyle wasn't the most likable guy on the face of the earth, but I keep getting this feeling that somebody out there is gunning for us."

Artie read the story carefully, taking his time though he already knew the details. Charlie didn't know about

Cathy or Chandler yet and when he found out, the shit would really hit the fan.

"I got a right to know," Charlie said quietly.. "You better believe Nathan already has Franny and me pretty upset. The kid could have killed us all. I feel like we're characters in *Ten Little Indians*, where one by one the suspects are knocked off." He pointed at the paper. "Did you know anything about this? And if you did, why the hell didn't you tell me? I'm not exactly an innocent bystander, Artie, not after the other night."

He was referring to Nathan again, Artie thought. He shook his head. "That's the first I've read about it, Charlie. Scout's honor."

Charlie studied him, trying to decipher the expression on his face. "You're lying like a rug, Artie. How long have you and I and Mitch been friends? More than twenty years now? You and he know something, and you're not letting me in on it. We all have our secrets, but this time it looks like my family's concerned. Not good."

He stared at Artie a moment longer, then motioned toward the bookcase. "The diaries are in the shopping bag there—I flipped through them and pulled the ones where I saw a mention of Cathy. I didn't read them closely. Why spoil the memories, right? Though right now they seem to be rotting pretty badly."

"Sorry you feel that way," Artie said quietly. "All Mitch and I are doing is trying to find out who killed Larry. I don't know about Lyle and Anya, though it looks like a lovers' quarrel."

"Coincidence stretched to the breaking point," Charlie snorted.

Something on his desk caught Artie's eye and he changed the subject. A box with a Walkman and a set of headphones draped over the sides. He pointed at it. "They won't let you have a radio in here?"

"Just trying it out—Christmas present for Nathan. This and a dozen tapes of his favorite bands. He loves 'em, I hate 'em, but this way he's the only one who's going to hear them."

Artie suddenly stiffened. When he got off the elevator, he hadn't seen anybody on the floor. It had been silent, the study rooms had been empty, and the Magazines and Newspapers Center was deserted. Now he sensed there was somebody outside the door. Probably the guard making his rounds, he thought frantically, and knew immediately he was wrong.

He smiled crookedly at Charlie, hoping it really was the guard and waiting for a knock on the door. A minute of staring at a puzzled Charlie. There was no rap on the door, no further sound of somebody walking in the corridor outside.

· But somebody was sure as hell out there; he could *feel* him.

"You know," Charlie said in a suddenly smug voice, "Mitch wasn't the only one who banged Cathy Deutsch. I had a piece of her, too."

Artie suddenly felt panicked. He had left the automatic back in the hotel room, hidden under the dirty clothes he'd stuffed in a drawer. Jesus, he should have known better.

Charlie had asked him to drop in at the library after hours, when he knew it would be deserted, and he had cheerfully obliged.

*you're a fool, monkey. . . .*

**For a moment life** was a series of freeze-frames. Charlie Allen, looking both smug and surprised at what he'd just said. The box with the Walkman and the tapes open on the desk, a long pair of newspaper shears at the top of the desk pad. The look on Charlie's face slowly shifting from one of surprise to one of watchful hostility. Then the little things: the telephone out of its cradle, the small green light signifying "On" for the phone recording system.

Setup, Artie thought chaotically. Whatever happened in that office would be recorded for Schuler to find later.

"You never struck me as a cocksman, Charlie," Artie said in a thin voice.

Charlie was a pudgy man but now there was a subtle change. He suddenly didn't strike Artie as weak or slow on his feet. Charlie was like a glove that something had put on and was now flexing its fingers.

"Those who do don't talk about it, Banks. I don't think Mitch ever got as far as he said he did."

"But *you* did?"

Charlie smirked.

"Why not, she was easy. So were Jenny and Mary." There was something behind his eyes that Artie couldn't read. "So was Susan."

Artie almost leaped over the desk at Allen, then realized that it wasn't Charlie speaking to him at all.

*the voice on tape is all that counts, monkey. . . .*

"You're a liar," Artie croaked.

Charlie shook his head in mock anger.

"It's okay for you and Mitch to talk about Cathy, right? But you ought to take a good look at Susan. She had a two-year-old kid, the boy needed a father, you were the closest thing to a virgin in the Club, and you even had something of a future. You were shy, she was physical, and a taste of flesh went a long way with you, didn't it? She's probably been a good wife and loyal, so you've had no complaints." He looked at Artie quizzically. "Or has she been? Loyal, I mean. She never struck me as very demonstrative, not the kind to run her fingernails down your back and spend half an hour telling you how great you were and how much she loves you. She ever done that, Artie?" He paused for a fraction of a second. "You don't have to answer—I never thought so anyway."

Artie felt himself go white.

"Has Franny ever done that for you, Allen? She

bowed out of the competition early, probably realized she was a loser all around."

He was almost shocked when he saw Charlie's fingers curl around the handle of the shears. Newspaper shears were long and pointed, and the grip would be great for either an underhand or an overhand thrust.

"Stop it, Charlie—he's trying to get to both of us!" For a moment the real Charlie flickered in Allen's eyes, frightened and confused. Then Artie found himself saying, "Cathy Deutsch wasn't the only punchboard. You sure Nathan's all yours, Charlie?"

First one, then the other. They were being played against each other. The argument was childish, but it wouldn't sound like that on the tape when Schuler discovered blood all over the desk and the walls, and a body on the floor, maybe two.

Raucous laughter inside his head . . .

*too late, monkey . . .*

He thought for a moment of going after Charlie, but Charlie beat him to it. He gripped the shears in his right hand and launched himself over the desk, rolling to his feet on the other side. Charlie shouldn't be able to do that, not even on a good day, and then Artie remembered the old man skating in Union Square.

The shears slashed through his coat and Artie felt a stinging sensation in his shoulder. A scratch, but probably a bloody one. He rolled backward in his chair and twisted so he was sitting on the floor, then caught Charlie in the stomach with a foot and the pudgy man went down. Artie rolled away and was on his feet, yanking at the doorknob.

He got as far as the corridor outside when Charlie was clawing at his back, and he went down again. Repeated jabs with the shears, catching mostly overcoat. Artie caught his wrist and tried to bend it back. Charlie was too pudgy, too out of shape—it should have been easy to take the shears away. It wasn't.

Charlie's other fist came up and caught him in the

throat. Artie rolled backward into an aisle in the stacks, shelves of books looming up on both sides. Charlie came after him, his face red with anger, using the shears like a broadsword to carve the space in front of him.

Artie reached out and swept books off the shelves onto the floor. Charlie danced out of the way, then slipped on one that had fallen open and went down in a flurry of torn paper. Artie turned and ran for the rotunda stairs.

He had started down when once again he was hit from behind, then was being forced over the railing. He grabbed the steel-pipe railing with both hands, caught a glimpse of the floor five stories below, then started to hoist himself back onto the stairs. When he looked up he was staring full into the face of Charlie Allen.

A very normal Charlie Allen who looked terrified and bewildered. He threw away the bloody shears and helped Artie over the railing.

"Christ, Artie, what's happening! What the hell are we doing?"

"Killing each other," Artie mumbled. His ribs ached and his shoulder felt sticky and wet. He sat on the steps, sagging back against the railing.

Charlie's face suddenly went blank and Artie tensed. "Wait!" Charlie turned and ran off.

If he had the brains God gave a goose, Artie thought, he'd get the hell out of there. Now.

Something was fingering the back of his mind again and the shelves of books just beyond seemed to ripple like the reflection of trees in a windswept pond. How easy it would be to hide in the stacks and catch Charlie when he returned. It would be Charlie Allen they'd find splattered over the floor below.

Suddenly he sensed confusion and anger, and his mind was free. He heard steps and turned to see Charlie running toward him, clutching the bag of diaries, the Walkman headphones covering his ears. He looked scared to death.

"What the hell's going on, Artie? It was me and it wasn't me. . . ."

Artie pointed at the headset.

"Why the phones?"

"So I can't hear myself think—and nothing else can, either. Metallica, Nathan's favorite. I can't stand them." He pushed the bag into Artie's hands. "Get the hell out of here. I got hold of the guard and he'll call the cops. I'll tell them some story about an intruder."

Artie grabbed him by the arm. "Let's both get out of here."

Charlie shook his head. "It can't follow both of us if we separate. My guess is it'll follow you—sorry, Artie, it's probably after the diaries. I'll be okay, just get out of here."

Artie clutched the bag and ran down the steps. Just before he reached the doors he staggered and almost fell, his mind caught for the moment like a baseball in a glove.

*you'll come to me, monkey. . . .*

**There was nobody back** at the hotel and Artie waited half an hour, patching up his shoulder with supplies he'd bought from a nearby drugstore. The shears hadn't gone very deep but the cut was bloody and hurt like hell. He cleaned it with alcohol and put heavy gauze and tape over it, then rinsed his bloody shirt in cold water and hung it over a towel rack in the john, turning on the ceiling heat lamp to help dry it. He watched the news on TV for a while, got bored, and ordered a ham sandwich and a chef's salad from room service—Mitch could order something for himself later.

He didn't want to start plowing through Charlie's diaries until Mitch showed. Best thing to do would be to skim one and turn it over to Mitch when he finished.

Maybe Levin would catch something he hadn't.

By eight o'clock, Mitch still hadn't showed up. Artie called Mitch's office, but there was only a recorded message telling the caller to leave his or her name and number and Dr. Mitchell Levin would get back to them. It was the same at home. No Mitch. He called his own house; no messages on his answering machine. And no messages from Levin at KXAM.

Mitch should at least have called him if something had come up, Artie thought, and that was funny because he'd blamed Mark for not doing it either. But something could have happened to him; Mitch was as much a target as he was.

Or was he?

He trusted Mitch because . . . he trusted Mitch. They were good friends who went back forever, but then so had he and Mary. So had he and everybody else in the Club.

He finished half the salad but had no appetite for the sandwich. Eight-thirty—where the hell was Mitch?

It gradually occurred to him that Mitch wasn't coming back and he remembered the phone call that morning. He'd had no idea what it was about except that it had concerned him.

And Levin had hardly been friendly afterward: "See you at the hotel tonight?" "Yeah, sure." But Mitch had said it offhand; he hadn't meant it.

By nine o'clock Artie had made up his mind, wondering if he wasn't already too late. Only one person knew where he was, but that might be one person too many. He put on his still-damp shirt and managed to slip into his coat, his shoulder protesting vigorously. He pocketed the automatic, picked up the bag of diaries, and took the elevator down to the lobby. He nodded at the desk clerk but didn't bother checking out. As far as anybody was concerned, that was where he was going to spend the night.

It was misting again but it was late enough so there

was no difficulty getting a cab. In case the doorman might overhear, he told the driver to take him to the Washington Square Bar and Grill. Once there, he got out, waited until the cab had disappeared from view, then caught another to Lombard Street.

There were dozens of cheap motels lining Lombard and he picked one at random. Checking in sans luggage was no problem; as long as your credit card cleared, you were golden.

The room was serviceable, the bed sheets on the gray side but clean, the towels worn but ditto. He took off his coat, set the gun on the other pillow, and lay down to watch the top of the late news. There was no story about the fight in the library, which was interesting. If somewhere Mitch were watching, he'd have no reason to believe that for ten minutes he and Charlie Allen had been intent on killing each other.

Unless, of course, Levin had been the prime mover all along, the Hound who had murdered Larry Shea a week ago and apparently had declared war against almost everybody in the Club.

Except . . .

He really didn't believe that. Nor did he believe the Hound had finally caught up with Mitch. No, Mitch had abandoned him and the only reason Artie could think of was that it had something to do with him.

For a moment he felt like he was back in the library, dangling from a railing in the rotunda, five stories above the floor. The only one he was sure of now was Charlie Allen. He'd *seen* what had happened to Charlie, just like he'd seen what had happened to the old man ice-skating in the square. Both had been subject to . . . control.

He wondered if Charlie had managed to get away, then guessed that he had. There was no way that the guard and a platoon of cops could have been manipulated all at the same time.

Artie closed his eyes and tried to will himself back

to the cave beside a meandering stream so many thousands of years ago, and when that failed tried to visualize himself at the breakfast table with Susan and Mark, wishing Susan well on her visit to her folks and bitching about almost everything Mark did that he thought was strange or uncalled for.

It had been so easy to forget that he was a teenager once. If he ever got the chance . . .

But he wouldn't.

Susan was gone, and so was Mark.

He opened his eyes and stared at the ceiling for a long moment, blanking his mind of everything, then spread the diaries out on the bed table and switched on the light.

He had a lot of reading to do.

# CHAPTER 21

**Reading about yourself** twenty years before was bittersweet, Artie thought. Charlie had been something of a naive writer at the start, but he hadn't missed much. He'd had a flair for characterization and description, even if his vocabulary had been that of a teenager, and he had been a meticulous chronicler of times and places. The later diaries were undoubtedly more sophisticated, but Artie couldn't believe they'd be as interesting to read.

You forgot so much: the characters drifting in and out of the coffee shop, a lot of students and a thick scattering of hippies. The early members of the Club would sit around a little table in back, sipping coffee and picking out which of the younger patrons might be interested in joining and those whom they wanted to ask. Arch—was anybody still named Archibald?— had been a jock from State and laughed a lot when they asked him to join, thinking they were putting him on. When he was convinced they were serious, he said he thought it would be a hoot. He had been the first to reach the top of the north tower of the bridge.

Arch. Gone now, a boobytrap in 'Nam. Screamed his lungs out until they got him to an evac unit and then he slipped away from an overdose of morphine. What the hell, it was front-line medical and everybody was so scared they were pissing in their pants; you couldn't blame them for occasional mistakes. Arch probably wouldn't have made it anyway.

A friend of Arch's had enlisted with him, and after being mustered out dropped in at the coffee shop to tell somebody, anybody, what had happened. How long had it been since he'd thought of Arch now? Ten years? Fifteen? If he ever wanted to feel guilty about something, he could always pick on that.

And the other members as they had drifted in. Mitchell Levin, toothy and nerdy and wearing John Lennon glasses even back then. Smart, the kind who bragged about it. His family had lived in the St. Francis Wood district and he'd gone to a private high school and bragged about that, too. But what you saw wasn't what you got. He'd had a wicked sense of humor, had taken martial arts classes along with Shakespeare and the History of the Renaissance, was fond of camping trips, and even had a small gun collection back then, carefully hidden from his father, who was one of the city's leading cardiologists.

Artie smiled to himself. Maybe it was because Mitch had been a fan of the Three Stooges that they'd gotten along so well. It had been strictly serendipity when they'd met up in 'Nam and he'd asked to be transferred to Mitch's unit. Intelligence was better than front-line duty, but then, to Artie's regret, the friendship had turned formal. It had been "Sergeant, I'd like you to do this" and "Yes, sir" unless things were really hairy and there was no time for bullshit. He'd been damned glad once the war was over and the friendship got back to normal. Or had it?

Larry Shea had been your typical average guy, so average they'd debated whether to ask him to join. He'd wanted to be a doctor even back then and had found a pigeon in Golden Gate Park with a busted wing, set it, and nursed the bird back to health. There was no debate after that; everybody wanted him in, even Mitch. Charlie Allen had been Larry's buddy and Larry had campaigned hard for him. For his part, Charlie had a flair for making himself useful. And he bugged them, showing up on escapades whether he was asked or not, dogging their footsteps no matter where they went. Finally it had been easier to ask him in than to try to keep him out.

Lyle had won the women's vote. He was somewhat surly, somewhat mysterious, and overwhelmingly sexy. A star of State's wrestling team, a below-average student, probably because he was a pothead but nobody had really objected to that—if you wanted a lid, Lyle could always turn you on to one.

The women had been something else. Mary had a stocky build and was somewhat self-conscious about it. She had been a music buff even back then, though she had no favorite among the rock groups—she liked them all. Her idea of a good time was to hang out at a rock concert, any rock concert. Somebody had reported seeing her going to the opera one night, but the idea was so outrageous that nobody had believed it.

She also loved art, and that was when Artie had become interested. She not only liked it, she studied it, and when he went to the museum with her it was like having his own private docent to explain the artists and their paintings. Mary had been his opposite, Artie thought. She had been energetic and extroverted. He had been fairly quiet, a bookworm with the saving grace of cycling and playing handball so he wasn't stoop-shouldered by age twenty.

It was Mary who had introduced him to sex, though he realized later that she had taken pity on him. He had tormented himself about masturbation; he hadn't been willing to admit that he was hormonally driven and had instead blamed it on his lack of enough courage to approach a girl. Mary had figured out the cause behind his occasional moody silences and invited him over for dinner when her roommates were away for the weekend, suggesting they play cards afterwards.

It had been a strange way to spend the evening, but he'd shrugged and thought, Why not? Mary had teased him into strip poker—later insisting it was his idea, which was all part of her therapy—and when he was naked and could no longer hide his feelings, Mary had sex with him. His first impression was that she had more teeth than the shark in *Jaws*. It was more comfortable face-to-face, but it was all over impossibly soon. Mary went out of her way to compliment him and help build up his ego. For all of a day or two afterward he'd lorded it over the girls in the Club because he had a prick and they didn't. Mary and he had slept together several more times after that until he figured out that for Mary it was more of a mercy fuck, and for himself it was because of loneliness. But they had been good friends ever since.

Until now.

After he had come back from 'Nam, it was Mary who had introduced him to Susan Albright, a widow with a two-year-old son. It had been love if not at first sight, then certainly by third. Ordinarily a little reserved and more thoughtful than adventurous, Susan was anything but that in bed. Mary had showed him how, but it was Susan who taught him to let go and enjoy the intricacies of lovemaking. One time when he'd held back— because, as Susan had told him afterward, of outdated "moral" reasons—she'd defiantly said, "It's my body and I'll do what I want with it," then smiled and added boldly, "and so should you."

But she soon became a lot more than a bed partner. When he walked into a room and she was there, he knew his eyes lit up and so did hers. He *liked* her, he finally decided. He liked the way she moved, her sense of self, how she thought and, of course, the fact that she liked him, that she seemed to like everything about him. When he realized she had become his best friend, he asked her to marry him. She had known he would all along; the only thing she had wondered about was when.

In his own mind—though not in Charlie's diaries— the other women seemed to play a minor role. Jenny had been the quiet goddess, the good scout who went everyplace you did and did everything you did and somehow never got her hair out of place. He couldn't remember her using much makeup but she was still a knockout. Quiet, too quiet, and she eventually gravitated to the company of Mary, who was brash and outspoken enough for both of them.

Franny had been the plump girl, too much aware that she was overweight, too anxious to please, too eager to do whatever the group wanted to do. She could be depended upon to show up with sandwiches and cookies for whatever trip they went on, sort of a self-nominated commissary. Charlie had caught her one day in a corner of the coffee shop crying to herself about her awkwardness when it came to the men in the Club. He had felt sorry for her, and they were a couple ever after. No regrets, Charlie had written enthusiastically. He'd found a diamond in the rough that all the others had overlooked. What he didn't admit in the diary was that Franny had figured out the road to his heart was through his stomach and, in his case, it had been a freeway.

Cathy had been the strangest one of the group. A beautiful girl who worried about her figure, worried about her complexion, worried that even in ordinary conversations she might say the wrong thing. She was driven by her insecurities and finally found a way to triumph over them, if only for a short time. She liked sex—a lot—and she was very good at it. It was in bed that she felt the most secure. It was the one place where she didn't have to worry about doing the wrong thing, because the "wrong" thing was usually the most exciting. And in bed, she had power over the boys.

According to Charlie's diaries, she spent a lot of time there.

But Charlie had been curious and didn't stop at merely reporting it. He had wanted to know why. As a fat little kid he had known what insecurity was all about—he'd had bouts of it himself—and wondered why a beautiful girl like Cathy should be insecure about anything. Her family was well off, the boys fell all over her, and she was certainly no dummy.

So, according to his diary, Charlie got himself invited over to the house for dinner and met the family. Her father had been a vice-president of Wells Fargo, her mother a socialite who went to every opera and play opening in town. She was very proud that she could call most of the singers and actors and actresses by their first names. There had been several members of the touring cast of *Jesus Christ, Superstar* at the house for dinner the night Charlie was there, and he had been properly impressed.

It was in Charlie's third diary that Artie found what he was looking for.

Cathy's great ambition in the world had been to be an actress.

But according to Charlie—Artie had no idea how he'd found out—her mother had discouraged her. Not that she disapproved of the profession, but compared to the professionals she'd met, her daughter had no talent and the mother didn't want her disgracing the family.

The lack of approval had bled into all phases of Cathy's life: she was no good at that, she was no good at anything.

But her mother's disapproval hadn't dampened her ambitions. She'd decided she needed a guru when it came to acting and she'd found one in the Club, one who'd played bit parts when touring companies filled out their casts with locals. One who had already made

inroads in the suburban theater scene playing juve-
niles.

The laugh-a-minute cutup, everybody's friend, one
who knew by heart every play on Broadway since the
Depression and could regale you for hours on end with
anecdotes that he'd plucked out of actors' biographies
and tell-all books about Broadway and Hollywood.

One who even then was talking about starting his
own theater company.

Dave Chandler.

But hardly anybody had known about Cathy's secret
desire. She had kept her ambitions under wraps until
she was "ready," and in Charlie's estimation—he'd
caught her in a minor role in a play Chandler had
directed for summer stock—she was never going to be
ready. A year later she finally bit the bullet, acknowl-
edged her lack of talent, and married Larry Shea, the
runner-up for her affections. Whatever else he was,
Chandler wasn't the marrying sort.

Had she ever gotten over Chandler, to whom she
had undoubtedly given heart, body, and soul? Charlie
Allen's precise handwriting indicated that he didn't
think so and expressed sympathy for Larry.

Artie put the diary aside and walked over to the window, watching the first signs of sleet whirl around a
street lamp outside. There wasn't any doubt that Chandler had been Cathy's first true love. And when she'd
fled her home in the Oakland hills last week and
wound up house-sitting for friends in the city, Chandler had to have been the one she'd called when the
loneliness had gotten to be too much for her. She
hadn't been afraid of him; she had trusted him im-
plicitly.

It never occurred to her that the man with whom
she had carried on a love affair for years, and in whom
she'd probably confided everything about her life—
and Larry's as well, including his latest project—was a
Hound from Hell for another species. Somebody who

regarded her with all the affection that a spectator regards a chimpanzee in the zoo.

Jesus.

It had been Dave all along, the one Artie would have voted least likely. Except that somebody had tried to dissolve Chandler's face with acid. It didn't make sense, but there was only one way to find out.

It was chilly in the room but he could feel the flop sweat start then. He and Mitch had been trying for days to find out who the Hound might be. Now he knew and he was the only one left who could go after it. Mitch had deserted him, and Charlie didn't even know what was going on.

He took a deep breath, held it for a moment, then let it out slowly and pushed everything else out of his mind. It was like going on night patrol in 'Nam, and God knew he had gone on enough of those. You never knew what was out there, who was waiting, but he had always managed to make it back. Mitch had once said that maybe whoever was the Hound should be afraid of him.

Maybe he was overmatched. But, with a little luck, maybe he wasn't.

And who was he kidding?

**It was three in** the morning, the witching hour for the city. The theaters had let out hours before, the bars had long closed, the Marina was deserted except for the occasional 7-Eleven. Artie had the cab circle the block twice to check who was on the street, then got out around the corner. There was a small side entrance leading to a walkway between Chandler's building and the one next door. It wasn't difficult to break the small lock and walk to the back. No dogs, no alarms.

Chandler's studio was three flights up.

Artie took his time climbing the stairs, slowly putting his weight on each tread so the squeak of wood wouldn't give away his presence. There were two apartments opening off the back porch, and he hesitated for a long moment, trying to decide which one was Dave's. There was a litter box outside of one door, waiting to be emptied in the morning. Did Dave keep cats? He couldn't remember any, then found a wooden slat on the porch and carefully dug into the box. It definitely hadn't been for a kitten, so the chances it was for a pet Chandler had recently acquired dropped considerably.

He worked with the lock of the other door for a minute, a simple eyebolt-and-latch affair, and managed to lift the latch with the thin blade of his pocketknife. The Manhattan mania for half a dozen dead bolts and chain locks hadn't hit this part of the Marina yet. There had been a time when almost nobody in San Francisco locked their doors and hardly anybody was ripped off, a far more innocent era that was now one with the ages.

He opened the door and slipped through, closing it noiselessly behind him. With good luck he'd find Chandler asleep; with bad luck he was probably in his theater/office watching an old movie.

He started down the long hallway that led to the front of the apartment. The office and home theater were about in the middle. It was gloomy but not completely dark; the door to the office/theater was open and the glow from the television screen suffused into the corridor enough so Artie could just make out the framed photographs and posters on the wall. Dave had been acting all of his life and was mediocre in most roles but superb in the most important one he had ever played: that of the *Homo sapiens* "Dave Chandler."

If Chandler were really the Hound.

Artie caught himself wishing desperately for Mitch Levin. With Mitch along, he'd have a decent chance. Without Mitch, he didn't stand much of one at all unless he caught Chandler by surprise and didn't make the fatal mistake of waiting. But what was he going to do, walk in and shoot Chandler where he sat? So far it was all surmise. If he were wrong, he'd spend the rest of his life regretting it. If he were right, then it was either him or Chandler—and he would have to be damned fast.

The Hound had come very close in the library. The next time, it wouldn't miss. He, Mitch, and Charlie Allen, all friends of Larry Shea's, were the only three left. And maybe Chandler, if he were wrong.

But he knew instinctively he wasn't.

A movement to his left caught his eye and he whirled. There was nothing there but one of the posters, the one of the beach scene in *From Here to Eternity*. But Burt Lancaster and Deborah Kerr were naked—and moving.

Artie swore quietly to himself. His hand holding the automatic was suddenly slick with sweat.

"It'd be easier if you turned on the lights, Artie. The switch is on the wall, a foot ahead to your right."

**Artie froze, then reached** out and flipped it on. The lights weren't blinding, as they had been in Mary's house. They were just about as bright as they would be in a theater auditorium before the feature started.

"Come on in, Artie—have a seat. Popcorn?" Chandler turned off the DVD player and the television screen flashed blue, then turned black.

*I said you'd come to me, monkey. . . .*

It was only a wisp of a thought, just enough to convince Artie he'd made no mistake. He should have shot Chandler when he came in the door but he'd hesitated a fraction of a second too long. Now he couldn't move a muscle.

Chandler was sitting behind his desk like he had been two days before. Artie stared. His voice was normal but his face was still covered with white ointment, though it obviously didn't hurt so much now because Chandler was smiling at him. Artie caught his breath. Chandler had disguised his voice the last time he and Levin had seen him. Now it was the familiar voice and a face he couldn't quite see.

Like Watch Cap at the skating rink.

"No sense in keeping this shit on any longer, though some of the neighbors might think I've made a miraculous recovery. But it wasn't for them, it was for you and Mitch." Chandler wiped at the ointment with a makeup towel. The red-furrowed, pink mask was peeping out at Artie now, and Chandler started peeling it off in strips. He had never gone to the emergency room, Artie thought. If he had, it would have been reported and Schuler would have been all over them the next day.

Then Artie stiffened. Under the makeup were raw, red scratches. The signs of Cathy's fight for life.

"I thought for sure I wouldn't fool you guys—you knew I was an actor, you knew I'd lived with makeup all my life. If you were watching a movie with special effects or a blue screen, you'd know it immediately. I guess this was just too simple." He looked at Artie in mock amazement. "And I was sure I'd blown it in the restaurant when I said I'd had lunch with Larry and he told me about his article for *Science*. Hell, you guys knew I wasn't that tight with Larry. Cathy told me about the article, what was in it." He shook his head. "A real no-no."

"What are you going to do?" Artie tried to keep the question casual but didn't succeed.

"What am I going to do? With you?" Chandler made a temple of his fingers and leaned back in his chair, his fingers directly beneath his chin. "How's your health, Artie?"

Artie could feel the sweat pop in his armpits and on his forehead.

"Fine. Why?"

282 ■ FRANK M. ROBINSON

Chandler shrugged. "Perfectly healthy people with normal checkups have heart attacks all the time. They're unpredictable. Little flaws in the pump or the circulatory system that doctors never catch beforehand. Fairly decent way to go, all things considered."

"And my body?" Artie asked.

Chandler glanced at his watch. "They're hardly going to find it here. I think the appropriate place for you to die would be home in bed, all tucked in and peaceful. A quick, painless exit from this world and the only people you'll be able to tell about me and mine will be those in the next."

"Mitch—"

"Levin? I'll catch up with him. I'm surprised you trusted him so much, Artie. You had almost as much to fear from him as you did from me. In one sense, even more."

He'd known it all along, Artie thought, he just hadn't wanted to admit it.

"He's one of you, one of the Hounds."

Chandler looked surprised. "Not one of ours, Artie. One of yours. You mean to tell me you never knew? And I thought he was one of your best friends." He studied Artie a moment. "You're something of a Hound yourself"—he shrugged, contemptuous—"but not a very good one. More of a hare."

Artie decided to try to bluff it out.

"You can't just give me a heart attack at will. . . ."

Chandler leaned across the desk and stared at him, his blue eyes hypnotic.

"Try and lift your right arm, Artie—the one holding your automatic."

Artie tried again. His right arm was as limp as spaghetti—he couldn't budge it.

"How do you do that?" He was more curious than frightened now.

"I can't tell you how, Artie. The best I can do is give you an example. Your species does it all the time, but mostly when you're kids. You're in a crowd at a theater or a store and just for fun you concentrate on the back of somebody's head and eventually they turn around in annoyance, wondering who in hell has been staring at them. A rather simplistic example of controlling somebody else with your mind. Give yourself thirty-five thousand years and you might become quite good at it. Even to the point of controlling somebody's autonomic nervous system."

"That's impossible," Artie said.

"Is it? A species can change a lot in thirty-five thousand years. You can learn to do a bunch of impossible things in that amount of time."

"And you pass it on, I suppose."

Chandler half smiled. "You have books, we have racial memory. They each have their advantages."

"Too bad you don't have a conscience," Artie said.

"Hey, good B-movie line, Artie. I'm impressed." Then, indignantly: "And you do? Jesus Christ, you were in 'Nam. Bad things happen in wars; that's the nature of them. You gave out medals for a lot worse than anything I've done. And whether you care to admit it or not, we're in a war. You and yours against me and mine. Like the IRA and the Brits, Hamas and the Israelis. You want a declaration of war? Hell, nobody declares them anymore."

"War," Artie said, feeling stupid.

Chandler looked surprised.

"War, Artie. The one that started thirty-five thousand years ago. You won all the battles back then but now it's our turn."

What did you do when the enemy looked like you, sounded like you, and wasn't wearing a uniform? It would be worse than the Civil War, much worse. You'd never know where the front lines were until it was too late.

"Cathy and the kids," Artie said slowly.

Chandler's handsome face was shadowed.

"Cathy knew more than the rest of you, and she knew it first. Whatever I did, no matter how much I stopped the leaks—Paschelke, Hall, Lyle—she was the important one who'd gotten away. I never would have found her if she'd stayed hidden. But then she called and asked me to come over." He shook his head. "I couldn't believe my luck."

"First you laid her, then you killed her," Artie said in disgust.

"I slept with the enemy and you think that was a bad thing." Chandler looked amused. "Everything's fair in love and war, Artie—it was love for her and war for me. I'm probably species amoral but then, we're not all alike any more than you're all alike. But I didn't rape her—she asked. I think she lived half her life in bed. They may be different species, but donkeys don't refuse to screw mares. And I'm sure they both enjoy it."

"And the boys?"

"They knew me, they saw me come down the stairs, and I had no idea how much they might have heard about Larry's project around the house. The stakes were too high; I couldn't take the chance. I did what was necessary."

He studied Artie's expression. "Okay, I see I'm still a monster. And you an ex-military man! Didn't the army ever give you a course in ethics? Or maybe it's morals, I'm always confusing the two—or maybe I've got the wrong word entirely. Say your platoon is lying in ambush along a roadside, waiting for the enemy. A young boy who doesn't know you're there starts across the road and doesn't see the first enemy tank coming—don't ask me why he doesn't hear it. Do you jump up and save the kid, thus giving away your position and endangering all your men, or do you let the tank run the poor kid down? Maybe it's a bad analogy, but you see what I mean."

Artie sat there, silent. Chandler suddenly hit the top

of the desk with the flat of his hand, his face grim.

"Don't talk to me about innocent bystanders, Banks! Nobody gives a shit about innocent bystanders in a war! How many women and children died in Dresden and Hiroshima and London? Tell me whether it makes a difference if you kill them face-to-face or from ten thousand feet up! I'd like to think that matters to your species, that you couldn't kill if it had to be done face-to-face. If it did, you would have had far fewer wars, wouldn't you? But then there were the ovens, and face-to-face it turned out nobody was exempt. Or go back to Agincourt, when Henry the Fifth had his soldiers slaughter the helpless French prisoners. Did you applaud in the movie when the English won? But that's right—they didn't show the slaughter of the prisoners, did they? Maybe if they had, the applause wouldn't have been quite so loud."

"That was war—"

"And what the hell do you call *this*?"

For a brief moment, Artie was back on the path by the river's edge, a member of the Tribe watching a Flat Face hold a young boy over the river and cut his throat.

"One of our racial memories," Chandler said. "Some things we wish we could forget but can't."

"That was thousands of years ago—"

"Not to us. If you're cursed with racial memories, it might as well have been yesterday, Banks."

"You have plans—" Artie started, desperate to stall.

"In the short run? To see that you have a heart attack—back home, safely in bed. It could be a lot worse. Artie. In the long run?" Chandler thought for a moment. "I'm not sure—not my department. But it's time for your species to go; nature made a mistake and it's time to rectify it. Frankly, I don't think it will be that hard. Your society is so interconnected that, technologically speaking, one man could bring it all down. But in what part of the machinery should he throw his wrench? It'll probably be something along biological lines—you're more vulnerable than you might think."

Artie didn't say anything and Chandler looked amused.

"Do you honestly believe your world can totter on for another thousand years? You know it can't, no way. Another hundred? Would you bet on it? A few years ago your Pat Robertson gave it all of five—five years to the end of your world! He's probably more correct than he thinks."

Chandler had become preoccupied with his arguments and Artie could feel a little strength flow back into his arm. He was careful not to move a muscle.

"We've been in tight spots before—"

"Meaning *Homo sapiens*? Come *on*, Banks, be real. The Black Plague nearly did you in, and that was only a few hundred years ago. You've survived this long only because you've been separated by oceans and your technology was primitive. You've tried to substitute political systems for wars and what's been the result? There hasn't been a year since World War Two without one. And each political system is convinced it's the best and anxious to convert the political heathen—by force, if necessary. Wasn't it Churchill who said that as a system democracy was crap, it was just better than any of the others?"

Artie could feel the butt of the gun in his hand and casually rested his finger on the trigger.

"What was it like, pretending to be human?"

"You mean pretending to be one of you?" Chandler leaned back in his chair, the light from the lamp illuminating the shadows of his face and reflecting off his vividly blue eyes. Artie was startled. He had never really looked at Chandler before, probably because nobody ever takes a clown seriously. Except for his slightly buck teeth, Chandler was one of the handsomest men he had ever seen. Cathy must have been obsessed with him.

"Fun, in a way. You learn what buttons to push and

you can have almost anything you want from anybody if your stomach is strong enough. You saw the photographs in the hallway? They're special, Artie—I slept with all of them. They're handsome or pretty, all of them famous, and most of you have wet dreams about them. But to be honest, few of them are any good in bed—or at much of anything else. I remember going to a party at a film convention in Vegas and by two in the morning everybody was either dead drunk or balling their brains out in the various bedrooms. I wandered into one looking for a place to crash and here was one of the biggest movie stars in the country screwing some hooker from the Strip. A big education for me, Artie. Take away the soft lights and the music and the romantic camera angles and what you've got left are smells and sweat and grunting. No whispered endearments, no tender moments. Just two animals rolling around on satin sheets rather than in the dirt." He laughed. "I know what you're going to say—'Hey, they're only human!' I couldn't agree more."

"Not as romantic as you and Cathy?" Artie said sarcastically. His finger was on the trigger and he had angled the barrel up just enough so he could catch Chandler in the groin.

Chandler shrugged.

"I suppose I meant something to her, but I never encouraged her. She fed her own fantasies. But she was a danger to us, Banks. She could have been responsible for the deaths of thousands—"

Artie tried to pull the trigger and his hand jumped slightly in the attempt. His fingers suddenly froze.

Chandler's face changed then. No longer smiling, no longer casually amused or arrogant. It was hard, furious, all angles and hollows, the lips thin bands against his large white teeth, which showed in a snarl. It was like somebody had morphed Chandler's face and White Beard's when the old chief had been angry and his heavy brows had become like stone, his eyes slitted and rimmed with red.

*you shouldn't have tried that. . . .*

Artie felt like somebody had jumped on his chest, knocking the wind out of him. He couldn't breathe and he started to struggle in his chair, then felt his sphincter give way and realized he had shit in his pants. His heart was going crazy and he could feel it tumble into a fast, erratic beating.

*your species or mine, monkey—you think I ever had a choice?*

Artie forced the chair sidewise and managed to fall to the floor and for just a moment felt the pressure on his heart lessen and his hand loosen up. He managed to get·off one shot and heard it shatter the front of the television set. But nobody would hear it outside the soundproofed room. The pressure abruptly returned and his vision started to fade, the room turning black. He was going to die right then and there. It was more than his heart now; it felt like something was tearing up his insides. His stomach was spasming with cramps and somebody's hands were squeezing the rest of his guts. In the distance he heard screaming and realized with mild surprise that it was himself.

He managed to roll behind a couch and for a second was free. He could feel a sly probing in the air around him and tried to crawl for the doorway. Then Chandler caught him again and Artie felt himself being squeezed like somebody might squeeze a balloon. It felt like his head was blowing up to a monstrous size and he could look down on the room and see himself lying on the floor and Chandler sitting calmly behind his desk, staring at him. He had no sensation of a body at all.

This was it.

Then there was the faint sound of another shot and he was back on the floor, acutely aware of his own stink. There was no pressure on his chest or guts, but he ached as if he'd run a marathon. On top of everything else, he was going to be sick from sheer exhaustion. It took a moment for him to realize he hadn't managed to get off a second shot after all. Somebody else—

"Artie!"

He was being helped off the floor and onto a chair. It took a moment for his eyes to focus.

"Charlie," he mumbled. "What the hell . . ."

He looked over at Chandler, who was slumped back in his chair, his eyes a dull watery blue with no life in them at all. Artie watched the blood pump from Chandler's chest onto his desk and then simply flow over his shirt and down to the floor.

Artie desperately wanted to get out of his clothes; he needed to shower badly. He looked up at Charlie Allen, staring in sick fascination at Chandler slumped in his chair.

"What the hell was he, Artie?"

"A hero to his own kind," Artie muttered. "To us, a homicidal maniac. Maybe we all are, depending on which side we're on."

Allen didn't know what he was talking about. "I listened to him for a couple of minutes. He never saw me—he was concentrating on you."

Artie took a breath. His heart had slowed, but it didn't seem by much.

"How did you know I was here? You must have reread your diaries after all—you must have figured it out."

Allen shook his head. "I never had time to go through them. But when I got home Franny and I started talking and she told me all about Cathy and Chandler. She was pretty hurt back then, pretty envious. She remembered everything. She insisted Cathy was still tight with Chandler. After you read the diaries, I figured you'd come right over here. Dave was a night person; he'd still be up."

Artie held his head; he had the start of a whopper

of a headache. He couldn't think straight. Not everything Charlie was saying made sense but he couldn't argue with his timing.

Charlie was looking at him with an almost belligerent expression on his face. "I'm not going to be left out this time, Artie. Larry and Cathy were friends of mine."

"He killed Cathy and the boys."

Charlie nodded sadly. "I heard him."

"Your gun," Artie said. Charlie was still holding it. "I didn't know you owned one."

Charlie looked down, surprised. His hand immediately started to tremble and he put the gun on the desk. "It isn't mine. I found it in the library months ago. Somebody had left it there, believe it or not. So I stuck it in my desk—too late to turn it in, the guard had gone home—and forgot about it. Until tonight."

He stepped closer to Chandler to look at him, and Artie was afraid Charlie was going to be sick.

"You didn't do a bad thing, Charlie, you—"

"Don't worry about me. Larry Shea was one of my best friends. So was Cathy. She played around but she was still a good person." He reached out to touch Chandler, his hand jerking back when he made contact. "I don't know how he did . . . what he did, I didn't understand a lot of what he was talking about." He glanced back at Artie, his face grim. "You're going to have to tell me, Artie. I'm serious—you owe me."

"Someday," Artie said. Then: "Take me home, Charlie. I need to shower down. I stink."

Charlie glanced around the room, frowning. Something had just occurred to him.

"Where's Mitch? I thought he'd be here with you."

# CHAPTER 22

**Mitch's house on Telegraph** Hill was eerily quiet. It was midmorning and everybody on the Hill had left for work and their maids hadn't yet arrived to clean up the mess from the night before. The BMW wasn't parked on the street above, and Artie sat in his car for twenty minutes, just watching. There had been a black-and-white at the corner and Artie guessed that Schuler was finally going to bring him and Mitch in, that too many members of the Club had died for Schuler not to think they were involved in some way. Especially with Chandler's death.

The police had left their squad car five minutes ago and sauntered down the hill to a coffee shop. They wouldn't return for a good half hour. Artie still had the keys Mitch had lent him some time back, and he let himself in the back door, hesitating a long moment for any sound of Mitch in the bathroom or his office. Nothing. Nobody. As far as Artie could tell, the house was pretty much as he had left it three mornings before. The sink had a coffee cup in it, and a rinsed-out cereal bowl sat in the drainer. Artie opened the cupboard out of curiosity. One box of bran flakes. The life story of the American male: you started with Cocoa Puffs and ended with All-Bran.

He glanced around the kitchen again and noticed the Mr. Coffee still plugged in, the little On light glowing orange. The glass carafe was half full and Artie rummaged around in the cupboard for another cup, poured some of the coffee in it, and tasted it. It was still light colored and not bitter; the unit hadn't been left on overnight. His guess was that Mitch had left the house probably not more than an hour before.

The good news was that Mitch was still alive. The bad news was that he had no idea where Mitch had gone.

Or why.

Artie wandered into the bedroom, feeling more like a spy than ever. Jesus, what was he doing here? For twenty years, Mitch Levin had been his best friend, ever since they had both collapsed in laughter watching old tapes of the Three Stooges in a crash pad just off Haight Street. For twenty years, they had been as close as brothers. He and Susan and Mitch had gone on vacations together, he had confided in Mitch about almost everything he had ever done or ever thought of doing, he had even asked Mitch to be a latter-day godfather to Mark.

He started for the door to leave, then shrugged. It was Mitch who'd failed to show up the other night, who had left him to face the Hound by himself. He didn't owe Mitch any apologies.

He glanced around the bedroom again. What the hell did he hope to find?

He hadn't been to Mitch's house all that often—when Mitch had offered to let him spend the night, he'd been surprised and touched. He couldn't remember Mitch ever throwing any parties there. But that made a sort of sense: it was easier for a bachelor to visit his married friends than the other way around. If you invited people over it meant you had to do the dishes and pick up your dirty underwear from where you'd dropped it on the floor.

He pulled open the drawers of the bureau and did a quick and careful search. Fancy-label boxers and T-shirts, a stack of carefully folded linen handkerchiefs. Along with his suits, Mitch's shirts were hung in the closet on hangers; they didn't come neatly folded with a thin paper band around them. Expensive designer shirts, Italian suits—nothing really ostentatious but enough good taste to choke on.

There were no surprises in the john. Two electric razors, one a barber's special for trimming sideburns, an electric toothbrush, a stand-up canister of Mentadent, mint-flavored Listerine, dental floss, a row of non-prescription cure-alls for headaches, constipation, and diarrhea. A small prescription container of Valium, another of Percodan. Apparently psychiatry had its occupational hazards.

One thing was missing, which left Artie puzzled. There had been no condoms in the drawer of the bedside table and there were none in the medicine chest, which surprised him. Mitch wouldn't have led a risky life in that respect. Which meant Mitch was something of an ascetic, reputation aside. Maybe it was a reputation he'd deliberately fostered, man-about-town, so none of the wives would keep asking why he didn't settle down and they knew a woman he would love to meet. Or maybe after listening to hundreds of patients over the years, he'd just turned off to sex.

Or maybe his personal life was more professional than that. Casual encounters deliberately kept casual, maybe play for pay, though in that case you'd think his medicine chest would be loaded with condoms and ditto the bed table.

But there was nothing very exotic about the average man's sexual life. It was when you looked at the emotional one that you found the variations, the odd and the unusual and the pathetic.

The largest room in the house was in the back, with a huge picture window overlooking the bay. Every home had one room for show, the one that usually sold the house to prospective buyers. Mitch had taken it and turned it into a combination office and den. The desk was separate from the computer area and clean of papers. A small table radio, a combination phone and answering machine, a notepad, desk calendar . . .

And two photographs, one a candid shot in a small, black frame and the other a studio portrait sandwiched between two sheets of clear plastic and standing upright in a black plastic base.

Artie picked up the smaller one first. The photograph was faded but he could make out a very young Captain Levin standing on the top of a small Japanese-style bridge in a city park, his arm around a young Oriental girl of perhaps sixteen or seventeen. They were both smiling for the camera. There was an inscription in the lower right corner that he could barely make out.

*Love you alway, your honeybunch Cleo . . . Saigon, 1975.*

An unlikely partner for Mitchell Levin, but there it was. A wartime romance in which Madame Butterfly had disappeared completely when the city had fallen. No way for Mitch to trace her even if he had wanted to. If he did now and succeeded he'd probably discover she was forty and graying, had a husband and three kids but no memory of Mitch from among the hundreds of GIs she'd serviced when she was a working girl so many years before.

The studio portrait was signed simply *For Mitch, all my love—Pat.* No indication who she was or what part she had played in Mitch's life, though it was obvious she must have had an important role. Artie started to replace it on the desk, then noticed a newspaper clipping taped to the back of the frame. It was dated September of 1981. A tabloid tragedy—Patricia Bailey had apparently dumped a boyfriend, who then showed up at her small carriage-house apartment late at night, dragged her into the courtyard, shot her, and then shot himself. The boyfriend had been a law student at a local university and had a history of mental instability.

Artie knew who she had dumped him for. Mitch would have had his first courses in psychiatry by then. Maybe he'd taken it upon himself to suggest she drop the old boyfriend, about whom she must have already had her doubts, and take up with good old stable, lovable Mitch. Perhaps she already had, and the old b.f. had shown up one evening after weeks of brooding about it.

Mitch had never told anybody. But it was obvious that he'd never really been a man-about-town—that had been a role he'd played, helped along by Cathy Shea's friendly praise when they were younger. In reality, he had been disappointed in love twice, and the last time must have been traumatic. After that he had become a man for whom life was all work and definitely little play. He was a top psychiatrist, but Artie now wondered whom he went to himself. It was like the quatrain from *The Rubaiyat*: "I often wonder what the Vintners buy one half so precious as the Goods they sell."

But what about the stories Mitch had told him and the others about his affairs? Not that many, not that gamey, but enough so nobody would wonder about his personal life. Or lack of it.

Artie glanced around the room, frowning. He'd overlooked something. He went back to the bedroom and opened the doors of the chiffonier. Behind them was Mitch's gun collection. Most of the guns dated from 'Nam, but the Uzi looked new and so did several of the others. All of them were polished and oiled and appeared ready for action. Disturbingly, there were four empty spaces, vague shadows on the wood indicating where the guns had been.

Artie hurried back to the closet and brushed aside the suits and shirts hanging in a neat row. At the back were a Samsonite two-suiter and several briefcases. Mitch should have had an overnight bag or two to go along with them, but there weren't any.

Among the lineup of suits and coats were several empty hangers, and Artie wondered what had been on them. One overcoat, that was for sure. Trousers, probably a jacket, and maybe a couple of sweaters.

When Mitch had left him in the Haight, he'd returned home and spent the rest of the day catching up on work and rescheduling appointments. This morning he had packed and left. For where? He'd taken an overnight bag and his car; he hadn't packed for an extended trip nor had he chosen to fly. Wherever he had gone, it was relatively close by. Not more than a day's driving, if that.

Artie wandered back to the office-den. Through the picture window he could see clouds rolling in from the ocean. The mist was turning into a light rain and he thanked God he'd stopped by the hotel to pick up his car. It would be hell trying to get a cab up there once the rain hit in earnest.

He looked around, then settled into the chair in the office area of the room. Unlike the desk, the computer table was cluttered with notebooks and a pile of opened letters. Mitch probably didn't use his computer much except for typing and maybe billing—though Artie was sure Linda did that—and E-mail. There was a small stack of it that Mitch had printed out.

Artie hesitated, then picked up the stack. If you were going to be a snoop, you might as well be thorough. He'd already checked out Mitch's sex life, or lack of one. This couldn't be any more embarrassing.

He riffled through the stack, then stopped abruptly at one message. DOD, Department of Defense. From a colonel in Intelligence, somebody Mitch had apparently kept in touch with from his 'Nam days.

No, the colonel had written, they had no information on other species, aliens, or flying saucers. But if

Mitch had proof . . . The humor was heavy-handed but friendly. Artie checked the date. A little more than a week ago. It had been sent the day after they had first talked to Paschelke. Mitch had been a true believer after all. When he'd gotten home that night, it was too late to phone so he had told his old colonel all about it via E-mail.

Artie hastily leafed through the rest of the correspondence. The ones from Washington got increasingly serious, the bantering tone dropping away. Mitch had kept them fully apprised. Paschelke's death, Hall's murder, Lyle's, Cathy's, the near suicide with the bottle of Valium and the scotch.

Artie felt his face gradually go white. There were mentions of himself, references to the various incidents he had told Mitch about. Not all the mentions were flattering, and he felt his face flush. The last E-mail said simply that the information Mitch had fed them was being bucked upstairs, but that they needed proof for the situation to be taken seriously. If Levin could offer something really solid, they would move on it immediately.

They hadn't trusted phones; they could be tapped. The E-mail had undoubtedly been encoded, and Mitch had a program for decoding when he printed it out.

Artie pulled open one of the drawers in the filing cabinet next to the table and started checking the correspondence at random. Mitch had never stopped playing the intelligence officer. He had kept a line open to Washington even after he had been mustered out, a part-time agent for the Bay Area. Attend the protest meetings for this and that—the Bay Area was full of them—and report back. He'd been something of an agent provocateur on at least one occasion. There had probably been others, but Artie didn't bother checking the rest of the files.

Even after his two true romances had fallen apart, Mitch still had a life. A lousy one.

What was it Chandler had said? That he thought Artie had as much to fear from Mitch as he did from Chandler? That he was surprised Artie had trusted Mitch? Levin, he had said, was a Hound.

For the other side.

It didn't make sense, Artie thought. He'd suggested to Mitch that they call in the Feds and Mitch had advised against it. Why? Because they hadn't known enough about what was going on? So Mitch could hog all the glory? So he could still play the game of intelligence officer?

The answer was probably simpler than that. A good Hound wouldn't trust anybody, and Mitch had never really trusted him. Mitch had wanted to watch him a little longer, see what he did, where he went, what happened to him. After Larry and Cathy, he had been the major player, and Mitch had treated him as bait.

Now Mitch had packed and split, and there was no indication of where he had gone. But after that morning, Artie knew it had to have something to do with him.

He leaned back in the chair and let the small stack of mail slip to the floor.

Twenty years of friendship had just turned to ashes. Twenty years of looking forward to nights of racquetball, to Sunday picnics, to drinking beer in one of the local bars and shooting the shit about the Good Old Days, which had never been all that good but you wanted to think they were. Susan had liked Mitch, had always looked forward to having him over for dinner. And when Mark had been younger, he'd doted on Mitch, who had played the role of uncle to perfection.

But the truth was that he'd been far more of a friend to Mitch than Mitch had ever been to him. He and Susan and Mark had been merely grist for Mitch's psychological mill, a family that provided occasional companionship and amusement but was more important as a family to be watched and studied.

For twenty years Mitch had pretended to be his best friend.

And for twenty years Mitch had lied to him.

**The campus of Bayview** Academy was deserted; apparently everybody had left for the holidays. The day had turned sunny and there were few clouds; the view of San Francisco across the bay was dazzling. With a little imagination you could almost believe the claim that when some visitors first saw the city, it struck them as something out of *The Arabian Nights*.

Artie felt tired but, for the first time in more than a week, relaxed. Schuler was probably out there looking for him but at least the Hound was dead. And then he suddenly wondered about Schuler. Had Chandler reported to anybody higher up? He must have. And who better than Schuler, who knew everything that happened in the city, who knew where the bodies were buried—literally, where people might hide, the places where people might run to. Lyle had never trusted Schuler and Artie would be a fool if he did.

Schuler was probably as good an actor as Chandler, maybe better. Probably all the Old People were. Acting, the ability to convince the observer that you were somebody else, would have become second nature. Kids were natural actors, but most of them lost the ability as they grew up. The Old People hadn't. For them the ability to masquerade as somebody else probably meant the difference between life and death. Schuler—

Paranoia. He would never be without it.

But at least he now had time to look up Susan and talk about any possible divorce. What had she chosen for grounds? The situation didn't make any sense but she wouldn't be at a loss for answers; he knew that. The immediate thing was to try to find Mark, put some pressure on Headmaster Fleming to tell him more than he had. He was Mark's father—he had a right to

know everything that Fleming knew. Somebody at the
school must know where Mark had gone.

Artie called out "Anybody home?" a couple of times,
then circled the administration building looking for
the caretaker. Nobody. At the rear, the door to the gym
hung open, creaking back and forth slightly in the
wind. Artie walked in.

The gym was empty. Even if nobody was there, he
still had expected to see the equipment, the climbing
ropes, the benches, the tumbling apparatus and tram-
poline, the barbells and exercise machines in the corner, the punching bag, the canvas-covered mats on the
floor.

It had been cleaned out. There was nothing but the
walls and the bare basketball floor.

The kitchen was as empty as the gymnasium. No
pots, no pans, no knife racks, empty china cupboards.
Artie opened several of the industrial-sized refrigera-
tors that remained. Some shreds of lettuce in one of
the bottom bins, a lone, half-filled plastic jug of spoiled
milk, half a stick of butter.

Empty, all of it gone. No silverware, no boxes of cereal, no toasters, no waffle irons, no stainless-steel trays
for the steam table.

He wandered into the big dining room. It was
cleaned out to the walls. No tables, no chairs, no steam
table, no setup for a cafeteria serving line. If he hadn't
had coffee there once, he wouldn't know the room
had ever been used as a dining hall.

The classrooms were just as barren, though the
blackboards still remained. On one of them, somebody
had chalked *Have a Merry Christmas!* and in another
room a small plastic Santa Claus dangled from a window shade. But the teachers' desks and the one-arm
student chairs were gone.

Artie hurried down to the one room he had wanted
to visit, the headmaster's office. The neatly lettered inscription on the door reading HEADMASTER: SCOTT V.

FLEMING was all that remained. The inside of the office was vacant. No desk, no lamp, no chairs, no filing cabinets.

Schools closed for the holidays but there were usually caretakers, janitors, somebody around. And the equipment was usually still in place, the tables and chairs still there, the library still had books, the gym still had its equipment, the dining hall its steam table and the kitchen its pots and pans and knives.

Bayview Academy hadn't closed for the holidays.

It had closed, period.

He walked outside to go back to his car when behind him, a familiar voice said, "What are you doing here?"

Artie turned. Collins.

"I could ask the same of you, Collins."

The boy studied him, wary.

"You didn't get the notice?"

"What notice?"

"The school's closed for good. The notices were sent out a week ago."

If Susan had gotten one, she would have told him. Christmas deliveries, the mails were slow.

"I haven't been home the last few days." But if the school had been due to close, it would have been discussed with the parents months ago to give them time to make other arrangements. He knew from experience there weren't that many schools for handicapped kids. "Kind of sudden, wasn't it?"

Collins shrugged. "I thought everybody knew."

Everybody but himself, Artie thought.

"They cleaned it out in a hurry, didn't they?"

Another shrug and Collins looked vague. He was an expert at looking vague.

"After the buildings and grounds were sold, I guess they sold the furnishings and equipment."

They'd had a week to do it, Artie thought. Everything was probably on consignment with an auction warehouse, and in another week or two there would be an ad in some newspaper. Or maybe a trade magazine that covered institutions; they would be the logical buyers.

"Somebody liked the view," Collins added. "I think they're going to turn the campus into a resort complex like the Claremont."

The breeze had started to pick up and Artie buttoned his coat. Collins was wearing a wool sweater and the sudden chill to the air didn't seem to bother him.

"You haven't told me what you're doing here, Collins. School's out—in more ways than one. Why hang around?"

Collins was staring out at the bay. He didn't look at Artie and Artie guessed that he didn't like being asked questions. When he was seventeen he hadn't liked talking to strangers either.

"Mr. Fleming asked me to drop around every few days, check for vandalism."

Artie didn't believe him. Collins was there because *he* was there.

"What does he care? It's been sold."

Another faint shrug. "I dunno, maybe the final papers haven't been signed yet."

When he'd seen the gymnasium door standing open, Artie had guessed that the school had closed for the holidays but had hoped that Fleming would still be there. When he hadn't seen anybody around, he'd thought of breaking into Fleming's office and going through the filing cabinets to see what records they kept on Mark. Maybe something in them would have given him a clue.

Now there was nothing at all. Except Collins, who had been something more than just a friend to Mark. Had Mark confided in Collins? And if so, what had he told him? Had he talked to Collins about running away, about the girl he was presumably running away with?

Hell, he must have. Kids didn't talk to their parents,

they talked to each other, and a lot of what they thought they knew about the world they got from other kids as ignorant as themselves. He had, and so had everybody else he'd ever known. It took a lifetime to figure things out as they really were.

He'd expected Collins to turn and walk away but the boy had jammed his left fist in the pocket of his sweater and was staring out at San Francisco across the bay. He was, Artie suddenly realized, waiting.

"What's your father do, Collins?"

"Nothing fancy, Mr. Banks." Collins started to walk back to the gymnasium. Artie didn't move. If Collins was really cutting him off, he'd chase after the little bastard and find out what he knew about Mark if he had to beat him bloody.

A dozen steps away, Collins stopped and waited for him to catch up.

They walked into the gymnasium together. Collins pulled the door closed after him. It was still cold—there was no heat in the empty building—but at least they were out of the wind.

Collins sat on the floor with his back to the wall. He pulled his legs up, gripped his right hand with his left, and wrapped his arms around his knees. Artie sat a few feet away.

"Your father, Collins."

"I told you, nothing fancy—we're not rich. He's in construction." He hesitated, as if he were trying to remember. "Dry wall, I think."

Artie stared at him.

"Like the character in *Roseanne*."

"The old TV show? I never watched it."

"You're putting me on, right, Collins?" He didn't try to keep the menace out of his voice.

Collins managed to look both surprised and hurt. "I told you it was nothing fancy, that we weren't rich."

Artie turned away. "Right. Sorry, Collins."

It was time for Collins to get up and split, saying he

had to be back home. Collins didn't move.

"Where is he, Collins?"

Collins picked at his shoelaces.

"Where's who?"

"Mark."

Collins shrugged. "I wouldn't tell you if I knew. I wouldn't rat on Mark."

Collins knew all right. He was lying. Artie pulled the automatic out of his pocket and placed it on the floor in front of him, out of Collins' reach or where his feet might kick it away.

"Mark is my son," Artie said quietly. "I will do absolutely anything to find out where he is. Do you understand, Collins? We're all alone; nobody saw me drive up. I don't think anybody will see me drive away."

Collins didn't look impressed.

"Then I couldn't tell you anything, could I?"

Artie kicked the gun across the floor and held his head in his hands.

"Okay, Collins, beat it."

Collins didn't move.

Collins was a lock and there had to be a key, Artie thought. Did he know where Mark had gone? Yes. Was Collins going to tell him? No. Why? Because Mark had told him not to tell anybody. But there was a key and Collins was waiting for him to use it.

Then he had the answer. All Collins really needed was an excuse.

"You love Mark, don't you, Collins?"

Collins nodded, mute.

"I don't care what happened," Artie said.

"I told you. Not much." Collins looked like he wanted to cry.

"Collins." Artie hesitated. "I can't tell you everything that's been going on but I can tell you one thing. I don't give a damn if Mark has chased off for a week's fling. More power to him—I had my own when I was his age."

He thought momentarily about Mary and wondered if his brief affair constituted a fling and if it had been anything like that for Mark. He doubted it; Mark seemed much more pragmatic about sex than he had ever been.

"I want to find Mark," Artie continued, "because his life's in danger."

Collins looked worried. "Medication?"

Artie shook his head. "No."

Collins said quietly, "Look me in the eyes and tell me his life's in danger."

Kid stuff, Artie thought with surprise; Collins was older than that. Then he looked into Collins' eyes and changed his mind. The boy's eyes were a steady gray, his face expressionless, and Artie had the uncomfortable feeling that Collins could tell a lie from the truth at a glance. For a moment all Artie could think about was Cathy and James and Andy and Chandler's face just before Charlie Allen had shot him. There was a chance, maybe only a small chance, that another Hound for the Old People would come after him and by extension Susan and Mark. He wasn't out of it; he'd probably never be out of it. But he desperately wanted them out of it. At the very least he owed it to them to tell them what they faced. There were no innocent bystanders, Chandler had made that pretty clear.

Artie said, "His life's in danger, Collins."

Collins stared at him a moment longer, then glanced away.

"Mark went up to Willow. To meet his mother."

"When?"

"This morning. A friend drove him up."

Nobody had answered when he'd called; communications had broken down somewhere up there. Mark's weeklong fling was over, but Artie had the oppressive feeling that Mark was driving into danger and Susan was probably up to her neck in it.

He stood up.

"Thanks, Collins."

What he had told Collins was the truth and it had been the key that had released Collins from whatever promise he'd given Mark. The thing that bothered Artie was the small expression of satisfaction on Collins' face just before the boy had turned away.

# CHAPTER 23

**It was a long** day's trip to Willow and it was getting dark by the time Artie drove into town. He hadn't bothered to pack anything—just stopped at an ATM to pick up several hundred dollars, then hit the road. He could buy a toothbrush when he got there and rinse his shorts out in the sink at some motel.

He'd never been close to Susan's parents, Harold and Sharon Albright. They'd been at the wedding, but they'd been openly hostile to him and he'd never visited them. For whatever reason, they hadn't approved of the marriage and made it plain they didn't care to see much of him. He'd obliged them, and Susan had taken care of the parental obligations, remembering them at Christmas and sending out birthday cards, calling occasionally, though Artie couldn't remember any time when *they* had called until the week or so ago when Susan's mother had phoned to say her father wasn't doing well. They had never sent cards or presents, not even at Christmas, not even to Mark.

Chalk one up for Mark: he'd never complained about them. Occasionally when Susan had visited them she had taken Mark along, but Mark never had much to say about them afterward. Probably out of deference to him.

Willow was a little town of a thousand at the foot of the Cascades. A Motel 6 on the outskirts, then a three-block-long Main Street with a clothing store and two small restaurants, a combination gift shop and bookstore, a small grocery plus some shops catering to occasional tourists.

Artie glanced at his watch—almost dinnertime. But if he showed up at the Albrights in time to eat, he knew damned well Susan's mother would be annoyed.

He parked in front of a little restaurant that had red-checked curtains in the window. The cold evening air cut through his thin jacket and half a foot of snow crunched under his shoes when he got out of the car. He should have taken the time at least to grab a sweater before leaving.

Inside, the restaurant was small but spotless, with half a dozen tables and a counter with eight stools. Only one of them was occupied—an old man reading a copy of what looked like the county weekly. Two teenagers were in back playing a pinball machine, and a middle-aged couple with two kids sat at a table along the side.

It looked very comfortable, very cozy.

Artie picked a table close to the front door. They probably didn't have much business this time of year, so there wouldn't be a draft with people running in and out. The table was covered with oilcloth that matched the curtains, the menu neatly typed and inserted in a little clip holder that also held an ad for Budweiser.

It was the little things that counted, Artie thought. The ketchup and mustard bottles were full, the tops carefully wiped off. And there were no signs of the previous diner on the oilcloth. It was a high-class establishment for a small town.

"Hi, stranger. What can I get you?"

She was chubby and smiling, midthirties, hair done up in a loose bun, wearing a spotless white apron and holding a little notepad, ready for his order.

Artie looked at the menu without really seeing it. "Any recommendations?"

"Everything's good." She pointed to one of the items. "I had the ham and sweets earlier this evening. The green beans are frozen but the biscuits and gravy were made tonight." Another smile. "Try the apple pie for dessert—my mother bakes it special."

"You own the place?"

"Me and Terry—he works the kitchen, I wait the tables. Good division of labor."

Artie had glimpsed a thickset man in a white apron in the kitchen just off the dining area. He'd caught Artie's eye when he came in, flashed a smile, then went back to his stove.

Friendly town, even the dogs were friendly. A shaggy collie lying on the floor at the far end of the counter had eyed him when he first came in, then went back to dozing.

The waitress left a copy of the paper for him to read while he waited, and Artie leafed through it. The usual small-town board meetings, apparently centering around getting prepared for a sudden influx of visitors. It didn't say why or when, but then small towns probably spent most of the winter getting ready for the rest of the year unless they were ski resorts.

The ham and sweet potatoes were the best Artie ever had—the hogs were raised on a farm just down the pike, the waitress said, and the farmer did his own slaughtering. The biscuits and gravy melted in his mouth, and the cook had even done something special to the beans. The apple pie was superb, and Artie ordered another slice, which he couldn't quite finish.

When he had finished the meal, he felt stuffed. There was nothing he wanted more than to go back to the motel and collapse on the bed—except one thing: to see Susan and Mark.

He dawdled over his coffee and stared around the

restaurant again. The kids in back were still going at it, the old man at the counter had been replaced by two giggling girls of high school age, and the middle-aged couple and their two kids had been exchanged for a younger family with a baby in a high chair.

Middle America, Artie thought.

Norman Rockwell country.

He paid his check, then just before leaving turned to the waitress and asked, "Do you have a hospital in town?"

She looked alarmed. "You sick?"

"Just wanting to check on a friend."

"We're kind of small for a hospital. Doc Ryan has something of a clinic—two or three beds—his wife helps out as his nurse. But that's the closest we come. Anything really serious, LifeFlight flies them to Redding or Eureka or some bigger town, depending on what's wrong." She looked dubious. "I didn't know Doc had an overnighter but you can never tell, I guess."

He hadn't really expected there would be a hospital in Willow. When he'd called they had told him there was only a clinic and old man Albright wasn't there. He'd hoped there had been a mistake and now it looked like there wasn't. Maybe Willow was a dry hole after all.

"We had one last year—young tourist girl was lost in the brush. It was three days before they found her and she was suffering from exposure pretty bad. I think they flew her to Redding for treatment."

Artie got the doctor's address, then went outside and stood on the sidewalk for a moment, filling his lungs with the chill night air.

Beautiful little town. He should have found an excuse to come up with Susan more often; the hell with her parents.

He started for his car, then glanced back at the restaurant. Not a gourmet's paradise, but some of the best food he'd had in years. He could see through the windows that the boys in back were still playing pinball, the young couple were spoon-feeding the baby, and the girls at the counter had their heads together in animated conversation.

Norman Rockwell country all right.

Kids in the city playing pinball wouldn't be nearly that quiet and well behaved.

**The Albright home was** a small, white clapboard house with a neatly tended lawn in front, familiar from the photographs Susan had shown him. Even in the dusk Artie could see it was well kept up. An old black Chevy in the driveway, a swing on the front porch, doghouse to the side.

The porch light was on and so were lights in the living room. Artie took a deep breath, got out of the car, and crunched through the snow to the door. It opened on the second ring.

"Yes?"

The man who answered certainly wasn't Harold Albright. He was twenty years too young and twenty pounds too thin. And friendly. He was still holding the paper he'd been reading and looked at Artie expectantly.

"I was looking for the Albrights," Artie said, expecting to be told that the whole family was up in Eureka or Redding because of the old man's illness and friends were house-sitting for him.

The man in the doorway looked apologetic.

"Sorry, but nobody by that name lives here, Mister."

Artie stared at him, not sure what to say.

"They . . . used to some years back." He hesitated, uncertain. "You have any idea where they might have gone?"

Somewhere in the house behind him a woman's voice said reprovingly, "Ask him in, Tom. It's cold out there—he'll catch his death."

The man opened the door wider.

"Come on in. No sense letting all the heat out."

Artie carefully wiped his shoes on the doormat. On the inside, the house had all the warm, rustic appeal of a country bed-and-breakfast. A slender woman in her forties was sitting on the couch knitting. She looked up at him over the tops of her glasses, then stood up, waiting to be introduced.

"My wife, Maude." Her husband turned his head slightly. "Maudie, our friend here is looking for the Albrights. You ever heard of them? Apparently they used to live in this house."

She shook her head, frowning and trying to look helpful at the same time. "Name doesn't ring a bell."

The man turned back to Artie and shrugged. "We bought the place seven years ago from the Mac-Dougalls. Got no idea who owned it before them." Still friendly but curious, "Why you looking for the Albrights?"

"I'm married to one of them—their daughter. She came up to visit them and I said I'd follow on the weekend." Artie started to back away toward the door. "Must have got the address wrong."

"Sorry, Mister." He looked genuinely regretful when he said it. "Ask at the gas station just out of town—they usually know where everybody lives."

He should have asked the waitress, Artie thought. She would've known. But then he had an even better source of information: the doctor.

In the door, Artie paused and said, "Thanks—thanks a lot." He turned and trudged back to his car. Friendly couple, but for a small town you would have expected them to have asked more questions, or else to have been curt and slammed the door in his face.

**The doctor looked like** he might have stepped out of an old Marcus Welby television show, white-haired, late sixties, ruddy-cheeked. And, like everybody else Artie had met, he went out of his way to be friendly and helpful.

"Hal Albright in the hospital?" He looked mystified. "I didn't even know the old coot was sick. Who told you that?"

He invited Artie into the living room, one with lace curtains and old, dark oak furniture whose legs had been carved or decorated. A lamp with a beaded fringe stood guard over the ancient rolltop desk and there were lace doilies on the arms of the big easy chair the doctor sat in and on those of the couch.

"My wife—I'm married to their daughter. Her mother called up and said that Hal was in a bad way, that he was in the hospital."

The doctor squinted at him, suddenly making the connection. "You're the fella who called, aren't cha?" Artie nodded. "Well, if Hal was in a bad way, he sure wasn't here then. Most serious thing I've handled aside from births and emergencies was an appendectomy with Liz handling the anesthesia." He turned and hollered to his wife in the kitchen. "Lizzie, that coffee ready yet?" Then back to Artie. "Your wife say what was wrong with him?"

Artie shook his head. "It was a short conversation. She sounded under a lot of stress. Maybe it was something the doctors hadn't diagnosed yet."

The doctor motioned him to a chair. "How's Susan? I haven't seen her in a coon's age. I remember when she was a little girl, all pigtails and energy."

Artie stared at him. Susan had gone up there, but the doctor, who should know everything in town, hadn't seen her or even heard she was around. Something was falling apart, Artie thought. If her father was as sick as Susan had implied, they would have airlifted him out to a hospital in a bigger town. Maybe Susan had called from a nearby city—one with a hospital— and just forgotten to tell him. But Mark would certainly have checked with her, would have known where she was. He wouldn't have driven all the way to Willow for nothing.

"I haven't seen her father in years," Artie said slowly. "We never got along very well; I never came with her when she visited him. I went to the address I had and they're not there. The couple in the house had never heard of them."

The doctor frowned.

"Your wife never told you her folks had moved or where to?"

Liz bustled in from the kitchen with coffee and a small plate with slices of coffee cake on it. "Thanks, Lizzie." They sipped their coffee in silence until she retreated to the kitchen.

"Sounds like you and your wife are having a bit of trouble." Ryan shook his head. "Not my business, of course."

"We're thinking of divorce," Artie said, surprised how painful it sounded when he mentioned it aloud. "That's what I drove up to see her about."

"Divorce." The doctor concentrated on his coffee cake. "Bad business, divorce."

"You know where they moved to?" Artie asked.

The doctor looked at him shrewdly.

"I'm taking a lot on faith, young man. How do I know you're who you say you are?"

"If you know their phone number, you could call them," Artie suggested. "Talk to Susan."

"I suppose I could do that." Ryan put down his coffee cake and walked to the phone on the desk and dialed. He waited for a long minute, then finally hung up. "Out of luck, young fella, just the damned machine. Nobody's home, or else they're not answering, which would be unusual for these parts."

"I need to see her," Artie said desperately.

The doctor hesitated, then said, "Let me see your driver's license."

Artie pulled it out and the doctor checked it over,

squinting at Artie to see if he matched the photograph. He wrote some information on a piece of paper.

"Just in case anything happens, the state police will know who to look for. Sorry if all this seems unfriendly, but all I've got is your word and I don't know you from Adam." He scribbled something on another piece of paper and gave it to Artie.

"The Albrights moved out of town, oh, I'd say ten years or more ago. Didn't ask why, they never told me—but Hal just never got along with people. Their place is back in the woods a ways, five miles out on Route 89. A little county road connects just about there. There's a white mailbox at the front of the driveway, can't miss it. They're about a hundred feet in, sort of a fancy log-cabin affair."

Artie stood up, tucking the piece of paper in his pocket.

"Thanks a lot, Doctor."

Ryan clapped him on the shoulder.

"Glad to help, son—sorry if I came across as too suspicious. Try and talk your wife out of that divorce— only people who benefit are the lawyers."

Artie left and drove slowly through the few blocks of the business district. A sweet shoppe—they even spelled it with two "p"s—with three or four cars out front, the type his father used to call jalopies. Young kids huddled in the booths, and Artie could hear music blaring from the jukebox but no rock, no rap. The residential part of town was a few blocks of old wooden houses with porches and dormers and big lawns, now covered with snow. There was a small brick schoolhouse, and right before the town ended and the woods began, a classic white painted church with a tall steeple and a cross silhouetted against the starlit sky.

Artie was on a slight rise and pulled over to the side of the road, stopping to look back. The perfect dinner in the perfect small-town restaurant with perfect small-town customers. The motherly waitress, the friendly

cook, the well-behaved kids playing the pinball machine, the friendly couple who didn't know where the
Albrights had gone and were genuinely sorry they
didn't know, the country doctor right out of central
casting.

A small village on a starry night, the snow softly falling, holiday lights twinkling in the windows below. It
could have been the model for a Hallmark Christmas
card.

A village right out of the nostalgic past with people
to match, everybody in costume and playing their
parts, like the characters at Disneyland.

If you were driving up Highway One along the coast,
Willow might not have looked out of place next to Car-
mel or Mendocino, pretty little towns overrun with cars
and noisy kids and chockablock with tourist traps. But
inland, you got a different type of small town. Old
working towns with an ancient grain elevator or lum-
bermill and the occasional dilapidated tractor sitting
in a farmer's front yard, roadhouses with a dozen pick-
ups and beat-up cars parked out front with large furry
dice or small plastic skeletons jiggling in the rear window.

In the back of Artie's head a flag went up.

Willow was too good to be true. It was in the wrong
place to be what it seemed to be—a picture-perfect
tourist town—when there was no lake or mountain or
seashore nearby to draw the tourists.

What was the old expression? A Potemkin village:
one of the fake villages that Catherine the Great's lover
built along the roads she traveled so she would never
see the poverty of the peasants.

Willow was a Potemkin village.

A few days ago somebody had given him a guided
tour of the Old People in the city. But they were in the
country, too.

In one sense, Willow wasn't a village at all.

It was a nest.

A nest of the Old People.

And then he took one last look and changed his mind. It was probably an experimental village by, of, and for the Old People. An example of what the whole world could have been like if *Homo sapiens* hadn't fucked it up.

# CHAPTER 24

The white mailbox was just where the doctor had said it would be, a few yards beyond the intersection of Route 89 with the county blacktop. Artie could see the driveway and the shadowy form of the house, the lights on in the living room downstairs. Nobody had answered the phone but somebody was home, or maybe they'd just left the lights on to make people think they were, a standard ploy in the city.

He cut the engine a hundred yards away and watched for a few minutes, then got silently out of his car and started up the road. There was a car in the driveway and he knew by the blocky outline that it was Susan's old Volvo. Hers was the only car there, which meant Susan was home unless she'd gone out with her mother and father for the evening. A few steps farther and he walked across the intersection with the county road. He automatically glanced down it, then abruptly stopped. There was another car on the road, he could tell by its silhouette against the starry sky. It had been parked about as far away from the Albright house as his, and for the same reason. The driver had probably killed his engine at the top of a small hill and coasted down the slight incline to a stop, trying to keep his approach as silent as possible.

Artie hesitated, felt for the reassuring bulge of the automatic in his pocket, and walked up the road to the car.

Mitch's BMW. He had driven around the town on the back roads because he didn't want to be seen. A BMW in a small country town would be a little hard to forget.

Artie felt like somebody had slugged him in the stomach. He'd probably been as blind as Larry. It had been a nice, little, incestuous club—everybody had been balling everybody else. Susan and Mitch had probably been a number back then. And they probably still were. Nobody would have told him, any more than they would have told Larry about Cathy.

And now Mitch had done what he hadn't been able to do. He'd found Susan and immediately gone up to see her.

Artie felt sweaty and sick. Why hadn't Mitch told him he was driving up? Because Mitch hadn't wanted him to know. After the phone call he'd made the previous morning, Mitch hadn't told him anything. Maybe Susan had left a message on his machine telling Mitch where she was staying.

Artie turned to the house and walked quietly across the lawn, keeping out of a direct line of sight with the front windows. With good luck, it would turn out that Susan's father was too mean to keep a dog. At least he prayed he didn't.

He sidled up to the edge of one of the living room windows and looked in. He felt the sweat start all over then. Mitch was seated with his back to the front door, Susan and Mark were sitting together on the couch, Mark with his arm around his mother. Mitch was talking but Artie couldn't make out what he was saying.

What the hell should he do? Artie wondered. Go around to the rear of the house and hope the back door was open? Crash through the window? Break down the front door?

He walked to the front door and rang the bell.

There was a pause, and then Mitch said in a loud voice, "Come on in, Banks—door's open."

Mitch was using his Captain Levin voice and Artie felt a momentary flash of relief. He wasn't interrupting lovers. This was about . . . something else. He tried the knob and walked in. Mitch was seated in a big easy chair, his legs crossed, relaxed and in charge. Susan and Mark sat on the floral-printed couch, both of them looking pale and frightened.

It was the same scene that Artie had glimpsed from the window except now he could see that Mitch was wearing his camouflage fatigues and had a gun in his hand. Strangely enough, over by the couch where Susan and Mark sat, no crutches or wheelchairs were in sight.

It was a different scene from the one he'd expected. One that didn't make much sense.

Cautiously Artie asked, "How did you know it was me, Mitch?"

"Just a guess—the old folks had left for the evening and I couldn't think of anybody else it might be. I don't think people drop in at this time of night without calling first." He looked curious. "That was you a few minutes ago, wasn't it?"

Mitch must have watched the house until Susan's parents had left and he knew Susan and Mark were alone.

"That's right." Artie glanced from Mitch to Mark and Susan and then back again. This time he took a closer look and felt the blood drain from his face. There were bruises and an open cut on Mark's cheek. Mitch had pistol-whipped him, one of the first steps in breaking down a prisoner.

"What the hell's going on?"

Mitch cracked a thin smile.

"Good question, Banks, one I came up here to find the answer to. And I think I have." He waved the gun at Mark. "Stand up, son. Take a few steps forward."

Mark looked shame-faced at Artie, then stood up, took a few steps, and sat back down.

"That should give you a clue, Banks."

Mark was taller than Artie had thought. How many years had it been since he'd seen Mark stand up straight, without leaning on crutches? Since he was twelve? For five years it had all been pretense, an act. Mark could probably walk and run with the best of them.

Artie's first reaction was to try to hold back tears, grateful that Mark wasn't crippled after all. But why?

"Things weren't quite how they appeared, Banks. Apparently, they never have been."

Artie looked at Susan, at the agony and fear on her face, then over at Mark, who was trying to keep a poker face but was plainly scared to death.

"What's going on?" Artie repeated. His voice was empty of emotion.

Levin dug in his pocket with his free hand and pulled something out. He held it up to the light so Artie could see it. Mark's earring, the one that Collins had given him a few days ago and that Mitch had borrowed to show a friend.

Artie glanced at it.

"Was it really Mayan?"

"A little older than that, Banks. My friend had it dated—it goes back something like thirty-five thousand years. You said it was a family heirloom, right?"

Artie could feel the hair stand up on the back of his neck. That had been the call Levin got on Haight Street. His friend had left a message about the date and Levin had called back to confirm it.

"That's what I was told."

Levin's expression was sardonic. "Apparently the family tree goes back a ways. But the boy's not yours, so it looks like you're strictly a recent graft. Did you and she"—he waved his pistol at Susan—"ever try to have children?"

"Susan said she couldn't."

"Oh, I think she probably could. The children would have been sterile, of course."

Artie took a breath.

"What are you trying to say?"

Levin stared at him in mock surprise.

"Christ, Banks. All the time you're looking for the Old People and they're right under your nose—you married one of them. Sort of like Jenny and Mary, though I suspect Jenny knew what she was getting into and you didn't. Right?"

Artie looked over at Susan and didn't know what he felt—relief at finally finding her, anger at the deception. She'd never told him she loved him because she never had. She wouldn't have been able to, even if she had wanted. And he was sure she'd never wanted.

"That right, Susan?"

Her face was expressionless, her eyes bleak. He had seen the expression once before, on the faces of the members of the Tribe when they were being massacred on the riverbank. None of them had expected mercy.

It was Mark who said quietly, "That's right, Artie."

For fifteen years his life had been a sham. Susan had married him, but not for love, and he had no idea what other reasons she might have had. At the time she'd certainly had her choice of men. Why him?

"How'd you find them, Levin?"

"You said Susan had left for Willow. Then you said she hadn't. Logical thing to do was check out Willow anyway, find out where her parents lived and pay them a visit. We"—Artie knew he meant the DOD—"went through the records. She never used her regular credit cards after she left San Francisco, but she had a Shell card and used that—it wasn't a joint card, it was in her name only. She bought gas twice on the way up and after that it was simply connect the dots. The manager at the Shell station just outside town had an address for the old folks."

How easy, Artie thought. But then Levin had the resources of the federal government. Chandler had been right. Levin was a Hound. For the other side.

Levin glanced at Artie, curious. "You drive through town?"

Artie nodded.

"I guessed it would be full of them—Christ, they had to be someplace—so I circled and came in from the back. I was right, wasn't I? The town's a staging area."

"In a sense," Artie said bleakly.

He was staring at Susan and Mark and trying to figure out the emotions that kept welling up in him. His marriage had been a sham; they had deliberately used him. As a cover, as a convenience. But why had they picked on him?

What had Susan told him about Mark's biological father? Killed in an industrial accident of some sort? He had never pushed her for details; it had obviously been painful for her. Painful because Mark's father must have been the man she had really loved, had probably never gotten over.

Levin glanced at his watch. "I figure we've got an hour."

Artie suddenly felt apprehensive.

"An hour for what?"

"Backup, Banks. There should be at least two choppers on their way; I phoned in and left a message for my old colonel. We can sweat the people in town after we get the proof back to Washington."

"Proof," Artie repeated, feeling stupid.

Levin nodded at Susan and Mark.

"Them. Government doctors and psychiatrists will examine them. There won't be any secrets then." Levin leaned back in his chair, the hand holding his gun never wavering, and whistled. "For thirty-five thousand years they've lived among us, Banks. Think of that. And nobody knew, nobody suspected."

Mark shifted on the couch and Levin was suddenly on the edge of his chair. "Don't try anything, son. The doctors can do an autopsy when you're dead. They'll take you apart bone by bone, do X rays and CAT scans and blood tests and come up with just as much information as they could if you were alive."

"Be careful, Levin. He's my son," Artie said in a dead voice.

Imagine the genocide, Mary had said.

The expression on Levin's face was one of genuine pity.

"I feel for you, Banks, I really do. You lived with them for fifteen years and from everything you said it was a happy marriage. But they were using you, can't you see that? It was probably the same all over the country, infiltration. Married to you, why should anybody suspect them? But don't forget, Cathy Shea left town the night of Larry's murder, and your wife left for Willow the next morning. Ask yourself why. Because she knew what was coming down? You were almost killed too. Being married to you was protection for her—it wasn't protection for you. Think she shed any tears over the possibility? You knew too much, even though you didn't think you did. She could have asked you to go to Willow with her but she didn't. She told you her father was sick; you could have gotten time off from work."

He studied Artie, reading the expressions flitting across his face. It's what Levin had done in 'Nam, Artie thought. It's what he did for a living in the States. The ace psychiatrist who listened to his patients and watched the flood of emotions on their faces and read them like a book.

Artie tried his best to look blank-faced. He'd had his own experiences in 'Nam, too, including the three months in a Charlie prison camp until he'd managed to escape. He'd learned to hide his feelings then.

"She didn't want you along," Levin continued, "but she wanted the boy, didn't she?"

Levin was an expert at painting the picture of a wasted marriage, of betrayal, but of necessity it was a distorted portrait. He had been there; Levin hadn't.

"Banks." In the light from the lamp, Levin looked hostile. "She's a different *species*. She's as different from you as you are from an ape. It doesn't take a military genius to figure out we're in a war. What do you think they want? Easy answer: They want their world back. The losers always want to turn back the clock. How do you think they'll get it? How *can* they get it? By eliminating us. It's the only way." He turned cajoling. "We're in a war, Artie, and war is vicious and brutal— you know that. Think of Dr. Paschelke and Professor Hall, Lyle, poor Cathy and the kids. Tell me what compassion they were shown."

"It was the Hound—" Mark started feebly.

"Shut up, son. You talk when I tell you to."

Captain Levin, Artie thought again. Levin loved it. And then he had a flash of guilt. So had he when he was in 'Nam, but not in the same way. He had loved the danger, the hunt. Levin had loved the kill. After you got out, you pushed it out of your mind. Everybody had done things they weren't proud of. But he guessed Levin had never forgotten it and never worried about it. He'd slipped into the friendly, slightly sardonic role of psychiatrist with no trouble at all. And Artie had taken him at face value. The Captain Levin in 'Nam had gradually become a vague memory. Now here he was, come back to life, the 'Nam Levin whom Artie had never really liked. The captain who inspired both admiration and horror. The captain who loved his job too well.

Levin was still staring at Mark.

"There're no Germans here but us good Germans, that it?"

The river's edge, Artie thought. The young boy being held over the rushing waters while his throat was
cut. For a brief time he had been a member of the
Tribe, he had been one of *them*, and they had been . . .
had been . . . What? Human. Very human. Even Professor Hall had suggested that.

"What are you going to do with them?"

"These two?"

"All of them."

Levin shrugged. "I imagine we'll develop DNA tests
so we can identify them. I suppose they'll be camps for
them, like there were for the Nisei during World War
Two."

"Gas chambers, Levin? Down the road?"

"Christ, Banks, what the hell are you thinking of?"

He couldn't tell whether Levin was really shocked or
not. Everybody had committed genocide at one time
or another, Artie thought. Nobody had clean hands.
And then he realized that after all of this was over,
Levin would be a hero. And he thought of Mary again:
*If you want to know what you were like in the past, look at
what you are today.*

"Susan's my wife," Artie said slowly. "Mark's my son."

Levin's eyes narrowed.

"Do you remember what Cathy looked like?" he
asked softly. "James and Andy? Their Hound did that,
all by himself—no proxy murder that time. Remember
Lyle? Nobody liked Lyle, but he didn't deserve what
happened to him. And Paschelke and Hall, did they
deserve it? And what about yourself? You almost did a
swan dive off your rear balcony—three stories up onto
concrete, Artie. Think you would have survived? They
would have picked you up with a blotter." He waved
his gun at Susan and Mark again. "Do you think they
would have shed any tears?"

That was one of the few things he had never told
Levin. That somebody had cried "Dad!" and the next
thing he knew Mark had pulled him off the railing and

was kneeling over him on the porch, the rain beating in his face, his wheelchair left behind in the doorway. Mark had dropped the pretense to save him; he had risked betraying his own species to do so.

"We can't give up the world, Banks—you know that. For events that only anthropologists care about, events that happened thirty-five thousand years ago? It's tragic but it's simple. It's us versus Professor Hall's Old People. Do you think they would let us live?"

No, Artie thought bleakly, no they wouldn't. They couldn't. But that didn't stop him from loving Susan and Mark. He'd always loved them more than they loved him, always would. That equation hadn't changed.

Or had it? In the back of his mind, a part of him was wavering.

Levin shrugged again.

"It's war, Artie. When you look at the world twenty years from now, what do you want to see?"

Garbage world, Artie thought chaotically. Poisoned streams, empty oceans, thousands of species that had died and hundreds of others that existed only in the concrete and steel confines of a zoo.

Levin cocked his head, listening.

"The choppers are coming."

Artie thought he heard something in the distance but he wasn't sure Levin was right; he'd served in 'Nam too long to be mistaken. Enlisted men knew the sound of choppers better than officers, probably because they spent more time in the front lines.

Mark suddenly lunged off the couch in a desperate leap at Levin. Susan screamed. Levin fired once and Mark crumpled to the floor.

For a split second time was stationary, impressions and thoughts flashing through Artie's mind. Levin would take Susan and Mark back to Washington and he would be the interrogator, the one who always got the information he wanted but whose methods would make you sick. Levin would ask Susan and Mark to identify the Hounds. He would never believe them when they said they couldn't. Captain Levin was firmly convinced there was always an answer, that there *had* to be an answer.

Artie fired twice then, right through his jacket pocket. His first shot hit the bulb in the lamp and the room abruptly went dark. There were only the stars and a full moon lighting up the room now—just enough moonlight to glint off the frame of Mitch's granny glasses.

After all these days of doubt and indecision, Artie finally knew exactly who he was and where his loyalties lay. Above all else, he was a man whose whole life was his family. How in the world could Mitch have misjudged that?

His second shot shattered the left lens of Mitch's glasses.

# C H A P T E R   2 5

**They got back to** San Francisco on Christmas
Eve, driving the whole way in silence. Dr. Ryan had
patched up Mark's shoulder, urging Artie to get further treatment for him in the city. The muscles had
been torn, nothing serious, but somebody should
check him for possible infection once he got home.

Levin had been mistaken. They weren't choppers,
though perhaps he had thought so because he'd been
operating with a 'Nam mind-set plus a bad case of wishful thinking. It was his chance for an intelligence coup,
to become a national hero. He must have called Washington, but the message had never been delivered. The
Old People had Hounds in D.C. as well as San Francisco and besides, Levin's old friend was probably
tucked away in a minor bureaucracy of the DOD. Without proof, who would pay attention to what a semire-
tired intelligence officer told them?

The "choppers" had actually been several cars from
Willow, the passengers armed. They had been too late,
and for that Artie had been grateful. Susan and Mark
would never have survived any shootout; it had been
bad enough as it was. Doc Ryan had been along and
helped Mark, but there was nothing to be done for
Levin. It had been a lucky shot, an instant kill.

Artie had left the house with his arm protectively around Mark's good shoulder. He'd glanced once at Levin lying on the floor and had felt everything from grief to pity to relief that he had been so lucky and Susan and Mark were still alive. Then he'd had a brief flashback to the days in the Haight when he had lived in a crashpad with half a dozen others, including Mitch, and spent more than one evening smoking joints and laughing uproariously at the Three Stooges on the tube.

But there was little connection between that Mitch and this.

The doctor and the others would take care of the body. Levin had left San Francisco in his BMW and disappeared. There would be an investigation, but nobody in Willow had seen either him or his car. The case would end up in an open file, be shuffled toward the back, and eventually forgotten.

Susan's parents had told her they would be back at midnight but Artie didn't want to stick around to meet them. Somebody else could fill them in. Susan had left them a note; she didn't want to stay either. He hadn't argued with her one way or the other; he couldn't care less.

Back at the house on Noe, he and Mark had taken a nap, then gone out shopping for a Christmas tree. Afterward he called Connie to wish her and the Grub a Merry Christmas and to report that his family was together again. He'd bitten his tongue when he said it, but was glad he'd told her. A little of the Christmas spirit had managed to infect Connie and the news had cheered her even more.

"Merry Christmas, Artie, and don't drink too much eggnog. Oh, yeah, Monday's a working day and you better be here, damn it—you've just run out of excuses."

They had spent late afternoon trimming the tree and Susan had eventually joined in. Mark was cheerful and talkative; Artie didn't have much to say. Susan said nothing at all.

They ordered out for pizza, waited an hour and a half for it to show up, and ate a cold mushroom-and-double-sausage in stony silence.

After he had finished one slice, Mark shoved his plate away, angry.

"You two got something to talk about but I don't think I want to hear it."

He stalked out to the porch and yanked the sliding glass doors shut behind him. Artie could see him leaning on the railing, looking out at the lights of the city twinkling in the gathering dusk. San Francisco at its prettiest. A fairly warm evening, the fog just beginning to roll in and a sea of colored lights below that seemed to go on forever.

Artie pushed his own plate aside and walked into the living room, Susan following. He sat on the edge of the couch, Susan on the edge of the big recliner, tense and uneasy. She still hadn't looked him in the eyes.

"Where do you want to start?" she finally asked.

"Why did you marry me?" He had wanted to be dispassionate and objective, but to himself he sounded despairing. *Women will break your heart all your life, Arthur.*

"Because I wanted a father for Mark. And for protection. I was afraid of what might be coming."

Like a few Jewish women did in Nazi Germany, Artie thought. Married to an Aryan, they had hoped for protection during the holocaust that had followed. If they married high enough up, it helped. But not always.

"Why me?" Artie repeated.

She looked at him then, a slight flush of anger on her cheeks.

"You want me to read off your virtues? You're brave, you're stable, and you're a family man. I realized that early on. You wanted a family badly and when you got one, I knew it would mean everything in life to you.

Do you remember the conversations we had after we first met? You wanted me, but you really wanted a family more. I couldn't give you everything you wanted— I warned you about that—but I could give you enough, and with Mark I could give it to you all at once. As I remember, you said you liked that."

"Protection," Artie said, sullen.

"That's right, and for protection. For myself and Mark. Especially Mark."

"But not for love," Artie said. It hurt to say it.

She looked away.

"No, not for love."

He had asked for the truth and gotten it, and now he was sorry he had asked. But he couldn't blame her for that.

"Your first husband—you've never told me much about him."

"I'd known Michael in college. We graduated during a recession and he ended up in construction, as labor. He was on a work site one day and a wall collapsed on him. He died immediately."

Artie knew better but he had to ask it anyway.

"You loved him."

"No."

He looked surprised and she said, "He was a friend. I wanted children and if you're one of us that means an arranged marriage. You have to be matched—both of you have to be species typed. My family knew his, and both families approved. My father thought the world of him."

Which explained why her parents hated him, Artie thought. They would probably have hated anybody who followed Michael.

"I hoped to grow to love him." Her voice was dry, emotionless. "I think I might have."

"You told me you couldn't have any more children. The truth is you didn't want any more, right?"

"That's not true. But they would have been sterile

and nothing on heaven or earth would have enabled them to have children in turn. How do you think they would have felt? How do you think I would have? I would have condemned them to a childless marriage. It wouldn't have been fair. Not to them. And not to you, either—you would have wanted grandchildren."

"They could have adopted," Artie said. "It wouldn't have mattered to me."

She stared at him, contemptuous.

"And you're so sure you can speak for them?"

**Hubris, Artie thought.** He was guilty of it, guilty as sin. But he couldn't help himself.

"Chandler was your Hound," he said. "Cathy was his lover and told him everything about Larry's research. She didn't know what he was." For just a moment he was back in Chandler's little theater, watching as Dave peeled off his makeup and became somebody Artie had never known, somebody who had almost squashed him like a bug. "Charlie Allen shot him."

"Chandler?" She looked surprised.

"You never knew?"

She shook her head.

"Of course not." Then: "You don't understand how . . . underground we've had to be. Nobody knows who the Hounds are. They're the only army we have, if you want to call it that. We couldn't tell you who they are even under torture because we don't know. We live in cells, little groups of us scattered around the country. There aren't many of us—there never were. A town like Willow, of almost a thousand, is unusual. I don't know of any others, though I'm sure there are some. A very few of us have contacts outside the group, like Dr. Ryan has contacts in Washington. But otherwise, we're in—"

"—deep cover," Artie finished.

"That's right. We have to be."

"Mark's school," he said. "It never was a school for the handicapped, was it?"

She looked tired.

"Schools, even private ones, have too many physical examinations, too much probing by doctors and nurses from the state. Maybe they never would have discovered anything unusual. Maybe they would have. We don't get sick very often—we're immune to most of your diseases. We couldn't take the chance that somewhere along the line somebody would get curious. Perfect attendance records, an *A* in health. Always. And stronger, much stronger, than average . . ."

"So you opened your own schools. Like Bayview."

"Mark and I have our own family doctor, too. You never knew."

"What happened with the academy? I met one of the students there; he said it had been sold."

She shrugged.

"It was time to fold it. State examiners were suspicious the last time they came around. They were due again right after the first of the year and we felt we couldn't risk it."

"Why not?"

She half smiled then.

"You saw Mark. None of the students were handicapped; it was a sham, a show for anybody who came around."

"Like me."

"Like you."

Collins had been very good. Artie would have sworn he had a withered right arm. And Mark had fooled him for five years. The car accident had been faked. Both he and Susan had gone out of their way to deceive him.

"You knew Larry was going to be killed."

She shook her head, denying it.

"I didn't know. Certainly not then. Cathy had told me what Larry was working on, swearing me to secrecy, and I knew it would be dangerous. I knew . . . eventually . . . a Hound would come after him. But aside from Mary and myself, I didn't even know there were any others of us in the Club. The police called Cathy shortly after Larry's death and she called me just before she left the house. She wouldn't say where she was going."

The timing would have been right, Artie thought. He wouldn't have known about the call; he'd been at Soriano's, waiting for Larry to show.

"So you called your folks and said you'd be coming up—maybe for an extended stay—and they were delighted. You decided to fake your father's illness."

"Something like that. Hal suggested it—I needed a last-minute reason for going. They didn't want you to come along, said you'd just bring danger up with you."

"You never left the house when you were in Willow, did you?"

"I didn't want anybody to know I had gone up there. After Larry was killed, I knew there would be an investigation, that sooner or later the police would want to talk to me. Perhaps to Mark. I didn't want to risk it."

Artie was suddenly angry again.

"You knew I was a good friend of Larry's, that I was one of those with his neck in a noose. You knew it all along, and you never warned me. That morning when you left, you asked me what Larry had to say at the meeting, and all the time you knew he was dead. You lied to me."

She sighed.

"Yes, Artie, I lied to you." Then it was her turn to be angry. "If I had warned you, I would have had to betray my own species and betray Mark. I couldn't do that. You should know about divided loyalties—they're not easy to handle, are they?"

He had a glimmering of the truth then, only a glimpse, and then it was gone.

"I would have sacrificed everything for you and Mark." He cursed the plaintive tone in his voice.

"That's why I married you. In turn, I would have sacrificed everything for Mark. I still would, I would offer up my own life for him as easily as I would offer up yours. I did my best to get him out of here. I ordered him to come up to Willow and he refused. We agreed on a day or two later, as soon as school was out. But school wasn't his reason for staying."

Artie couldn't hide his bitterness. "A week of romance. An early Christmas present to himself." •

She looked at him, startled.

"You can't really believe that!"

Artie didn't answer her. He was lost in a flashback of the last dream he'd had, when he had stood watch in front of the cave, looking at the wolf just beyond the firelight and wondering if it could be trained to guard the cave in return for scraps of meat.

"You married me to be a watchdog," he said with sudden insight.

She had shifted slightly so her face was in shadow. "Not against any of our Hounds—against yours. And you were a very good watchdog. You more than lived up to expectations." There was a sudden tinge of pity in her voice. "I knew that somewhere along the line you would have to make a choice. I didn't think it would turn out to be the particular one you had to make."

Moe and Curly and Larry on the tube and a very young Mitch Levin sitting beside him on the dirty floor mattress, doubled up in laughter.

"You felt nothing for Shea?" he said at last. "For Lyle? For Cathy? I thought she was your closest friend."

She started to cry then, silently, the tears glistening in the glow from the lights on the Christmas tree.

"Yes. They were good friends, and I betrayed them by keeping quiet. It was just as difficult a choice to make as yours." She was suddenly furious, at him, at herself, at the choice she'd had to make. "And there was no way I would betray Mark!"

Artie sank back in his chair. Everything had gone to hell; everything bad that could happen to him had happened.

"Mitch was right," he said slowly, "and so was Chandler. It was war and it was either you or us. I was as familiar with that as Mitch was—we were both graduates of the same killing fields."

Pity flowed over her face like water.

"There isn't going to be any war, Artie. We've won and you've lost."

Artie frowned. "What the hell are you talking about?"

She looked away. "Go ask your son."

"He's not my son," he said angrily.

"He thinks he is. You raised him; he's got your values, your outlook. He might as well be your flesh and blood. He earned it. He saved your life. He stayed behind to take care of the beloved watchdog. I hadn't planned on that."

"I owe him," Artie said reluctantly, remembering the time on the porch.

She saw the image in his mind. "That wasn't the only time."

He held his head in his hands, trying to make sense of everything she was telling him. There were huge gaps, but he was too tired to ask her to fill them in now.

"There were other times?"

Her voice was curt. "How do you think you stayed alive? You should have died a dozen times over. Ask him."

"Maybe tomorrow."

"Tonight. You don't know him—you should at least make a start. He's not like you, but he's not like me either. I would like to think he has the best of me." She paused. "And the best of you. You should be proud of him. And you should be willing to show it."

"If he saved my life more than once," Artie said sarcastically, "then he must have known Chandler was the Hound. Why didn't he just kill the bastard? You people seem able to do anything else."

"He doesn't have the genes for it," she said, her voice ice. "He didn't kill him because he couldn't kill him."

Artie looked up, confused and angry once again.

"You're going to have to explain that one."

She shook her head.

"Not me—Mark. Go talk to your son, Arthur."

# THE ENDING

**It was darker now,** and a wind had started to whip the trees along the side of the house. Artie had brought out a sweater for Mark and handed it to him, then leaned on the railing beside him and looked down the block at the decorations on the houses and the flickering Christmas lights in the windows. A few doors away a window sign was blinking MERRY CHRISTMAS, HAPPY YOU-ALL.

It wasn't like back East, where he'd grown up as a kid. In Chicago there would be a foot of snow on the ground and he'd be bundled up to his ears with a thick coat and gloves stiff from making snowballs, plus a woolen cap and earmuffs and heavy galoshes. He missed it, but if he ever moved back there, he knew the winters would kill him.

"I heard some of the argument," Mark said.

He had to talk to Mark about it sooner or later, Artie thought.

"Your mother and I—"

"Yeah, I know." Then, curious: "Are you and Mom still friends?"

Artie felt defeated. "I don't know, Mark. I just don't know. She doesn't—"

"Has she asked for a divorce?"

Artie suprised himself with the answer.

"No she hasn't."

"Maybe you asked the wrong questions," Mark said quietly.

He would have to think about that. Marriages among the Old People were usually arranged, they were seldom for love. Why should he and Susan have the same frame of reference? She had married him because she had wanted a father for Mark and protection for them both. He had married her because he had wanted a family. Both of them had gotten what they wanted.

"I don't know if I ever thanked you."

"For what?" Mark asked.

"Saving my life. Here on the porch."

Mark grunted.

"Susan told me there were other times," Artie said.

"Yeah." Mark laughed quietly at the memory. "You almost ran into me at the museum that first day. I thought for sure you'd seen me."

Artie remembered the hour spent with the Tribe in the Visions of the Past room and he was suddenly uneasy.

"Those were *your* memories, weren't they? Racial memories?"

Mark shrugged.

"You were there to find out about us, where we came from. I thought I ought to show you. It was pretty grim, but I thought you needed to know about us, what it had been like for us back then."

It had all been part of his education as a watchdog. You have to know who you're guarding—and against what. He was suddenly puzzled.

"I used to have dreams—"

Out of the corner of his eye he could see Mark smile.

"Those were supposed to be my wet dreams, not yours. I was broadcasting in my sleep and didn't realize it."

Artie laughed and then immediately sobered.

"You placed the phone call to me when I was about to leave the museum that day with Dr. Hall."

He could sense Mark nod in the dark.

"I followed you when you drove away. Chandler almost got you then—you would have killed the guy in the car."

"How did you stop him?"

"Set up an interference pattern. That was about the only thing I could ever do. . . . And I was at the zoo, admiring the Siberian tiger. I almost got to the station parking lot too late." He was silent, remembering. "It was the same thing at the library. And I had Charlie Allen chase after you early in the morning when you went to Chandler's apartment. His wife didn't want him to go." Another silence. "He could do what I couldn't."

"There's a lot that Charlie is going to insist on knowing."

"He won't remember," Mark said gently. "I'll see that he doesn't."

He had a lot to ask Mark, Artie thought, but he didn't know where to begin.

"I gave you the guided tour of the city when you were staying at Levin's house," Mark continued. "Maybe I should have stuck around longer, but I was pretty tired by then. I read about the fire later."

"I was worried about you," Artie said slowly. "You could have let me know you were still alive."

Mark laughed in the darkness. "I was too busy keeping you alive. And I had Collins tell you his father was in dry wall. I guess you didn't pick up on that one—I thought you were sharper than that."

"You arranged with Collins to tell me at the end, didn't you?"

"It was time you found us; it was time you came up to Willow. I knew Chandler was dead, that you were no longer in danger. And I knew your friend"—Mark paused, aware he had used the wrong word—"was looking for Mom and me. I knew he would come to Willow searching for us." He suddenly sounded distant, remote. "I had done my best to save you. It was time for you to save us. You just made it."

All his married life he had been their faithful Hound. And to save them he had killed his best friend. But that wasn't true. Mitch hadn't had any friends, only patients and old army buddies.

Cautiously: "Collins struck me as a decent kid."

"Collins likes me too well," Mark said easily.

"I guessed that."

"I think the world of Collins—I wouldn't have turned him down. But what he wanted meant so much to him and so little to me his pride would have been hurt. I could have lied to him but he would have known." Mark hesitated. "A friend of his loves him, but Collins doesn't realize it yet."

Artie didn't say anything. It wasn't any of his business—and then he realized that of course it was. If it mattered to Mark, it mattered to him. He stared into the gathering night and after a moment said, "Susan claims the war is over. That it was over before it really began. That we lost—that is, *Homo sapiens* lost."

It was Mark's turn to be quiet, and Artie had a sudden premonition about what he was going to say.

"Doc Ryan talked to me about it before we left Willow. He'd just gotten a message from a friend at the Centers for Disease Control."

Artie was silent, waiting.

"He said it was in the papers, though they didn't print everything. Maybe they couldn't. Rift Valley TB. That's where they found 'Lucy,' isn't it? One of the earliest fossils? In the Great Rift Valley?"

"I think so." It took a moment for Artie to recall where he'd heard of the disease, then he had it. A TV news show in the hotel room with Mitch. And Watch Cap—Chandler—had mentioned it.

He knew Mark was looking at him in the dark, uneasy.

"Where the Rift Valley cuts through Ethiopia . . . there were a lot of mercenaries involved in their latest civil war and they were the first to come down with it. You go fighting in old boneyards and I guess you run the risk of catching whatever killed the owners of those bones to begin with."

"What's it like?"

"Doc Ryan said it's something like TB—but a lot worse. He said it was multidrug resistant and ultraviolet radiation doesn't kill it. Incubation period of a month or so, then a week of vomiting blood and that's it."

"They'll find something for it."

Mark shook his head.

"Doc didn't think so. Said there's only one drug that's good for TB now and it doesn't touch this. It's incurable."

Artie felt the first touch of fear.

"Did he say anything else?"

Mark cleared his throat. He suddenly seemed reluctant to talk about it.

"That it's species specific. That we're immune."

But *Homo sapiens* wasn't. Mary had been right. They had done it to themselves. But if it wasn't this, it would have been something else. TB was airborne and by now it would have spread all over the world, mercenaries going home and passing through Heathrow—all of London would have been exposed. You couldn't quarantine a city, and it was too late now, anyway. After that, New York, Paris—wherever the flights went. There were no oceans to protect them, no mountain ranges that would seal it off.

"Doc said the Old People are withdrawing. Moving out of the cities into the country, into uninhabited areas. Collins knows of a little town in Alaska, about a hundred miles out of Anchorage. Kodiak Creek. It's one of ours." Mark looked over at Artie. "We could move there."

"Maybe," Artie said. He'd like it in Alaska, he thought. "And maybe we'll be lucky."

But he knew they wouldn't be.

Mark changed the subject.

"Did you love your grandfather?" he asked.

Artie turned, surprised, trying to read his face in the darkness.

"Yes, of course."

"And your father?"

Artie smiled. "Him, too."

"Neither one of them were like you, were they?"

"In some ways, of course they were. In a lot of other ways, I suppose not. But that didn't affect my loving them."

"I'm not like you," Mark said.

"I know that."

"I'm not like Mom, either."

Something was bothering Mark, and Artie remembered what Susan had said: "He doesn't have the genes for it. . . ."

"Susan told me that. I didn't understand her."

Mark walked over to the porch light and stood beneath it.

"Look me in the eyes," he said quietly.

Mark's eyes were just as gray as Collins', but there was a depth to them that Artie had never seen in anybody's eyes before. Mark was suddenly more naked than if he had stripped off all his clothes. The only thing Artie could compare it to was when he was on the line in 'Nam and friends who were scared shitless talked to each other about themselves and their lives with absolutely no pretense and no lies. How they felt, things they had done, what they thought. It was when they were in extremis that you finally saw the real person beneath all the bullshit and the real person was usually . . . beautiful.

He was seeing everything Mark was or ever would be. Mark could show his soul at will and it was overwhelming.

And there was something else.

Mark could also see him as he really was, without the mask that everybody wore almost all their lives.

Artie looked away.

He had been staring into the eyes of the Buddha.

How long had Susan known? he wondered. Probably shortly after Mark was born. She had kept his secret ever since. Mark was the person who meant the most to her, the one person she could never betray, the one person she would gladly die for. She had never lied to him about that.

Mark suddenly yawned.

"Would you have shot Collins?"

Artie shook his head. "I was trying to bluff him. That was silly, I know."

"Yeah. He thought so, too." Mark opened the sliding glass doors and stepped inside.

"Good night, Dad."

**Ever since he was** *a kid, he had thought it would be fun to play God. Most kids probably did.*

*But he'd had his chance.*

*And it hadn't been fun at all.*

Artie leaned against the railing and looked out at the city below, the lights winking in the darkness. The streets downtown would be jammed with last-minute shoppers, the restaurants crowded, the theaters filled. It was probably the same across the country, around the entire world. *Homo sapiens* going about its business of shopping, eating, making children, making war, making plans for a thousand tomorrows that would steadily diminish until finally there were no more.

A few might linger for a while in small patches here and there. The species was too genetically diverse to be wiped out by a single bug. There might be a few farmers, maybe even a tiny village. An insignificant self-endangered species dependent upon the kindness of the other species surrounding them. Chances were they would still be warring among themselves until Cain once again slew Abel and they vanished for good.

They were going to go away. All of them. How many years? He didn't know. But sooner rather than later.

Something would take their place. Something that had been in hiding for thousands of years. Mankind would dwindle, realizing what was happening but powerless to stop it. As powerless as the dinosaurs had been when the meteorite had plunged into the sea millions of years ago and they had gone away, leaving their world to the tiny mammals hiding under the leaves of the forest.

But of all the teeming billions, he was the one truly Damned because in whatever small way, he had been the Instrument. He'd had to make a choice: his best friend or his family, his species or theirs.

But even if he had chosen Mitch—and he knew he never could have—it wouldn't have made a bit of difference in the outcome, only in how bloody it might have been. The Old People would have been blamed for spreading Rift Valley TB, and the pogrom that followed would have been everything that Mary feared.

Perhaps the Old People deserved the earth. Perhaps they had been meant to own it after all, at least for a while. Evolution had stopped for *Homo sapiens*; there were no isolated pockets of them that could throw up a mutation and then breed true. The world of *Homo sapiens* was all one; the constant mixing would have diluted it all too soon. But it hadn't been like that for the Old People. They had lived in tiny patches scattered around the world, isolated socially if not geographically. Evolution might have hesitated for them, but it had never stopped. And they'd had thirty-five thousand years for a change to show up. Time enough plus the tides of chance.

Artie turned away from the railing. The world would continue. The genus would continue. Hominids would continue. But *Homo sapiens* would disappear and so, eventually, would the Old People. Mark's genes would dominate, and after so many millennia the Old People would be replaced themselves, like every species was slated to be.

With Mark, nature had thrown the dice once again, willing to try a new combination rather than giving up the game altogether.

Artie smiled to himself.

Mark would be a surprise to them, one the Old People hadn't counted on. But at least they would let him live rather than burn him at the stake or dissect him in a laboratory or cage him in a zoo.

He wondered what their scientists would call Mark. *Homo* what?

**"If we're all here."** Grossman grunted heavily, "why should we delay?"

Tanner nodded to Petey, who started to read the minutes of the last meeting. *"Saturday, May twenty-second. The meeting of the Navy Committee for Human Research was called to order . . ."*

Tanner waited until she had finished reading the minutes, then made a show of fumbling with his pipe, wondering briefly how many of them knew it was Young Man with Prop.

"During the last year," he started easily, "we've been doing primarily survival research—why some men live and some men die under different stresses and environments. Under battle conditions, certain men are smarter, more efficient, and more capable than others. Having determined the qualities necessary for survival, we've been trying to figure out how the successful ones, the ones who *do* survive, get that way, what factors play a part."

He champed a little harder on his pipe and squinted through the smoke. "Hunting for people with these characteristics has been a little like hunting for a needle in a haystack, so John Olson suggested a questionnaire—where you can cover a lot of people quickly at a small cost. Those who showed promise on the questionnaire could be given more exhaustive physical tests later. As you recall, the questionnaire we drew up covered an individual's past medical history, psychological outlook, family background, and heredity—all the items we had agreed were important, and many of which can hardly be tested in a physical sense anyway." He smiled cautiously. "We all agreed to take the test ourselves last week—sort of as a dry run. None of us signed our names, for which I'm sorry. John's compiled the results and I must admit there were some pretty fantastic answers on one of them."

DeFalco looked curious. "Like what?"

Tanner held up one of the questionnaires. "The person who filled it out, if we take it at face value, has never been sick, never had any serious personal problems, never worried, and has an IQ close to the limits of measurability. His parents came from two distinct racial stocks and for what it might be worth, his father was a water dowser and his mother a faith healer."

There was a ripple of laughter around the table and even Professor Scott was grinning. Tanner put the questionnaire aside. It had been good for a chuckle at least.

"If there are no more suggestions, I'll have Petey send the form to the printers, then . . ."

"Professor Tanner!"

He glanced down at the end of the table. Olson's pudgy face was covered with a light sheen of sweat that glistened in the sunlight coming through the windows.

"Do you think that questionnaire was on the level?"

Tanner felt annoyed. If Olson had had doubts about it, why hadn't he asked him about it in private, rather than bring it up now?

"You mean, did I fill it out as a gag? No, I didn't—but obviously somebody did."

Olson wet his lips again. "Are you so sure of that?"

There was an uneasy silence, then Professor Scott snorted, "Rubbish!"

Olson didn't give ground. "Maybe there's something to it. I think we ought to . . . look into it."

Nordlund edged into the conversation. "If it's on the level . . ."

"It isn't," Tanner said curtly.

"But if it was?"

*One layman in the crowd and you spent the whole damned afternoon explaining the ABCs.*

"If it was on the level it would mean the person who filled it out was a very unusual human being, perhaps a very superior one. But I hardly think we should take it seriously. And there are a lot of important things to cover today."

Olson's voice rose to a nervous squeak. "Maybe you don't want to admit what it means, Tanner!"

They were all staring at Olson now. His face was damp and his eyes a little too wide. The eyes of a man scared half to death, Tanner thought cynically. Then he could feel the sweat start on his own brow. He had a hunch that Olson was going to blow his stack right in the committee room.

He tried to head him off, to get the frightened man to talk it out. "All right, John, just what do you think it means?"

"I think it means the human race is all washed up!"

Tanner glanced over at the Navy man and could see that Olson's outburst was going over like a lead balloon with Nordlund; there was a look of shocked surprise on the other faces. A moment of embarrassed silence followed, then Petey, looking as if she were about to cry, said, "John, I think we better . . ."

Olson didn't look at her. "Shut up, Pat."

Nobody said anything. They were going to let him handle it, Tanner thought uneasily. It was his baby. He held up the questionnaire. "Who filled this one out?"

Another strained silence, one where a slight, uneasy

movement in a chair or an embarrassed fumbling with papers sounded very loud.

"Don't you think we ought to skip this?" Van Zandt said impatiently. "I don't see how it's getting us any place."

Tanner flushed. He was trying to humor Olson and Van Zandt knew it but then, this was the academic jungle. Van had won his spurs a long time ago, but he still liked to keep in practice.

He dropped the questionnaire. "All right, we'll forget it for now." He nodded to Olson. "See me after the meeting, John, and we'll talk about it then."

"You're scared!" Olson screamed in a hysterical voice. "You don't want to believe it!"

Tanner could feel the hair prickle at the back of his neck. Take the survival tests and couple them with an inferiority complex and maybe you ended up with a superman fetish. Something half akin to religion—a willingness and desire to believe in something greater than yourself. But why was Olson so frightened about it?

Olson was trembling. "Well? What are you going to do about it?"

It was like watching an automobile accident. It repelled you but you couldn't tear your eyes away. There was a sort of horrible fascination to this, too—the sight of a man going to pieces. He waited for Van Zandt to say something, to squelch his younger colleague with a few broadsides of logic. But Van said nothing and only stared at Olson with a curious, speculative look in his eyes. Nobody knew Olson better than Van Zandt, Tanner thought, but for reasons of his own, Van was letting John dig his own grave and wasn't going to argue him out of it.

He was sweating. There was nothing left to do but go along with Olson. He turned to Marge. "Do you have a pin?"

She found one in her purse and handed it over. He

stood a book on end on the table, imbedding the head of the pin between the pages so the point projected out about an inch. Then he tore off a tiny fragment of newspaper, folded it into a small, umbrella shape, and placed it on the pin point.

"Maybe we can prove something this way, John. I'm assuming that our . . . superman . . . has mental powers such that he could make this paper revolve on the pin merely by concentrating on it. The paper is light, it's delicately balanced, and it wouldn't take much to move it. Okay?"

There was a round of snickers but Olson nodded and Tanner felt relieved. It was the only thing he could think of on the spur of the moment. A kid's game.

"Anybody care to try?"

Marge said, "I'm willing if everybody else is."

The others nodded and she stared intently at the pin. The paper hung there quietly, not stirring. After a minute she leaned back, holding her hands to her head. "All I'm doing is getting a headache."

"Van?"

Van Zandt nodded and glared at the paper umbrella. If sheer will power could do it, Tanner thought, Van Zandt was his man. But the paper didn't move. Van Zandt leered. "My superior talents apparently aren't in evidence this morning."

Olson himself and then DeFalco tried and failed. Nordlund stared intently at the pin and then looked bored when the paper didn't even tremble. It was Professor Scott's turn next.

The paper hat tilted slightly.

There was a thick, frightened silence. The condescending attitude had vanished like a snap of the fingers and Tanner could feel the tenseness gather in the room. All eyes were riveted on the suddenly trembling old man. *My God, I didn't . . ."*

"Very simply explained," Grossman said quickly. "A door slammed down the hall, though I doubt that any of you heard it in your concentration. I am sure that a slight draft would be enough to affect our little piece of paper."

The old man looked enormously relieved and some of the tenseness drained away. Grossman tried it next, with no result.

Tanner shrugged. "Well, John?"

Olson was suddenly on his feet, leaning his knuckles on the table and glaring down the length of it. "*He* won't admit it, he hasn't got the guts! If he wouldn't admit he had filled out the questionnaire, he wouldn't show himself in a test like this!" His pudgy face was red. "He hasn't got the nerve, Tanner, he's hiding!"

*What the hell do you do in a case like this?* Tanner thought. They were babying a neurotic but they had gone this far and it wouldn't hurt to go a little farther. He'd play along just once more. *I feel embarrassed for the poor guy. And it's partly my fault; I should have done something about it a week ago.*

"We'll try it again, only this time all together." Olson's superman could still hide and yet reveal his powers—if he wanted to take on Olson's dare. When nothing happened, maybe then John would be convinced. Except that you could never dissuade a neurotic when they wanted to believe in something. . . .

He nodded to the others.

On the street outside there were the faint sounds of automobile traffic and the muted vibrations of conversation. Some place far away tires screeched. Equally remote were the indignant complaints of a housewife, shortchanged at a sidewalk fruit stand. In the room itself, there were no sounds, not even the muffled sighs of breathing. And there was no motion, other than that of the small motes of dust floating in the bars of sunlight that streamed through the window.

And the tiny paper umbrella which trembled, tilted, and then spun madly.